Alexandra Potter was born in Bradford. She has lived in LA and Australia and worked as a features writer and sub-editor for women's glossies in the UK. She now writes full-time. Her previous novels are *What's New Pussycat*, *Going La-La* and the widely-acclaimed *Calling Romeo*: 'a cracking summer read' *Heat*.

Also by Alexandra Potter

CALLING ROMEO

and published by Black Swan

DO YOU COME HERE OFTEN?

Alexandra Potter

BLACK SWAN

DO YOU COME HERE OFTEN?
A BLACK SWAN BOOK: 0 552 77004 3

First publication in Great Britain

PRINTING HISTORY
Black Swan edition published 2004

1 3 5 7 9 10 8 6 4 2

Copyright © Alexandra Potter 2004

Set in 11/12pt Melior by
Falcon Oast Graphic Art Ltd.

Black Swan Books are published by Transworld Publishers,
61–63 Uxbridge Road, London W5 5SA,
a division of The Random House Group Ltd,
in Australia by Random House Australia (Pty) Ltd,
20 Alfred Street, Milsons Point, Sydney, NSW 2061, Australia,
in New Zealand by Random House New Zealand Ltd,
18 Poland Road, Glenfield, Auckland 10, New Zealand
and in South Africa by Random House (Pty) Ltd,
Endulini, 5a Jubilee Road, Parktown 2193, South Africa.

Printed and bound in Great Britain by
Cox & Wyman Ltd, Reading, Berkshire.

Papers used by Transworld Publishers are natural, recyclable
products made from wood grown in sustainable forests. The
manufacturing processes conform to the environmental
regulations of the country of origin.

For Lynnette

Acknowledgments

There were some pretty tough moments during the course of writing this book, and I'd like to say a huge thank you to Lynnette for brainstorming with me in Earls Court, drinking way too many cosmopolitans with me on my birthday, and for being an all-round fantastic friend. Another big thank you goes to my wonderful family – my mum and dad, Ray and Anita, for all their love and support, and also to my sister, Kelly, her boyfriend Steve, and Karma the dog, for our memorable road-trip to Mexico!

I'm also very lucky to have some great friends and I'd like to thank Katie & Jeremy (and baby Mia, just for being gorgeous); newlyweds Kate Rosen and Melissa Scales; Georgie; Ashleigh; Bev in Yorkshire; Rachel and Kate in Sydney. And a special mention to Justin for all his help and kindness – and for looking after me in the desert!

Finally, thanks as always to my editor, Diana Beaumont at Transworld for her enthusiasm, under-standing, not to mention patience! And a big hug to my agent Stephanie Cabot at William Morris, for giving me lots of advice and encouragement – and for taking in a poor homeless author – thank you!

Prologue

'*. . . So listeners, that brings us to our next love letter, this time it's Cindy from Paddington and she's looking for someone special to mend her broken heart . . .*'

It's past midnight. Dark and drizzly. Across the length and breadth of the capital traffic-choked roads are eerily empty, thronging high streets have turned into hostels for the homeless, and tucked snugly away in a million bedrooms, under a million duvets, millions of Londoners are sleeping, snoring, dreaming.

Most, but not all.

In the slow lane of the A40 a casualty doctor is driving home from his shift in his knackered old VW camper van; on a gold velvet sofa in a high-rise in Streatham a middle-aged couple are cuddling up to a nightcap, and above Baltic Travel in Paddington, a single mum is pacing up and down her flat, waiting for the telephone to ring. Different people, different places, different lives. And one connection. A radio. An FM frequency. And the fact they're all listening to the same show.

Luther Vandross singing 'Endless Love' is faded out as the DJ strikes up.

'*Hi this is Dr Cupid and have I got some late-night-lovin' for you. The author of tonight's love letter is a woman whose life was shattered when her partner walked out on her and their son. Hi, Cindy, are you there?*'

There's the sound of a nervous vacuuming of the throat. '. . . *Er . . . yes . . . hello.*'

'*Welcome to the show, you're speaking to Dr Cupid. Now tell me Cindy, it sounds as if you've had it pretty tough recently.*'

'*. . . yes . . . sort of . . .*'

Cue a tut and lots of sympathetic noises from the DJ. '*So tell us a bit about yourself.*'

'*Erm . . .*' her voice is wavering with nerves.

'*Don't be nervous,*' soothes the DJ. '*Take a few deep breaths.*'

There's a pause, the chink of a glass of water, and then, '*Well, I suppose I'm rather creative. I used to be a make-up artist for all the glossy magazines, which was great as I got to travel the world meeting lots of interesting people, but then I had my little boy and . . . well . . .*' she sighs, part wistfully, part lovingly, '*. . . then I became a full-time mum.*'

'*And in your letter you say you're looking for that special someone.*'

She lets out a throaty laugh. '*Oh yes, I did, didn't I.*' Even across the airwaves it's obvious she's blushing with embarrassment. '*But then, isn't everyone?*'

'*Absolutely,*' gushes the DJ. '*Which is why* Do You Come Here Often? *is here, because we're going to find you your soulmate.*'

'*You are?*' replies Cindy, unable to hide the disbelief in her voice.

'*Yes, indeedy.*'

'*Oh . . . right . . . super . . .*' She makes an attempt to match his level of enthusiasm and then breaks off and giggles nervously. There's the sound of her inhaling hard on a cigarette . . . '*That's a relief, because you wouldn't believe the last date I had, it was a total disaster – that's why I wrote to you. I mean, to be perfectly honest, I don't actually believe in dating agencies, or trying to find your soulmate,*' she admits, almost as if she's forgotten that she's confiding in the DJ and a lonely hearts radio show. '*I believe in destiny, in fate, in the magic of the universe. I believe we have no control over love. Either it's going to happen or it's not . . .'*

Hearing his whole show being demolished live on air, the DJ interrupts. *'London's full of single people searching for that special someone. Why don't you describe your soulmate, Cindy?'*

'Well, I don't know until I've met him, do I?' she replies in confusion.

'Try, Cindy,' cajoles the DJ, anxious to fill airtime until the next record. *'Don't be embarrassed. Remember, you're talking to Dr Cupid, and I'm here to fix that broken heart of yours.'*

Silence, followed by an awkward laugh. *'Oh, well if you insist.'*

'I insist.'

'OK, well let's see . . . he's funny, and kind, and faithful . . .'

'Of course,' agrees the DJ, being all matey.

'. . . and spiritual and passionate and warm and romantic . . .' As Cindy warms up, her nerves disappear: *'and he's the kind of man that if you're at the supermarket together and you go off to get the Earl Grey teabags or something and lose him . . .'* now she's on a roll, there's no stopping her *'. . . you start searching for him in the aisles, until suddenly, right in the middle of the sea of trolleys you see him. And only him. Because although he's surrounded by lots of other men with their trolleys, it's as if they simply don't exist. The Italians have a word for it, un colpo di fulmine. It just hits you and wham, thunderbolt city.'* As her voice trails off in a dreamy reverie she lets out a deep wistful sigh. And quickly comes back down to earth. *'To be honest, I'm not really sure what he's like, but I'll definitely know it's him when I meet him.'*

'And so will we, won't we, listeners?' cheers the DJ, hastily moving the show quickly up a beat. Absorbed in her supermarket story, he'd completely lost track of time, until his producer caught his attention by

11

gesticulating wildly and dragging a finger across her throat. '*So if you think you're Cindy's soulmate, why don't you pick up that phone and give us a call here at* Do You Come Here Often?' – the same irritating jingle as before begins playing – '*but first, here's* 'Hello' *by Lionel Ritchie.*' As the jingle is crudely faded out, the opening chords of a record are heard: '*And remember. Don't waste another minute as love waits for no-one . . .*'

As Lionel Ritchie's velvety voice croons over the air-waves, the casualty doctor smiles to himself and whacks up the volume, the middle-aged couple gaze lovingly at each other and hug each other even tighter. And in that cosy, fairy-lit flat above Baltic Travel, a pretty, dark-haired woman is wondering what on earth possessed her to call up a national radio station, and to an audience of thousands of listeners, ask Dr Cupid to sort out her love life. Waiting by the telephone, she lights up another cigarette.

And she hopes.

Chapter One

Snuggled deep into the womb-like depths of their king-size sleigh bed, Grace was drifting in and out of sleep. In a distant, disconnected place her brain was trying to tell her to get up, get ready, and go to work, but her body wasn't responding. Her limbs seemed to have been paralysed overnight. Even her eyelids were refusing to open. She was just lying there. Thinking nothing. Doing nothing. Just breathing in. And breathing out. Slowly, dreamily, blissfully.

There was a flash of blinding light as the curtains were yanked back.

'*What the . . . ?*'

Diving for cover, she scrambled back underneath the safety of her duvet. Breathing in the warm darkness she released a deep sigh of relief. Grace had enjoyed a lifelong affair with her bed, be it her childhood bunk bed, single, badly sprung university mattress, twenty-something, backbreaking futon, or her current grown-up expensive oak number from John Lewis. Like lovers, they'd all had their good points and bad points, but she'd adored them all and never wanted to leave any of them.

Unfortunately it was Friday morning, and as a designer at a graphic design agency in West London, she had to get up for work. Groaning dully, she toyed with the idea of snoozing for five minutes. Fat chance. Sun was streaming in through the window and in the background she could hear the TV blaring away in the kitchen. Spencer had obviously left it on again, she thought, feeling a wave of irritation. Living with someone for three and a half years meant getting to know all of their annoying habits, and one of Spencer's was getting up, flicking on the portable in the kitchen, and then getting distracted and forgetting all about it.

But then Spencer's attention span was incredibly short. He was the kind of bloke who started things with good intentions, but then got sidetracked, changed his mind, and never finished them. Like running a bath but never getting in it, putting bread in the toaster but never eating it.

Getting engaged but never getting married.

'Babes, are you awake?'

Why did people do that? Deliberately wake you up and then ask if you're awake? Emerging from her goosedown lair, Grace prised open her welded eyelids. She blinked blearily, trying to focus on the grey shape in front of her.

'Uh . . . what time is it?' she mumbled.

'Seven-thirty.'

'*Seven-thirty!*' she screeched, her body jolting awake in indignation. She could have had another forty-five blissful minutes of sleep. *A whole three-quarters of an hour.* Grace felt robbed. Groggily peeling her tangled hair out of her eyes, she blinked again, her vision snapping into focus. The instigator of this heinous crime was wearing just a towel and leaning across the bed holding a *pain au chocolat* with a single pink party candle stuck in the middle. Grace felt the seeds of irritation wither away.

'Happy birthday to you, happy birthday to you,' he began singing. His voice was a remarkably good baritone and whereas other blokes might have trailed off self-consciously, he proceeded to belt out the whole verse: 'Happy birthday dear Grace, happy

14

birthday to you.' He finished with a little flourish on the end. 'Happy Birthday, Babes.'

Blimey. Of course. *Her birthday.* Sleep had caused a delay in registering, but now the last reluctant smudges evaporated and it clicked. Grace smiled up at Spencer. Just out of the shower, his dark blond hair was still wet, his tortoiseshell-framed glasses slightly steamy, and tiny drips of guava and citrus scented water were trickling across his enormous freckled shoulders and running down the dip between his pecs. For someone nudging his late thirties he was still in incredibly good shape, she thought proudly. It caused her to smile happily. What with his nakedness and the promise of a chocolate fix, it was a vision of loveliness.

And too good to be true.

In the four birthdays Grace had spent with Spencer, he'd never woken her up singing Happy Birthday. Never brought her breakfast in bed. He didn't go in for all that slushy sentimental stuff. And anyway, he was usually in too much of a rush, always in a hurry to get to the office, always promising to make it up to her later. Her mind began whirring up to full speed, clicking through the possibilities: he hasn't had time to buy me a present, he's got to work late tonight; he's forgotten to book a restaurant . . .

Spencer interrupted her thought process. 'Can't a man wish his woman a happy birthday without there being something wrong?'

'No,' she yawned, shaking her head.

His offended expression dissolved into a shrug of admission. 'You know me too well.'

Grace sensed her good mood was about to be crushed underneath one of Spencer's excuses, and folding her arms she leaned back against the pillows, a judge in PJs. 'So come on then, own up,' she demanded, but she was smiling. Well, it was a ceasefire of sorts.

'It's just that there's this case I've been working flat out on and it's being heard in court tomorrow.'

'So we can't go out tonight,' she concluded, cutting short what was no doubt going to be a long story. She'd lost count of the number of times plans had had to be cancelled because of Spencer's work commitments. If it wasn't some drinks party to welcome foreign clients, it was a corporate dinner, or a late meeting, or a pressing deadline.

'Hey Babes, let me finish.' He pulled a face. If there was one thing Spencer hated, it was being interrupted. 'Of course we're going out tonight. I've already booked the restaurant for nine, although admittedly I might have to meet you there a little later as there's this cocktail thing after work and I've got to show my face, have a quick drink . . .'

'A quick drink?' repeated Grace, grinning. 'Isn't that an oxymoron in your case?'

'No in my case there's a couple with three kids, two lovers and a million-pound house, and I'm the one trying to clear up their messy divorce,' he snapped irritably. As one of London's top divorce lawyers, Spencer was kept incredibly busy. He sighed, 'Sorry Babes . . . it's just I've been working so hard on this case and . . . well . . . I know it's no excuse but I haven't had a chance to buy you a present.' Taking off his glasses Spencer wrinkled his forehead so that the blond lock of fringe that always hung over his forehead, fell into his faded, denim blue eyes. To the innocent observer it would appear a spontaneous action, when really it was a technique that had taken years of practice. And one which, he knew, made him look adorable. 'Would you mind if I just gave you cash instead?'

Now normally, Grace would be the first one to feel hurt if her boyfriend hadn't taken the time and effort to choose her a gift: she would assume he didn't care, that he couldn't be bothered, that he didn't love her. But with Spencer, she was actually relieved. She didn't mean to be ungrateful, it was just that, whereas she always bought him impulsive, outrageous, extravagant presents that had caught her eye, he always bought her presents that were – dare she say it – terribly *practical*.

Last year she'd unwrapped a leather box and flipped it open, thinking it was jewellery, only to discover a Mont Blanc pen. It was lovely, it must have cost a fortune, and it was extremely useful, but it was hardly the figure-hugging, chocolate satin Ghost dress she'd been dropping hints about for weeks. The year before it had been a mountain bike – again it had been lovely, again it must have cost a fortune, with extra chunky tyres and fifteen gears and all the extras, but she'd been exhausted just looking at it and was secretly relieved when it had been nicked less than a week later. And the year before that it had been a bag, but not a ridiculously dinky shoulder bag in the softest chamois leather she'd been craving, but a sturdy leather briefcase from Mulberry which, yet again, must have cost a fortune, and was so extremely practical for work. Which, as far as Grace was concerned, was the kiss of death for a present. By their sheer nature they had to be impractical, luxurious treats. Practical, she mused, was by no means perfect.

'Am I forgiven?'

God, he's trying to be so nice, thought Grace, feeling suddenly guilty. And I'm being such a cranky, narky old girlfriend. She threw him a big smile. 'Don't be silly, of course you are.'

'So does this mean you're going to blow out your candle and make a wish, or am I going to have to sit like this all day?' He checked his wristwatch.

Grace rolled her eyes. 'Shucks, you're so romantic.'

'I have my moments,' he smiled, leaning forward to kiss her.

Feeling his lips against hers, the smell of naked skin and damp aftershave, Grace felt her mind wandering off in an unexpected direction. Usually the morning routine involved the usual coupley stuff: Spencer rushing around with a hangover, scraping burnt toast

17

into the sink and losing his keys while she poached herself in the bath, looked for tights without ladders, and found his keys down the back of the sofa. But the coupley stuff didn't stretch to sex, not lately anyway, not even with the help of two espressos and a soak in a tub of honey and tangerine bubbles. Then again.

'That depends . . .' she murmured.

'On what?'

Pulling back, Grace tilted her head, closed her eyes and blew through the crook of his shoulder. A wisp of smoke began rising from the candle. 'On whether or not I get my wish ...' Still keeping her eyes closed she ran her hand over his bare chest, tracing her fingers through the smatterings of hair. She smiled happily. She hated hairy chests but Spencer's was deliciously sexy. She couldn't think of anything nicer than resting her head between his broad shoulders and snuggling into its furry softness. But that's love for you, she thought, as her hand began weaving its way down underneath the towel. Or was it just lust?

'I better get dressed, I'm going to be late.'

Snapped out of her X-rated reverie, Grace opened her eyes to see Spencer untangling himself from the duvet and standing up. She felt a pang of disappointment, followed by rejection, followed by irritation as she watched him retucking the lilac towel firmly – a little too firmly – around his middle. What did he think she was going to do? *Rape him?*

'I've got a deadline and . . .'

'Sure,' she nodded, making an attempt at nonchalance. It wasn't easy. One minute she'd been immersed in a warm, happy, sensual bubble bath of expectation, and the next she'd been plunged under an icy cold shower of reality.

And no sex.

Annoyed at being made to feel like some kind of nymphomaniac, and on her birthday, Grace didn't say anything as Spencer pulled on a clean pair of Calvin Kleins, chose a shirt from a dozen identical ones that hung in his wardrobe, all drycleaned, all from Thomas Pink, and pulled out his suit.

'Which do you reckon? The silver, or the gold?' He was holding up two pairs of cufflinks.

'You choose,' she snapped sulkily. There she was, all naked and warm and ripe for sex, and he wanted to talk about *cufflinks*?

Oblivious to her feelings, he shrugged. 'I think I'll go with silver,' he muttered, fastening them into place. 'Oh by the way, about tonight . . .'

'Yes?' she hissed, overemphasizing the 's'.

He didn't notice. 'What were you thinking of wearing?'

Grace bristled. Spencer had an annoying habit of always suggesting what outfit she should wear whenever they went out. He liked her to look 'classic' and was always sticking Boden catalogues under her nose and talking about 'quality not quantity', and how she should invest in a few designer pieces that would last her for years. *Last her for years?* The thought nearly killed her. She was a high-street fashion junkie who got bored with things within weeks and was attracted to anything with an 'As recommended by *Glamour* magazine' ticket around the coat hanger.

'I don't know.' She attempted a smile. It was more of a snarl. 'Why?'

'You'd look great in that little black dress.'

'What little black dress?' she demanded suspiciously. She didn't do little black dresses, she did jeans with flowery chiffon tops, or spangly vests, or spaghetti-strap dresses in rainbow colours.

'You know, the one with the long sleeves.'

'You mean the dress I wore to your grandmother's funeral?'

'Oh, is it?' he said, sitting on the side of the bed to lace up his brogues. 'Never mind. I just thought it would be nice to see you in something other than jeans for a change,' he grumbled, giving her a quick peck on the forehead before striding out of the bedroom.

* * *

With still half an hour left before she had to get up, Grace lay in bed listening to the blurred babble of TV in the kitchen, the turning on of the bathroom light and its noisy extractor fan, the sounds of Spencer cleaning his teeth, the hiss of antiperspirant, the buzz of his electric razor. How could it be that one minute she'd been feeling happy and horny, and the next Spencer had managed to use something as trivial as a pair of cufflinks to set off a whole series of nagging doubts?

It's not as if I even care about what type of cufflinks he wears, or whether he wears any at all, thought Grace feeling inexplicably irritated. That wasn't the point. The point was that they were another example of the little things that had lately begun to niggle her about Spencer. His increasing hangovers, his diminishing sex drive, his suggestion she should wear her funeral dress on her birthday, his refusal to set a date for the wedding. First one, then another, and another, and another. Once they'd started toppling over it was like one of those record-breaking domino lines you see in American shopping malls on the telly.

His jangle of keys broke into her thoughts, and she was about to call out and remind him to turn off the TV before he left, when she heard him yell goodbye and the front door slam. Abruptly the flat fell into silence, emphasizing Eamon Holmes's chuntering which wafted into the bedroom.

'Huh,' she tutted, feeling out of sorts and disgruntled and not really understanding why. Sinking down into the bed, she tugged the duvet up under her chin, forgetting the plate of *pain au chocolat* balancing on top, and hearing it fall clattering onto the white wooden floorboards. Ignoring it, she flung out her arm with the intention of hitting the snooze button on her alarm but with characteristic clumsiness managed to knock over the snowglobe that perched beside it on the IKEA shelving.

For a split second she blearily watched it roll towards the edge until, with somewhat impressive reflexes, she jerked upright, shot out her arm and caught it. The globe felt cold and smooth in her hand, and uncurling her fingers she placed it upright on the flat of her outstretched palm. It was one of those you could put a photograph inside and magnified through the clear plastic was the image of a couple ice skating in Central Park. Noses Rudolph red from the falling snow, they were wrapped up in silly woolly hats and stripy Dr Seuss scarves, smiling idiotically as they clung to each other, trying to stay upright on the slippery ice.

Looking at the photograph, Grace felt a glow of nostalgia. It had been just before New Year's Eve, a few months after they'd met, and Spencer had whisked her away to New York for the weekend, fulfilling in one fell swoop every romantic fantasy she'd ever imagined. And some more she hadn't. That Polaroid had captured a perfect moment and preserved it for ever. The moment when, at twenty-seven years old, she'd realized she'd finally found her Mr Right.

Impulsively Grace shook the globe and as the millions of tiny white snowflakes began swirling around inside, fluttering and twirling, her mind flicked back over their relationship, thinking about the times they'd spent together, the rest of their lives they were going to spend together. Lost in her thoughts, she didn't notice the snowflakes gradually settling until she looked back at the globe and all at once saw the clearer picture. And it was then, on the morning of Grace's thirty-first birthday, that all those doubts, all those differences, all those fears clicked into place, like one great big jigsaw.

And a disconcerting thought hit her.

If Spencer was Mr Right.

Why did he feel like Mr Wrong?

Chapter Two

*So this is it. This is the bit where I'm supposed to say
goodbye. Where I'm supposed to give her a quick kiss
on the lips, put my arms around her shoulders, and
give her a hug. The whole thing should only take a
couple of minutes, and then I'm supposed to let go.*

Jimi didn't want to let go.

Standing on the rainsoaked pavement outside
Departures, he wrapped his arms ever tighter around
Kylie's bare midriff and continued kissing her. They'd
been at it for ten whole minutes. Beginning with a self-
conscious peck on the lips, the feathery, polite kind
reserved for public places, and swiftly progressing
into something a little more full-blown. Lip tugging.
Teeth licking. Tongue thrusting. Bumping wet noses,
he was about to pause for breath when he felt her
tongue stud rubbing rhythmically against the roof of
his mouth. It was strangely erotic. Tightening his
grasp, he began kissing with renewed vigour.

Normally Jimi wouldn't be seen dead indulging in this
kind of toe-curling behaviour. At thirty-one, he had a
high-flying career as a journalist, a designer loft, and a
pair of tweezers which he religiously used to make
sure his eyebrows never grew into a Noel Gallagher
monobrow like his father's. He played pool, watched
DVDs and hung out with work colleagues and friends
in trendy restaurants and gastro pubs across London.

He didn't do teenage displays of affection. Not in public. And most definitely not somewhere as clichéd as Heathrow Terminal 3.

Or at least he didn't used to. Now everything had changed. Not only was he locked in a farewell clinch that was like a scene from a bad movie, but, more importantly, *he didn't care*. Neither did Jimi care that he – who prided himself on being the epitome of cool – was surrounded by hordes of people throwing him curious looks. Nor did he care that the new suede Nikes he'd had Fed-Exed over from the States were going to be ruined in the downpour. Or that he was going to have to let his stonking great big erection go to waste.

Why?

Simple.

Jimi Malik was getting married.

After God knows how many flings, several half-hearted relationships, and too many one-night stands, it had finally happened. He'd met a woman who was worth giving up his bachelor ways for. A woman who'd miraculously turned the word 'monogamy' into something desirable, instead of something he'd been running away from his entire life. In short, after a whirlwind romance of six months, he knew he'd found his dream woman.

Predictably, he'd found her in a bar. He'd spotted her as soon as he'd walked in. Not that Jimi didn't often spot women he fancied in bars, in fact if the truth be known he usually vaguely fancied every woman he laid his eyes on. But she'd been different. Not just vaguely fanciable, but truly stunning. Physically, she was everything he desired in the opposite sex: straight glossy hair – hers was the colour of honey and poker-straight; long and leggy – she was a size eight and towered above him in trainers; pert, round little breasts – hers were the perfect handful. But there was a catch.

Her name: *Kylie*.

Forget spinning around, her name had sent Jimi's heart sinking to the bottom of his snakeskin Patrick Cox wannabes. He'd always assumed his soulmate would be called Lola, or Sasha, or Liberty. Not something that, however hard Ms Minogue shook her booty in those itsy-bitsy golden hotpants, still flashed up scary images of a blue-eyelinered Charlene and *that* dodgy poodle perm. Worse still, Kylies were either sixteen-year-olds from Essex, or Australians. Not that Jimi had got anything against people from Essex, or Australia for that matter, it was just that he was used to dating women from New York, Paris, Milan, London. Somewhere funky, edgy, cool.

Two vodka, lime and sodas later, and Jimi had discovered Kylie was from a small town in Canada and had only recently moved to London. He also discovered she was twenty-one, a model, and he was the envy of every man in the bar. And so he'd done the usual of asking her out to dinner, booking his usual table, and putting clean sheets on his bed for later. But then something had happened that he hadn't bargained for. During his shitake mushroom and grilled polenta starter, he'd looked across at Kylie and realized he was genuinely enjoying her company. She was funny, and interesting, and when she laughed an adorable dimple appeared in her left cheek. And it was at that moment he'd made the startling discovery that he didn't want a one-night stand, on the contrary, he wanted – cue the crashing of loud piano chords, da-da-daaaaahhhh –

A Relationship.

The realization had shocked the hell out of Jimi. Even more shocking was that instead of sleeping together on the first date, he'd patiently *and faithfully* endured a whole month of celibacy while they 'got to know each other'. It had been the longest four weeks of his life. Twenty-eight days of trying to make smalltalk with her commune of flatmates, of pretending to coo over her several small, sneezy, moulting cats that wrapped themselves around his legs and covered him with long, ginger hairs. Of having to sit through the entire boxed video set of *Cold Feet*.

Twice.

If there was one actor Jimi really couldn't stand it was James-I-think-I'm-so-bloody-funny-Nesbit. That cheeky Irish grin bugged the hell out of him. Unfortunately, Kylie thought his cheeky Irish grin was adorable, and so to prove his love Jimi had forced himself to laugh through clenched teeth at 'lovable rogue' Adam's twinkly-eyed escapades, until finally when he couldn't take another episode and was about to admit defeat, Kylie had taken pity on him, put him out of his misery.

And slept with him.

Jimi shifted from one foot to the other.

His hard-on was killing him.

Pressing himself up against Kylie's Maharishi combats, he concentrated on kissing her deeper, and deeper. Her mouth tasted of Diet Coke and Marlboro Lights. Which was another thing, he thought, letting his hands slide down her slender waist and rest on her skinny hips. Before Kylie he'd always made it a rule never to go out with smokers. 'Who wants to kiss an ashtray?' he used to scoff. Usually in a very loud voice next to a female dragging on a Silk Cut. Oh, the irony. Now here he was wanting to spend the rest of his life with a woman with a thirty-a-day habit.

A crackle of lightning splintered the skyline. What had begun as a humid September morning was now turning into a fully fledged storm. Overhead, clouds were huddling together like great big dirty black sheep, blocking out the sunlight and plunging everything into an eerie darkness. A spooky, gusty type of wind had whipped up out of nowhere and was stealing straw hats from holidaymakers and whirling along the kerb. And it was pouring down.

Mammoth raindrops began pelting the collar of

25

Jimi's T-shirt and trickling slowly across his shoulder-blades. He continued kissing Kylie, but it wasn't the same. Now all he could think about was the soggy cotton sticking to his back. It was supposed to be an Indian summer, for Godsakes. What had happened to early morning sunshine? Hazy warmth? *The pollen count?* Dryness would be nice too, he thought, feeling the rain bouncing up his legs and beginning to seep through his Diesel jeans. Obviously this was heaven's way of trying to dampen their ardour.

Right on cue there was a rumbling explosion of thunder.

'Well, I guess this is it.' Reluctantly breaking away, he attempted a jovial smile. It didn't come easy. He'd spent his lifetime perfecting a whole range of smiles — brooding, roguish, dashing, laconic — he wasn't used to doing jovial. It made him look constipated. Sniffing vigorously, Kylie glanced up at him through the Gucci sunglasses he'd bought her, and nodded mutely.

She's going to start crying, thought Jimi, feeling at once concerned and responsible. And also secretly chuffed. He felt immediately guilty. He loved Kylie, and of course he didn't *want* to upset her, but years of loving himself was a hard habit to break. Part of him couldn't help feeling comforted by how upset she was. At how upset she was to be leaving him.

'Hey come on, it's not like it's for ever.' Tilting her chin with his thumb, he wiped away the hair that had flattened itself to her forehead.

'A week feels like for ever,' she sighed, screwing up her bee-stung mouth into a sulky pout. Jimi felt himself melt. Kylie looked so darn sexy when she did that. Then it hit him. Seven whole days without sex. 'It seems like a lifetime to me, too,' he murmured, heaving a sigh.

'Do you promise you'll call every day?' Raising her eyebrows, Kylie shot him a look that said if he didn't, she'd kill him.

Jimi felt hurt that she'd even had to ask. 'Of course I

promise,' he protested. Once upon a time he would have choked upon those words. Jimi Malik? Promising to call a woman every day? Who would believe it?

'You know what, I'll call twice a day – three times even. You'll be sick of me calling, you'll take the phone off the hook,' he heard himself blathering piteously.

'I could never be sick of you,' Kylie giggled.

'Yes you could.' Now he was the one pouting. 'But I'll never get sick of you. Not even if you slob around on the sofa in sweatpants all day watching *Ready, Steady, Cook* and eating Big Macs with grease dribbling down your chin.'

'I'll never be sick of you. Not even if you shave your chest, grow a handlebar moustache and wear a jock-strap on the beach.'

This was one of their favourite games. Taking it in turns to argue about who loved each other the most. It was truly sickmaking.

Him: 'Not even when you're seventy with a perm and a blue rinse.'

Her: 'Not even when you're ninety and you've got long black hairs growing out of your ears.'

The rain showed no sign of easing off and they were both soaking, yet neither made any movement to go inside.

Until finally Kylie spoke. 'I better make a move.'

Jimi felt a wrench. 'You're leaving. *Already?*'

Pulling her sodden army jacket around her, she smiled tearfully. 'I know it's really early but it takes hours to go through all those security checks, to make sure I'm not carrying a dangerous weapon like my nail-clippers,' she tried to joke but it failed sadly. 'I don't want to miss my flight.'

'No . . . I guess not,' he mumbled, part of him wishing she would. Despite all his tough-guy posturing, he knew he was really going to miss Kylie, even if it was only for a week. He ran his eyes over her face, saw the liquid eyeliner that had been tested to its waterproof limits and was running freely down her cheeks. He missed her already.

'I love you, Goofy.' She was gazing dreamily at him. He gazed back. 'I love you, Minnie.'

Pet names. In six months. *Incredible*.

Chapter Three

Chuffed with her rather nifty bit of reverse parking,
Margaret Chapman lit up her second Lambert & Butler
cigarette of the morning, blew out the blackened
match and tossed it decadently out of her car window.
Sucking hard on the filter, she drummed one set of
freshly painted fingernails on the steering wheel, tilting her wrist ever so slightly so as to squint at the new
bracelet watch she'd just bought in duty-free. Gold and
dinky, it looked rather fabulous against her Puerto
Banus tan. Unfortunately the only problem was she
couldn't see the hands, as her eyesight was going.

But that was the gruesome reality about getting
older, she thought, taking a long, satisfying drag. Once
you hit fifty, bits and pieces started to wear out, like
the heels on an old pair of boots. Not that she was
ready for the knacker's yard just yet, she mused, snorting two jets of smoke down her flared nostrils. At
fifty-five, she was the same age as Cher and Felicity
Kendal and that wasn't bad company to be in, she
decided, tugging open the glove compartment.

Inside lurked her guilty secret. Scanning the street
to make sure no-one was looking she furtively fished
out a gold chain from the glove compartment, on the
end of which hung a pair of tortoiseshell glasses. She
glared at them hatefully, even more hatefully because
they were blurred, and then reluctantly perched them
on the very tip of her nose. As everything snapped into

perfect focus she tutted irritably. Crikey Moses, just look at the state of her French manicure. What on earth would people think? It looked a right old mess. As if one of her grandchildren had done it with Tipp-Ex and a paintbrush. Exasperated, she began furiously scraping the untidy white splodges of varnish off her cuticles with her thumbnail. Then she remembered.

She wasn't just losing her eyesight, she was losing her marbles. Gasping irritably, she stretched out her arm so that the sleeve of her lacy cardigan slid back, revealing her wristwatch. And the time. *Twenty-five minutes past nine.*

With a sharp intake of breath, she realized they were going to be late for work. She would be too late to make the MD his usual morning coffee with milk, no sugar, to run through his diary with him, to cancel his afternoon appointments so he could take his mistress to lunch . . . As the list began unravelling she whipped off her glasses, sending them swinging pendulously across her ample chest and, with all the force she could muster, crashed both palms down hard on the horn.

'*Beep-beep.*'

'Uh . . . huh?' Face down on her mattress, Grace stirred.

'*Beep-beep.*' A car horn sounded again outside her window.

'Shurrup,' she growled dozily, jamming the pillow harder around her ears and burying her face even further into her quilted mattress protector.

'*Beep-be-be-be-beep . . . beep-beep.*'

It sounded again. This time more urgently, despite the foil of jaunty tune. Grace groaned wearily. Why the hell did they have to make that racket in her street? And, by the sounds of it, right outside her frigging flat.

Oh shit.

Erupting from the duvet in a tangled volcano of arms, legs, boobs, hair, Grace bolted across to the bedroom window and yanked up the wooden slatted blind. Directly opposite, in the street below, a spearmint green Fiat Panda was parked with its engine running. The driver, a deeply suntanned fifty-something wearing a pink silk headscarf wrapped around her head in a kind of turban, an abundance of chunky silver jewellery, and clashing brick-red lipstick, was leaning out of the car window. A cigarette clamped between her teeth, she had both hands pressed firmly, and uncompromisingly, on the horn.

'*Beeeeeeeeeeeeeeeep.*'

Oh God.

It was her lift.

Margaret Chapman – Maggie to friends and work colleagues – was PA to the managing director of Big Fish Design, an international art and design agency where Grace had worked for the past three years. Despite the age gap, she and Maggie were firm friends. Many saw their relationship as one of mother and daughter, but what they didn't realize was that although Maggie might be in her fifties, she had the energy, vibrancy and *joie de vivre* of a teenager, not to mention the dirtiest sense of humour, and jeans that showed off a bottom Grace would kill for.

She was also Grace's lift. Every weekday morning she would leave her high-rise in Streatham at precisely 8.45 to make sure she arrived at Grace's at 9.15 'on the dot' so they could leave at 9.16 precisely and be in Kensington by 9.45. Free-spirited and bohemian when it came to her wardrobe, Maggie was a stickler when it came to timekeeping. Which, thought Grace, ducking down behind the reproduction Victorian radiator before Maggie could spot her in all her naked glory, could only mean one thing. She'd overslept.

Oh fuck.

Forgoing her beloved bathtub and all those luxurious, boutique-hotel-type-bottles of bath milk, body moisturisers and scented soaps she'd splurged on at Aveda last weekend, Grace went into overdrive. Throwing on everything that had lain over the end of the bed from the day before, not including underwear, she dashed around the flat haphazardly chucking things into her leather briefcase. Despite the general messiness – neither she nor Spencer were particularly big on housework – it was relatively easy to find her belongings as they stood out against the neutral décor. Spencer preferred all things plain and preferably magnolia whereas she was drawn like a magnet to anything shimmery, spangly or brightly coloured: Indian tapestry make-up bag, furry leopardskin pencil case, acid pink plastic hairbrush, flowery mobile, spangly flip-flops . . .

Her stomach gave a loud, gurgling, rumble. *Breakfast.* Glancing quickly around the kitchen – blond-wood-effect units, cream-tiled splashback, white butler sink – and finding nothing edible – she and Spencer weren't particularly big on food shopping either – she joyfully remembered the live yoghurt drinks she'd bought a couple of weeks ago when she was having a virtuous moment in Sainsbury's local. Diving on the integrated fridge-freezer she yanked it open, spotted them lined up proudly like miniature pale pink soldiers in the sliding side compartment, and grabbed one, only to realize too late that it was past its sell-by date, had swollen to twice its size and was ready to burst.

Which it did. All over her sleeve.

Swearing profusely she threw it in the swing bin, missed, left it, dabbed her sleeve with a dishcloth covered in coffee granules, dotting little black specks all over her favourite Whistles cardi, and finally, with one deft brush of her elbow along the fake marble kitchen work surface, swept the loose change/ wallet/keys into her bag. Maggie, meanwhile, sat outside and honked like a goose.

'Coming . . .' Tugging her arms into the skinny

sleeves of her denim jacket, Grace pounded down the hallway, kicked a wedge of mail out of the way with her flip-flop, slammed the door closed behind her, and hurried down the front steps.

'Take your time, doll, it's not as if we're in a rush,' grumbled Maggie, revving up the Panda as Grace yanked open the door and threw herself onto the passenger seat.

Before she'd had the chance to pull the door closed, Maggie was accelerating down the leafy street towards Wandsworth Common, Spanish conversation blaring out of her tape deck. Due to take early retirement in a few months, Maggie and her other half, Sonny, were buying a villa in Spain, and she was determined to chat with the locals. Unfortunately she'd discovered that when it came to languages, she wasn't a natural. Despite having had the 'Teach yourself Spanish in a weekend' box set out on loan from the library for the past six months, she was still only on tape one. This morning it was restaurant ordering.

'*A litre carafe of house red, please,*' intoned the voice on the tape, before repeating in fluent Spanish, '*Una jarra de litro de tinto de la casa, por favor.*'

There was a gap for Maggie to repeat. Which she did. Badly.

'Oona harra . . . er . . . deh la kah-si paw-va-floor,' she repeated, single-handedly demolishing the Spanish language.

They were speeding past large Victorian family houses, scores of four-wheeled-drives, and droves of white, affluent, middle-class mothers. Pushing three-wheeler Landrover-buggies, they were all heading towards the cluster of pine-filled teashops, overpriced grocery stores, two terribly nice chintzy boutiques and a Pizza Express which hung a sign proudly in its window boasting 'Babies and pushchairs welcome'.

If Chelsea was where Sloaney PR girls went to meet their Prince Banker, then Wandsworth was where they went to live happily ever after with two kids and a four-wheel-drive, mused Grace as she half listened to Maggie's atrocious Spanish accent that sounded like a bad take-off of *Fawlty Towers*'s Manuel. Gazing out of the window, she noticed a floppy-fringed, thirtysomething male in a pastel Ralph Lauren shirt kissing his identikit wife and toddler goodbye on the doorstep. Idly watching him striding away from his wife and children, briefcase in one hand, gym bag in the other, and climb purposefully into his navy blue Cherokee Jeep, a disconcerting thought popped into her head.

He looked like Spencer.

At a push, of course, and obviously not half as good looking, but there was something about him. He had the same athletic build, same suit, same stride, same car. Even the same expression.

Which was followed by another disconcerting thought.

She flicked her eyes back to his wife, who was still standing in the doorway, baby on hip, toddler around her ankles. Whereas Spencer bore a similarity to your average Wandsworth husband, not by any stretch of his imagination did she look like your average Wandsworth wife.

Followed by disconcerting thought number three.

To be quite frank, she didn't want to.

Oh dear. Grace felt a flutter of alarm. What did this mean? Why had she never thought this before? How come she'd spent the last three and a half years tramping across the common with these people, nodding hi, passing comment about the weather, not thinking anything was out of the ordinary, and now all of a sudden she felt like something out of *The Stepford Wives*?

'. . . I know it might only be five minutes but it throws the entire journey off kilter . . .' Breaking off from ordering paella in pidgin Spanish, Maggie was chattering away gaily as she shifted down into first at the lights.

But Grace wasn't listening. Not for the first time she'd caught herself wondering how on earth she'd ended up living in Nappy Valley. She liked Spencer's flat, it was big and comfy and grown-up, but sometimes she felt a yearning for her old, tiny, cluttered flat in Camden. For its multicultural neighbourhood, its fusion of Chinese restaurants, Indian takeaways, Thai cafés, Sudanese diners, the lively reggae bars, the colourful market, the graffiti, the litter, the mix of young and old. The abundance of neon and the complete absence of pastel-coloured shirts . . .

'. . . a few seconds, that's all it takes, and then you're slap, bang in the middle of rush hour. I dread to think what the traffic's going to be like going across that bleedin' bridge, it'll be a right nightmare . . .'

Adopting a suitably apologetic expression Grace zoned back into what she called Maggie's 'traffic speech' which she knew off by heart as it was given every morning. And almost immediately zoned back out again, Maggie's voice fading into a background hum as she gazed back out of the window, and thought about Spencer.

He'd proposed two years ago. It was memorable, not for its romance, but for its mundanity. As with a lot of occasions that are supposed to be momentous – losing your virginity, smoking your first cigarette, discovering yoga – Grace had learned over the years that all the hype and fermented anticipation that surrounds such events can make the reality seem something of a disappointment.

Take the marriage proposal. She'd been led to believe that this involved bended knees, tears of joy, waiters applauding. Not for one second during twenty-nine daydreaming years had she envisaged a drizzly midweek evening, her pottering around the kitchen cooking dinner – well, not so much cooking as removing cardboard packaging and pricking plastic sleeves with a fork – Spencer, who'd just got in from work, crashing around in the cutlery drawer, rifling among the biros, takeaway menus, drill bits and all the other crap that ended up in there, trying to unearth a corkscrew so he could open a bottle of red.

All normal, ordinary, un-proposally-type stuff, you might think.

And so did Grace until, midway through a conversation about what wedding present to buy his sister – 'Why don't we get her one of those Perspex loo seats with shells and fish and things in it?' – Spencer had gone all quiet and thoughtful, as if he quite liked the idea of the Perspex loo seat, and replied, 'Why don't we get married?' At which point the microwave had pinged to signal their Tesco's Cod Mornay was ready.

OK, so it wasn't exactly up there in the echelons of romance, but the subsequent congratulations, cards and traditional trip to Tiffany's helped to make up for it. And anyway, it didn't matter *how* he'd asked her, she'd thought consolingly while excitedly showing off her baguette-cut diamond in its platinum setting to her cooing girlfriends, surely all that mattered was that he'd asked her. To marry him. To spend the rest of her life with him. *To be his wife*.

Grace made no apologies. For all her talk of independence, equality and female emancipation, of opening her own doors and going Dutch in restaurants, of being nifty with a Black & Decker but not being able to iron an item of clothing without it bizarrely melting. For all that she always ticked the box marked Ms when she was filling out forms, and refused to tip when cabbies called her 'luv', deep down she was as romantic as the next girl.

And over the moon. After Spencer's proposal her life had taken on a whole new meaning. Entire days revolved around such weighty issues as whether to go for rice or hand-picked rose petal confetti, weeks were spent choosing his'n'hers helium balloons, and then there was the weekend she spent surfing the web for special offers on white doves. And she did it without the slightest snigger. She, Grace Fairley, a woman who'd always called it an outdated, old-fashioned tradition, who declared that white wedding malarkey was just a ridiculous waste of money, had been amazed to discover she couldn't get enough of it. Church or register office? Summer or winter? Big or small? Traditional or funky?

Only after a few weeks of avidly perusing Virgin Bride brochures with the kind of cricked-necked devotion she usually reserved for a new issue of *Glamour*, did it dawn on her that Spencer had gone awfully quiet.

Grace couldn't put her finger on it. Call it being forgetful, careless, indifferent or oblivious, blame it on a short attention span, a low boredom threshold, or just straightforward absent-mindedness, whatever adjective she chose to use, once the diamond was sparkling on her finger Spencer was hit with a kind of inertia. He became bewilderingly vague, couldn't decide about setting a date, the guest list, where to have the ceremony, where to hold the reception. In fact, for a man who prided himself on being extremely opinionated, he couldn't decide about anything.

Despite his protestations that no, of course he hadn't changed his mind, and yes, of course he wanted to marry her, the months wore on. And nothing happened. Always wanting to talk about 'it' later, he was always inexplicably – and, Grace began to suspect, *conveniently* – busy later. Until gradually her magazines became out of date and she chucked them away, her special offers on white doves expired, the platinum on her ring scratched and dulled and the diamond seemed to lose its sparkle. And life went on. She stopped mentioning it, Spencer stopped avoiding it, and for the time being they forgot about it.

Well, almost . . .

'Y'awright doll? You've hardly said a word.'

'What? Oh yeah, yeah,' stuttered Grace, as they set off jerkily from a zebra crossing. 'Look, about this morning . . . I'm sorry about being late. It's my birthday and . . .'

'Ooh sweetheart, you should've said,' remonstrated Maggie, slapping Grace's thigh affectionately and beaming at her brightly.

'Mags. The road,' reminded Grace on autopilot.

'So come on, how old?' Without missing a beat Maggie flicked her eyes back to the road.

'Thirty-one,' grimaced Grace, wrinkling up her nose at the thought of being a real-life thirtysomething. It sounded so mature, *so old*. Still, looking on the bright side, at this rate she'd be lucky to make it to thirty-two, she thought, clutching the frayed fabric of her seat as they jumped the lights. In the opposite direction an old, classic Citroën DS pulled out in front of them.

'Mags, the car . . .' shrieked Grace, bracing herself for a head-on.

'I see it, I see it,' lied Maggie, clipping its wing mirror as she swerved sharply. There was a sickening screech of brakes and the driver began honking his horn furiously.

Maggie, however, seemed completely oblivious.

'Awww, still a baby,' she was chuckling happily, the cigarette hanging lazily from the corner of her mouth.

That woman has got to have nerves of steel, thought Grace, sitting rigidly in the passenger seat, her face a whiter shade of pale.

'I tell you, it's when you get to my age you need to start worrying,' continued Maggie, sounding not the least bit worried.

Grace had to smile. 'I don't see you worrying.'

'I know. You're right,' she nodded gaily, shifting gears. 'I need to hurry up and start.' Laughing loudly, she turned her attention back to the cassette, which had moved on to hotels.

'*There is no toilet paper in the bathroom . . . No hay papel higienco en el cuarto de bano*'

'Oh for Godsakes,' gasped Maggie stubbing out her cigarette in the overflowing ashtray. Reaching out a manicured fingernail she pressed the eject button. 'Stick your bleedin' bog roll up your arse.'

Chapter Four

Time can be a real pain. One minute it's dragging its heels, not wanting to go anywhere very fast at all, and then the next moment, wham — it's hurtling into the future at such a speed it feels as if it's all over before it even began.

Kissing Kylie one last time, Jimi could feel it starting already. Someone had jammed their size nine on time's accelerator and all at once she was gathering up her bags, telling him she was fine, to stop fussing, that yes she'd drink lots of water and do her leg exercises on the plane, that no she wouldn't talk to any strange men, that of course she'd email him the minute she arrived in Toronto.

And before he knew it his hands weren't holding onto her skinny, naked midriff, they were jammed deep into his pockets and he was watching her walking away, dragging behind her the biggest trolley Samsonite had ever constructed. Watching her waving and sniffling, and smiling that gorgeous, dimply smile of hers. Then suddenly she was gone, vanished behind those automatic sliding doors like some kind of David Blaine illusion, and he was standing by himself on the pavement. *Alone.*

And with a lump in his throat.

Jimi was horrified. Kissing in public was one thing, but lumps in throats? What had got into him? He'd be crying next, he thought, swallowing hastily. It might have made Gazza a national hero, but that was different. *That was football.*

Turning, he began slowly walking back to his car. Jimi never hurried. Not even when he could see the traffic warden taking down the details of his number plate. If anything, that made him slow down to a saunter. Traffic wardens were his enemy number one. After hundreds of parking tickets and thousands of pounds' worth of fines he'd rather have his car towed than rush over and beg the warden to tear up the ticket. He wouldn't give him the satisfaction.

He was right by his car when the breast pocket of his jacket began vibrating. It was his mobile. Deftly attaching his earpiece, he answered the call.

'Hey dude, have you bin messin' about with my woman?' A terrible attempt at a Canadian accent blasted down the earpiece.

Jimi had to smile. Despite his unmistakable Etonian vowels, his oldest friend Clive could never resist pretending to be someone else on the telephone. It would be pitiful for a fifteen-year-old, but Clive was thirty and a casualty doctor at St Mary's Hospital in Paddington.

'Hi Clive.'

There was an exasperated gasp. 'How did you know it was me?'

'A wild guess?' In ten years, Jimi had never known him to actually fool anyone with one of his impersonations.

'So I take it you're ready for this evening?'

'Well that depends on what you've got in mind.' Glancing at the clock, he turned the key in the ignition, flicked on his wipers and watched as the ticket began sliding backwards and forwards across his windscreen. There was something so gratifying about seeing how long the ticket could cling on before it fell fluttering into the drain. Especially when combined with the expression on the traffic warden's face. Jimi grinned, glancing across at the clock again. So far his best time was fifty-four seconds.

Oblivious to this great sporting moment, Clive continued. 'It's all sorted. The boys are meeting at mine, we're going to pick you up in the cab on the way, ETA eight-thirty . . .'

The ticket, which had tangled its plastic wrapping around the wiper in a vain attempt to hang on for dear life, was suddenly flung sideways, skidding and catapulting across the bonnet like a stunt double. Forty seconds on the nose. A new record. Jimi grinned widely. Unlike the traffic warden, who was now advancing, scowling. Indicating right, he pulled out.

'. . . and then we're going to hit the town for some serious drinking and who knows what else . . .' Clive was interrupted by the sound of him being paged by the Tannoy: *'Dr Eddington to A&E immediately. Dr Eddington to A&E immediately.'* He cut short the call. 'I have to go, duty calls and all that.'

'Aren't you at least going to tell me where we're going?' asked Jimi, suddenly curious.

'That's the whole point, old son. You don't get to know where you're going. It's your stag night.' There was a snort of laughter and the line abruptly went dead.

My . . . stag . . . night. Silently mouthing the words, Jimi glanced at himself in the rearview mirror, trying to give himself a reality check. It sounded so alien, so weird, *so not him*. He still couldn't believe it was actually happening to him, and not somebody else. That in a matter of days he would be flying to Canada to say his marriage vows. That after all those years of being single he was giving it all up to become a faithful, devoted husband.

The concept drank up his attention and before he knew it Hammersmith roundabout was looming ahead. Seeing the traffic lights turn to green he put his foot down, then braked sharply.

What the hell . . . ?

From out of nowhere a car shot in front of him like a bullet, smashing into his wing mirror as it careered past. He gasped angrily. Would you believe it? *Would you bloody believe it?* Accelerating, he pulled along-side and turned to glower at the driver, eager for a showdown. Which is when he saw that it wasn't a sportscar being driven by some city boy, but a Fiat Panda. A spearmint-frigging-Panda and it was being driven by some mad old coot in a turban.

Jimi gawped in astonishment. Women drivers. Shouldn't be allowed on the roads, he fumed, sounding his horn as he raced ahead. He was in a hurry. He had a stag night to get ready for. And with the Panda fading fast into a spearmint blob in his rearview mirror, Jimi suddenly found his face splitting into a delighted grin.

My stag night.

Finally it had sunk in.

Chapter Five

A few miles away, in the scarlet satin and black PVC depths of Anne Summers, Rhian was absent-mindedly chewing the iridescent varnish on her thumbnail as she studied the selection of sex toys. She was spoilt for choice. There was the pair of shiny silver handcuffs with bubblegum-pink fur trim, diamanté studded cat-o'-nine-tails whip, leopardskin eye masks with matching his'n'hers G-strings, tubes of chocolate body paint . . . Her eyes lingered over those, though more from hunger than lust, she thought, her stomach making loud, approving gurgling noises.

And then of course there were the vibrators. Talk about a selection: there was an entire shelf unit dedicated to them. Rhian was mesmerized. It was a bit like the tinned tomato section in her local Tesco's, she thought, peering closer, and then hastily drawing back as she realized there was slightly more variety here than merely chopped or plum. Feeling her neck flushing, she hurriedly glanced away. She'd got side-tracked. She wasn't here to purchase a dildo – heavens, no. At the very thought the flush on her neck began spreading like a bush fire up across her cheeks. She was here for the underwear. She was here, thought Rhian, feeling a fizz of nervous excitement, *because she had a date.*

Rhian was thoroughly enjoying the novelty of shopping for naughty underwear, of imagining fastening and trussing herself into garters and stockings, satin knickers and a velvet balconette bra. The excited anticipation that a man might glimpse a lacy bra strap beneath her dress, or perhaps run his hand up her thigh and feel the knobbly fastener of her suspender instead of the thick elastic waistband of her greying tummy control knickers, was secretly thrilling. After months of feeling rejected, of her confidence being at rock bottom, she wanted something to give her a boost, to make her fabulous, provocative, sexy, fun. And not how she usually felt: a dumpy single mum.

'Excuse me, but I'm afraid children aren't allowed.'

Rhian broke off from fingering a purple lacy thong and wondering if it came in a size sixteen, and turned around. Behind her, she saw the assistant peering at her disapprovingly across the counter of scented lubricating oils. 'Excuse me?'

'Only over-eighteens. And babies,' the assistant added pointedly, puckering up her face so that her thickly caked foundation cracked like the glaze on an old terracotta pot.

They both looked at her three-year-old son Jack who was spinning around on the carpet: wrapped up in a hooker red feather boa he was humming some tune or other to himself. Lady Marmalade eat your heart out.

'But he *is* a baby,' protested Rhian. *He's my baby*, she added silently, and adoringly.

Only the assistant wasn't having any of it. Whereas Rhian might be looking at a three-year-old on the floor and seeing a cute little angel, all the assistant could see was an annoying little brat. And her P45, if the manager popped back early from lunch at Bella Pasta.

'He's not in a pushchair,' argued the assistant tartly, pursing lips that were coated in more layers of gloss than an old radiator. 'Babies in pushchairs are allowed. But no children.'

'Jack, do you want to sit in your pushchair?' cooed Rhian brightly, patting the tartan seat of the buggy as if he was a puppy.

Jack threw her a murderous look. He was having far too much fun with the feather boa to be coerced into the confines of a tatty, second-hand pushchair.

'For Mummy?'

The desperation in Rhian's voice was tangible. All at once she felt her hopes for this evening in danger of being snatched away like a handbag on Oxford Street. She'd had it all planned. She was going to set out with Jack to nursery, and on the way pop into Sainsbury's and pick up some fish fingers for his tea later, scoot into Boots for toothpaste, leg-waxing strips, condoms – well, you never know – which left just enough time for her to dash across the road and splash out on some ridiculously risqué underwear in Anne Summers.

Rhian had never been in Anne Summers before. Her underwear came in packs of three from M&S, chucked hurriedly in her wire basket along with bags of broccoli florets and their 3-for-2 fishcakes. She'd often walked past the shop on the way to the supermarket, glanced with curious interest at the window displays of flimsy bits of lace and tightly laced satin corsets, allowed her mind to wander as she'd trotted off to do some boring errand or other, imagining what it would be like to wear that kind of stuff. It looked so uncomfy, so impractical, so tarty.

So much fun.

And fun wasn't something Rhian had been having a lot of lately.

It was eighteen months since Phil had walked out and, after going through a heartbreak diet of shock, tears, grief and despair, she'd given up hope that he was going to come charging back on his white horse, begging her to forgive him, telling her he'd made a huge mistake, that he'd panicked at fatherhood, that he still loved her. She had to face facts. He had a new girlfriend, a new life in the States and a new future, and although she might be the mother of his child, however hard it was for her to face it, she was also his past.

Rhian had never intended it to end up this way. It was nine years since she'd moved to London from Cardiff to pursue her dream of becoming a make-up artist. She'd been quickly successful. In a world of combats and trainers, head-to-toe-black and fake tan, twenty-six-year-old Rhian had stood out from the crowd in a look that was more Grace Kelly than the Appleton sisters. Pale-skinned to the point of alabaster, her teenage years had been spent trawling second-hand shops and market stalls for vintage clothes long before they were fashionable, and she had a wardrobe consisting of Jackie O suits in peacock green satin, antique gold Chinese dresses embroidered with dragons, and fluffy mohair cardigans decorated with sequins and mother-of-pearl buttons. Never one to do casual, she teamed them with strings of pearls, real fur stoles, crocodile-skin clutch bags, not forgetting her trademark red lipstick and sweeping black eyeliner.

And heels.

From being a child dressing up in her mother's clothes, Rhian had discovered early on in life that heels changed everything about herself, from the way she looked, to the way she walked, to the way she felt, and from then on her tiny, size three feet were never seen in anything with less than a two-inch stiletto, kitten or mule. Even barefoot she walked on tiptoe, due to habit and shortened calf muscles from never having walked on the flat.

But there was nothing flat about Rhian. She was curvy through and through. With hourglass curves, a glossy raven bob, and the kind of deep-throated laughter that put Mariella Frostrup to shame, she exuded old-fashioned sexiness combined with a wide-eyed innocence that was fascinating to women and men alike. Not that she had the slightest clue, of course. Where men were concerned she hadn't had much experience. Unfashionably traditional, Rhian liked men to be men, and women to be women, and in twenty-first century London, the roles were all a bit too blurred for her.

Phil, on the other hand, had seemed like the perfect gentleman. She'd met him on a photo shoot. He was the photographer, she was the make-up artist and it was the oldest cliché in the book. She'd fallen for him immediately. He was achingly handsome and incredibly charming and when she'd fallen pregnant she'd thought life couldn't get any better. She was right. *It didn't.* Eighteen months after Jack was born Phil came home from a fashion shoot in the Bahamas, confessed he'd fallen for someone else, and moved out the very next day.

Overnight she'd become a single mother. At first she believed the hype – this was the millennium, she could have it all, she could be a high-flying make-up artist and a devoted mother. But after cancelling yet another job because her babysitter blobbed, spending all night with a colicky baby and all the next day with a stroppy celebrity, she decided that women quite simply couldn't have it all, and to be quite frank, she didn't want it all either – it was too bloody exhausting. And so she'd given up her career, her salary, her pension plan and private health insurance, and become a single mum on benefits – an even bigger cliché and one with stigma attached.

Those first few months had been tough, days spent numbly going through the motions, nights spent lying awake staring into the darkness, but slowly, gradually, amazingly, new life began creeping in around the edges. She moved into a housing association flat in Paddington, enrolled Jack in nursery, found herself a great babysitter. And tonight she even had a date.

Hence the mission for new underwear, thought Rhian, leaving the shop. Knickerbox was much more her anyway, she decided, trotting along the busy pavement, oblivious to the blazing red feather boa grasped in Jack's dimpled knuckles that was trailing jauntily behind her.

In fact she was so caught up in her lingerie hunt that it wasn't until she was halfway down the high street that Rhian remembered. Oh my goodness, she hadn't wished Grace happy birthday. Unclasping the crocodile-skin handbag, she manoeuvred her ancient mobile phone that was the size of a small black brick out of the faded folds of the lining. Usually she text-messaged – it was a lot cheaper – but today I'll make an exception, she thought, beginning to dial.

'Aha, the usual suspects.'

On the second floor of a grand, Victorian red-brick building in Kensington, at the far end of the de-ceptively large, open-plan office, Grace and Maggie had arrived late and, in desperate need for a coffee, were trying to slip unnoticed into the tiny kitchen.

They didn't stand a chance. Barely through the door they were pounced upon by Janine, senior designer and senior pain-in-the-arse. Grace's heart sank. 'Someone's taken my Purple Ronnie mug,' she glared accusingly at Maggie.

'Really,' breezed Maggie, lighting up another cigarette, taking just about the biggest drag a pair of human lungs could ingest, then directing a cloud of carbon monoxide fumes all over Janine's sleeveless viscose tunic.

She coughed dramatically and began waving her fleshy arms around as if doing the butterfly stroke, her bingo wings jiggling. 'For Christsakes, Margaret,' she barked. Stomping over to a window, she yanked it wide open. 'There is a smoking room, could you please make use of it.'

The smoking room was actually a smoking cupboard down the corridor. Measuring about six foot by four, it had metal grilles on the windows and could only fit in two people at a time who huddled there, wedged up against the grey metal filing cabinets, like outcasts from society.

'Sorry, doll,' cooed Maggie, her voice dripping with

barely concealed sarcasm. 'I'll just get some caffeine into these veins and then I'll be out of your hair.'

Janine huffed – she did that a lot – and ran her thick, solid fingers through her own heavy streaks. These were not natural, golden, Cat Deeley-esque highlights, these were showercap streaks that came in one unnatural shade – ash-grey – and were favoured solely by women who incorporated not just one hairdressing horror, but two: short-back-and-sides with a curly perm on top.

'And not only has someone stolen my mug, but they've replaced it with this.' With the tenacity of a terrier, Janine waved a freebie Esso mug at the few other office members who were hungrily making toast and trading telly gossip.

'Anyone for a Jaffa?' interrupted Maggie, waggling a fresh packet she'd pulled out of her handbag.

Janine glowered. Biscuits always caused the ranks to dissent. Flinging a teabag into the hateful Esso mug, she began stomping around the tiny kitchen area, slamming the fridge door, rattling the cutlery drawer, furiously clanking the teaspoon as she stirred in her two-level-and-one-half teaspoons of sugar.

Grace watched her. That was one of the ten commandments she'd learned about office life. Thou Shalt Not Use Someone Else's Mug. She wouldn't have believed it if she hadn't witnessed it at first hand, but normally sane, sensible men and women turned into crazed maniacs when it came to mugs. They hung onto them like grim death. Some would even fight over them to the death, she mused, watching as Janine threw her a thunderous expression.

'Mmm, Jaffa cakes,' enthused Stuart, comic-strip genius and general peacemaker. Studying a notice pinned to the staff noticeboard, he stretched out his hand, located a biscuit and began nibbling off the chocolate around the edge of the orange jelly. 'Great.'

Janine scowled and sipped from her Esso mug. She wanted to throttle Stuart.

'Have you seen this?' Stuart started on the sponge bottom.

'What?' asked Grace, wandering across and peering over his collar. Stuart was twenty-nine, devilishly handsome and, unfortunately for her, gay.

'This.' He jabbed his finger at the overflowing cork board on which was pinned a piece of A4 with a photo of Sydney Opera House and the headline 'Big Fish has swum all the way to Australia'.

'Going down under are you, luvvie?' Across the tiny kitchen Maggie winked at him as she spooned out Nescafé into two mugs.

'I wouldn't say no,' he winked back like some latter-day Dick Emery. 'What about you, Mags? Fancy a bit of Manley?'

Grace smiled at Maggie's expression. 'Oohh, I like the sound of that,' she laughed, pouring out two glugs of semi-skimmed. 'What the hell's that when it's at home?'

'It's a beach,' snapped Janine churlishly. 'But you're not eligible, Margaret. The agency is opening a new office in Sydney and they're looking for designers, not secretaries. You need a professional qualification,' she added smugly. Giving her a crocodile smile, she tittered loudly. 'And I'm afraid shorthand doesn't count.'

Maggie refused to rise. 'I don't think my Sonny would be too keen. He's not the surfing type, more a sangria kind of man,' she smiled, walking over with two steaming mugs and passing one to Grace.

'What jobs are being advertised?' asked Grace, look-ing at Stuart and sipping her coffee. To be honest, she never read any of the stuff that was pinned up on the noticeboard as it usually consisted of the odd ad for a second-hand car, out-of-date flyers, or one of Janine's furious marker-penned reminders about not leaving teabags in the sink. Which only made Maggie start building a PG Tips dam in the plughole.

'Oh, the usual – illustrators, web design, graphics . . .'

'Mmm, just think of all those Aussie fellas,' grinned Maggie, winking at Grace.

'Christ, just imagine,' groaned Stuart wistfully, scanning the kitchen. 'It's like a witches' coven in here.'

'Aren't you supposed to be finishing designing that book cover, Stuart?' barked Janine as she marched authoritatively back out into the office.

'Thanks for reminding me, Janine,' he smiled sarcastically, and giving Maggie and Grace a rueful smile, headed back to his desk.

'What about you, Grace?' Raising her eyebrows, Maggie gestured to the notice.

'Me?' replied Grace with genuine surprise. The thought had never even entered her head. 'It'd be pretty amazing, I mean living in Sydney, wow . . .' For a moment she felt a flicker of the old yearning. She'd always planned to travel around the world, but then she'd moved to London, met Spencer and somehow her life had taken a different path. A much better path, she added to herself as an afterthought. 'No, it's not for me.' She shook her head decisively.

'Why not?'

'I'm happy with my life the way it is, thanks,' she smiled. 'Anyway, all that sun's bad for your skin. I don't want to end up like a wrinkly old prune now, do I?' she joked.

'Like me, you mean,' quipped Maggie, waving her fag around like an air freshener and grabbing her coffee. 'If you need me I'm just popping next door for my nicotine,' she smiled, wafting out with her coffee which, Grace suddenly noticed, just happened to be in Janine's Purple Ronnie mug.

Smiling, she sipped her coffee and her eye drifted back to the photograph. Sydney, Australia. The other side of the world. A whole, new, completely different life, full of beaches and sunshine and . . . for a brief moment she found her mind vaguely toying with the idea, before quickly abandoning it. She was being ridiculous. Spencer could never move to the other side of the world, and she could never go without him, could she?

The shrill ring of a phone pierced her thoughts.

'Will somebody get that?' snapped Janine's voice irritably.

'It's Grace's, she's in the kitchen,' piped up Stuart timorously.

'No I'm not,' answered Grace, rushing across to her desk and diving for her phone. 'Hello, Grace Fairley speaking.'

'*Happy birthday to you, happy birthday to you, happy birthday . . .*' It was Rhian. Best friend and frustrated lounge singer.

'*Happy birthday dear Graaa-ceeee –*' there was a tremulous warbling as her voice shifted octaves and began building towards its final crescendo – '*Happpeee, birth-daaaayy, tooooo,*' followed by a final gasping of air.

Wait for it. Grace held the handset away from her ear in readiness. Any minute now . . .

'*Yoooooooo.*' There followed the kind of high-pitched tremulous wail that went on for ever, rather like Mariah Carey. Until finally . . . Silence.

'Aww, thanks Rhian, that was great.'

'Oh it was nothing,' she panted heavily, sounding delighted. 'So, how does it feel to join the thirty-something gang?'

'Liberating.'

'Really?' Rhian was impressed by Grace's nonchalance. When she'd turned thirty-one she'd spent the whole week in sunglasses and a headscarf, convinced she'd suddenly wrinkled like a fruit on a time-release film.

'Actually I'm lying,' confessed Grace, sinking into her chair. 'It's a complete headfuck.'

There was a sharp intake of breath at the end of the line. Grace smiled, picturing Rhian's shocked expression. With Rhian, she always felt like the naughty little sister, foolish where Rhian was sensible, impulsive where she was cautious, clumsy where she was careful.

'Thirties are the new twenties,' consoled Rhian brightly.

'What magazine did you read that in?'

'*Cosmopolitan*. So it must be true.'

This, it has to be noted, was said without a hint of irony.

Grace couldn't help smiling. Whereas some people found answers to life in religion, or yoga, or even alcohol, Rhian's philosophy was garnered from an eclectic mix of superstition, spiritualism, astrology – and a stack of glossy magazines. Her handbag was always filled with crystals, Mexican worry dolls and a bottle of Australian Bush Essence; her bookcase was stuffed with self-help manuals, astrological guides and back issues of *Marie Claire*, and as for her CD collection – Rhian had to be the only person who still listened to Enya. *With a straight face.*

'By the way, about tonight . . .'

'You are still coming, aren't you?' urged Grace.

'Try stopping me,' smiled Rhian. 'The babysitter's booked, the dress is ironed, I've even shaved my legs . . .'

'Sounds like you've got a date.' It was meant as a joke but the silence that followed showed that Grace had unexpectedly hit on the truth.

'Oh my God, Rhian, you have, haven't you?'

'Well you see I was having a drink at the Windsor Castle with my friend Suzie . . .' Rhian began gabbling guiltily '. . . and she was late, so I ended up chatting to the barman. His name's Noel,' she admitted, almost apologetically.

'You're a dark horse.'

'It's nothing serious, just a bit of fun,' she began nervously.

Sensing her friend's grave doubts, Grace hastily switched from teasing to encouraging. 'Good for you, that's great.'

'I don't know about great,' murmured Rhian doubtfully. Reaching Knickerbox, she paused at the doorway to stare at the window display. Her stomach began fluttering as if she'd just released a cage of butterflies in there. 'To be honest, it's all pretty terrifying. That's why I wanted to bring him along tonight, for a bit of moral support, and so you can see what you think.' Squashing her nose against the glass, she stared at a pair of cream lace knickers. Was it just her, or were they getting smaller? 'When it comes to men, I'm not exactly the best judge of character, am I? I thought Phil was my soulmate and look what happened.'

Grace slugged back a mouthful of coffee. 'Do soulmates really exist? Or is it just a concept they use in articles about Posh and Becks to make us mere mortals feel dissatisfied?'

'What about Spencer?' protested Rhian. Her belief that everyone had a soulmate was as fundamental as a five-year-old's belief in Santa Claus. 'I thought he was your soulmate.'

Grace hesitated. She thought about earlier that morning: the snowglobe, those nagging doubts that hadn't disappeared but were lingering like a dull ache. For a moment she considered telling Rhian how she felt, confiding her fears, asking her advice. And then changed her mind. She brushed it off. 'He is,' she said firmly. Too firmly.

'Lucky you,' sighed Rhian, manoeuvring Jack's pushchair through the doorway and into the satin jungle of push-up bras and G-strings. Taking a deep breath she steeled herself to take that first step back into the land of dating.

'Yeah I know,' agreed Grace, saying her goodbyes and hanging up. Taking a sip of hot, sweet coffee she stared distractedly out of the window. The dull ache twinged.

Lucky me.

Chapter Six

It was all in the hips.

Swaying tantalizingly in the amber glow of the candlelight, they sent ripples spreading across her pale naked belly. A gentle quivering that began below the diamond solitaire glittering in her bellybutton and quickly rose upwards until the soft fleshy rolls were trembling and shaking. Jiggling and wobbling. This was a stomach that had never done a sit-up, felt the burn, or counted calories. It wasn't the kind seen on catwalks, in *Vogue* magazine, Hollywood blockbusters or Special K ads. Proudly undulating to the rhythmic beat of the music, this was the kind of stomach that was usually kept firmly, and ashamedly, under wraps. It was flabby. Covered in stretchmarks. *And it had cellulite.*

Grace was mesmerized. Sitting at a table in the crowded restaurant, she gazed at the bellydancer with a mixture of disbelief and awe. Having been brought up on a diet of Pamela Anderson, Kate Moss and Kylie, not to mention a punishing regime of thrice-weekly gym sessions since she was eighteen, she was dumbfounded to realize that this rather plain fortysomething woman wearing false eyelashes and a balding sequined bikini top with a fraying C&A label, had the sexiest, most desirable belly she'd ever seen. And, by the look on the faces of the diners, she wasn't alone in her revelation. If the women squeezed into their Earl jeans were hypnotized, the men were positively drooling.

Including Spencer.

'Isn't she fantastic?' Reaching across the table littered with falafel crumbs and half-eaten bowls of meze, she stroked his forearm to get his attention.

'What? Oh yeah . . .' Spencer nodded, blushing self-consciously as he reached for his wine glass and took a large gulp. 'Though I have to say I'd rather be looking at you in a bikini,' he whispered, running his thumb down the side of her face and leaning forwards to give her a kiss.

Grace smiled happily. Normally, catching Spencer ogling another woman wouldn't be cause for merriment, but in this instance she couldn't help feeling amused as she watched his cheeks flush ketchup red. Despite a smattering of grey hairs around his temples and an air of relaxed confidence that came with athletic good looks and partnership in one of the best law firms in Covent Garden, Spencer looked like a naughty schoolboy when he was embarrassed.

'Do you suppose it's really difficult?' asked Rhian, who was sitting opposite, trying to make smalltalk with Noel, her date. Looking incredibly striking, with her large doe eyes, sleek plum-coloured bob, and the kind of curves befitting a fifties sweater girl, on the outside Rhian appeared every inch the confident, attractive, sexy woman. But it was a different story on the inside, where nerves, awkwardness and insecurity bubbled like a Jacuzzi in the pit of her stomach.

'Apparently it's all to do with rhythm.' Seeing Rhian getting no response from Noel, Grace tried helping her out.

'Isn't everything?' quipped the horsy blonde at the end of the table.

This was Tamsin. For anyone who didn't know her, she could be summed up in three words: 'Works in PR'. An old university friend of Spencer's and the archetypal smug married, she would orchestrate any conversation to talk about her 'amazing' beach ceremony in Barbados and preach to other 'less fortunate singletons' how marriage was the best thing in the world and they didn't know what they were missing. A statement which she usually directed at Grace with a look of pity and condolence.

By rights, her husband Matt should have been equally unbearable, but surprisingly he couldn't have been nicer. Owner of an organic café in Shepherd's Bush, he was funny, faithful, kind and caring – in fact, there was only one problem with Matt. And that, unfortunately, was his bloody awful wife.

'Wouldn't you say, darling?' Catching her husband's eye, Tamsin smiled conspiratorially, and then batted her eyelids around the table to make sure everyone had clocked her. It was impossible not to, thought Grace, blithely. Tamsin was forever harping on to anyone who would listen about how often she and Matt did it, how amazing their sex life was, and how her nickname for him was Marathon Man.

So much so that Grace suspected she hadn't had a shag in yonks.

'Actually, I once watched this amazing documentary about a woman who took belly-dancing lessons,' ventured Matt, seemingly oblivious to Tamsin's attempts at sexual nuance. 'In six weeks she went from a suburban housewife to some kind of Mata Hari.'

'Yeah, I saw that,' interjected Noel, pausing for a moment in between mouthfuls of deep-fried Haloumi cheese. It was the first thing he'd said all evening. Apart from 'Mine's a Stella.'

'*Really?*' A surge of hope flooded Rhian's perfectly made-up face.

Grace knew what she was thinking, as she was thinking the same thing.

He watches documentaries.

'Wow, that must have been really interesting,' prompted Rhian, surreptitiously extracting a sliver of iceberg lettuce from underneath a falafel and nibbling at it. She hadn't touched any of the starters, due partly to her nerves, partly to her latest diet, and mostly to her dress, which she'd dug out of the back of the wardrobe and which was so tight the cotton on the seams was squeaking. 'It was pretty boring, actually,' mumbled Noel, not looking up from trying to wipe the pattern from his plate with a rag of pitta. 'I flicked over to watch J Lo on *Top of the Pops*.'

'Do you think I'd make a good bellydancer?' giggled Tamsin, tossing back her polished hair and blatantly fishing for compliments. Grace pretended not to hear. Tamsin had the most annoying habit of always trying to drag the conversation back to her favourite topic of conversation, which just happened to be herself.

Even more annoying was how it was only women who seemed to notice this. Men, on the other hand, always thought she was 'really sweet'. It was as infuriating as it was disconcerting.

'Because I've always secretly fancied having a go at it,' continued Tamsin, determined to hoik out some words of flattery if it killed her.

'Me too,' enthused Rhian, inadvertently stealing her limelight. She glanced shyly at Noel. He was much younger and alarmingly trendier than she'd remembered from last week in the pub, but like she'd said to Grace earlier in the loos, so what if he was only twenty-six? On paper he'd ticked all the boxes. Single. Attractive. Employed. Available.

He couldn't be that bad. Could he?

'*You*? Bellydancing?' There was a snort of laughter from across the table. 'Well, you've certainly got the hips for it,' joked Noel, winking playfully at Rhian and blowing her a kiss.

She laughed good-naturedly. Well, fat people always laugh at themselves, don't they? thought Rhian, giggling loudly. It came with the territory and the thighs. But when she thought no-one was looking, her face crumpled and she silently concertinaed the lipstick-stained filter of her cigarette down hard into the blackened ash.

Across the table, Grace caught her friend's hurt and glared at Noel. Well, that answered that question, didn't it?

Yes, he bloody well could.

They were having dinner at Zagora's, a Moroccan restaurant tucked away in a side street in deepest Elephant and Castle. On first impressions, it would seem a bizarre choice to celebrate a birthday. It didn't have a fashionable postcode or a listing in *Time Out*, Madonna had never been spotted there and the only clue it was there at all was the flickering neon sign hanging lopsidedly in the window. In fact, to be brutally honest about it, with its cold and unflattering strip lighting, white scuffed Formica takeout counter and misspelt Day-Glo stickers advertising 'free chilly sauce' and 'battered onion rings' stuck higgledy-piggledy against the back wall, it looked like the kind of place you'd only ever venture into after the pubs had shut.

But that was the thing about first impressions, Grace had thought earlier as she'd pushed open the door and walked boldly inside: they were always misleading. Which was a real shame, because hidden away at the back was an archway draped with a tasselled velvet curtain, and what most people didn't know about, and would most probably never *get* to know about, was that stepping through it was a bit like stepping into Narnia. Except on the other side it wasn't a winter wonderland, but a bustling restaurant decorated with sepia-painted walls and glowing lanterns, filled with people and music and, best of all, perfumed with the most amazing scent of exotic spices.

Breathing in the mouth-watering aroma, Grace looked around the table at her friends. Spencer had gone a long way to make up for his lack of present and lack of sex, not only by booking a table at her favourite restaurant, but also by remembering to actually invite their friends, instead of his usual habit of forgetting until they'd arrived at the restaurant, realizing nobody else had turned up, and then doing a frantic ring-around. In expectation, she'd spent all day planning what to wear. Determined to wow him with such a knockout outfit he'd never again suggest she wore that horrid, old black dress, she'd had it all planned. She was going to glam up in something tight and sexy, attempt to blow-dry her wavy hair straight, paint her toenails gold and wear a ridiculously high pair of heels.

Unfortunately she'd run late at work and only just made it home in time to dive into the shower, pull on her jeans, and leave her hair to dry – *naturally*. It wasn't a particularly good look. Heroines in novels might look great with just a slick of lipgloss and a pair of flip-flops, but this was real life and she needed time, effort, and a scary-looking mountain of products.

Something which had been kindly pointed out by Tamsin, who'd turned up at the restaurant with a swingy curtain of golden hair extensions, a new Diane von Fürstenberg dress, and a salon-applied fantasy tan. And had greeted her with a stiff little perfumed hug, cooing, 'Ooh, is grunge back in?'

'. . . and so this oldish bloke walks into my office and says, "I want to sue my wife for criminal damage, I want her locking up . . ."' The Merlot had waved its magic wand, and as an animated Spencer began regaling them with one of his anecdotes, everyone leaned forward to listen. Including Grace, despite having already heard the story.

'. . . when I ask why, he confesses, "I was having an affair and when she found out she left me . . ."'

'Hear, hear,' heckled Rhian, taking a slug of vodka tonic.

'". . . but not before she'd poured paint stripper on my Mercedes, cut off the arms of all my suits, hid a bag of frozen prawns under the mattress",' continued

Spencer, his voice getting louder, his mannerisms more theatrical. 'And so I say, "How long were you married?" And he replied, "Twenty-five years".' Draining his wine glass, he refilled it generously.

Grace noticed, and felt a pang of worry. That was his fourth glass of wine and they'd been there less than an hour.

'Now this man is as bald as a coot, severely over-weight, and he stinks of BO. At which point my partner, Rupert, walks in and, taking one look at him, says . . .' Drawing himself up, Spencer twisted his face into a growl and barked, ' "Quite frankly dear chap, if I was the judge I wouldn't lock her up, I'd give her a bloody medal".'

There was a burst of appreciative laughter from around the table, the loudest surprisingly coming from Noel, who clutched his Adidas tracksuit top and brayed like a donkey. Thankfully, with perfect timing the food arrived, and he was silenced by a generous mouthful of lamb tagine, the juices of which dribbled down his chin like wax from a melted candle.

'Mmm, this place is really fabulous,' enthused Rhian, catching Grace's worried expression and giving her shoulder an encouraging squeeze. 'The food looks amazing.'

'Shame about the wine,' replied Spencer, gulping down the rest of his glass. 'They really need to get themselves a decent wine list here.'

'Well you seem to be drinking enough of it,' quipped Grace, trying to be all light-hearted and not sound like a nag, and failing miserably and sounding exactly like one. She couldn't help it. When Spencer drank, his whole personality would change. At first he'd become happy and amiable, the life and soul of the party, the last one to leave. But unfortunately the problem was he never knew when to stop and he'd inevitably turn moody, irrational, argumentative. She looked at him, his face already flushed, his body language more animated, his expressions exaggerated, and felt a knot tighten in her stomach. Just for once, could he not get completely hammered. Not tonight. Not on her birthday.

Defiantly he began refilling his glass. 'I've had a couple of mouthfuls,' he protested, even though it was blatantly obvious he'd had a whole lot more. His unsteady hand caused him to overfill and wine sloshed over the brim. A large scarlet puddle began seeping into the Persil white tablecloth.

'*Spence . . .*' Gasping, Grace began dabbing it with her napkin.

'Don't panic, it's only a tablecloth,' he replied calmly, picking up the offending bottle.

She continued blotting.

'Grace, just leave it.'

'But it'll stain.'

'It's a restaurant, I'm sure they can cope with a few wine stains.'

Reaching for the salt cellar she began sprinkling the tablecloth.

'*For Christsakes, will you stop fussing.*'

The chattering at the table fell silent.

Grace looked away, her face blazing. It had started already; the alcohol was affecting his temper. An awkward void opened up, which Rhian immediately attempted to fill.

'Ooh, are those the chicken kebabs? Don't they look delicious.' Leaning across the table, she began sniffing the pile of decorated bowls. It crossed her mind to wonder whether it was possible to actually inhale calories.

'Shall I order another bottle?' Emptying the last few drops into his glass, Spencer looked expectantly around the table.

Leaning back in his chair, Matt shook his head. 'I'm on the beers, mate.'

'Not for me, I'll stick with the vodka,' said Rhian loyally.

'And I'll stick with you,' grinned Noel, reaching under

the table and giving Rhian's thigh a flirty squeeze. Unused to the male attention, she blushed vermilion.

'You know, you should try this detox that I'm doing, it's really amazing . . .' trilled Tamsin, smiling engagingly at Spencer and angling her body towards him. 'You'd feel like a whole new man.'

But for once Spencer wasn't listening. 'Grace?' he interrupted, making eye contact while Tamsin gasped huffily in the background.

'No thanks.' Shaking her head, Grace reached for the water.

'Oh c'mon, Babes, you're supposed to be celebrating,' he coaxed, taking a generous mouthful and clinking his glass apologetically against her own. 'I'm sorry,' he mouthed, reaching across for her hand and smiling, his usually white teeth stained purple.

Feeling his fingers interlacing through hers, Grace gazed into Spencer's bloodshot eyes. She knew that look. She'd seen it all too often. Alcohol-induced adoration. Weaving its way through his veins like an anaesthetic, the wine had erased his guilty defensiveness and embarrassment, leaving behind a warm, woozy sentimentality.

'I'm fine, honestly. Don't order another bottle. Not just yet anyway . . .'

But as she said it she knew he wasn't going to take a blind bit of notice. And she was right. Picking up the empty bottle by its neck he dangled it in the air between finger and thumb and raised his eyebrows at Ahmed, the monobrowed owner, who was getting carried away on the dance floor clapping wildly, and enthusiastically wiggling a tenner down the bellydancer's generous cleavage. Catching his customer's eye, he prised himself reluctantly away from her breasts, hitched up his already impossibly high-waisted trousers to conceal his erection, and scuttled over with a fresh Merlot. Ahmed might be a self-confessed breast man, but he was a businessman first and foremost.

Turning back, Spencer's grin lost its edge as he caught Grace's expression. 'I just fancied another glass,' he shrugged defensively.

You mean another six, she corrected silently, trying not to let it get to her. But watching as Ahmed filled up Spencer's glass, she couldn't help thinking how selfish he was being. About getting blotto, about not buying her a birthday present, about choosing cufflinks over her, about *not setting a date*. She pulled away her hand and, noticing the ring that was still sitting on her finger, a silent reminder, Grace finally realized there was no point pretending.

It got to her.

Big time.

Chapter Seven

Stifling a yawn, Jimi poured the rest of the beer in his glass, tilting it sideways so that the amber liquid swirled gently, gazing as the bubbles began exploding to the surface, bursting into a white frothy head before slowly dispersing.

He zoned back in.

Jesus, anyone would think he was stoned. Thinking about it, he wished he was. He took a swig. The beer was warm and soapy. Rolling it around his tongue he held it in his mouth, savouring its bitterness, while surveying his surroundings.

Never again.

According to Clive, the restaurant was one of London's best-kept secrets. According to Jimi, who'd been eagerly looking forward to a bar in Notting Hill or a restaurant in the West End, it was the unofficial London Dungeon. Wedged between 'the first coin-operated launderette in the world' and 'Terry's Taxis', it was the kind of place he'd never dream of entering sober. There was no doorman to unhook a little gold rope for them, no queue they could jump, no guest list to be on. Instead there was a garishly illuminated take-out section at the front with mummified chickens rotating on spits and a lamb shank oozing grease on a kebab stand.

Stepping out of the cab into the warm, pungent air, his spirits had shrivelled up with disappointment like a crisp packet on a naked flame. He wasn't a snob, he was into all things 'urban', he dug things that were edgy, but stepping over a tramp asleep outside on the pavement, Jimi hadn't been able to help feeling it was all a bit *too edgy*. Up and coming areas might be cool in grainy black and white photo shoots in *ID*, but he didn't want to actually spend his stag night in one. He wanted to be somewhere that had up and come.

And what was that smell?

Walking inside, he'd inhaled a powerful whiff of incense that had made his eyes water. Breathing through his mouth, he'd followed the rest of the party into the stifling hot restaurant. It was an assault on his senses. As well as the pungent aroma, loud, wailing drum music was being piped over the speakers and there was a middle-aged woman jigging around in the middle of the room – *in a bikini*.

Jimi let the beer trickle slowly down the back of his throat. He'd spent the last hour trying to enjoy himself, and failing miserably. He was bored, disappointed, and fed-up. In fact, to be perfectly honest he wouldn't mind going home.

Early.

On his stag night.

As the thought struck, he expelled it at once and forced himself to take another swig of beer. Unfortunately, the same couldn't be said for Clive.

'*Avago*.' Stumbling back from the toilet he leaned across the table and slurred loudly in Jimi's face. His breath stank of beer, spicy food and the smouldering cigar wedged in the corner of his mouth. Despite being a non-smoker he'd happily bowed to the tradition of men and celebratory cigars, and was puffing – and spluttering – on a Monte Cristo.

'What?' yelled Jimi, trying to make himself heard above the restaurant din.

Mistakenly assuming it was the volume of the music and not his lack of coherence that was the problem,

Clive leaned even closer. He slurred again. Only this time even louder. '*Avago.*'

Jimi shook his head. It was useless.

But Clive wasn't about to give up. Swaying dangerously in the ancient pair of Allstars he'd had since Eton, he attempted to fix him with a bleary frown. He was having trouble focusing. Forehead wrinkled, eyebrows raised, he began to blink rapidly, while at the same time his mouth began opening and closing, his cigar wobbling dangerously. It all seemed to take a lot of effort and an interminably long time before finally he managed to articulate one word. 'Bellydancing . . .' There was a pause as his brain grappled through the alcoholic fog to string it all together. 'Why don't you . . . there was a beery pause '. . . have . . . a . . . go . . . at . . . bellydancing,' he finally announced, smiling triumphantly and taking a Churchillian puff of his cigar, which was beginning to resemble a small, soggy brown turd.

Jimi smiled. He knew Clive was only trying to get him to enjoy himself, but there was nothing worse than being sober among drunk friends. 'I think I'll sit this one out, thanks.'

'Nahhhh, you can't do that,' the three remaining members of the stag party butted in like backing singers from the far end of the table. 'Nahhh, you can't do that,' they wailed the chorus into their Casablanca beers.

'You wanna bet?' laughed Jimi, slumping down in his seat and consoling himself with his beer.

'But it's your stag night,' they chorused. As Jimi's oldest mates, Andy, Stu and Kev had made the trip down from Manchester especially for the occasion. They were not, under any circumstances, going home empty-handed.

'I never thought I'd see the day . . .' began Kev. 'It's like the end of an era . . .'

'But who can blame him for wanting to spend the rest of his life with the adorable Kylie?' slurred Clive wistfully. As a hopeless and unfulfilled romantic, he lived vicariously through other people's relationships. 'Who isn't envious of him marrying such an amazing woman, sharing his life, his soul, his body . . .'

'Wooooahhhhh!'

His speech was interrupted by an explosion of *double entendres* as Clive gasped with irritation, 'Gentlemen, please, do you have to drag this down into something so base?'

There was a chorused reply of yes as Clive broke into a good-natured smile and swigged his beer in defeat.

'It's Jimi's last night of freedom, we're not going to let him disappear off to Canada without making his last night a memorable one, now are we, lads?' declared Stu. Taking over the stag party mantle from Clive, who'd peaked way too early and was now collapsed in a chair, he was getting into his stride. 'No, we're most certainly not,' he repeated, beginning to sound scarily like one of those warm-up acts they always use to get studio audiences all fired up before game shows.

'You're not . . . ?' asked Jimi dubiously, stretching out the question and leaving it hanging. He was greeted by a trio of shaking heads.

'. . . no we're bloody well not. Do you think we're going to let you sit there all night?'

'Well, I was thinking maybe we could head over to Notting Hill,' suggested Jimi hopefully. 'I'm a member of the Electric so there'd be no problem getting us all in . . .' His voice trailed off as the rest of them burst into loud beery laughter.

'What's so funny?'

'You are,' they chorused.

Jimi felt a pang of panic. Normally he was the one cracking the jokes, but tonight the joke appeared to be on him, and before he knew what was going on he was being hoisted up from behind the table, hauled up above the empty beer bottles and half-eaten plates of food and dragged towards the dance floor. It was only afterwards, with the luxury of hindsight and time to do a few action replays in his head, that Jimi realized he should have put up more of a fight. Unfortunately, at the time it all happened so fast he wasn't sure what was going on. One minute he'd been drinking his beer and minding his own business, and then the next he was slow-dancing with the woman in the bikini.

'Oh Christ, it looks like a stag party,' muttered Spencer, giving himself a top-up as he watched a rowdy group of men tugging their mate out from behind the safe house of the table, and enthusiastically pushing him towards the gyrating bellydancer.

Still wearing his leather jacket and a woolly hat which he'd pulled down over his face in a futile attempt to hide, Jimi was self-consciously jigging up and down on the dance floor, while the other diners clapped along good-spiritedly. The bellydancer, meanwhile, who'd been so delighted at such handsome company that she'd wrapped herself around him, had been prised off by Ahmed and was now circling him with her shimmery veils, twirling and leaping around like something out of Kate Bush's 1978 'Wuthering Heights' video.

'Has Spencer set a date for his stag night yet?' piped up Tamsin. Feeling left out of the conversation, she consoled herself by having a quick stir. 'Or are you two still set on a long engagement?' Pointedly raising her eyebrows at Grace, she did her 'concerned friend' look. Grace bristled, and was about to launch into her 'long engagements are fashionable' speech when unfortunately – or perhaps fortunately – one of the stag party, a ginger-haired man in a REM tour T-shirt, hoisted himself up from his seat, lost his balance and fell backwards into their table.

'What the . . . ?'

Spencer swore loudly as their table shook violently, sending plates crashing Greek wedding style, cutlery clattering to the floor, and the fresh bottle of Merlot toppling towards his lap. He staggered to his feet, but he was too late. The alcohol had dulled his reactions and the red wine had already splattered all over his shirt. A large stain began spreading across his crotch, echoing the thunderous look on his features.

Typically the stag party thought this was the most hilarious thing that had ever happened. Fuelled by alcohol and bawdy humour they whooped and jeered as Ahmed and his army of waiters swooped upon the table. Cursing in Arabic they started clearing up the mess, helped by Rhian, who immediately grabbed a dustpan and brush and fell on her hands and knees, while Spencer and Tamsin took it in turns to see who could complain the loudest.

'It's just outrageous, look at my Jimmy Choos, they're brand new . . .'

'Jesus Christ, what a bunch of idiots . . .'

Grace glanced at Spencer. Red-faced and wine-stained, he was standing legs apart, arms raised while Ahmed doused his crotch in white wine and began dabbing tentatively. She glanced away, and taking this as her cue to use the loo, began weaving past Noel and Matt who were calmly sipping beers and talking football, past the bellydancer who was treating the impromptu interval as a fag break, towards the back of the restaurant.

And it was then she saw him.

It was the man from the dance floor. Taking off his leather jacket, he was straightening the collar of his loud, floral shirt, making sure it was just so. She watched him. Something about the way he was doing it struck a familiar chord. He vaguely reminded her of someone. But no, it couldn't be. She was being ridiculous.

She continued walking and as she did, he turned towards her, his face partly concealed by the stupid teacosy he was wearing on his head. For a split second Grace thought, *she hoped*, she'd made a mistake, that

she'd got it wrong. After all, it had been a long time –
her mind flicked back – it seemed like a lifetime ago.

She paused.

Tugging off his hat he ran the flat of his palm over
his shaved scalp, his head bowed, his face hidden in
the shadows. Until with a shrug of his shoulders he
looked up.

And it seemed like only yesterday.

When will I be famous?

Manchester 1988

He drove a Ford Capri.

Tangerine orange with go-faster stripes, huge, shiny chrome fog lights, and a spoiler that rose like a shark's fin, it would accelerate into the school carpark every morning, windows down, stereo cranked up, Bros's anthem 'When Will I Be Famous' blasting from its super-woofer speakers.

And everyone would turn to stare. To gawp enviously at the sixth-former who, in his aviator sunglasses and tight white T-shirt, thought he was Grangeville Comp's answer to Nick Kamen, his heavily streaked hair wet-gelled carefully into a spiky flat top, a cigarette hanging nonchalantly from his lips.

The driver's name was Jimi Malik. Cocky, confident and outrageously good-looking, he was the lead singer in the band, Carnal Knowledge, sported a Navajo eagle tattoo on his shoulder, a full chin of real stubble that put to shame the pathetic fronds of bumfluff on every other boy's top lip, and — get this — not only had he passed his driving test, *he had a car*.

You couldn't get much cooler. All the boys at Grangeville Comp secretly wanted to be Jimi Malik. All the girls secretly wanted to be *with* Jimi Malik.

Except Grace.

Grace couldn't stand the sight of him. She thought he was a complete idiot. She thought he was vain, sexist, big-headed, talentless – and every other word she could find in her pocket thesaurus. She loathed the way he was always cracking jokes, hated how he swaggered around the corridors with an ever-present crocodile of third-formers who devotedly followed him like a fan club, despised how he always insisted on wearing sunglasses and clinging to his microphone when he was on stage with his band, like some kind of wannabe Bono. Everyone else might have fallen under Jimi Malik's spell, but she saw right through him. Right through his strategically ripped 501s, right through his black leather biker's jacket with the sleeves pushed up way past his elbows, right through his red and white paisley bandanna.

Jimi Malik, for his part, couldn't stand Grace either. When he wasn't driving past her at the bus stop, purposely going too close to the kerb to splash her new Miss Selfridge white denim jacket with dirty water, he was taking the mickey out of her taste in music – so what if she knew all the words to every song ever written by Everything But the Girl? But worst of all was his greeting whenever she walked by. Clicking his tongue and winking at her he would take the greatest delight in sneering, 'Still a virgin?' and watch her turn a violent shade of cerise, throw him her filthiest look and stomp off in the opposite direction.

This went on for two whole years. Right through lower sixth to upper they were sworn enemies, arch-rivals, Den and Angie of the sixth form common room, until mercifully, on 15 June 1988, the credits had finally rolled on this particular soap opera. The last A-level exam over, Grace had walked out of the assembly hall, down the corridor and out through the fire doors. It was raining, but even that hadn't dampened the surge of jubilance she'd felt as she watched Jimi climb into his car, jack up the stereo and accelerate, tyres screaming, third-formers sniffling, out of the car park.

And out of her life.

For ever.

There'd followed two glorious months of doing nothing. No having to stay in every night underlining Shakespearean sonnets with a luminous green high-lighter pen. No having to frantically redo revision timetables as the exams loomed ever closer. No having to miss the *EastEnders* omnibus to learn the dates of Wolsey's foreign policy. It had been sheer bliss. Hanging out with her friends in the park, shopping trips to River Island to purchase lots of things in black Lycra, Tiffany's nightclub on a Friday night wearing the aforementioned Lycra.

Grangeville Comp became a distant memory. A past life that had faded quickly as the future burned bright with feverish anticipation. Thoughts of university, leaving home, new people and new places filled Grace's every waking moment as turning eighteen, she passed her driving test, opened her first bank account and got legally drunk on Malibu and pineapple. In those two months she quite literally, threw up and grew up.

So it was this new adult Grace who, on a hot, muggy Wednesday morning in the middle of August, joined the stream of anxious eighteen-year-olds as they descended for the last time on the Victorian redbrick comprehensive to receive their long-awaited A-level results and then retired across the road to the pub to celebrate – or commiserate. Unfortunately she was one of those commiserating. On opening the brown paper envelope and seeing she'd gained a grade A at Art, but unclassifieds in the rest of her subjects, her first re-action had been to burst into tears, but her second had been to bury her aching disappointment and join the rest of her friends in the beer garden.

As soon as she'd sat down on the grafittied wooden bench, she'd realized it was a big mistake. Surrounded on all sides by sixth-formers comparing grades and discussing universities was bad enough, but even worse, she just happened to have managed to sit right next to the swotty straight-A brigade who kept congratulating each other and discussing the merits of Oxford versus Cambridge. For someone who was now looking at the prospect of having to go through clearing to scrape a place at some godforsaken place like Coventry poly – *if she was lucky* – it was torture.

Bored, miserable and wondering how long she had to sit there being polite before she could escape, she'd been consoling herself with a bottle of Diamond White and a packet of scampi fries, when she thought she heard music. It was coming from a car stereo. Strains of Bros wafted towards her, followed by the roar of a Capri engine, the skid of tyres on the tarmac, and an overpowering whiff of Kouros aftershave. Just Great.

That was all she needed.

She didn't have to turn around. She knew it was Jimi Malik. Instead she resolutely persevered with trying to listen to the conversation about freshers week and sipping her warm, flat cider. But she was bursting with curiosity. She could imagine everyone crowding towards Jimi as he climbed out of his car. See him swaggering, posturing, full of himself as he swigged from a Grolsch that had been passed to him by one of his cronies.

Even more galling was hearing him laughing and joking, doing high-fives and boasting about his 'wicked results'. Her ego bristled. What was so wicked about them? What were they? Were they better than hers? Worse than hers? The same as hers? Inside she felt the familiar annoyance. And then. Quite suddenly. She heard something else.

'*Oi. Paki.*'

The words resounded through the excited chatter of the beer garden. All at once it fell eerily quiet, just the sound of a few drunken giggles and someone nervously clearing their throat. 'Are you fucking deaf? I'm talkin' t'you. *Yeah you, you fuckin' Paki.*'

Despite the sweltering heat, Grace's insides turned to ice. She turned around. Standing only a few feet away at the entrance to the carpark was a gang from the local housing estate. There must have been about six of them, all late teens and early twenties, all wearing their uniform of tatty football shirts, steel toe-capped Doc Martens and with thick blue tattoos etched onto their forearms. All swigging cans of Special Brew from the offy. She'd seen their type before. Out of work and on the dole, they blamed everything on the Asian community – the litter, the unemployment, the lack of housing, the price of a pint. And so, bored and bitter, they formed little gangs and took up a new hobby.

They called it Paki bashing.

And Jimi was today's target.

A knot of fear tightened in Grace's throat. She looked at Jimi. Sitting with legs astride one of the wooden picnic tables, the obligatory Grolsch in one hand, the obligatory cigarette in the other, he looked the same as always. Same Sun-Inned hair now grown long enough to be tied into a tufty ponytail, same biker's jacket, same stubble. Yet he looked different. Seemed different somehow. Watching him taking a drag, she saw his body stiffen, his mouth tighten. Noticed his hand waver ever so slightly. And it was at that moment, with a total, unpredictable, sudden clarity, that Grace realized the reason.

Jimi looked different because she was *looking* at him differently. She was seeing a different Jimi. He wasn't the enemy any more.

They were.

'Why don't you go away and leave us alone.'

Grace had the surreal experience of hearing a voice that sounded exactly like her own, looking around to see where it had come from, and then realizing that it was her own.

76

'What did yer jus' say?'

For a split second she toyed with the idea of playing dumb, turning the other way, staying out of trouble. But then she'd never been one to shy away from trouble.

'Are you deaf?' she retorted. 'I said why don't you go away and leave us alone.' OK, so she was hardly Arnie Schwarzenegger in the threatening stakes, but it took a serious amount of balls. And although her voice was shrill, it didn't waver.

'Grace, keep out of this.' Jimi had stood up and was staring at her. Expecting to see gratitude, she was startled to see angry pride.

'And who the fuck are you?' snarled a wiry Jack Russell of a man. Jaw jutting out, his fists were curled, his body coiled, ready for action.

Jimi's expression caused Grace to falter momentarily. She should really shut up. Stay well out of it. Except she couldn't. She and Jimi were on the same side now and all at once she felt frightened for him, protective of him, and as indignant as hell. Digging her fingernails into the palms of her hands, she summoned up every last drop of teenage bolshiness.

'I'm his girlfriend. Why? *Who the fuck are you?*'

God only knows whatever possessed her to come out with that. Where it sprang from. She never did find out. Even years later, when Grace looked back on that moment, she still couldn't say why she'd stood up in front of the entire upper sixth and a gang of racist thugs and declared herself to be Jimi Malik's girlfriend. She didn't know who was more taken aback. Them or her.

Or Jimi Malik.

Staring at her with an expression of pure confusion, he was stopped from speaking by the appearance of the pub landlord, a colossal bear of a man, who lumbered down the front steps, a Fred Perry that had seen better days stretched tightly over his enormous girth.

'Ger'owt of it,' he said gruffly, advancing towards the skinheads. 'Go on, ger'owt of it,' he growled again, his sovereign rings glinting threateningly in the sunlight. Bob the landlord had been a well-known wrestler in his heyday, and although his Jumbo the Great days were over, his hulking frame was still a force to be reckoned with. Seeing their moment of fun was over, the gang didn't hang around. Jeering and swearing they scattered like marbles, jumping on each other's shoulders and scraping keys along the row of shiny parked cars as they left. Anything for an afternoon's entertainment.

'What the hell did you say that for?'

'Say what?' Blushing with embarrassment, Grace feigned innocence. After her outburst and the ensuing commotion she'd decided it was time to leave and, when no-one was looking, she'd scooted out of the beer garden and dived into the bus shelter across the road. For the last ten minutes she'd been praying for a number 602 into town to arrive. Unfortunately the only thing to turn up was Jimi in his Capri. And he was furious.

'Don't give me that, you know exactly what I'm talking about.' Pulling up next to the kerb, he'd turned off the engine and was now shouting. 'I can look after myself, you know. I don't need a girl coming to my rescue. You made me look like a complete twat in front of those morons!'

'You don't need me to do that,' muttered Grace under her breath.

'What did you just say?'

'Nothing.' Checking her watch she peered up the road. Just typical. There was never a bloody bus when you needed it.

He gasped. 'Jesus, what is it with you?'

Grace hopped from one foot to another. Her new Ravel cowboy boots had rubbed a huge blister. She glowered. '*What is it with me?*' she hissed, screwing up her eyes as she stared up the road, desperately willing that bus to appear. 'There isn't *anything* with me. I was trying to do you a favour. I was trying to save your skin.' That was it, she couldn't stand it any longer. Sitting down on the kerb she yanked off her boot, peeled off her cerise ankle sock and wriggled her bare suntanned toes in the warm air. The relief. 'Though God only knows why. To be honest, I wish I hadn't bothered, you ungrateful little shit,' she huffed loudly, grabbing hold of her boot and beginning to rub her toes furiously.

From the safe bunker of his car, Jimi watched her. Leaning against the bus shelter, she cut a scrawny figure. Sunburned a deep Hawaiian Tropic tan, the tip of her nose, which was far too large for her freckled face, was pink and peeling, her corkscrew perm had frizzed into a bath sponge in the humidity, and her electric blue eyeliner was smudged around her eyes like a child's crayon drawing. She was wearing faded Levis belted high on her waist and some kind of top that wrapped so tightly around her ribcage it drew attention to her pathetically flat chest. He noticed she wasn't wearing a bra, noticed her tiny button nipples, visible through the flimsy fabric. He gazed at her. Despite her determined expression she looked appealingly vulnerable.

Grace looked up and saw Jimi staring at her, his features all screwed up as if lots of stuff was going on inside his head. Obviously he's thinking of some insult or other to throw me, she thought, indignantly waiting for the avalanche of abuse.

It didn't happen.

What did happen was entirely unexpected. Leaning across to the passenger door, he released the catch. 'Are you hungry? There's a new McDonald's opened up in the precinct.'

Taken aback, she eyed him suspiciously. Was this some kind of joke? Hugging her fraying knees to her chest, she replied defensively. 'I'm a vegetarian.'

He didn't miss a beat. 'I'll buy you a cheeseburger without the burger.'

Try as she might she couldn't resist smiling. 'What about fries?'

He smiled ruefully. 'You get those too.'

She hesitated, her foot throbbing, her stomach gurgling, her pride wavering. Oh to hell with it. Grabbing her shiny new cowboy boot she hopped, limped, and almost tripped into the infamous passenger seat. The seat she'd watched other girls vying for and swore she'd never be seen dead in. She sank down into the soft, squishy leather. It was surprisingly comfy. Too comfy. Strapping on her seatbelt she turned to face him.

'Before you get any ideas, Jimi Malik, I would hate to be your girlfriend.'

Flipping down his Raybans, he turned to face her.

'Before you get any ideas, Grace Fairley, I would hate you to be my girlfriend.'

Faith

Justin, the pimply-cheeked assistant at McDonald's, was completely thrown by Jimi's request.

'Scuse me?' he grunted, his pale, greasy brow furrowing beneath his jaunty red and yellow striped cap.

'A Big Mac without the Mac.'

Jimi and Grace looked at each other and smiled.

'Er . . .' Clutching his name badge, which proudly boasted four stars and was pinned to his skinny chest like a medal, Justin faltered over the cash register. There was no button to press. No mention of it on the illuminated menu behind him. No memory of it being mentioned in the daily staff meeting. 'You want a Big Mac . . .' he began doubtfully, studying their faces for some kind of clue.

'Yesssss.' Jimi nodded without batting an eyelid.

'Without the two all beef patties . . .' he nodded, mirroring Jimi.

'That's right.' Grace grinned, folding her arms on top of the counter and staring at Justin who was cupping his bare elbow with one hand, and with the other was agitatedly picking his flaky benzoyl-peroxided chin.

'Is that a problem?'

'Er no . . . no, problem.' His reply was cautious. And then remembering the three-step-policy of smile, speed and service, he hurriedly flashed them both a lopsided grin. 'A Big Mac without the Big Mac coming right up,' he announced, before adding quickly in a hushed voice, 'I won't be a tick, I'll just go and ask my manager.'

More than a few ticks later, Grace and Jimi were walking back through the precinct, stuffing their faces with the contents of their yellow polystyrene containers. Teeming with droves of harassed shoppers, the Arndale shopping mall was a mecca for mothers, their pushchairs laden down with squawking toddlers and carrier bags full of shopping balancing on each handle. Gangs of schoolchildren congregated at the top of the escalators, smoking cigarettes and watching out for the security guards, while old-age pensioners huddled on benches next to the decorative fountain, nursing swollen ankles and eating vanilla slices from the baker's on the corner.

Meandering past them on their way to the NCP multi-storey carpark, Grace chewed on her burger-less burger and mulled over the afternoon's events. An ardent vegetarian, this was her first ever Big Mac experience and, although it was basically just cheese slices melted onto a sweet, soggy bun, a few gloops of ketchup and a bit of grated iceberg lettuce, she was surprised to discover it was actually rather delicious.

An even bigger surprise was Jimi.

At first she'd regretted her decision to get into his car. In fact no sooner had she climbed in than she'd wanted to climb out again. Fastening her seatbelt, she'd silently berated herself. What on earth had she been thinking? Neither of them had said a civil word to each other in the whole time they'd known each other – what on earth were they going to talk about for an entire lunch? How long did it take to wolf down a cheeseburger and fries? Five minutes? Three minutes? Two and a bit if she didn't chew every mouthful like her mother always insisted. Feeling panic rising as they raced off towards the city centre, she'd decided there was nothing else for it but to plot her escape route at the first available moment.

But then something weird had happened. Expecting a long and awkward silence, she'd been amazed to discover that only a few minutes later they were chatting nineteen to the dozen. God knows how it happened, or who had said what, but before she even had time to think about it they were hopping from a debate about whether Dirty Den should leave Angie, skipping on to discuss whether Mrs Collins, their maths teacher, should bleach or shave her moustache, jumping into an argument over which was the best flavour of crisps: just for the record, Jimi was a cheese'n'onion man, whereas she was firmly in the prawn cocktail camp.

Even more amazing is the realization that we share the same sense of humour, thought Grace, sneaking a sideways glance at Jimi as they sauntered past Etam, past a group of young teenage girls who nudged each other furiously and gawped lustfully at him. She couldn't believe it. After all those years of steadfastly ignoring Jimi Malik, she'd spent the last hour listening avidly to him cracking jokes, tears running down her cheeks as he did a faultless impersonation of Justin handing over their order with a baffled expression, taking off his cap and scratching his head like a latter-day Stan Laurel.

Something they didn't share, however, was their taste in music and as they rode up the escalator he whooped with delight.

'HMV. Ace,' he said, hurrying up the last few steps as the store loomed up in front of them. 'I wonder if they've got the new George Michael, it's been sold out everywhere.'

HMV? Ace? Grace stared dolefully at the pink and blue neon sign. Record shops were her pet hate. They were so intimidating, with their blaring music, trendy assistants and puzzling maze of music sections. She hated trying to navigate around them, past the hard-core musos flicking professionally through the indie-slash-punk-slash-acoustic section, heads bobbing to the tinny beat emitted by the Walkmans superglued to their ears. Either that or super-cool DJs selecting twelve-inches by the dozen, doing high-fives with other brothers they'd bumped into next to the house remixes.

It was all too much for someone whose musical collection was made up of one *Super Trouper* album *circa* Christmas 1980, the Band Aid single, her mum and dad's old Beatles records, and about a hundred home-recorded cassettes of the top forty, all muddled up and in the wrong cases. Hovering nervously in the unfamiliar surroundings, Grace was never quite sure where to go, how to find anything, what to look for, and usually ended up blurting out something stupid to one of the ultra-hip assistants who would roll their eyes, sigh, and point vaguely into the recesses of the shop.

But with Jimi it was different. This man was a pro. Acknowledging respectful nods from the assistants, he plunged enthusiastically into the thumping, pumping depths. Noisily sucking up the last slurps of chocolate milkshake, she reluctantly followed as he strode confidently down the aisles providing a running A–Z of music. It was quite amazing to watch him. Without pausing to check what bit of the alphabet he was up to, he began deftly plucking out album covers, giving reviews, making comments, throwing out bits of information as he went.

'. . . did you know U2 have already sold half a million copies of *The Joshua Tree*? . . . Oh wow, look, this album's had a wicked review in the *NME* . . . God I love this – Prince. 'Alphabet Street' – have you heard the backing vocals? They're something else . . . Did you ever see this band on *The Tube*? These guys gave a fantastic performance . . .'

Grace trotted behind, nodding knowledgeably, raising her eyebrows to show interest, making agreeable uhhmms and ahhhs and ohhhs. This was all a ruse to make Jimi think she had at least some clue as to what he was talking about. In the past she'd occasionally switched on *The Tube*, but it wasn't for the bands, it was to see what Paula Yates was wearing, and as for *NME* – wasn't that just for people who drenched themselves in patchouli oil and wrapped red and white tasselled scarves around their necks, like something out of *Lawrence of Arabia*?

Finally, after lingering for what seemed like ages over the new Compact Disc section with Jimi enthusing over how they were going to replace vinyl one day, he found his treasured George Michael twelve-inch. Clutching it triumphantly to his chest he turned to her, beaming.

'What are you buying?' he asked, eyebrows raised with interest.

'Buying?' On the spot, Grace faltered from trawling through a nearby rack of black and white Athena posters. She wasn't buying anything, although she wouldn't mind the man with the tyres and the six-pack on her bedroom wall, she thought, scanning the top ten hurriedly. Her attention was caught by a jaunty cover. 'Oh, I thought I'd get this,' she shrugged, feigning nonchalance.

'*Fairground Attraction?*' Jimi could barely conceal his contempt.

Damn. Wrong answer. Grace immediately wished she'd chosen something else. U2 maybe, or that bloke with the funny name, Terence Trent something or other.

'What's wrong with Fairground Attraction?' she said huffily, hackles rising, chin jutting defensively.

Jimi cursed silently. Shit. Why did he do that? Why couldn't he just have smiled approvingly, lied, pretended it was one of his favourites? He really liked Grace. In a million years he'd never have believed they'd get on so well, but now he'd gone and ruined it. He double-checked Grace's expression. Yep, if he didn't do some serious damage limitation he was in danger of falling out with her all over again, and he didn't want to. Not even if she did have appalling taste in music. Back-pedalling furiously, he grinned. 'Nothing's wrong. It's a great single.' Draping his arm around her shoulder, he pressed his mouth to her ear and began crooning the chorus.

Grace's initial reaction was to push him away, tell him to sod off, go back to where they began, but feeling his warm breath on her neck, she thawed reluctantly. Enveloped in the crook of Jimi's denim shoulder, she felt snugly comfortable. She hadn't had much experience with boyfriends, but of the few encounters she'd had, none of them had been this effortless, this easy, this enjoyable. She had to admit, this did feel strangely perfect.

Except for one thing. Walking towards the cash register she tried and failed to stifle an unflattering snort of laughter.

'What?' Frowning, he stopped crooning.

'Nothing,' squeaked Grace, clamping her hand over her mouth.

Jimi might know an awful lot about music, but he couldn't sing to save his life.

The afternoon seemed to slip away and by the time they'd located the car in the rabbit warren of the NCP carpark it was rush hour. Joining the gridlock of traffic trying to nudge its way out of the city centre, Jimi coasted along in neutral and glanced at Grace. Resting her chin on her knees, her face hidden by spirals of sun-frazzled hair, she was closely studying the sleeve of her record, imagining it sitting proudly on her MFI shelving. She made a mental note to get rid of her *Super Trouper* album. God only knows what Jimi would say if he should ever see it.

'Sorry . . .'

His apology interrupted Grace's mental interior designing. Taken by surprise she jerked her head up, her face puzzled. 'For what?'

He hesitated, trying to choose his words carefully. He gave up and blurted it out. 'You know, earlier . . . at the pub . . . I didn't mean to fly off the handle.'

'Oh . . . that.' She shrugged, feeling a flush of embarrassment. 'It's OK, I guess it was a bit stupid, I just didn't think. Those idiots just made me so angry.' As the scene began playing back in her head, like videotape in slow motion, she felt her toes curl. Oh God, Jimi must have thought *she* was the idiot. Standing up in front of everyone like some kind of

Joan of Arc. Trying to save the day. How ridiculous. *How naive.*

'You know, you're pretty frightening when you're angry.'

'I am?'

'Absolutely terrifying.' He was smiling at her, his large lazy mouth swept back in amusement.

'Well you better keep on the right side of me then, hadn't you?' she retorted with mock-seriousness.

'I think I'd better,' he agreed, his eyes twinkling.

After a few minutes the traffic slowly began to crank forwards, widening small gaps, making spaces. It was vehicle orthodontics, and moving quickly Jimi nipped and cut, swerving and squeezing, until leaving behind the city centre they began moving quickly past the ugly concrete high-rises that hung sulkily around the outskirts, the sprawling university campus thronging with baggy-jumpered students, the steep, sombre rows of run-down Victorian terraces.

This was late eighties Northern England. Untouched by the financial boom and bypassed by yuppiedom, it was a world away from the affluent South. Here there were no wealthy city boys, no glut of Porsches, no rage in mobile phones, no boom in property. Harry Enfield's Loadsamoney was just a character on TV, not a reality. Here nothing had changed. Life here was like a Talking Heads lyric, thought Jimi, accelerating past a launderette, catching sight of the weary-faced women inside, unloading driers, folding sheets, matching socks. The same as it ever was.

A road sign rose up before them. Straight ahead to Grace's house, left to his. Pulling up at the lights, he turned to her. 'Are you in any rush to get home?'

Reminded of her results, she shook her head. 'No. Going home means telling my parents I won't be going to uni.' As she spoke she remembered her crushing disappointment, the loss of her hopes of moving away, of achieving something, she wasn't sure what yet, but *something*. Only a few hours before it had felt as if her whole world had collapsed, yet now, with Jimi, somehow things didn't seem so hopeless.

'So, it's your life, let them be furious.'

She smiled sadly. 'They won't be furious.'

'So what's the problem?'

'That *is* the problem.'

'Eh?' Jimi was confused.

Grace sighed, a mixture of frustration and indignation. 'I *want* them to be furious. I want them to be outraged and upset and appalled. But they won't. They don't expect straight As, or Oxbridge, or a high-flying career. They expect me to get a nice steady job, something with a nice uniform and a good pension. There are no great expectations, and that's what hurts so much.'

As Grace spoke she could picture her dad putting his paper down, patting her on the shoulder and saying she'd done her best, her mum putting the kettle on and dropping great big clunking hints about how she'd heard WH Smiths were looking for a trainee assistant manager. Oh God, she couldn't bear it.

'No, I'm definitely not in a hurry to get home.' She turned to look at Jimi, and as she did a chink of hope surfaced. 'Why?' she asked cagily.

'Because I'm not exactly in a hurry to go home and face the firing squad. I've got the opposite problem. My dad thinks I'm going to Oxford to study medicine.'

She smiled. How ironic. 'You didn't get the grades?' she guessed. Almost hopefully.

He shook his head. 'Oh no, I got the grades all right.'

Grace felt herself deflate. 'So why will there be a firing squad?' She tried to hide her jealousy.

'Because I'm not going.' Jimi's jaw set defiantly. 'I'm going travelling. I've been saving up for ages and I've already bought my ticket. I just haven't told the olds yet. Mum'll be cool. She's Irish and still a bit of an old hippie. She travelled a lot in the sixties. That's how she met dad, in a restaurant in Delhi.'

Grace was intrigued. 'Your mum's Irish? So you're not . . .' she faltered.

'. . . a Paki?' finished off Jimi.

'Are you calling me a racist?' she fired back hotly.

'Course not,' he smiled, amused by her indignation. 'Not for a minute. I was being ironic.'

'Well don't be,' she said huffily, staring out of the window. 'Anyway, I thought you said she met your dad in Delhi. That's India, not Pakistan.'

'Most people don't know the difference,' he shrugged.

Grace turned to face him. 'But I'm not most people,' she said quietly.

A look passed between them. Neither gaze wavered.

Until a car hooting behind them broke it, and looking away Jimi put the car into gear and turned right.

Perfect

As they blasted over the curve of the hill, the pale skeletal walls of the ruined abbey rose up against the riverbank and the densely packed woodland that stretched neatly behind like a backdrop of bottle-green Velcro. Braking sharply, the Capri rattled over the cattle grid and began following the dirt track that twisted its way down towards the car park. Usually it was home to rows of cars, coaches and tourists, but it was growing late. Apart from a few straggling picnickers, most people had left for the day.

'Where else are you going?'

They'd been having this conversation the entire journey, Grace asking Jimi where he was going to visit on his trip around the world. Eager to talk about his plans after keeping them secret for so long, he was only too happy to comply.

'I've read about this amazing island, off the coast of Thailand called Koh Samui.'

'Cosamooey,' repeated Grace, rolling the strange word around on her tongue as if she was tasting it. It sounded exotic and exciting. 'And where else?' she pestered.

'Australia. That's my dream. Heading into the outback. Travelling across the desert. Seeing Uluru, that's the Aboriginal name for Ayers Rock,' explained Jimi, his eyes wide with anticipation as he yanked on the handbrake and skidded the Capri into a parking space. He could never resist. Something about watching *The Professionals* when he was a kid. Switching off the engine he reached into the glove compartment, grabbed the cans of Coke they'd bought on the way, and opened the door. 'You know you can ride around it on a Harley-Davidson.'

'You can?' Grace didn't know what was so exciting about getting on a motorbike and riding around some great bloody big rock in the middle of nowhere, but she tried to look suitably impressed.

'Why don't you come along? You could ride pillion,' he enthused.

'What? You and me?' scoffed Grace. 'Travelling around the world together?'

'Well why not?' Now he was really getting carried away.

'Because . . .' began Grace, '. . . because . . .' She paused. Come to think of it, she couldn't think of any reason why not.

Scooping a can out of the plastic bag he began shaking it. 'If you don't, you'll live to regret it,' he laughed wickedly.

'I believe you,' she yelled, screaming and running away as he pulled back the ring-pull and chased after her, spraying her with a fizzing jet of Coca-Cola.

They made their way through the ancient graveyard that surrounded the abbey, stepping in between the gnarled and mossy stones that stuck out of the earth, crooked and chipped like old men's teeth. Unlike Jimi, Grace always found graveyards fascinating. Reading the inscriptions, she would imagine faces to fit names, and trace with her fingers the carved lettering that had grown worn and smooth. Complaining it was ghoulish, he jogged ahead, down to the river, across the stepping stones and into the woodland where he found a small clearing, tucked away.

Catching him up, Grace threw herself down and thankfully tugged off her cowboy boots. Out of breath she dug her bare toes into the soft earth and looked out towards the abbey, at the last smudges of sunshine fading into a marmalade sky, filtering an amber sheen over everything. It was like being a kid again, holding toffee papers up to the light and looking through them.

'Isn't it gorgeous?' She looked at Jimi, who'd plonked himself down next to her and was rummaging around in his plastic bag.

'Umm, s'OK,' he mumbled uninterestedly as he

located whatever it was he was looking for. He pulled it out jubilantly. 'Do you smoke?'

'What? Oh, yeah, occasionally,' she nodded, trying to be all cool and attempting to blot out the image of her nearly throwing up and choking to death the one time she'd taken a drag of a cigarette. 'As long as it's Silk Cut,' she added, injecting a little detail to try and sound knowledgeable.

Jimi burst out laughing, his eyes wide with amusement. 'No, I mean dope, you dope. You know, hash, marijuana, spliff . . .'

'Oh,' gasped Grace, feeling horribly foolish. 'No,' she shook her head. What was the use in pretending? She'd already blown it. First the single, and now this.

She watched with curious interest as he pulled out a small blue packet, slipped out two tiny pieces of tracing paper, ran his tongue along the edge, and stuck them together. Next he sprinkled in some tobacco, produced what looked like a small piece of Oxo cube and lit the edge of it with a match. It produced a soft, sweet aroma, and he began crumbling it along the line of tobacco. Finally, rolling it up he tore off the edge of the packet, curled it between finger and thumb, and slipped it inside.

'Hardly the Camberwell carrot, but it'll do.'

Grace looked at him, nonplussed.

'*Withnail and I?*' He attempted to jog her memory.

Grace frowned. What on earth was he going on about?

He gave up. 'It's a film,' he explained. 'You've got to see, it's hilarious.'

'Oh, yeah,' she murmured dispiritedly. How was it that this morning when she'd got out of bed she'd felt adult and reasonably well informed whereas now she felt like a kid with huge gaping holes in her knowledge? She glanced at Jimi who was confidently twisting the end of the Rizla paper, burning it with a match, blowing away the charred ends. In contrast he seemed to know about everything. Music, films, travelling, smoking marijuana. Suddenly she understood why all those girls hung off his every word. She was hanging so hard her arms were aching.

'Now your turn.' Blowing out the smoke, he held out the skinny, papery cigarette. It looked entirely innocent. He passed it to her. She swallowed hard, determined not to look like a complete novice, and tentatively took it from him.

'Go on, it won't bite, you know.'

She smiled nervously and, putting it to her lips, took a deep breath. As the smoke whooshed into her lungs her knee-jerk reaction was to cough long and hard, to splutter for all she was worth, but she resisted. She felt a rush, as if she'd dived into the sea and was heading back up to the surface. Her fingers went tingly and felt a long, long way from her wrists. She wriggled them, and found herself giggling. This was actually rather nice.

'Do you know, I've spent the last two years hating you,' she blurted, before she could help it. Embarrassed, she clamped her hand over her mouth.

He smiled. 'Believe me, I know. I've spent the last two years hating you too.'

'But you're nothing like I imagined,' she added hastily.

'Neither are you.'

They passed the joint between them in silence.

'Do you remember when I drove through those puddles and sprayed you with all that muddy water?' he asked, looking sheepish.

'How could I forget?' she deadpanned, attempting to look serious. Taking a puff of the joint she passed it back. 'I never did get the stain out of my white denim jacket.' Her mouth twitched. 'God, that jacket, it really was dreadful, wasn't it?' Unable to suppress them any longer, she broke into giggles.

Relief flushed Jimi's face.

'Still, I did stand in the front row of one of your gigs and heckle,' she confessed.

'I know, I could have killed you,' he laughed, shaking his head, smoke leaking out of his flared nostrils. 'There was I thinking I looked totally cool, doing my best Bono impression, and all I could hear was you in the audience yelling, "Rubbish, get him off!"' His eyes began watering as he laughed, and then broke into coughing. He lay on his back, trying to draw breath. '"Get him off."' He wheezed faintly, pinching the crook of his nose, his eyes screwed up with mirth.

His laughter was infectious, and Grace began giggling, ticklish, bubbling giggles that swelled into loud belly chuckles that creased up her middle into a white cotton concertina. 'Oh God, don't, you're making my sides ache,' she protested, clutching her stomach and hugging it tightly.

'"Gerr . . . 'im . . . off . . ."' spluttered Jimi, his body shaking as he tried raising the joint to his lips. He was prevented by a surge of laughter. Rolling over onto his side, he wiped his eyes with the sleeve of his leather jacket. 'Christ, I'm wasted,' he eventually managed to gasp, his mouth stretched wide as he smiled broadly.

'Me too,' grunted Grace happily, gazing down at him. He had the whitest teeth. Big, square, white teeth that stood out in two neat rows against his caramel-coloured skin. She'd never really noticed them before, or his eyes, which she'd always thought were just plain, boring old brown, but were actually the colour of conkers, with amber flecks around the edges. *Oh dear.*

Suddenly she felt her head lurch. Once, twice, and then it was off like a carousel, spinning lazily around. Except she couldn't get off. Feeling decidedly strange she flopped backwards onto the warm mattress of earth and closed her eyes. 'Totally gone . . .' she murmured, her voice trailing off as she took a few deep lungfuls of woodland air.

Closing her eyes she felt herself drifting, floating, aware of nothing but her body, the feeling of the soft, velvety moss grass beneath her bare feet, the smell of leaves and tree stumps and soil, the rhythm of her breathing as it began to slow right down.

And then it happened.

Later, lying awake on her bed, staring up at her bedroom ceiling, Grace couldn't recollect the details, they were all fuzzy and blurry, like not knowing all the words to a song but being able to remember the chorus. Jimi kissing her, the musky smell of his naked body, the feeling of warm, bare skin against warm, bare skin.

And the excitement.

Everybody had always said the first time was disappointing, but this had been everything and more than she'd ever imagined. More scary, more clumsy, more nerve-racking, more exhilarating, more natural. She couldn't describe it. It had just been more.

Afterwards they'd giggled and hugged and grinned at each other. They hadn't spoken, they didn't have to. There was no awkwardness or regret, just a happy, buzzing glow. The kind of glow that came from deep inside. Pulling on their discarded clothes, they'd walked back to the car, Jimi with one hand around her shoulder, she with one hand around his waist, and he'd driven her home, squeezed her hand, kissed her cheek, stroked the nape of her neck.

And promised to call.

The next day she'd loitered in the hallway, getting in the way of her mother's vacuuming, putting up with the taunts of her brothers who immediately sussed with teenage perception that she was waiting for a phone call *from a boy*. But Grace hadn't cared. She didn't care about anything except Jimi. She'd fallen in love. Completely, utterly, head-over-heels in love and it felt like nothing she could have ever imagined. It was liberating and fantastic and freeing. Finally, everything made sense. Finally she knew what her big dreams were. And every single one of them belonged to Jimi.

Grace sat in that hallway for two weeks. Two whole weeks. Watching. Waiting. Hoping.

Two whole weeks for her heart to break into a million little pieces.

Jimi Malik never called.

And she never saw him. Ever. Again.

Chapter Eight

Until now.

Thirteen years later and there he was. The first man she'd ever slept with, the first man she'd ever fallen in love with, the first man she'd ever trusted. He'd promised he'd call and she'd believed him. Totally, utterly, completely. That he'd broken his promise had broken Grace's heart. At eighteen years old she'd thought she was never, ever going to get over it. But of course she had, and she'd gone on to fall in love with lots of different men, some of them nice, some of them not-so-nice, and some of them – the Greek waiter in Corfu being a case in point – who were, quite frankly, pretty revolting.

And yet now, standing in the restaurant, face to face with Jimi Malik, it brought it all back again. For a brief, *hopeful* moment she thought it was a case of mistaken identity. Wasn't everyone supposed to have a double? An identikit person roaming around in the world that one day you'd come face to face with. Just like that French film she'd once watched when she was going through her arty World Cinema stage at the video store. What was it called? Ah yes, *The Double Life of Véronique*. In which case this could be life imitating art. This could be The Double Life of Jimi Malik.

Except in the nanosecond it took to hurtle desperately through this assault course of thoughts, she heard a voice.

'I'm really sorry, things got a bit out of hand . . .'

That voice. It sent her reeling back into the past. Although his accent had mellowed over the years, it was still pure Pennines. And unmistakable.

'My friends seem to have had a little too much to drink, obviously I'll pay for any damage . . .' Still utterly charming, he was passing over his card and smiling at Ahmed, who he now had completely eating out of his hand. '. . . and can I just say what a wonderful place you have here, it's such a shame that we have to leave so early . . .' By their expressions it was obviously news to his friends, but before they could protest Jimi Malik had unhooked his drunken red-haired friend from his beer, like a coat from a peg, and was guiding him out of the restaurant, followed by a rather subdued stag party.

Grace watched him with bitter irony. It was 1988 all over again. Jimi was still the leader. Still with his ever-present crocodile of faithful fans. Except one thing had changed. She had. She wasn't some vulnerable, insecure virgin any more, drowning her A-level sorrows in cider, unsure what her future held. She'd grown up, got a life, and grabbed hold of the confidence that came with it. Now she had a career, a sex life, *a fiancé.*

'Your table is ready.' Interrupting her thoughts, Ahmed reappeared and began clapping everyone on the back, motioning for them to sit down. 'Please, I send over more wine. On the house. No problem.'

'Don't worry, we're fine, honestly.' Grace smiled politely.

'Speak for yourself.' Running his fingers through his ruffled hair, Spencer grabbed hold of one of the glasses of wine Ahmed was hurriedly dispensing, and promptly knocked back a large mouthful. 'Look at me, I'm covered in red wine.'

Without missing a beat, Grace glanced across at Spencer. 'For goodness sake stop fussing, it's only a shirt,' she said and smiled sweetly, unable to resist.

Everyone began making their way over to the table, scraping back chairs, fluffing out napkins, but Grace hung back slightly. She glanced over at Jimi, leading his friends out of the restaurant like the Pied Piper. She watched as he shook hands with Ahmed at the door and felt a great sense of relief. He was leaving. And, as luck would have it, after all that panicking, he hadn't recognized her after all.

Her relief was tinged with hurt pride. Was she really that unmemorable? So forgettable? So inconsequential? She was feeling vaguely aggrieved, and it was at that precise moment he chose to look back and caught her staring.

They locked eyes.

He smiled.

She fumed.

Because as soon as Grace caught sight of that arrogant, self-satisfied, smug little smile of his – *ping* – she was hit by all those old emotions. All at once she wasn't thirty-one any more. Throwing Jimi Malik her filthiest look, tossing back her hair and stomping – which in flip-flops wasn't easy – towards her freshly laid table, she was that self-conscious, awkward, eighteen-year-old all over again. And she hated him for it.

It was nearly midnight by the time they left the restaurant. The last to leave was Rhian. Lagging behind in the pretence of putting on her cape, a hooded, scarlet, Red Riding Hood number which she'd unearthed during one of her regular forages in her local Christian Aid shop, she paused in the doorway to tug Grace to one side. 'What do you think of Noel?' she whispered hopefully in her ear.

'Actually I didn't get much of a chance to talk to him.' Grace smiled tactfully. She wanted to add that it was because he'd been too busy stuffing his face all evening, but didn't. This was Rhian's first date, she had to tread softly.

'No, he's more the silent type,' gushed Rhian, fiddling around in her crocodile-skin clutch bag. Locating a cigarette, she clamped it between her china doll teeth and lit it. Grace couldn't help noticing it was with Noel's lighter. Blowing out a cloud of smoke, she grinned excitedly. 'I've asked him to come back to mine for coffee.'

Grace felt a pang of alarm. 'You have?'

Rhian narrowed her eyes and pouted. 'Don't look at me like that.'

'Like what?'

'Disapprovingly.' Locating her lipstick, she unscrewed the lid and began dabbing her mouth determinedly. 'I can't remember the last time I had sex.'

Grace was taken aback. In all the time she'd known Rhian she'd never heard her talk about her sex life. They discussed everything else in endless detail, but as soon as the S word was mentioned, Rhian would always go bright red with embarrassment and change the topic to horoscopes, or caramel-flavoured rice cakes, or how Marks & Spencer's were doing packs of thongs for ten pounds. And she didn't even wear thongs.

'Oh c'mon, it can't be that long . . .'

'Fifteen months, one week and three days,' rattled off Rhian matter-of-factly.

'Fifteen months?' Grace's forehead wrinkled with confusion. 'But I thought it was eighteen months since you broke up with Phil?'

'It is,' nodded Rhian. 'But we ended up doing it a couple of times on his access visits, before he moved to the States,' she confessed sheepishly, taking a puff of her cigarette. 'I never mentioned it as I knew you'd disapprove, but you don't know what it's like, you're in a relationship.'

Grace didn't say anything. Why was it that people always assumed that if you were in a relationship you were at it constantly, like rabbits? That there was an abundance of sex, when in fact it was quite the opposite? Probably because no-one wants to admit it, she considered, thinking about Spencer's scuttling out of the bedroom that morning, and deciding to join the conspiracy of silence by not fessing up to her own less than satisfactory sex life.

Mistaking her silence for agreement, Rhian continued. 'My next-door-neighbour Georgie's got Jack for the whole night. I can't afford to miss an opportunity like this.'

'Like what?' Grace motioned towards Noel who was standing under the street lamp, playing Snake on his mobile.

Rhian continued puffing on her cigarette. 'If you were single you'd know exactly what I'm talking about. It's a desert out there.'

'And what's Noel? An oasis?' joked Grace.

'Something like that,' grinned Rhian, dropping her cigarette onto the pavement and daintily stubbing it out with the heel of her stiletto. She hesitated, her expression turning pensive, and she looked up at Grace. 'When Phil left I thought I was going to die of a broken heart. But I didn't. I'm still here. OK so now I've got a child, and I've got the stretchmarks to prove it, but I'm only thirty-five and I haven't given up hope. Everyone's got a soulmate, Grace, I truly believe that. It's just a matter of finding them.'

Grace stared silently at Rhian. In her crimson cape and baby-blue stilettos and with a crocodile-skin clutch bag tucked under her arm she looked like some modern-day Mary Poppins. If anyone else had come out with a speech about soulmates and true love, Grace would have found it difficult not to feel more than a little cynicism, but Rhian said it with such sincerity, and without the merest hint of irony, that she couldn't fail to be moved. After everything that had happened to Rhian, all the shit she'd been through, nobody would have blamed her for being the most disillusioned, bitter, negative person around. But instead she'd emerged from her tunnel still as hopeful and positive. Her rose-tinted specs might have taken a bashing, but she was still refusing to take them off.

Although that appeared to be all she was refusing to take off. 'But while I'm waiting, I might as well have a bit of fun with what's on offer,' she whispered, grinning mischievously.

'You have a good time,' said Grace, smiling as she kissed her friend on both cheeks. 'But be careful, don't wear the boy out,' she teased, gesturing towards Noel who, in his Kangol cagoule looked even younger than his twenty-six years.

Rhian giggled. 'I'll call you,' she winked, linking up with Noel and teetering on her four-inch-heels towards the tube.

Grace watched her. Rhian had never been a public transport kind of girl. Even now, with her appalling finances, she insisted on driving everywhere in the little Smart Car her parents had bought her, even to the corner shop to buy a bottle of Fairy Liquid. She looked at Noel who was busily rummaging around in his trousers, pulling out his travel card for the tube in readiness, and a depressing thought struck. All that talk about having a soulmate was lovely and romantic, but what if you couldn't find him?

Followed by an even worse thought.

What if there wasn't a special someone waiting in the wings for everyone?

What if her soulmate didn't actually exist?

'Grace?'

She looked up to see Spencer. Standing a little way ahead of her, he was jangling his jacket around trying to locate his car keys. Finding them in his breast pocket, he pulled them out and pressed the alarm. A few feet away a Jeep Cherokee flashed and beeped.

'You're not thinking of driving, are you?' she asked, walking up to him and sliding her arm around his waist.

'And why wouldn't I be?' he replied, immediately defensive. She felt his back stiffen.

'Maybe because you've been drinking?' teased Grace, ignoring his snappiness and kissing him on the lips.

'I've had a couple of glasses of wine. *With dinner.*' Pulling away from her, he walked to the car, grabbed hold of the handle and stubbornly opened the door.

'It was a bit more than that.' She smiled, calmly trying to reason with him. The easy laughter she'd felt with Rhian was draining away and a familiar knot was tightening in her stomach. But Spencer was anything but calm or reasonable.

'No it wasn't,' he retorted, adamantly denying it.

She persevered. 'Oh c'mon, Spence, you drank nearly two whole bottles, and then there were those brandies. You're way over the limit.' There, she'd said it.

'Jesus, Grace, what were you doing all night? Checking up on me?' Annoyed, he threw her a scowl.

Grace stared at his face: it was tight and moody. It was truly amazing, she thought. How could you go from loving someone to hating them in less than thirty seconds? And she did love Spencer, for all the problems in their relationship, she really did love him. She took a deep breath. 'I don't want to argue, Spence, really I don't. I'm tired, you're tired . . .' She wanted to say drunk, but resisted. 'Why don't we just get a cab?' It was late and she wanted to go home. It had been a long evening.

'What? And leave the car here?'

'Why not?'

'It'll get nicked, that's why not,' he replied, huffily. 'And anyway, I'm perfectly OK to drive.' Climbing inside, he put the key in the ignition and started the engine. He eyed her challengingly. 'Now, are you getting in or what?'

Grace hesitated. This had happened so many nights like this and every single one of them she'd given in and said nothing. She'd silenced her fears, climbed inside, strapped on her seatbelt, and stared out of the window as they'd driven home in silence.

But not this time.

She looked at him. The alcohol had made his mouth slack, his denim blue eyes faded and dull. He didn't look like the Spencer who'd woken her up that morning wishing her happy birthday. Probably because he wasn't, she thought, sadly. She'd left him behind after the first bottle of Merlot.

She shook her head. 'No.'

If he was shocked he didn't show it. Instead he just shrugged in feigned nonchalance.

'Suit yourself,' he said. He slammed the door, put the car into gear and revved the accelerator. Standing on the pavement, Grace looked at his profile and could see the muscle in his jaw twitching in annoyance. She heard the engine roar, and felt a stab of doubt. Surely he wasn't going to drive off and leave her. He wouldn't leave her. He *couldn't* leave her.

Could he?

She was still wondering as he drove off.

Chapter Nine

Terry's Taxis was minute and overcrowded with the kind of people that Grace really didn't want to be sitting squashed up against at quarter to midnight, on a hot and sticky Friday night. Bloodshot eyes, sovereign rings, trackie bottoms, they were mostly male, mostly drinking cans of Red Stripe, and mostly eyeing her up.

Poised at the graffitied doorway her nerves nearly failed her. Until she reminded herself of the alternative – a night bus – and decided that as scary as this was, it wasn't as scary as spending the next two hours trying not to be caught in the crossfire of blood, urine and projectile vomiting. So, screwing up her courage in both hands, thanking God she was wearing jeans and a T-shirt and not the dress and heels she'd planned, she looked straight ahead and boldly flippety-flopped inside.

Inside was bright. Deathly bright. Grace felt her skin fade to grey as she stepped into the glare of the fluorescent strip lighting that buzzed and flickered overhead, attracting moths to join the mouldy funeral pyre already trapped inside. In the far corner a badly tuned radio was playing loud, jangling reggae and there was the strong smell of spliff wafting from behind the counter, which was barricaded by a thick, metal grille.

A lifetime's worth of newspaper headlines about lone women being attacked sprang to mind like some macabre cuttings library. She tried blocking them out. Under no circumstances was she going to crumble into tears. Big, fat, salty tears that she could feel welling up threatened to spill down her face as she ducked down and, sniffing loudly, whispered through the grille, 'Er, excuse me, I'd like a cab to Wandsworth.'

This isn't really happening, piped up a little voice inside her head. It's just a horrible nightmare. It will all soon be over. I'm just a cab ride away from being snuggled up in bed underneath that new gingham cover Mum sent me for my birthday, along with the matching pillowcases and fitted sheet 'for my bottom drawer'.

Veering off at a tangent, Grace's mind attempted to block out its surroundings by concentrating on her mother's obsession with filling her bottom drawer. To date Mrs Fairley had managed to fill a whole chest of drawers, a pine trunk and the cupboard under the hallway, much to the chagrin of Spencer, who'd recently discovered his beloved tennis racquet squashed underneath two mattress protectors, a paisley valance and a patchwork eiderdown. Throwing a wobbly that McEnroe would have been proud of, he'd stomped petulantly around the flat in his Cliff Richard tennis whites, yelling, 'For Christsakes, Grace, the next time you speak to your mother, will you kindly remind her we've only got one fucking bed.'

'You wanna go to where, sugar?' A bald head, as shiny and as round as a bowling ball, appeared from underneath the counter.

'Erm . . . Wandsworth, just by the common,' blurted Grace, trying not to think about Spencer. It was impossible not to. How could he do this to her? OK, so they weren't one of those perfectly in-tune couples who never had a cross word to say to each other. Over the years there'd been plenty of rows and sulks and shouting – he'd even driven off and left her once before, over an argument in IKEA about whether or not to go for a tiled splashback in the kitchen, or brushed steel panels. It had been a Sunday morning and if she remembered rightly, he'd had a hangover then, which was why he'd been so bad-tempered. But in the end they always made up.

This, however, was different. This wasn't IKEA on a Sunday morning, it was Elephant and Castle on a Friday night. She was alone. It was dangerous. *And it was her birthday*. Digging her mobile out of her pocket she stared hopefully at the screen. It stared back silently. No missed calls. The disappointment was crushing. Regret began sprouting. Maybe she shouldn't have stood her ground. He drank and drove all the time. What was so different about tonight? Why had she chosen tonight to make a stand? If she'd just kept quiet and got in the car she'd be at home, in bed. *And not here*.

Grace glanced up at the head behind the counter. 'If that's OK . . . please . . . thanks.' She threw in a smile. With any luck it might help her with a bit of queue jumping. Ladies first and all that.

It didn't.

''Fraid it's gonna be a bit of a wait.'

Any hope she might have harboured quickly disappeared. Avoiding eye contact with her audience, all of whom had now ceased their drunken banter and were watching her curiously from the wooden benches lining the scuffed grey walls, she folded her arms tightly across her chest like an Egyptian mummy and leaned closer to the grille.

'How much of a wait?' Despite her desperate mood, she attempted to inject a note of optimism. Maybe it would rub off.

The head behind the counter drew heavily on a joint. Inhaling deeper and deeper, it seemed to go on for ever, like the last note of an aria, until finally, when it seemed impossible for his lungs not to burst, there was a loud exhaling and a smokescreen drifted up through the grille. 'I think you better si' down, sugar . . . It's gonna be a tidy sum o'time.'

Which translated means hours, thought Grace gloomily, feeling the eyes in the back of her head and realizing that if she wanted to sit down she was going to have to face the welcoming committee, ask someone to move up, and squeeze in. *Tightly*.

She hesitated – oh what the hell, things could hardly get any worse – and turned around.

Jesus, she hasn't changed at all.

Sitting in the far corner, wedged up on a bench in a line-up that looked like something out of *The Usual Suspects*, Jimi was witnessing Grace's discomfort. Having come to his earlier conclusion that stag nights were naff anyway, and he really didn't want to be stripped naked, tied to a lamppost in Trafalgar Square and sprayed with shaving foam, he'd jumped out of the limo at a red light, leaving Clive and Co. to head off to Spearmint Rhino, while he'd headed for Terry's Taxis.

He'd been there half an hour, eyes closed, half dozing, half listening to some wicked reggae, when he'd sensed a ripple of testosterone, and looked up to see the cause of it. Grace Fairley.

Jimi still hadn't got over the shock of seeing her in the restaurant. Although he prided himself on think-ing nothing ever ruffled him, after all those years it was such a blast from the past. He'd recognized her immediately, even without the *Dirty Dancing* shaggy perm, dodgy blue eyeliner and that godawful white denim jacket. There'd been no mistaking that stomp, that huffy way of tossing her hair, that filthy look. Not that she recognized me, he mused. In fact she's obviously *forgotten* all about me, he concluded, irked that it irked him.

Watching Grace looking for somewhere to sit he felt a pang of concern. He'd been going to say hi earlier in the restaurant, but you know how it is, she'd been with a bunch of friends, he'd been with a bunch of total pissheads – so all in all it hadn't exactly been a good time for a trip down memory lane.

But now, seeing her looking so vulnerable conjured up a flashback. He couldn't remember the exact date, or the name of the pub, or the names of most of the other sixth-formers, but he remembered the skinheads, remembered Grace sitting by herself at the bus stop, remembered shouting at her with angry pride for trying to come to his rescue. Out of the corner of his eye, he saw the guy in the corner pause from eating his kebab to leer at her rather snug little bottom, and felt oddly protective. Now it was his turn to try to come to hers.

'Grace?'

Hearing her name and expecting to see Spencer standing in the doorway looking remorseful, Grace was already halfway through rehearsing her furious reply to his apology as she turned and caught sight of a face lurking in the corner. Jimi Malik. His presence threw her. Where the hell had he just sprung from? Her mind did a U-turn and began firing questions like poison darts. Beginning with confusion: What was he doing here? Where were his friends? Why was he by himself? – and turning quickly into humiliation as she realized what he must be thinking – What is she doing here? Where are her friends? *Why is she by herself?*

Grace felt her cheeks turn from washed-out grey to deepest burgundy. Awkwardness, insecurity and foolishness tied themselves up in a knot in her stomach. Why oh why did she have to bump into him again here? Now? Of all places? Why couldn't she be looking cool and gorgeous? Why couldn't she be all dolled up in some fabulous bar, one hand entwined around a glass of some fabulously expensive cocktail, the other around Spencer, who'd be wearing that lovely Prada shirt she'd bought him for his birthday and gazing at her longingly? Maybe even nuzzling her ear. Or laughing appreciatively at some terribly witty observation she'd just made.

She pulled herself together.

'Oh, hi,' she said breezily in a tone which she hoped

made her appear confident and indifferent and didn't betray how she was really feeling – unattractive, awkward, and horribly self-conscious. Unlike Jimi, who looked cool, comfortable and, thought Grace feeling a stab of infuriation, quite staggeringly handsome.

'Hey, fancy meeting you here,' he enthused, feeling unexpectedly nervous and trying to cover it up by jumping up and grinning broadly.

Grace was taken aback by his greeting. Having assumed it would be a lot more cool, it completely buggered up her whole nonchalant act. Over the last decade and a bit she'd done her fair share of imagining what she'd say if she ever bumped into Jimi again. Now it was actually happening all those witty put-downs had legged it.

'Yep, fancy that. Do you come here often?' she replied. And cringed. What the hell did she have to go and say that for? Mortified by her showstopping opening line, Grace smiled tightly, hunched up her shoulders and stuffed her hands in the back pockets of her jeans to stop herself curling up with sheer embarrassment.

'I thought it was you in that . . .' Jimi hesitated, searching for a polite adjective, and then gave up, '. . . that Moroccan dump.'

There was a disgruntled growling noise from the man in the far corner whose dark, almond-shaped eyes glared menacingly above the pitta parapet of a lamb kebab.

'You mean Zagora's,' retorted Grace defensively.

'Whatever,' he shrugged uninterestedly. 'To be honest, the sooner I forget about that dive the better,' he continued, completely oblivious to the fact that her face was setting quicker than cement. So much so he even threw in a jokey compliment, 'But you. Now I could never forget you . . .'

Oh Christ, nothing had changed, groaned Grace inwardly. He was still a smoothie.

'Wow, it must have been ten years . . .'

'Thirteen,' she corrected before she could help herself. Damn.

His eyebrows shot up with surprise. 'Jesus, you're right.'

Of course I'm bloody right, was what Grace wanted to hiss venomously, but instead she summoned up every ounce of thirtysomething maturity and smiled politely, wondering where exactly all this chummy reunion stuff was going to end up.

As did the rest of the waiting room who, devoid of a TV set, were slumped on the benches watching these two strangers as if they were the latest reality show, wishing they'd hurry up and start arguing, and thinking it wasn't a patch on *Big Brother*.

Unfortunately for them their hopes were dashed by the head behind the counter. Rising up until the crown was just visible, it boomed over the reggae like some kind of oracle. 'Mr Malik? Going to W9?'

'You live in London now?' asked Grace, feeling oddly miffed. She looked at Jimi. He'd gained a few crinkles around the eyes, swapped the ponytail for a buzzcut, and ditched the ripped 501s for an old pair of baggy Diesels, but he was still Jimi from Manchester. He'd always be Jimi from Manchester. In her mind she'd frozen him in time, expected him to be exactly the same, even though she'd changed, but of course he wasn't. He was Mr Malik from W9, this new person, and it felt weird to think she didn't know anything about his job, or the music he now listened to, or what he'd been doing for the last thirteen years. She didn't know anything about him any more.

'Yeah, I moved down in '91. I only meant to stay a couple of years, but you know how it is. I got a job, a flat, a life . . .' he laughed warmly. 'What about you?'

''93,' she replied, annoyed that it felt like a competition. And she'd just lost.

'Funny we've never bumped into each other, hey?'

'Yeah, funny,' she said. Fucking hilarious, she thought.

111

'Mr Malik. Your cab's waiting outside.' Its message delivered, the head resubmerged itself in the spliffy depths.

'Look, I better go . . .'

'Well it was nice to see you,' she butted in, sticking out her hand. Of course it wasn't. Disconcerting, maybe. Weird, definitely. Awkward, absolutely.

But nice?

Jimi glanced at Grace's outstretched hand. Her formality surprised him. He'd been going to suggest they swap numbers, maybe keep in touch, but now he changed his mind. She obviously still bore a grudge. Even after all these years. Christ, women were like elephants.

'Yeah, you too.' He made his handshake brisk and perfunctory. Two could play at that game. 'See you around, maybe.'

'Maybe,' she ventured, aiming for the right level between uninterest and cockiness. Christ, after all this time, it was pathetic. But necessary, added her pride stubbornly. She didn't want him getting the wrong impression. Knowing how arrogant he is, he probably assumes I still fancy him, thought Grace tartly. The thought galled her. She'd never fancied Jimi Malik, she'd just fallen for him.

There was a difference.

For a moment they both hovered awkwardly, an uncomfortable silence sitting between them like one of the tattooed meatheads on the bench opposite.

'Well . . . bye, then.' Not waiting for him to be the one to walk away first – which showed that there was at least *one* pearl of wisdom she'd garnered over the years – Grace turned, walked over to the small space left between the kebab man and an elderly gentleman who'd nodded off, head back, mouth open, a steady flow of spittle drooling out of the corner of his mouth, and sat down. She felt squashed but triumphant. So what if she had to

112

wait another hour while he drove home, snug and safe.

'Do you want a lift?'

Hadn't she heard that line before? Glancing up, her eyes narrowed, she fixed him with a stare. 'No, thanks,' she replied curtly. She was determined to play it cool. She wasn't going to accept any favours from Jimi – *sorry*, *Mr* Malik, and she certainly wasn't going to accept any lifts. After what had happened last time? No siree. She was going to shake her head, affect a regal-cum-blasé Mona-Lisa-type smile and politely say no, she was fine, she'd wait for her own cab, thank you very much. Feeling strong and determined she glanced up at the lopsided clock on the wall. *Midnight.* For one small, self-pitying moment all she wanted was to be curled up in her pyjamas.

'Are you sure?'

Feeling her nonchalance unravelling she glanced over at him. He was hanging back in the doorway. She could hear the sound of a minicab hooting outside.

'Look, it's no problem.'

She opened her mouth to refuse, when the man asleep next to her chose that precise moment to let out an amazingly loud, amazingly eggy fart. Jolted awake he sat up and threw her a filthy glare as if she was the perpetrator. 'Do you mind?' he hissed indignantly. Lost for words, Grace was trying to think of some cutting remark when she caught sight of Jimi in the doorway, silently killing himself with laughter.

Try as she might to resist, it was infectious. She stifled a giggle.

'Actually, on second thoughts . . .'

Chapter Ten

'So how's things?'

'Great,' she lied. 'And you?'

'Yeah, great.'

Like two boxers sitting in opposite corners of the ring, Grace and Jimi eyeballed each other across the back-seat armrest of the Nissan Micra. The irony of their situation didn't escape either of them. Being by yourself, in a dodgy minicab that still retained the manufacturer's plastic seat covering, on a sultry Friday night, wasn't exactly the Oxford Dictionary's definition of 'Great'.

Of course neither was going to admit it.

'So whose stag party was it?' Squashed up against an ashtray littered with old bits of chewing gum and tab ends, Grace upheld the pretence of polite chitchat. If the truth be told, she wanted to pin him to the plastic seat covering and blurt out, 'Why didn't you fucking ring?'

'Mine,' he said matter-of-factly.

'*Yours?*' She was incredulous. '*You* are getting married?'

He nodded, and a big, lazy smile engulfed his face. 'Sure am.'

Grace shook her head. 'I can't believe it,' she laughed.

'Why's that so funny?' said Jimi, keeping his tone light. It was a struggle. Why did she have to keep going on about it? he thought, beginning to feel annoyed. Was it that ridiculous that he should settle down? Everyone did eventually. Even Liam Gallagher. Well, sort of. 'It happens to us all, you know,' he added, tugging his cableknit hat down low over his eyes.

'I know, but you . . .' Her voice tailed off as she momentarily forgot her predicament and started laughing again.

Listening to her throaty giggles, Jimi felt strangely miffed. 'So, what about you?' he asked, determinedly turning the spotlight back on her.

'Me?' Abruptly Grace stopped laughing. 'Oh, I'm engaged.'

'Congratulations,' he replied.

Sarcastically, thought Grace.

There was a tense silence. Grace found herself desperately wishing the cab would get a move on, but they were stuck in traffic, even at this time of night. Jimi turned to gaze out of the window. She immediately did the same, pretending to concentrate on what was outside, but really studying what was on the inside. Namely Jimi, who was reflected in the window. Bathed in an orange glow from the street lamps, he was slouched down on the back seat, legs stretched wide, arms folded, head resting against the window. He still had that air of arrogance about him. Even after all these years it still irritated her.

'So, when's the big day?' asked Grace, more for want of something to say than actual interest.

'Next weekend,' he answered casually. *Seven days, and twelve hours and about forty-five minutes*, he thought nervously.

'In Manchester?'

'No, Kylie's Canadian so we're doing it in a hunting lodge in the Rockies,' he enthused, his mind flicking up the image of a lavish ballroom lit by flickering candelabra, with him drinking ice-cold champagne in landscaped grounds and Kylie looking amazing in a figure-hugging dress.

'Wow, lucky you.' Grace's reaction hid her own crushing disappointment. Talking about weddings always made her wistful.

'What about yours?' Having discovered that not only was he rather enjoying all this wedding talk, Jimi found himself genuinely interested. 'When are *you* getting hitched?'

'Oh, we're having a long engagement,' she quickly replied.

'A what?' Jimi was nonplussed. Being a man, all those phrases women bandied around as part of every-day vocabulary were like a foreign language. Commitment-phobes, transitional relationships, surrendered singles, it was all so bloody confusing.

'It means we haven't set the date yet,' she explained.

'In other words you've got cold feet.'

'No.' She was indignant at his interpretation. 'Nobody's got cold feet. It's just complicated,' she added feebly.

'It couldn't be *more* simple,' argued Jimi. 'He asks you, you say yes, you get married. It's hardly rocket science.'

Grace glared at him across the armrest. She didn't know what it was about him, but he had a knack for annoying the hell out of her.

Realizing he'd overstepped the mark, Jimi tried backtracking. 'When did you get engaged?'

'Two years ago.' She could feel herself being defensive.

Jimi's jaw dropped open like a ventriloquist's dummy. 'C'mon, you've got to be joking,' he laughed.

'Why should I be joking?' she retorted hotly.

Christ, she really wasn't joking. Jimi's face became serious. 'So, what are you waiting for?'

Without hesitation Grace launched into her well-rehearsed speech. 'We've just been so busy with our careers and we've been doing up the flat, and you know how expensive weddings are . . .' She gave one of her customary sighs and looked at Jimi. By his expression it was obvious he didn't believe a word she was saying. And you know what? I don't believe a word I'm saying either, thought Grace suddenly realizing in the middle of her speech, in the middle of Clapham High Street, that actually, she wasn't fooling anyone. In fact the only person she'd been fooling was herself.

'We haven't got married because Spencer doesn't want to,' she blurted.

Wow. There. She'd said it. Grace was taken aback.

But not as much as Jimi. Shite, this was all getting a bit heavy. For a moment he considered swiftly changing the subject to house prices, or how Manchester United were doing. After all, this was none of his business, it wasn't as if they were friends; more acquaintances. Only it didn't feel like that. He glanced across at Grace. She was visibly upset. This was obviously about much more than a marriage proposal.

'Do you want to tell me what it was about?'

He caught her off guard. 'What?'

'The row.' He turned towards her. 'Why else would you be in a cab rank by yourself?' he added quietly.

Still reeling from her admission, Grace felt defensive and on the verge of telling him to sod off and mind his own business, she looked at him, looking at her, and something made her change her mind. She paused, shrugged, and then opened her mouth.

It came pouring out.

'It's my birthday and he got completely hammered.' She began by firing this straight off, and then, seeing his reaction was more *So, what?* than *What a bastard!*, she became defensive: 'And I know you probably don't think that sounds like anything to get upset about . . .'

'Oh it does . . .' Jimi nodded, ignoring memories of getting completely rat-arsed himself.

'But most people don't think that,' said Grace, looking at Jimi in a favourable new light. 'Most people think he's great because after a few drinks he's the life and soul of the party, always buying another round,

117

always cracking jokes, always having a laugh, but when he drinks he doesn't know when to stop and we always end up having a row . . .'

'You do?' Jimi's attempt at sympathy came out sounding like an accusation. He cringed. 'I mean . . . shit, that's too bad.'

'. . . and he knows I hate it but he still went and did it anyway, and then when we left the restaurant he insisted on driving home, even though he was way over the limit . . .' With horror Grace felt her eyes beginning to water, spilling salty drizzles down her cheeks. 'And usually I don't say anything, usually I just let it go.' Feeling like an idiot, she choked back the big, meaty sobs, wiping her running nose on the back of her sleeve, trailing a silver snail of snot and spit along her denim jacket. 'But tonight I didn't. Tonight I refused to get in the car. And you know what he did?'

Jimi had a pretty good idea, but he acted as if he didn't. 'No, what did he do?' he asked compliantly.

'He drove off!' she gasped indignantly. 'He drove off and left me.' Her anger vanished as quickly as it had arrived and, feeling her tears returning, she put her head in her hands.

Stiffly sitting on the seat next to her, hands stuffed firmly in pockets, head tilted on one side, Jimi felt extremely uncomfortable. He craned his neck ever so slightly. At this angle he could see tears plopping off the end of her nose and soaking into her denim knees. What the hell was he supposed to do now?

And then before he knew it, he was reaching across, gently stroking away the straggle of hair sticking to her damp cheek, putting his arm around her and saying, 'Here, cry on my shoulder.' And Grace was sniffing tearfully, resting her cheek against the soft leather of his lapel, and closing her eyes.

Feeling the warmth of Grace's face on his chest Jimi tensed up, his body pinned against the plastic seat covering like a crash-test dummy on wind-tunnel test. Until, slowly, gradually, he felt himself relaxing. For someone who'd only ever used sympathy and affection to try to get a woman into bed, this was a whole new experience, and it wasn't so bad. In fact, it was rather nice, he thought, protectively stroking her fluffy, freshly washed hair, inhaling her soft, sweet, musky perfume, feeling a pleasant stirring in his Calvin Kleins.

A *what*?

Jimi's heart threw itself into his mouth. No . . . it was impossible . . . it couldn't be . . . he couldn't have . . . But with the determination of a pantomime audience, his penis was saying oh yes he could. And oh yes he did.

He had a stiffie.

Oh shite.

There was no doubting it now. In his jeans a huge erection was trying to burst out of his button-fly. What was going on? He was getting married in a week and yet here he was with a ginormous hard-on, feeling utterly, unexpectedly, and inexplicably *horny*.

Grace fidgeted.

Jimi freaked. Squeezing his thighs together he tightly clenched his buttocks. He had nothing to worry about. This was just a physical reflex, like blinking if you got something in your eye. Yes, that was it, Grace was just like a piece of grit, or an eyelash, or a dodgy contact lens or something. Not to mention the fact that he was missing Kylie, missing the physical contact, and didn't that do funny things to men? Weren't prisons full of big butch men who'd gone onto the other side, so to speak, because they were desperate for a bit of how's-your-father?

But his hard-on wasn't convinced. Wide awake and determined, it refused to budge. His mind could try and intellectualize it, but his basic instinct was to grab hold of Grace, rip her clothes off and shag her senseless. Jimi panicked. This was getting him nowhere. He took a few deep breaths and tried with all his might to concentrate on the world's unsexiest things, like having a root canal, or cleaning out those bits of food that always got stuck in the plughole, or kissing Anne Robinson . . .

Well, it just goes to show how you can get people so wrong, thought Grace, nestling comfortably into Jimi's lapel. She felt guilty, yet gladdened. It proved that people really could change. I mean, just look at Jimi. He isn't a sex maniac, or a slimeball or a shithead any more. On the contrary, he's caring, he's getting married, and maybe he *is* going to stay faithful and monogamous for the rest of his life. And if that trans-formation was possible, who was to say Spencer couldn't change?

Eyes closed, she felt herself relax. She wasn't speak-ing, but then neither was he. She didn't feel the need to. There was just the blurred sounds of the car radio, the slowing of her breathing, the faint thudding of his heart. It was oddly comforting. There was something so familiar about being with Jimi, he reminded her of home, her childhood. It was a bit like finding an old teddy bear she'd had as a kid. Except of course the teddy bear wouldn't have slept with her and then broken her heart.

Abruptly she sat up.

'Where are we?' Cupping her hand around her eyes she leaned across him and peered out of the window. They had pulled off the dual carriageway and were now passing parades of closed shops, their windows hidden behind iron grilles like corrugated eyelids, the odd late-night Chinese takeaway sign throwing a gaudy light against the smog-blackened Victorian buildings.

'Er, not far,' said Jimi, hastily crossing his legs and covering his groin with his jacket. Sitting upright, he felt horribly self-conscious. The back of the cab was claustrophobic. Leaning forwards he addressed the driver. 'Erm . . . excuse me, do you have any music?'

Muttering grumpily under his breath the driver flicked on the radio and began twiddling the dial, just a little bit to the left, a little bit to the right. It was like keyhole surgery. Until finally.

'... *so for all you listeners out there looking for Mr or Ms Right you need look no further. Write to us here at* Do You Come Here Often? *and we'll find that special someone for you ...*'

'What the hell is that?' murmured Jimi.

'Ah ... this is very good. This is a very good programme.' The minicab driver had perked up. It was his favourite. Mistaking Jimi's question for interest, he turned up the volume.

'... *Just think, that special person could be out there right now, listening to this programme, just waiting to hear from you ...*'

'It mends broken hearts,' added the minicab driver, catching Grace's eye and nodding pointedly.

She smiled appreciatively and glanced out of the window, recognizing the familiar leafy streets, the common, the bus stop on the corner, Spencer's car parked further up the street. She felt a mixture of anger and relief. At least he'd got home safely.

'Just here, thanks.'

The cabbie pulled in and, sensing the rather frosty reception for his choice of radio station, turned down the volume.

Fishing around in her suede fringed bag Grace pulled out her wallet, but Jimi stopped her.

'Hey, don't worry, it's on me.' He grinned. 'Call it a birthday treat.'

'Thanks.' She smiled, and all at once she was glad she'd bumped into him. Things had changed, they'd moved on, they were both older and wiser but it was like listening to an old record and discovering that you still knew all the words. After all those years the connection was still there.

There was a pause. It was time to say goodbye, but they were both waiting for the other to make the first move. Grace broke first.

'Bye, then.' She went to kiss him on the cheek, just

as he turned his face a fraction, and like a parachutist coming in to land, she realized she was way off course before it had even happened. She crash-landed and kissed him fully on the lips. He looked surprised, but not as surprised as she was by the blast of sexual energy that rushed straight from her lips and burned straight to her groin.

And all that in the fraction of a second.

Where on earth did that just come from? Taken aback, she broke away from Jimi, her cheeks burning, her mind whirling, her heart racing. What on earth had just happened? Was she just feeling emotional, tired, upset, or had she felt something? And had he felt it too? They looked at each other in stunned silence. It was a moment when either of them could have said something and set things off on an entirely different course altogether. But all too quickly it slipped away and was filled by a hasty unravelling of goodbyes.

'Well, I hope you live happily ever after,' she joked awkwardly.

'Er yeah – you too.' Jimi was nodding. 'Maybe I'll see you around . . .'

'. . . Yeah maybe,' she agreed, both of them knowing they'd never see each other again, that after tonight they'd both slip back into their lives and forget all about it, but for some reason they both felt compelled to say it.

And then before either of them had time to think about it Grace slammed the door and stepped out into the warm boozy Friday night air.

Behind her she could hear the cab pulling away, the wheezing of the clapped-out engine as it changed through the gears and at the last minute Grace had an urge to turn around. God knows why. Old times' sake? Maybe. Sentimentality? Probably. Because he was a sod and never did bloody tell her why he never rang? Most definitely.

Whatever the reasons, Grace did look back. She didn't know what she expected, but if the nostalgic part of her was hoping for something, it was disappointed. This was real life, not the movies. There were no lingering glances or soulful eyes meeting or significant waves. Instead she saw the back end of a rusty old Nissan Micra driving away down the street with its exhaust hanging off.

Watching it, she absent-mindedly put her finger to her lips.

They were still tingling.

Chapter Eleven

The aroma of sizzling bacon wafted up from the frying pan.

Mmmm. Spatula in one hand, pan handle in the other, Rhian closed her eyes and took a deep lusty lungful. *Mmmmm.* Forget Calvin Klein's Obsession, this had to be the most wonderful scent in the whole world. Dipping her head closer to the frying pan, she stuck her nostrils inches away from the streaky rashers that were beginning to curl and brown with the heat of the oil and inhaled languorously. God, that Danish rindless smelt so damn good, it was almost orgasmic. Her mouth watered.

Her resolve wavered.

Feeling a swell of guilty anticipation, Rhian peered from underneath her lashes. Bubbling and fizzing, the streaky flesh almost looked as if it too was salivating. Oh Lordy, she groaned inwardly, this was going to be a toughie. Immediately she began her mental chant. '*A moment on the lips, a lifetime on the hips, a moment on the lips . . .*' but it was just a backing track for the lead vocalist in her head '*Maybe if you have just a nibble. Just a taste. Just that little teensy-weensy crispy bit just there, tucked away in the corner.*' While her mind sang a duet, her body hesitated, debated, yearned, agonized. '*. . . a lifetime on the hips.*'

And then it was all over in a cartoonish blur. Faster than a newt flicking out its tongue her hand shot out, grabbed a rasher and popped it into her mouth. Blink and you'd have missed it. For a heavenly moment she remained completely still, her guilty secret melting against the roof of her mouth and then, unable to contain her rapture, her tongue wrapped itself around it, embracing it like a long-lost lover. *Mmmmmfuckingmmmm.*

'Hey, what are you doing in there?' hollered a male voice. It was Noel. Down the hallway, in the bedroom, he was lying spreadeagled and naked on her quilted satin bedspread. Starving hungry, he was waiting impatiently for his promised fry-up.

Nearly choking, Rhian swallowed hard. 'Er, nothing . . . honey,' she jabbered, her cheeks burning with shame. Mortified, she dived across the kitchen and yanked open the fridge door. It was covered in bright plastic alphabet letters and several pieces of jotter paper scrawled with biro and crayons.

To the untrained eye these might just look like scrawls, but to Rhian the funny blue splodge thing was quite obviously a house, the orange squiggle with a thumbprint looked uncannily like her, and the swirl of yellow crayon was Jack to a T. Looking at them she always felt a blush of pride. Not because she was his mum, but because at three years old Jack was a talented artist. Possibly even the next Damien Hirst, she thought, grabbing the cardboard six-pack of free-range that lay on an otherwise empty shelf.

'How do you want your eggs – fried or scrambled?' she cooed, hurriedly cracking them into the pan.

Hitching his naked body up against the garlands of fairylights wound around the white iron bed frame, Noel reached for his cigarettes and lit up a post-coital fag. Framed by a glittering multicoloured con-stellation, he drew in a lungful of Benson & Hedges finest and scratched his bollocks contentedly, a satisfied smile spreading over his face. 'Poached.'

Oh. Poised with her thumbnails pierced deep into her third shell, Rhian stared with dismay at the fast-solidifying whites. Hissing and spitting at her it was almost as if they'd guessed their fate before she had. She hesitated, fighting with the shadow of irritation that threatened to overcast her mood, and then banished it. After all, he wasn't doing it to be awkward, was he? Scooping broken yolks and egg whites into the sink, she said gaily, 'Coming right up.'

It was the morning after the night before, and despite the dull thudding of a hangover Rhian was feeling deliciously happy. The sun streamed in through the garlands of purply-pink plastic flowers that hung like a blind at her open window, sending a dappled, lilac light dancing over her spotlessly clean work surfaces, rack of sparklingly polished wine glasses and neatly lined up jars of tea, coffee and Candarel. Outside was the usual bustling din of inner-city London – buses rumbling along the busy main road, a dog yapping in next-door's garden, a car alarm wailing on the street below – but this morning it floated vaguely over her like the background noise of a TV set.

Lifting the lid of her cream enamel bread bin, she pulled out a new loaf of Hovis wholemeal from its pristine, crumbless interior. She didn't care what all those magazine articles said about being single and independent and pleasing yourself, there was nothing nicer than waking up on the weekend with a man spooned behind you. Absolutely nothing, she thought, tap-tapping across the kitchen lino in her pink fluffy kitten heels and new cream satin bathrobe, her mind wandering back to last night.

Her cheeks flushed at the memory. After all that waiting, all that build-up, sex with Noel hadn't been exactly amazing. To be honest, for all her anticipation and for all his swagger and confidence, he'd fumbled around a lot, grabbing and jabbing at things like an overexcited little boy in a sweetshop, sucking her nipples, licking her face, nibbling her earlobes but, rather disappointingly, choosing not to eat anything from what her Nanna Jones used to call 'the dessert trolley'.

But then she could hardly blame him for fumbling, could she? After all, she was the one who'd insisted on closing the curtains and turning off the lights. Plunged into pitch darkness he'd stumbled around with his bulging erection, treading on a rogue piece of Jack's Lego, stubbing his toe on her exercise bike and swearing vociferously. Eventually he'd managed to locate the bed, in which she was already lying hidden under layers of satin nightie and feather duvet, with the bedspread pulled firmly up to her chin.

Rhian had been determined Noel wasn't going to see her naked. She'd never been one of those tall, skinny girls, but even so, she used to be rather proud of her petite frame and generous curves. However, since having Jack her body was barely recognizable. Her handspan waist had broadened and thickened, her full, firm bottom had sagged and dropped, and her voluptuous breasts were now just plainly huge. She was, quite frankly, enormous.

Rhian knew she'd 'let things go'. She knew people were only trying to be kind when they described her as curvy. Because she knew what they really meant to say was fat. She was plain old fat. No longer able to look at herself in the full-length mirror, she'd stuffed it behind the wardrobe along with the Christmas decorations, and the bright, colourful, shiny garments that hung in her wardrobe no longer got past the dimples in her knees. They were like a metaphor for her old, colourful, vibrant life. It didn't fit any more.

But this morning she'd been allowed to glimpse what life could be like, cooking breakfast for her man, enjoying a lie-in, having sex. She flicked on the radio. 'Respect' by Aretha Franklin was playing, and smiling to herself she began to tap her feet and hum along. There was a real art to a fry-up, she mused a few minutes later as she finished ladling the food onto a plate and turned off the gas. Pleased with her culinary expertise she checked her reflection in the glass units, shook back her hair and padded into the bedroom.

'Mmmm, gorgeous,' enthused Noel, a large smile stretching over his face.

For a moment Rhian wasn't sure whether he was referring to her or his breakfast. She smiled uncertainly. She'd been OK last night, when it was dark and the lights were off, but in the bright light of day she felt vulnerable and self-conscious.

'I'm starving.'

It was the latter.

She passed him the large flute-edged plate, piled high with steaming food, and watched his eyes widen with gluttonous delight. Resting it on his knees he took a final drag of his cigarette and then stubbed it out in the mug on the pine chest, next to the bed. Rhian flinched. It was her favourite hand-painted bone-china one she'd found on a market stall in Paris and haggled in pidgin French to buy. But she didn't say anything. After all, he wasn't to know, was he?

Ignoring her, he began tucking in. Perching on the edge of the bed, she attempted to snuggle up to him, all the while tugging down the satin hem of her dressing gown which for some reason seemed intent on riding up her legs.

'Ree . . . ?'

He was looking at her, a frown clouding his large, baby blue eyes. She felt a wave of embarrassment. Oh please God no. Please God don't let him have seen. Even she felt sick at the sight of all that horrible lumpy cellulite up the backs of her legs. Sticking her legs under the bedspread to hide them, she hurriedly pulled it up to her waist.

'Er . . . yes, honey?' she purred. God, she felt ridiculous. She was not – and was never going to be – a seductress. Not with these thighs.

'Don't I get any fried bread?'

'What?'

He was staring at his plate, his bottom lip stuck out

petulantly. It reminded her of Jack when she wouldn't let him watch *Teletubbies*.

'Oh . . . sorry,' she began to apologize, mentally cursing herself. 'I made toast instead,' she began hopefully, but his expression didn't change. 'I can make you some fried bread if you want.'

'No, it's OK,' he grumbled, sighing like a martyr. 'The beans will be cold by then.'

He ploughed on regardless and within minutes he'd finished, wiping up the last smears of yolk and sauce from the beans with the toast, every last crumb of which he'd managed to eat. Balancing the plate precariously on the china cup and giving a satisfied burp, he reached for his cigarettes. Noticing Rhian sitting next to him, he looked surprised. 'Are you not eating anything?' he asked, affectionately running his fingers through her hair.

'No, I'm not hungry,' she lied, ignoring the protestations of her stomach.

Lighting his cigarette, he stretched out languidly on the bedspread and admired his penis. Shiny pink and circumcised, it was as smooth and flaccid as the rest of his body and rested proudly on its pale blond nest. Reaching over, he took her hand and placed it on top. Rhian felt something stir underneath the palm of her hand as he leaned across and began to kiss her. His tongue probed her mouth. He tasted of fried bacon and cigarettes. In her starved state it was delicious. She kissed him back, feeling his hands sliding up underneath the satin hem, grasping at her buttocks, kneading her thighs. As they worked upwards, she sucked in her stomach and held her breath.

'You know what you've got, don't you, Ree?'

'No – what?' She felt the faintest glimmer of confidence. OK, so she was no Kylie Minogue, but size wasn't everything.

Enthusiastically squeezing a breast, he grunted, 'You must have one of those slow metabolisms.'

Disappointment seared. 'Yeah . . . maybe,' she

murmured faintly, feeling suddenly, horribly, pain-fully foolish.

Of course size was everything. It was everything and a whole lot more.

Chapter Twelve

'I suppose you're still mad at me.'

Tucked away in the corner of their local pâtisserie, between the glass-fronted counter filled with over-priced slices of *tarte tatin* and an industrial-sized double buggy, Grace looked up to see Spencer lumber-ing towards her nursing an almighty hangover and a double espresso. Crumpled and dishevelled, he was still wearing yesterday's clothes which reeked of alcohol, spices and cigarette smoke. Last night the cocktail of aromas had seemed deliciously intoxi-cating; this morning it was a pungent mixture of stale and sour, like takeout curry gone off. Taking off his smeared glasses he roughly rubbed his eyes with the flat of his hand, grazing his thumb down along the pale blond stubble coating his jaw. Replacing them, he gazed at her blearily.

She gazed back. For over an hour she'd been sitting by herself, trying to make one weak cappuccino last, outwardly flicking through the papers, inwardly thinking about last night. And now Spencer had turned up with an apology. At least that's what she presumed it was. It was amazing how he could make an apology sound like an accusation. How, after every-thing that had happened, he'd managed to turn her into the aggressor. *She was still mad at him?* What had happened to *him* being mad at *her*? So mad, in fact, that he'd driven off and abandoned her.

'Don't turn this around, Spence.'

'Turn what around?'

He looked the picture of innocence. The wronged man. No wonder he'd never lost a case. What jury would convict him?

'Last night. *My birthday*,' she added. Lest he needed to be reminded.

His face crumpled. 'Babes. I'm really sorry. I'll make it up to you, I promise,' he pleaded quietly, sitting down beside her.

Grace didn't answer. Sober promises, to be boozily broken.

'I've been so stressed out,' he continued hastily. 'What with work, and this stupid million-dollar divorce case, I don't know what the hell came over me last night.'

'Probably because you were too drunk to remember,' she couldn't help replying.

His jaw tightened. 'I know you're right. I've been drinking too much, I'm going to stop . . .' Hanging his head, he looked at her for sympathy. 'Another hangover like this is going to kill me.'

He didn't get any. 'Well if they don't, I will,' she muttered angrily.

It was just after 9 a.m. Eight hours after Grace had arrived home last night, let herself in and discovered the stereo on, some opera or other blaring loudly, and Spencer crashed out on the sofa. Arms dangling, thighs splayed, his trousers ridden up his leg to expose a hairy calf muscle, his mouth hanging open. He'd been snoring as well. And not just any old snoring, but a loud, phlegmy, boozy, smoker's rattle – *grroink-grrroink-grrroink-grroink* – as if a stick was being dragged along metal railings.

Flicking off the stereo, she'd looked down at him, and instead of feeling angry she felt only sadness. Sadness that she'd grown used to seeing Spencer arrive home drunk, watching him getting out the

Glenfiddich 'for just a nightcap', selecting a CD from his beloved opera collection, turning up the volume until her votive candles on the shelf rattled in their frosted glass containers. She was used to his 'second wind', him looning it up in the living room, waving his arms around as if he was a conductor, singing at the top of his voice like Pavarotti, before collapsing onto the sofa.

Then there'd be silence. The heavy breathing. Her realization that he'd passed out. That she was going to have to try and wake him up, steer him stumbling and staggering into the bedroom where he'd belly-flop onto the bed, and she'd begin the lengthy process of undressing him. First would be his shoes, then his socks, yanking arms out of sleeves, tugging legs out of trousers, until finally she'd cover him with the duvet, climb in beside him and lie with her eyes wide open, staring at the dark ceiling until finally she fell asleep.

But not this time. This time she'd left him where he'd passed out, had gone into the bedroom and in the silent, spacious luxury of having the king-size all to herself, spread out like a starfish. She'd slept soundly. Whereas most people might have lain awake for hours, mulling over what had happened, Grace's mind automatically switched off as soon as it hit a duckdown pillow.

Until she'd woken up that morning, jumped out of bed and tramped across the common. Somehow she'd ended up in a coffee shop and she'd perched herself on a stool by the window, absent-mindedly watching the invasion of McClaren baby buggies, gazing out of the window and flicking idly through the Saturday morning papers. She hadn't bothered to read anything. She couldn't concentrate. Everything was all churned up.

'You didn't even call to see if I was OK,' said Grace, looking accusingly across at Spencer.

'I tried your mobile but it was switched off. That's why I came to look for you,' he protested quickly.

'I wasn't talking about this morning,' gasped Grace.

'Oh, yeah . . .' he muttered, running his fingers through his rumpled hair. Gazing at her, he shrugged remorsefully. 'I don't blame you for being angry.'

But that was just it, thought Grace, she was a whole lot of things but angry wasn't one of them. She looked across at Spencer. Was it really only four years ago since she'd first laid eyes on him? He'd been standing right next to her, at a bar, and when he'd chatted her up and asked her out she'd said yes. When, six months later, he'd asked her to move into his flat in Wandsworth, she'd said yes. And, eighteen months later, when he'd asked her to marry him it was a foregone conclusion. Well that's how relationships are supposed to work, aren't they?

Except this one wasn't working any more, thought Grace, gazing at Spencer. Sitting opposite her he was cricking his neck, trying to read the upside-down sports headlines on the newspaper that lay on the table in front of her.

'We need to talk.' Her voice was quiet but determined.

He looked up. 'About last night, look, I know . . .'

But this time Grace was determined not to be interrupted. 'No, it's not just about last night.'

'It's not?'

Grace couldn't believe he actually seemed surprised. 'It's about lots of things.' She paused, wondering where to start and then deciding to start with the most obvious. 'One of them being why, after being engaged for two years, we're still not married.'

For a split second he hesitated. It was just a beat. A heartbeat. One breath. The time it takes for your eyelashes to sweep lightly down against your cheek in a blink. To most people it wouldn't have been discernible, they would never have noticed, but Grace wasn't most people. And she did notice.

'You know why,' he began, launching into their speech. 'Because we've been busy, and we were going

134

to finish doing up the flat, it's going to cost a small fortune to do that extension . . .'

'Spence, this is me you're talking to,' cut in Grace. She knew that speech so well, she'd written the bloody thing. 'What are we waiting for, Spence? Forget all this organization rubbish, why don't we elope? We could fly off to Vegas next weekend and have an Elvis wedding, or go to Barbados and do it barefoot on the beach.' Getting carried away, it was as if saying her marriage vows was like saying abracadabra and waving a magic wand and all her nagging doubts would disappear. Her voice trailed off as she caught Spencer's expression. He was staring at her, bemused by her suggestion of something so spontaneous. Leaning closer, he put his arms around her, his forehead leaning against her. 'We're OK as we are, aren't we?' he murmured, kissing her gently, his stubble brushing against her top lip.

Held close in an embrace, his face nuzzling her neck, all the upset, the worry, the anger, the fear faded away. This felt safe and snug and familiar. Closing her eyes, Grace rested her cheek on the soft curls of his hair. It would be so easy to slip back into the status quo. To just forget about last night, record over it as if it was a blank videotape. But she wasn't going to.

'No we're not OK. I'm not OK.' Pulling away, she shook her head. Because it wasn't really about last night, about her birthday, about him getting drunk, about him leaving her. It wasn't even just about their engagement. It was about everything. About that black dress he'd 'suggested' she wore, the drunken jokes she'd heard a hundred times before, the weekly trips she had to make to the bottle bank with his empties, the photograph in the snowglobe of the couple skating in Central Park. The couple she no longer recognized.

'This isn't what I want,' she confessed sadly.

Spencer frowned. Lulled into thinking everything had been sorted out, that he'd been forgiven and everything was back to normal, he was surprised. And annoyed. 'Is this your way of giving me an ultimatum?'

Was it? Grace wavered. If she was giving Spencer an ultimatum she had to mean it, and she wasn't sure. Because that was the problem. She wasn't sure about anything any more.

Her silence fanned his indignation. 'So what are you saying? That if I don't give an answer about our wedding and set a date right this second, you're going to walk out on me, that you're going to walk out on us?' he demanded.

There he went again. Turning things around.

'Well, if you're going to put it like that, yes I am,' she snapped back.

And then stopped. Oh God, what was she saying? This wasn't supposed to be how it worked out. For all her bravado, Grace felt suddenly afraid. It was all very well threatening to leave Spencer, but in reality would she? Could she imagine a life without him? Being single again?

The thought wasn't appealing. She was thirty-one, not twenty-one. She was a *thirtysomething* and she knew all about the fate that awaited her. It was well documented. She'd read *Bridget Jones*, she'd seen the movie, and she had enough single friends who'd bought the T-shirts and regaled her with tales of 'the desert' and how it was 'desperate out there'. Spencer might not be perfect, but neither was she, and weren't relationships about compromise, working at it, giving and taking? Wasn't that why they called it 'settling down'?

As all these thoughts and fears whizzed through her mind she looked across at Spencer. Clutching his throbbing head, he slugged back a mouthful of bitter espresso. Cocking his head on one side, he met her gaze. 'Christ, Grace, don't you think this is a bit heavy for nine-thirty on a Saturday morning?' he sighed wearily.

He looked so gorgeous, so remorseful, so familiar she felt her anger vanishing. 'You don't have to answer right this second,' she smiled, regretting her outburst and trying to make a joke out of it. 'Think about it over the weekend,' she said. Reaching her hand across the table, she laced her fingers through his.

'*Great*, so I've got all this stress at work, what with a case that's due in court on Monday, and now I'm going to have more stress thinking about this all weekend,' grumbled Spencer. Tugging his hand away, he pressed his thumbs against his temples and began rotating them roughly.

For a moment Grace just looked at him. Then she stood up and, without saying goodbye, began weaving her way through the assault course of pushchairs, tables, toddlers and parents until she reached the doorway. Pausing, she glanced back at Spencer, but he was already bent over the sports pages and didn't see her. Turning away she whispered to herself, 'You shouldn't have had to think about it.'

Chapter Thirteen

'Eurggghhh.'

An inhuman retching noise was coming from the bathroom. Obscenely loud and almost guttural it sounded like an animal howling in pain. On second thoughts, more like a werewolf howling in pain, considered Jimi, spooning Lavazza into his espresso machine. He paused to listen.

'Eurrggggghhheurrggghhh.'

There it went again.

Shaking his head, he clicked the coffee into position, curled his fingers around the silver handle, and slowly drew it down. This was a heavy-duty machine, a real Italian stainless steel Gaggia that was all knobs and dials and levers and temperature gauges. Jimi adored gadgets of all kinds, and it sat proudly on his granite worktop alongside his stainless steel coffee grinder, 1950s-style blender and a state-of-the-art juicer aptly named Hercules.

Jimi's stainless steel possessions were like a suit of armour, to protect him, give him strength, show him what he'd achieved, prove himself. It was just ten years ago that he'd returned from his round-the-world trip to discover that at twenty-one, not only was he penniless and jobless, but he was homeless. Tariq Malik had never got over his son's refusal to go to med school, and despite Colleen, his wife, begging him to reconsider, he'd thrown Jimi out of his house with as much emotion as if he'd been throwing out a binliner of rubbish.

Jimi had promptly picked himself up, dusted his rucksack off, and moved to London where he'd found himself a job flipping burgers on Tottenham Court Road, and a bedsit in Soho. Those first few months had been grim and he'd endured many times when he'd wanted to give it all up and head back home to his parents' comfy semi in Manchester, back to his old stomping ground, to his old mates.

But he didn't. Like his father, he was too proud, too headstrong, and too ambitious. So what if he wasn't going to be a doctor? He was going to be a journalist. And so he'd sat in night after night applying for jobs in the *Guardian*, eating eggs he'd boiled in the kettle, listening through the stained, paper-thin walls to the couple having sex next door, and waited for his big break. It had duly arrived in a brown A4-sized envelope. Inside had been a letter inviting him for an interview for a job he'd applied for, as editorial assistant on a trade magazine. The money was shit, the hours were long, and there were two hundred other applicants, but it was a start, and Jimi had wanted it more than anything in the world.

At his leaving party two years later the editor told him that he'd been so charming the job had been his the moment he'd walked into her office. It was the same time and time again – he'd move to a new job, swiftly learn the ropes, then leave. From a features assistant on a teen title, to a writer on a male glossy, to the editor of *Geezer*, one of the UK's top-selling magazines for men. And as his reputation as a funny, witty, irreverent writer grew so did his success with the ladies, and it wasn't long before he found himself in *Tatler*'s 'One Hundred Most Eligible Bachelors for 2000'. It had been a crazy start to the millennium, and with a great job, gorgeous new apartment, a fantastic salary, and a never-ending string of sexy women to date, Jimi had thought he'd achieved everything he'd ever wanted.

Except one. He wanted to write a novel. He wanted to be the next Nick Hornby, he wanted to see his name on a big chunky paperback, to catch people on the tube with their noses buried inside his pages, to get into the *Sunday Times* top ten. *He wanted his dad to be proud.* Jimi's relationship with his mum was still as close as ever, he regularly phoned her for chats, she often caught the train down to London to visit, and she was flying out to Canada for the wedding. But his father was a different story. They hadn't seen or spoken to each other in nearly ten years, not since their row in '91. It hadn't been intentional, but by the time their anger had faded, bricks of resentment had begun to build, hurt had set in them like cement, and before he knew it, an impenetrable wall had been built between them.

It was six months since Jimi had handed in his resignation and gone freelance and the commissions had never stopped: comment-pieces for the *Telegraph*, travel features for *Chic Traveller*, male-point-of-view articles for the women's glossies. And so he'd bought himself a funky glass-topped desk, state-of-the-art laptop, a fabulous leather swivel chair, and got to work. The plan had been to divide his time between his commissions and writing his novel. So far it was all going perfectly to plan. Despite foreboding tales of writer's block, warnings of rejection and other pessimistic responses, his plot had poured out onto the screen, his characters had sprung quickly to life, and he had high hopes for this future best-seller.

Watching the thick, treacly black liquid streaming into a small glass cup Jimi listened with satisfaction to the machine's gentle hissing. It was somewhat spoiled by being intermingled with sounds of retching. Poor old Clive. He had the hangover from hell and back. Releasing the handle, Jimi reached for the sugar shaker. He kept trying to give up sugar, as it wasn't exactly trendy to be seen ladling silver spoon into your Chai tea. Frustratingly, however, he was finding it impossible; he had such a sweet tooth, thanks to years of being brought up on Tetley's with two sugars.

Padding barefoot across the kitchen floor he leaned against the exposed brickwork and stared across his loft space. A slave to deconstructed minimalism, his loft was usually flooded with light and not much else. But now, his polished oak floorboards were cluttered with the sprawl of sleeping bags, comatose bodies, piles of discarded clothes and scrunched-up Heineken cans.

The lads.

Jimi stared at them with sympathy and genuine affection. He felt guilty about leaving them last night and wanted to make it up to them. He'd tried waiting up for them to arrive back, but in the end he'd given up and gone to bed. God only knows what time they crawled into their sleeping bags and passed out on the floor. God only knows what state they'd be in when they woke up. So far only Clive had risen and, well, by the sounds of things, he wasn't doing too good.

Something stirred in the navy blue nylon depths.

'*Ughhh* . . .' One of the bodies began moving.

'*Uhuh?*' Followed by another one.

'*Bleugghh.*' And another.

We have lift-off, mused Jimi, watching them slowly coming back from the dead. It was hard to believe these ball-scratching, phlegm-clearing, wind-passing specimens were the same men who only hours earlier had been impeccably groomed men about town.

'Anyone for coffee?' he asked, purposely chirpily.

'Fags . . .' There was a faint murmuring. 'I need fags . . .'

Someone chucked a packet of Marlboro Lights across the room like a missile.

'Milk . . . two sugars,' came a piteous moan.

'Got any booze?' rasped a feeble voice.

One by one the corpses sat up in their sleeping bags. Blearily they eyed a freshly showered, clean-clothed, bright-eyed Jimi.

'What happened to you?' they demanded accusingly.

'Oh shite, I'm sorry, guys, I just couldn't keep up in my old age.' He smiled apologetically. 'But I promise I'm going to make it up to you. What do you say to a lovely fry-up?' he suggested brightly, and then began describing it in full detail while everyone's faces began turning puce. Clive reappeared momentarily from the bathroom, overheard – '. . . and I could fry up some mushrooms and onions . . .' – before promptly diving back in again.

Thankfully, Jimi's vivid description was interrupted by a strange high-pitched noise. What was that? He glanced around the room. Everyone was looking as nonplussed as he was – heads tipped to the side, eyes darting left to right, foreheads creased, eyebrows scrunched. It was clearer now, more like an electronic jingle, a vaguely recognizable tune that sounded almost like . . .

'*Rhubarb and Custard*,' called Clive authoritatively, his voice echoing loudly from the depths of the toilet bowl.

They all turned to look in the direction of the bathroom.

'You know, that kids' cartoon. Back in the seventies,' he explained, re-emerging from the U-bend and staggering into the living room, jubilation at his immense knowledge of trivia replaced by his feeling like a prat for being able to name that tune in one.

'Oh shite, it's one of those novelty ringtones,' mocked Jimi, ready to launch into some serious leg-pulling. But nobody owned up. In fact, everyone was looking at everyone else, trying to locate the source of the noise. He began tracing it with his ears. It seemed to be coming from the jacket draped over the armchair.

His jacket draped over the armchair.

'Oh shite, that's mine. It was Kylie's idea,' he explained hurriedly. 'For a laugh,' he added. Rather ironically, he thought, considering he was the only person *not* laughing.

The posse of sleeping bags burst into raucous guffaws. 'Wooahh, going soft in your old age,' they hollered bawdily.

'Oh for Christsakes, grow up.' All this time no-one had actually answered the phone. Losing his patience, Clive strode across to the chair, stuck his hand into the jacket and tugged out the offending mobile. '*Yes?*' he growled. 'Oh. Kylie. *Hi.*' Immediately his voice rose a couple of octaves and was imbued with uncharacteristic lightness and cheeriness. Clive had a soft spot bordering on a crush for Kylie.

Jimi's face split into a wide grin. 'She must be missing me already,' he said, feeling secretly chuffed to bits. Eagerly he motioned to Clive to pass him the phone. Clive ignored him. 'Hey, mate. She's already taken,' Jimi winked, holding out his hand impatiently. Again no response.

'For Christsakes, Clive . . .' Feeling agitated, Jimi tugged the phone away from him, held it to his ear, opened his mouth to speak. And then stopped. The line was dead.

'*You cut her off,*' he gasped, with frustration. 'Jesus Christ, Clive, sometimes you take a joke too far.'

'She put the phone down.'

'What?'

'She said she didn't want to speak to you.'

'What are you going on about?' complained Jimi. Messing about last night was OK, but now the stag party was well and truly over and it wasn't funny any more. He would have liked a chat with Kylie. It might have only been twenty-four hours but you know what? *He'd missed her.* 'I know it's tradition not to see the bride before the wedding, but I thought you could speak to her,' laughed Jimi, but Clive's expression brought a nervous edge to his laughter.

'That's just it.'

'What's it?' he asked, looking at Clive in confusion. He wasn't in the mood for guessing games.

Only afterwards did Jimi wish he had been. Because

if he had he would have had another few minutes, maybe half an hour of his life as he knew it. Instead it was like yanking the needle off a record. His life stopped playing. He stopped singing.

And Clive just shrugged.

'There isn't going to be a wedding.'

Chapter Fourteen

'Well, I'll be off, then.' Tugging on his hooded grey sweatshirt which had GAP emblazoned across the chest in five-inch-high navy blue letters, Noel grabbed his keys and mobile off the bedside cabinet.

Rhian paused at the doorway, a cup of freshly brewed Earl Grey in each hand. Having expected to return from the kitchen to find Noel still naked under the covers, she was surprised to see him up and fully dressed. 'Already?' she asked, and then immediately regretted it.

'It's gone eleven,' he said matter-of-factly.

'I was thinking we could go for a walk in the park,' she suggested brightly. Jack was next door with the neighbour, so she didn't have to pick him up until later. Which meant she had the whole day free if she wanted. 'Or what about having some lunch down by the river?'

'Lunch?' repeated Noel, his forehead furrowed in surprise. ''Fraid no can do,' he said, shaking his head as he turned on his mobile and began deftly texting a message.

Ignored, Rhian hovered awkwardly in the doorway, wishing she was wearing something rather more substantial than her skimpy nightie. Watching his thumb move quickly over the buttons, his mouth hanging open in concentration, a flutter of insecurity unleashed itself in the pit of her stomach like a clockwork toy. Who was he texting? A woman? *A skinny woman, with slim thighs and no stretchmarks?*

Pressing SEND, Noel stuffed his mobile into the back pocket of his voluminous olive-green combats and, looking up, caught Rhian staring at him. 'Anyway, Ree . . .' he added, patting his stomach and smiling pointedly, 'some of us are watching our figures.'

Noel proceeded to make a sharp exit. After a trip to the loo for 'a quick leak' he kissed her on the forehead, ruffled her hair and when she'd tried to give him a hug, he'd laughed awkwardly and pulled away, gesturing to his sweatshirt and reminding her to 'mind the gap'. Noel didn't 'do' affection, he couldn't see the point – unless of course it was foreplay and then it was a means to an end. He'd let himself out, his mobile beeping a text message as he strode down the street, shoulders see-sawing, chin jutting, in an Oasis-type swagger.

For a few moments Rhian remained by the door, unsure what to do next, before finally surrendering to what she always did when she was at a loss, and opened the cupboard. It was the same every time – but whereas some people might reach for the bottle, Rhian reached for the vacuum cleaner.

Rhian *luurrrved* housework. She was addicted to it, as some women were addicted to shoes, or Cadbury's Crunchies, or Zara. Show this woman a yellow flannel duster and a bottle of Pledge and she was in seventh heaven. Combine it with a cookery programme, preferably Nigella with her lashings of cream and all-butter puds, and she was off into another galaxy.

Housework was her solace. Vacuuming, dusting, wiping, polishing, scrubbing – these were all activities that struck fear into the hearts of women like Grace, but Rhian embraced them with a religious fervour. She adored cleaning the cooker, scrubbing off the blackened bits around the gas burners with a Brillo pad. Felt a surge of contentment as she sprayed bleach around the rim of the loo and attacked the limescale in the U-bend. Discovered a spring in her step as she charged around the flat with the vacuum, swapping attachments like a pro and jabbing hard-to-reach corners with the nozzle, feeling a glow of satisfaction as the crumbs down the sofa whooshed away by magic and Jack's rogue Rice Krispies disappeared in a flash.

A tidy house makes a tidy mind, was Rhian's motto, and she was going to stick to it. She had to. Because by making everything around her clean, tidy and in order, it helped in some small way to ease the guilt she felt over the mess she'd made of her life. On the inside she might be in chaos, but on the outside she was a shining, showroom example.

Finished with the hoovering, Rhian turned to the washing up. Padding into the kitchen, she was hit by a whiff of fried bacon still hanging around in the air. Her stomach rumbled wistfully. She ignored it, and busied herself with filling the sink, adding a generous squirt of Fairy Liquid, tugging her pink pair of Marigolds off the wire-shaped hand that sat upright next to the sink.

Grabbing the saucepan, she pressed the pink satin toe of her fluffy mule onto the pedal bin. The lid flicked up and she began scraping beans into the white plastic liner. Cold and congealed, they formed a solid tomato lump in the bottom. Yuk, she thought, wrinkling up her nose at the sludgy remnants on the wooden spoon. She continued scraping. Uggh, how disgusting. Scrape, scrape, scrape. How really revolting.

But how delicious.

Before Rhian knew what was happening, her tongue was licking the spoon with the same rapturous slurps she'd once upon a time reserved for white chocolate Magnum ice-cream. Her teeth bit off the welded beans, her mouth enveloped the wooden shaft, her lips clamped tightly around it. This had to be the best blowjob she'd ever given, she mused, a faint moan of desire escaping from her lips as she sucked feverishly.

She was hungry. Bloody hungry. In fact she was more than that.

She was starving.

Oh Lordy. Her appetite ignited, Rhian felt an almighty craving. She struggled against it. *No, no, no.* The thin person within screamed weakly from the top of the slippery slope. *Yes, yes, yes,* bullied the great fattie pushing her down it. There was to be no stopping her now and, hastily dropping the spoon like a discarded lover, she dived on the frying pan which lay on the draining board, glimmering moistly in the sunshine. Grabbing the handle she cradled the pan against her breast and ran her finger around the greasy insides. It was wrong, she knew it was wrong, but God it felt so right. Licking her fingers, chewing the bits caught underneath her fingernails, running her tongue along the non-stick surface, she gave the pan her utter devotion.

Until her peripheral vision spied the loaf of Hovis.

On autopilot her arm shot out. No time for the twiddly, fiddly fastener she'd retied now. Oh no. Ripping through the plastic she grabbed a slice, her oily fingers ripping it in two as she plunged it into the pan and began frantically mopping up the salty grease, the charred bits of rind, the scraps of mushroom. Stuffing the wholemeal sponge hungrily in her mouth, she swallowed without chewing. And then another slice, and another, until the frying pan was licked clean. But still there was no satisfaction.

She yanked open the fridge door, her eyes darting, her chest hammering. Its white, sterile shelves were bare but for Jack's food. Rhian deliberately kept nothing in there to tempt her, but now everything was a temptation: baby rice pudding, a half-eaten tin of alphabet letters, a six-pack of junior Yoplait yoghurts, some organic turkey balls . . .

Turkey balls. Grabbing one from its greaseproof packet she squashed it in whole, but as quickly as she was trying to chew her mind had raced on to yoghurts. Normally choosing which flavour would take Rhian a good ten minutes, comparing the calorie content, weighing up the pros and cons of black cherry versus prune and apple, slowly peeling off the lid and carefully licking every last drip that had congealed on its underside, before carefully, respectfully, expectantly slipping her spoon into the creamy depths and savouring her first mouthful.

But not today. Today she ripped off the packaging and drank it straight from the carton, mixing it with a spoonful of uncooked fisherman's pie, a forkful of alphabet letters in tomato sauce, the remnants of the turkey balls. And what about the rice pudding? She mustn't forget that. Tugging off the ring-pull, she began scooping in the creamy, sweetness with her fingers.

Buuuuuzzzzzzzzzz.

Startled by the sound of her buzzer on her front door the tin slipped from between her fingers. It fell, splat, onto the kitchen tiles, its full-fat contents spilling across her spotless lino, splashing her shiny red units, speckling her lilac-painted toenails with pearly splodges. For a moment she stared at it, watching it seep like magnolia lava into the crack underneath the washing machine. And then she heard something. It sounded like a dog panting, a heavy, rasping breath loud and urgent in her ear. A globule of rice pudding trickled down her chin and dripped onto the floor. And she realized with guilty horror. It wasn't a dog making that sound. *She was.*

Buzzzzzzzzzzzzzzzzzzzzzzzz.

Snapping out of her trance, she flustered around the kitchen, stuffing empty cartons and packaging in the bin. It was Noel, he'd come back, he'd forgotten something. Racked with guilt and self-loathing, she wiped up the gloopy mess before hurrying down the hallway. Passing the bedroom she quickly cast her eye inside but there didn't appear to be anything he'd left. She pressed the intercom that released the main door of the building, hastily checking her reflection in the hallway mirror. A few splodges of grease lingered around her mouth, and wiping them away she took a couple of deep breaths and flicked back the brass Yale latch.

'It's over.' Standing in the hallway, arms folded, eyes hidden by sunglasses, was a familiar figure.

'*Grace?*'

'Yep, it's me.'

Shocked, Rhian took a step backwards. 'Oh Gracie, darling . . . I wasn't expecting you.' She popped her head out and looked up and down the hallway just in case. 'I thought it was . . . I mean . . . what's happened? Are you OK?' As she spoke, what Grace had just said suddenly registered. '*What's over?*'

'Me and Spencer. Our relationship,' she said matter-of-factly, shoving her sunglasses on to her head to reveal suspiciously red-rimmed eyes.

Rhian looked like she'd just witnessed a murder. Her jaw visibly dropping, she blanched. Clutching the satin collars of her dressing gown, she gathered them tightly around her throat. 'You and Spencer are over?' she whispered, her voice breathless with shocked disbelief. 'But you're engaged.'

'Tell me about it,' sniffed Grace, smiling weakly.

Her calmness threw Rhian. Wasn't she supposed to be sobbing and wailing and clutching her broken heart? Wasn't that what happened when you split up with the man you were supposed to be spending the rest of your life with? Or was that just what happened if they left you? she thought, as buried memories of Phil's departure floated to the surface of her mind like the debris of a shipwreck. It still hurt. Eighteen months later. And it still hurt.

But this isn't about me, Rhian reminded herself, this is about Grace. Reaching out, she squeezed her hand supportively. 'No, you tell *me* all about it.'

Chapter Fifteen

'Where do I start?' Grinding the small cube of chalk on the tip of his cue, Jimi stalked around the side of the pool table glaring at the multicoloured balls as if he wanted to obliterate them, not pot them.

Sipping his warm pint of scrumpy, Clive leaned groggily against the flashing fruit machine. He looked every inch a man with a hangover. His faded surf T-shirt hung misshapenly from his scraggy shoulders, his unwashed jeans hung immodestly low on his hips, and his eyelids were draped heavily over his bloodshot eyes. Taking another medicinal slurp of cider, he caught Jimi staring at him. Pointedly. What were they talking about? Oh yeah, Kylie's bombshell. 'Oh, er . . . at the bit where she told you why she'd called the wedding off?' he suggested helpfully.

Tact was not one of Clive's strongest qualities.

Jimi frowned. 'Tell everyone, why don't you?'

Clive peered around the gloomy depths of the pub. Apart from a middle-aged couple in the corner it was completely deserted. Which was hardly surprising considering it was a Saturday afternoon, gloriously sunny and about seventy degrees outside. 'There's no-one here,' he whispered innocently.

'It was a criticism, not an observation,' grumbled Jimi, never taking his eye off the green baize as he concentrated on weighing up the different options and angles.

Clive quietly sipped his cider. 'I'd go for the yellow if I was you.'

'Well you're not me, are you?' snapped Jimi, deliberately going for the green.

'*Right*, I see,' said Clive, sticking out his chin and scratching his twenty-four-hour beard. It itched naggingly. 'I get it. Take it out on me. Shoot the messenger.'

'And what's that supposed to mean?' Having bent down low over the pool table, Jimi changed his mind and stood upright. The green was no good. He'd go for red instead.

Clive shifted uneasily on his unlaced Allstars. 'It means that just because I told you the wedding was off, it doesn't make it my fault. I'm not responsible, you know.' Looking at Jimi, who was trying to hide his hurt by being angrily defensive, he wondered how far he could take it. Oh what the hell, someone had to tell him. 'Don't take it out on your mates, Jimi, it's not our fault, it's Kylie who called off the sodding wedding,' he blurted out loudly.

Jimi stood stock still, the words hitting home like a wooden cricket bat bashing him around the head. What was that about the truth always hurting? This was agony. Self-pity raged and he opened his mouth to bawl Clive out. Then stopped. 'You're absolutely right,' he sighed woefully, his body crumpling against the pool table. 'I'm sorry, mate, I'm just gutted,' he admitted, finally dropping the tough guy act and allowing his true emotions to show through. 'I just can't believe it's over. She doesn't want to be with me, she doesn't want to marry me.' He raised his eyes to Clive. He looked crushed. 'She's dumped me,' he whispered piteously.

Draining his pint, Clive shrugged sympathetically. 'It happens to us all, old chap.'

'But it's never happened to me,' said Jimi.

'There's always a first time,' murmured Clive sagely, shaking his head.

Numbly, Jimi turned back to the pool table, balancing the cue between his fingers before sliding it back. The ball shot across the baize, bounced against the corner, headed towards the pocket – and missed.

Clive sighed. 'Bad luck, mate,' he commiserated.

He meant the shot, but Jimi's mind was somewhere else entirely. Namely Canada. And Kylie.

He shrugged defeatedly. 'Yeah, bad luck,' he agreed sadly.

They were cooped up inside the grotty depths of The Earl of Percy, one of the few pubs in West London to still have dodgy carpet, a pool table and a cardboard rack of pork scratchings hung at the side of the till. It even had flirty barmaids that called everyone darlin' and traded *double entendres* over pints of Guinness, rather than the scowly bar staff in gastro-pubs who stomped about on the stripped wooden floorboards if you so much as dared ask for a couple of glasses of Chilean and a bowl of marinated olives.

They'd gone there after 'The Phonecall', a defining thirty-minute conversation which Jimi had proceeded to have with Kylie after Clive had dropped the bombshell. It had been bizarre, really. His life had been crashing down around his ears yet he'd been remarkably calm, finding the code for Canada, dialling her number, politely passing the time of day with Kylie's mum, 'Hello, Mrs Collins, how are you? How's the weather? Oh wonderful, you're having a barbie? That's nice, that's just fabulous,' before eventually being passed to Kylie. She'd been crying.

Talk about ironic. He was the one who'd been jilted, so how come she was the one sobbing down the phone? How come *he* was the one who had to keep it together, to remain stoic, strong, sympathetic? It hadn't seemed real. It had been as if it was happening in a film, or on TV. As if his life had turned into some hideous *Cold Feet* plot line which, considering it was her favourite show, couldn't have been more apt.

So, while the rest of his stag party had crawled out of their sleeping bags, slapped his shoulder supportively, and slipped off to catch the train back to Manchester, Jimi had sat in his leather armchair listening to his now ex-fiancée telling him how she'd had second thoughts, she was sorry but she couldn't go through with the wedding, and she was staying in Canada.

'And then she turned.'

'Turned?' repeated Clive, ripping open a packet of Walkers smokey bacon and hoovering them up with a suction only seen in the likes of a Dyson.

'Yeah, she went from being all upset and apologetic to coldly critical.'

'*Kylie? Coldly critical?*' parroted Clive, crisp crumbs sticking to his chin. 'But she doesn't seem capable.'

'She's a woman. They're capable of anything.' Jimi was trying to cling onto misogyny as only a jilted bridegroom could. Swigging back his drink he motioned to the pool table. 'Your shot.'

'Oh . . . yeah.' Hitching up his saggy jeans, Clive grabbed this cue.

'But that's not all,' continued Jimi, sounding wounded. 'She said I don't know what being in love means.'

'She did?' Expertly flicking his cue, Clive skimmed the white and sent two balls gliding into their pockets. 'Blimey. You and Prince Charles.'

'What?' Confused, Jimi frowned at Clive who was loping around the table potting balls with alarming ease.

'You know, with Lady Di in that BBC interview when they announced their engagement.' As another ball plopped silently, Clive began flicking through his library of trivia and settled on 1981. 'They're going on about how happy they are, and the reporter says, "And I suppose *in love*?" Diana says "Of course" and Charlie – wait for it, goes like this . . .'

Prepared for one of Clive's appalling impressions,

Jimi was surprised by an astonishingly good one of Prince Charles, all *Thunderbird*-jawed, ruched forehead and terrible awkwardness. Fiddling with an imaginary signet ring, he mumbled disparagingly, '"Whatever 'in love' means."'

'But I know what being in love means,' protested Jimi. 'I was in love with Kylie. I still am in love with Kylie,' he added forlornly.

Reluctantly dropping the impression, Clive turned his attention back to his drink. 'I know, I'm just saying . . .'

'Well don't,' cut in Jimi. 'You're my best man, and I'm the jilted bridegroom, you're supposed to be making me feel better.' He sighed; he felt horribly depressed. 'It's your job to tell me I'm better off without her.'

'You mean lie,' corrected Clive bluntly.

'If you have to, yes,' muttered Jimi, smiling wryly. 'You're supposed to be offering support and sympathy. And more drinks,' he added, holding up his empty glass. They'd gone down there under the pretence of shooting some pool, but they both knew it was so Jimi could drown his sorrows. Unfortunately they were proving to be bloody good swimmers. 'Mine's a vodka Red Bull. A large one.'

Clive took his glass.

'And a cigarette.'

'You don't smoke,' Clive reminded him. 'You hate smokers. You think smoking's a mug's game,' he deadpanned, repeating Jimi's mantra, but it was lost on Jimi who was already making his way across the pub to ponce a cigarette.

Glancing around the murky depths, his gaze had already fallen on the only other people in the pub, a middle-aged couple who were tucked up on the leatherette sofa in the corner, looking at some brochures. The grey-haired man was sipping a pint of Guinness and sucking on a pipe, while the woman was wearing some kind of pink turban thing on her head.

Jimi watched her nattering animatedly, a spire of smoke slowly curling from her nostrils.

'. . . my head's telling me to go for this one, the town house just on the outskirts of Alicante. It's bigger, we could always rent it out if we needed to, and we'll be near your sister Veronica's place . . .'

Taking a drag of her cigarette, Maggie waggled the estate agent's details of their proposed retirement home in Spain under Sonny's nose.

'Although on second thoughts, maybe that's not such a good thing.'

She'd just spent the morning visiting Veronica. It hadn't been what she'd call an enjoyable visit. A strict Catholic, Veronica had offered them weak tea, stale scones on doilies and the priest – Father O'Reilly, who'd chitchatted about original sin and redemption. If the religion hadn't killed Maggie, the scones nearly had, and after twenty minutes she'd left in desperate need of a G&T and a fag in the pub on the corner.

'. . . but then again my heart's telling me to buy the beautiful old *finca* in Jerez de la Frontera,' she paused and pointed to the photograph. 'It's so pretty – just look at all that bougainvillaea . . .'

'Hi.' Jimi switched on his most charming smile and waited expectantly for a pause. There wasn't one.

'. . . I've got a feeling this is it. This is the one.' Jubilantly Maggie beamed at Sonny.

'I'm sorry to interrupt,' Jimi butted in. 'But could I bum a cigarette?'

'Uh?' Sonny bit down hard on the stem of his pipe.

Frowning, Maggie looked up. Instantaneously the corners of her mouth rose upwards, her forehead relaxed, her glare was replaced by a beam. Well, *hello*. A very exotic, *very handsome* young man was staring down at her. Just like a young Omar Sharif, she thought, feeling her irritation melt away like the ice in her G&T.

'No problem,' she said gaily, her cheeks glowing

156

pink beneath her terracotta tan. 'A smoker in need and all that . . .' and began fishing around in her handbag while Sonny stared at her, aghast. Was this the same woman who usually guarded her cigarettes with her life?

'Thanks,' Jimi nodded, accepting the cigarette and her offer of a light. He inhaled deeply, the smoke embracing his lungs like a long-lost lover.

'Take two,' she cajoled.

Sonny nearly choked on his Guinness. 'Mags,' he spluttered.

'Sonny.' She glared at him.

Jimi obliged, it would have been rude not to, and then avoiding a domestic he made his way back over to the snooker table where Clive was setting up the balls in the plastic triangle for the next game.

'Do you want to break?'

Grabbing his cue he stalked over to the table and then turned. 'Do you know what?' The nicotine had triggered an epiphany.

'What?'

'I've had a lucky escape. Marriage is suicide. Why do you think it's called tying the knot?' he announced decisively. 'I couldn't see it before, but now I can. Kylie's actually done me a favour. What was I thinking of? Me? Settling down? Promising to only sleep with one woman for the rest of my life?'

'Is it me you're trying to convince, or yourself?' asked Clive, seeing right through Jimi's bravado.

But Jimi chose to ignore him. 'If I'd married Kylie I'd probably have never had sex again. Did you know married couples don't have sex? It's true. Statistics prove it. They go to IKEA instead.' Shaking his head he crouched low over the table, his cigarette gripped between his teeth. 'Christ, what was I thinking? I must have been crazy.'

'You weren't crazy,' corrected Clive. Jimi's little speech hadn't fooled him. 'You said it yourself. You were in love.'

With a loud crack Jimi's cue hit the white, smashing the neat triangle of coloured balls and sending them scattering across the smooth green baize.

'Well thank God I got out,' he replied determinedly.

Chapter Sixteen

Bathed in brilliant sunshine, Hyde Park was bursting at its grassy seams. Tourists filled the wooden benches, clutching *A–Z*s and melting ice-cream cornets, children swarmed over the adventure play-ground, scraping knees and playing make-believe, while troops of sweating joggers, determined power-walkers and illegal cyclists zigzagged through the vista of half-naked bodies. Stretching as far as the eye could see, from Bayswater Road to Hyde Park Corner, pro-fessional, bikini-clad sunbathers lay nut-brown thigh to mahogany stomach with amateurs who'd stripped down to their mismatched underwear to expose pasty limbs that were fast turning scarlet and blotchy in the heat of the midday sun.

It was late September but London was in the sweaty grip of an unplanned summer. It was hot. Stiflingly hot. Pinned high on the ivy-clad wall of Kensington Palace the mercury inside a shiny brass thermometer was creeping stealthily into the high seventies. A chocolate brown Labrador gave up chasing a wasp and collapsed panting into the shade, its ear cocked to the hazy, lazy buzz. Squeals of childish laughter, easy picnic banter, the soft thud of a football, the faint hum of a radio intermingled with the rhythmic *whoosh-whoosh* sound of rollerbladers weaving in and out of a row of plastic cups.

Overhead, a Virgin plane trailing two streams of

white across the cloudless stretch of blue sky. To the passengers on board, peering out of their porthole windows as they headed towards Heathrow, the park was just a multicoloured blur of figures, a patch of green, a flash of gold. But as they began descending the green became Kensington Gardens, the gold became recognizable as the Albert Memorial, the blur began to focus into matchstick people, into mums and dads, into two women, a three-year-old boy and a pushchair, strolling towards the Serpentine lake deep in conversation.

'So let me get this straight. *He* gets drunk and abandons you in the middle of Elephant and Castle, then *you* get mad and ask him to get married in Las Vegas, and then *he* gets annoyed and says no.' Trying to grasp the situation as hard as she was grasping Jack who was bombarding the swans with pellets of stale Hovis, Rhian stared at Grace in confusion.

'No, that's just it, he didn't *say* anything,' replied Grace, squinting in the sunshine and tugging her sunglasses down from her forehead. The last hour of intermittent crying had left her with a thumping headache.

'So that's it? It's over?' Rhian dabbed away a bead of sweat from her forehead. Swaddling herself in black might hide a multitude of sins, but she might as well have wrapped herself in tinfoil and put herself in the oven. 'It just seems so sudden, I can't believe it.'

'Neither can I,' murmured Grace, fishing a slice out of the plastic wrapper and tearing it into white, foamy ribbons. After all this time she couldn't believe it had come to this. Yet a part of her wasn't surprised. 'But it's been brewing for a long time, I've just been fooling myself like everyone else.' She shrugged resignedly.

'But you can't break up with Spencer,' argued Rhian. She was refusing to accept it. She'd known they'd been having a few problems recently but she hadn't expected this. 'I mean, you guys have been together for ever,' she urged. 'You're engaged.' There she went again.

Grace turned to her. 'And do you see us planning a wedding?' she said pointedly.

There was silence.

'Exactly. When Spencer proposed I was the happiest girl in the world, I imagined our whole future together, you know, dogs, babies, the whole roses round the door thing . . .' Her voice trailed off as she smiled wryly. 'Not that I think I'm ready to have a baby right this minute, to be honest, I don't think I'm ever going to be ready, but I look at you with Jack, and well . . .' Grace shrugged.

Turning back to stare out across the lake, she sighed heavily. 'It's time to face up to it. Spencer doesn't feel the same way about things. He doesn't *want* to get married.' After months of denial, now that she heard herself say it out loud, it seemed the most obvious thing in the world.

And the most terrible, thought Rhian, visibly shocked. Her own life might not have turned out as she would have liked, but she'd always looked to Grace and Spencer as proof that happy endings still existed.

'It's not you,' she said, shaking her head. 'He's already been divorced once, he's probably terrified of the commitment.'

'But what's so terrifying about being committed to me?' protested Grace, her angry indignation threatening to dissolve again into tears. Spencer had been a complete shit, but he was her shit, and despite everything that had happened she didn't hate him, she loved him. Albeit begrudgingly.

'If you want a man who's committed, go look in a mental hospital,' quipped Rhian, trying to rescue the situation. 'Mae West,' she added as explanation.

'Well Mae was bloody right,' agreed Grace. 'Spencer just wants to keep things as they are.'

'That's because he's in the comfort zone.'

'The what?'

'There was a whole debate about it in *Marie Claire*,'

161

confided Rhian. 'It's when men have got everything they want. Spencer's got you, but he's still got his independence. Why get married when he can live with you and get all the perks anyway.' She raised her eyebrows so high, the arches nearly got lost in her hairline. 'It's like that saying, "Why buy the cow when you can milk it for free".'

'And who's the cow in this analogy?' gasped Grace incredulously. 'Me?'

Grace had spent the last hour cocooned in Rhian's flat, drinking tea while Rhian exhausted her usual ways of cheering her up – 'Bach's Rescue Remedy? An aromatherapy massage? My relaxation tape?' – until finally Rhian had suggested a walk in the park. Grace had accepted. Partly because, emotional turmoil or not, it was too nice a day to be stuck indoors, and mostly because now they'd collected Jack from the neighbours, he'd refused to be palmed off with a Postman Pat video and had promptly started bawling his head off.

It was also a chance to analyse, dissect and justify – both to herself and to Rhian – why she should break up with Spencer. Apart from getting drunk and deserting her on her birthday – and wasn't that a good enough reason by itself? – there was his lack of interest in their wedding, and even more worrying, in recent months, their sex life. 'And there's all the other reasons,' continued Grace, who was discovering it was very cathartic to get everything off her chest. So far she'd been speaking for fifteen minutes straight without a break. 'He hates me wearing jeans and wants me to wear funeral dresses . . .'

Rhian threw her a bewildered look.

'. . . don't ask. And he tells the same jokes and they weren't funny the first time, he's always got a hangover and when I suggest he shouldn't drink so much he gets all defensive and says red wine's good for you and then tries to turn it around by telling me I'm

162

unhealthy because I don't do enough exercise . . .' Plonking herself down on the grass under the shade of one of the huge oak trees, she said indignantly, 'And he always manages to find the most boring thing on TV, and then watch it.'

'All men do that,' consoled Rhian, finally managing to get a word in edgeways. 'If there was a documentary on military battleships on some obscure cable channel, believe me, Phil would find it.' Unfolding a tartan picnic blanket, she began laying it neatly on the grass. 'It's like Coldplay.'

Grace looked confused. 'What is?'

'Men and Coldplay. Haven't you noticed? It's like they have this inbuilt radar. Phil and I would be in the car and I can guarantee, out of all the radio stations, he would manage to track them down. Then he'd turn up the stereo so loud the glove compartment would rattle and then he'd do this . . .' And Rhian began head-banging for all she was worth, her mouth open wide in silent yelling, a look of anguish contorting her features.

Despite her predicament, Grace couldn't help laughing. 'Oh my God, that's Spencer. He does that too,' she snorted, taking a gulp of Evian and feeling the rush of water as it shot the wrong way up the back of her nose.

'What did I tell you,' giggled Rhian. 'I mean . . .' She parked Jack, who was curled up asleep in the pushchair that he'd grown too big for, his arms and legs dangling out of the sides.

'. . . what was all that "Yellow" business about anyway?'

'Oh God.' Grace brushed away the tears of mirth that were trickling down her cheek. 'I know. I don't get it either.'

Rhian shook her head. 'I'm telling you. It's a man thing.'

'What about wanting to drift along? Is that a man thing too?' After the high of the laughter, Grace quickly dipped into the low of reflection.

'No, that's more of a couple thing,' said Rhian, bobbing down and extracting Barbie from Jack's podgy fist and stuffing her in the bulging plastic shopping bag among the babywipes, breadsticks, toys, bits of Lego, stale bread for the ducks, and beaker of fruit juice. Oh for the days of being able to leave the house with just a mascara.

'I read an article about that. It's called thirty-something drift.' Flopping down next to Grace, she lay on her back, tugging at her T-shirt to make sure it hadn't ridden up to expose her stomach.

'What haven't you read an article about?' asked Grace. Every month Rhian splurged on every women's magazine on the shelves, and then squirrelled herself away to read, digest and quote from every article in there.

'No, seriously,' protested Rhian. 'It's a new phenomenon. It's about when infatuation turns to indifference,' she continued, reciting the opening line from memory.

'I'm not indifferent. I love Spencer,' protested Grace. 'It's just . . .' It wasn't *just* anything. It was a whole load of things.

'You love him, but are you sure you're *in* love with him?'

'Of course I am,' retorted Grace.

'You're not distraught.'

'I'm upset.'

'You're resigned,' she corrected quietly. 'You're sad, and disappointed, and scared.'

'Of what? I'm a big girl now,' refuted Grace.

'Of not knowing how the story ends any more. Of not being part of a couple. *Of being alone*,' Rhian attempted Garbo with a Welsh accent. 'Believe me I know, I've been there.'

'You're saying you need a man to be happy? That my life is going to stop because I don't have a boyfriend?' argued Grace, but deep down inside it was herself she was trying to convince. 'Being single isn't a terminal disease.'

Rolling away, Rhian closed her eyes and muttered. 'Try telling that to my mother.'

Lying next to her on the grass, Grace looked up through the dappled leaves of the trees. She breathed in and out. Felt her ribcage rise and fall. On the outside she was quiet and still, but on the inside she was noisy and restless. Her emotions were all over the place, her head was a mess, her heart was confused.

Unexpectedly, a tear prickled her eyelash and fell trickling down the side of her nose. She brusquely wiped it away. 'I'm doing the right thing, aren't I?' she murmured quietly, turning to Rhian.

Rhian hesitated. This was her window of opportunity. As Grace's best friend she knew her role was to be a silent, supportive, sympathetic listener who occasionally uttered things like 'absolutely' and 'I don't blame you' and 'mint Aero or plain?' But as a single woman on the wrong side of thirty she felt it was her responsibility, nay *her duty*, to grab Grace by her tanned shoulders and shake her violently, whilst screaming at the top of her lungs, 'Are you nuts? Hang on to him for dear life, it's a fucking desert out there.' Instead she compromised. 'Why don't you two have a break,' she said.

'A holiday?' Grace smiled sadly at her friend's naivety, or was it just optimism? 'A fortnight on a beach isn't going to make much difference. Apart from the suntan.'

Rhian tutted. 'No, not that kind of a break, I mean a separation. Maybe Spencer needs to miss you. Maybe some time apart will shock him into realizing what life's like without you. How much he loves you. Before you know he'll be begging you to make an honest man of him.' She smiled cheerily at Grace.

She looked miserable.

Reaching out, Rhian squeezed her hand. 'Don't forget, Grace, this isn't just about Spencer, it's about *you*, it's about the rest of your life. Maybe *you* need time to decide if Spencer really is the right man for you. This isn't just about his lack of commitment, it's about lots of other things, you've just said it yourself . . .' Her dark eyes wandered out into the distance as she continued speaking. 'Maybe his attitude towards the wedding is why you've got all these doubts and fears and angry feelings. But maybe it's not. Maybe in fact it's not Spencer that's got the cold feet . . .' Breaking off, she paused. And meeting Grace's gaze said quietly, but determinedly,

'Maybe it's you.'

Chapter Seventeen

The following Saturday, in a bedroom painted bubble-gum pink and filled with satin heart-shaped cushions and far too many soft toys, a pretty blonde was sitting up in bed.

'You've got to go to the funeral of your grand-mother's cat?'

Clutching the sheets up against her perky breasts, her collagen-enhanced mouth pumped wide open like a blow-up doll, she was pouting sulkily.

'Sadly, yes,' affirmed Jimi. Stark bollock naked he was hopping around with one foot looped inside his Calvin Kleins, trying to yank them on while he continued to search for the rest of his clothes. 'Our family are huge animal lovers. Felix was thirteen. Fit as a fiddle –' locating his jeans tangled up in the bottom of her sheets he thankfully tugged them on '– and then the post office van came around the corner and . . .' he made a croaking noise as he dragged his finger across his throat. 'Everyone's devastated.'

'But it's seven-thirty a.m.,' she protested.

'Granny Malik is an early riser,' he explained, calling off the hunt for his socks and sticking his bare feet into his Puma trainers. 'It's kind of a tribute.' Grabbing his keys he leaned over, intending to give a quick kiss goodbye, at which point his getaway plan went awry because, before he could gasp, 'I'll call you later,' his head was thrust into an armlock and he was being suffocated by a pair of pink inflatable lips . . .

Jimi had met Sammy-Jo at a party a year ago. She hailed from Texas, worked in 'promotions' and had the biggest pair of breasts Jimi had ever seen. They'd gone on a couple of dates, and at first they'd seemed to have so much in common – this was a woman who wanted no-strings-attached sex, watched Sky Sport, and kept a shoe-box brimming with a pick'n'mix of condoms next to her bed. Until he'd discovered they had a bit *too* much in common when he'd caught her in a bar one night, huddled in the corner with her tongue down someone else's throat. And he'd only nipped to the loo.

Unrepentant, she'd paused, smiled, and given him an open-ended invitation to call her any time. Which he'd forgotten all about until yesterday when, lying in a bath that had long since gone cold, feeling depressed, frustrated and contemplating yet another unsatisfactory wank, he'd suddenly remembered. Sploshing Radox footprints down the hallway in his urgency, he'd dug out his phone, scrolled down to her number and dialled.

'Do you really have to go?' Coming up for air, Sammy-Jo slid her fingers underneath Jimi's T-shirt and began running her acrylic fingernails up his spine.

' 'Fraid so,' he said, doing his best to give a rueful smile.

'Wouldn't you prefer to pay tribute to my pussy?' she twanged coyly.

Jimi blanched. Normally he'd have needed no encouragement. He and Sammy-Jo might not have much in common, but with a body to die for and more enthusiasm than a reality TV show contestant, it wasn't her personality he was attracted to. But after last night he just wanted to get the hell out of there. 'Can't keep the congregation waiting, you know,' he winked jovially.

Her response was to rip open his button-flies, stick her hand down his trousers and lasso his penis between her thumb and forefinger.

'*Agghhh*,' yelped Jimi.

'*Oh*,' squeaked Sammy-Jo, a gasp of surprised disappointment escaping from her lips. Expecting to feel it hard, throbbing and ready for action, she was dismayed and perplexed to feel something warm, soft and sleepy in her hand.

Jimi was mortified. Oh no, not again. He wanted to sink through the mattress and disappear into the bowels of hell. Anything had to be better than this torture, he thought, feeling his dick shrink even smaller in shameful disgrace. Once was bad enough, but twice?

Frozen, they stared at each other, eyes wide, mouths open, her hand still stuffed down his boxers, his crown jewels still held hostage in those acrylic nails. Until finally, Sammy-Jo released her grip and sighed heavily. 'Jeez, you really are in mourning, aren't you?'

Last night Jimi had gone round to Sammy-Jo's for a reason, and one reason only: he wanted to have good, old-fashioned, uncomplicated sex. He wanted to bury his face in her big, blond hair extensions and forget all about Kylie. A barrier-bonk was supposed to help draw a line underneath their relationship, help him try to get over the disaster that was supposed to be his wedding, restore his ego and make him feel like a man again, rather than the victim. Or at least that was the plan.

After buzzing the intercom to Sammy-Jo's flat, bypassing unnecessary smalltalk and diving straight onto her baby-pink bedspread they'd begun enthusiastically ripping off each other's clothes. Initially everything had been going to plan – Stevie Wonder on the stereo, tealights on the windowsill, condoms on the bedside table. And then something unimaginable had happened. Something that, never in his deepest, darkest nightmares, had ever happened to Jimi before.

He couldn't get it up.

Even now, twelve hours after the event, he could barely bring himself to think about it. It had been so excruciatingly embarrassing, especially as Sammy-Jo had been so tenacious, working on his lifeless penis like a paramedic in A&E. She'd tried everything – and he meant *everything* – baby oil, a dodgy Swedish porn video, an even dodgier nurse's outfit which came complete with a tube of KY and a thermometer which she'd proceeded to make use of. Until eventually, after forty-five exhausting minutes – each minute seeming like an eternity, and there'd been *forty-fucking-five* of them – a wrist sprain had forced her to admit defeat.

The shame had nearly killed him. *And* not only was he in mental agony, but he was physically exhausted. Unlike Sammy-Jo who, just when he'd assumed that surely, in God's name, it couldn't get any worse, had only gone and produced a vibrator and demanded he use it on her. It was every man's idea of purgatory. A naked, gorgeous, sexually frustrated blonde, a limp penis that didn't want to play ball, and a rock hard dildo that was every inch the man he wasn't. And a lot more. Because, if the frustration hadn't been bad enough – and it was – as she'd thrust the black rubber dildo into his hand, whatever scraps of his ego had managed to survive promptly committed hara-kiri.

It had been ginormous.

Over the years Jimi had received plenty of compliments about size and girth but compared to 'King Kong' he was hideously inadequate. He'd been crippled by paranoia. Had he just been fooling himself all these years? Had all those women just been polite? Had he really been replaced by a latex-covered rolling pin with batteries? And it was scarily lifelike. He'd gazed at the veiny member in his hand. It had made his eyes water just looking at it. Unlike Sammy-Jo who, alarmingly, hadn't shared his concerns.

Elbowing him in the ribs, she'd grumbled impatiently for him to get a move on.

'I better go,' gasped Jimi, finally managing to extricate himself from Sammy-Jo's in a manoeuvre Houdini would have been proud of. 'I'm reading a poem I've written and I need to rehearse.' God I'm good, thought Jimi, surprising himself. He was beginning to believe this story himself. He even felt a bit weepy.

Sammy-Jo eyed him with intrigue. 'You know, Jimi, I'd never have put you down as a sentimental type of guy.'

'You wouldn't?' He smiled, feeling rather pleased with himself.

'No.' She shook her head. 'You always seemed kinda heartless.'

'I did?' In the past such a criticism wouldn't have bothered him, but now it stung. He was still hurting from Kylie's accusation on the phone that he didn't know what being in love meant. Despite all his bravado, it had left him feeling uncharacteristically sensitive, and now, to top it all off, here was Sammy-Jo telling him he was a heartless bastard. Jimi felt troubled. He realized that a common theme was beginning to emerge. And he didn't like it.

He tried to redress the balance. 'When you get to know me you'll see I've actually got a sensitive side, you know, helping little old ladies across the road, donating to charity, watching weepie movies . . . I mean, I must have seen *Titanic* a hundred times.'

'You have?' ventured Sammy-Jo suspiciously.

'Oh yeah.' He nodded, stretching his arms out wide like a crucifix and humming Celine Dion. '. . . It's sunset, Leonardo's got his arms around Kate, she's on the ship's helm, there's nothing as far as the eye can see . . . "I'm flying, Jack, I'm flying,"' panted Jimi, his voice high-pitched and heavy with emotion, and then he slumped and shook his head, sighing, 'Christ, it gets me every time.'

171

He looked across at Sammy-Jo. She had tears in her eyes.

'Oh jeez, Jimi, that's so beautiful,' she whispered, shaking her head. 'I had no idea.'

'Not many people do.' He shrugged, unable to believe she was actually falling for this load of old rubbish. 'I'm a real softy, you know.'

Immediately he regretted his choice of words.

Without missing a beat, Sammy-Jo crushed him back down to size. 'Oh I think I know that already,' she grinned wickedly.

He'd left, promising to call and knowing he never would. If the refusal by his dick to spring back into action had proved one thing, it was that he couldn't take up where he'd left off. Mentally he didn't want to slip back into his pre-Kylie habits, back into his bachelor days, and physically he couldn't anyway.

Nursing his crushed ego, he'd driven back to his flat, slumped at his desk and tapped the keyboard of his laptop. It sprang into life, throwing up his Rachel Stevens screensaver. He'd spent the whole week trying to work on his witty, humorous novel, but after months of flowing creative juices he'd completely dried up.

Sighing loudly, he stared dolefully at the screen. He envied the days when journalists used typewriters. At least then they had the luxury of being surrounded by scrunched-up balls of paper, of being able to dramatically rip out pages, screw them up and play basketball. Now he just pressed the delete key and everything disappeared. Vanished. Gone. A bit like Kylie, he reflected miserably.

Jimi couldn't help wishing his life was on that laptop. At least that way he could press the delete key, get rid of the last week, the last few months, and erase the memory of Kylie. Instead he had to put up with the hurt, and it really *did* hurt. He'd never felt like this before. Instead of going out, hitting the town, bouncing back, since Kylie's bombshell he'd spent most nights staying in, eating takeout, drinking Jack Daniel's, while an anaesthetic of TV soaps sent him to sleep. It was deeply depressing. Being jilted was one thing, but actually looking forward to *Emmerdale* was another.

A nasty whiff broke into his gloom and he wrinkled up his nostrils. What on earth was that smell? It was heinous. Stagnant. Rancid. Where the hell was it coming from? And then it dawned on him.

It was coming from his flat.

The place stunk. It absolutely whiffed to high heaven. Any minute now and neighbours would be getting the police round to knock down the door, expecting to find an undiscovered corpse. And instead they'll find me, thought Jimi, springing up from his chair. What was happening to him? Normally he was the embodiment of tidiness, cleanliness, pro-activeness. He was letting himself go. He needed to pull himself together and sort himself out. And he needed to start with this flat.

Feeling the first chink of positivity he reached into a cupboard, tugged out his Dyson, and then faltered as he stared at the huge task ahead of him. On second thoughts, he decided, grabbing the Yellow Pages, he'd just been dumped by his fiancée, let down by his manhood and abandoned by his self-esteem, the last thing he needed was to do the washing up. Hastily he dialled 'Rent-a-duster'.

A few minutes later he hung up, left forty quid on the table for the cleaner and, grabbing his Visa card, let himself out of the flat, putting the key under the mat. He'd tried lying comatose on the sofa watching soaps, he'd tried getting completely legless on Jack Daniel's, he'd even tried having sex with an ex. Nothing had worked. Which meant there was only one option left to try.

Retail therapy.

Chapter Eighteen

Break. (*brāk, noun*)
Rest, respite, interval, breathing space, lull, recess,
stop, pause, interlude, breather, time out, gap, split,
parting, separation, suspension, discontinuation,
termination, bust-up, halt, severance, rupture, falling-
out, gulf, chasm, estrangement, split, break-up.

There were many ways of saying it, but there was no
easy way to do it, thought Grace, squeezing down the
magazine aisles in WH Smith past the throng of
women gathering by the celebrity magazines. Whoever
said a week in politics was a long time had obviously
never broken off their engagement. Never gone back to
the home they'd shared with someone for three and a
half years, to the person they'd shared their life with
for four years, to their future they were going to
share for ever, and taken the huge gamble of saying
they wanted a break, that they needed some time
apart, that they were moving out.

But she had.

Picking up a copy of *Loot*, she surreptitiously
flicked to the flatshare ads and began scanning. It had
been one of the biggest, scariest, most momentous
decisions of her life and, true to form, after the build-
up, the agonizing, the doubts, the fears, when Grace
finally blurted it out there had been no thumping
EastEnders drumbeat, no cataclysmic reaction from

the gods, no histrionics, no wailing and beating of chests. Instead Spencer had calmly continued opening a bottle of wine, squeezing together the silver outstretched arms of the corkscrew and, with an expert flick of his wrist, easing out the cork with a muted pop.

The sound had been sadly ironic. The jubilant explosion of champagne corks had heralded their engagement, and now this unceremonious plop of a plastic cork being removed from a bottle of Penfolds had marked its demise. 'Aren't you going to say anything?' She'd looked at Spencer. Just back from a run, he was wearing a pair of blue Adidas shorts and a T-shirt which clung to his shoulders in damp sweat patches. Standing with his back to her he'd poured himself a generous glug of wine, swigged back a large mouthful and turned to face her. Leaning against the cooker, he'd sighed resignedly.

'What do you want me to say?'

Don't go. We can work this out. I want to spend the rest of my life with you. What are we waiting for? Let's run off to Gretna Green tomorrow. I love you. I'm sorry.

The obvious list of possibilities screamed loud and furious through Grace's head. Any of those would have done, if he'd said just one of them it would have caused her to hesitate, reflect, reconsider. Maybe even change her mind and stay. But he didn't.

And she didn't.

'I'm going to stay at Rhian's for a couple of days, and then I'll look for a place to rent.'

'For how long?'

'I don't know. However long it takes to work things out. Or not . . .' she added, her voice tailing off as the cold reality set in. It was hard to believe she was actually doing this. In her moments of greatest fear she'd imagined this moment hundreds of times and it always involved tears, and rows, and emotions, yet now it was happening it was all so matter-of-fact. So calm. So mundane. She shook her head. 'I'm not the one with all the answers,' she said quietly.

'You don't have to do this, you know,' he answered, deflecting her question.

'Yes I do.' She'd waited, wanting – hoping for – a reaction. For Christsakes do something, Spencer, say something, anything, she thought desperately. Convince me I'm wrong, argue your case, be that big bold effusive lawyer who wins every time. Fight for me goddamnit, fight for me, fight for us, *fight for our relationship.*

But he just stared at her sadly. 'Well if that's what you want I can't stop you.'

You mean you're not going to try, she'd thought, feeling a searing crush of disappointment as he'd silently refilled his glass, picked up the bottle and disappeared into the living room to idly flick through TV channels with the remote.

His reaction had strengthened her resolve. His answer was the wrong answer. Which only reinforced her fears that he was the wrong man. The right man would be begging her to stay, declaring how much he loved her, doing everything in his power not to lose her. There'd be a reaction. Tears. Anger. Desperation. Passion. And love. Lots and lots of love. But instead all she'd got was a few lousy words. A calm shrug of his shoulders. A cold, impassive stoicism.

A total cop-out.

Unexpectedly, Grace had felt angry. She'd felt cheated. That was the most Spencer could give. Four years together and this was the sum total of what she meant to him? She'd suddenly thought about his ex-wife, Sam. Grace had never met her but she knew she'd walked out before their first wedding anniversary and was now married to a doctor, had a couple of kids and lived on the coast. When Spencer had first told Grace, she hadn't been able to understand how any woman could leave him, but hey, one woman's loss was another woman's gain, she'd thought, too busy falling in love to care. But now *she* was the one leaving and for the first time things seemed different.

Thinking about his first wife now, she wasn't quite sure who had lost, and who had gained.

Canned laughter, football commentary and the whining roar of Formula One engines filtered down the hallway, providing a backing track as she'd walked into the bedroom and tugged down a holdall from the top of the fitted IKEA wardrobes they'd once argued over. It seemed so petty now, she thought, her anger giving way to heartbreak as her mind tossed up dozens of happy memories: the warmth of his fingers squeezed tightly around her frozen mittened ones as they skated in Central Park; the salty smell of his grizzly beard after he'd been away for a week sailing; the thrilling buzz of exhilaration the first time he'd told her she was beautiful.

Panic seized Grace by the throat and she faltered. What if I'm making a horrible mistake? What if I lose the best man that's ever going to happen to me? What if no-one ever tells me I'm beautiful again? And then something made her stop. Rewind. *Remember*. Something had caught her eye. In the corner, hidden beneath the radiator was the *pain au chocolat* Spencer had brought her in bed on her birthday. She'd forgotten all about it, but now this stale pastry reminder triggered memories of the night at Zagora's, sitting alone in Terry's Taxis, the next morning in the coffee shop; churning up feelings of hurt, disappointment, anger, rejection. And a realization. Spencer's actions spoke louder than any words. Even the ones he used to tell her she was beautiful.

Tugging open the pale beech door of the wardrobe, she grabbed a random handful of clothes and unzipped the holdall. Well, here goes ... She hung back. The reality of what she was doing caught at the back of her throat as she paused to stare into the empty holdall, to wonder how the hell her life had gone from a glossy fairytale romance into a mundane kitchen sink drama, to feel sorry for herself, to realize just how much she loved Spencer. And to let a big, angry, fed-up, fucked-off, frightened-to-death tear escape from underneath her eyelashes, roll down her cheek, and drip unceremoniously onto the black nylon.

That tear was the first thing she'd packed.

Paying for her copy of *Loot*, Grace stepped through the automatic sliding doors of WH Smith and into Kensington High Street. The pavement was streaming with weekend shoppers and for a moment she paused, watching them zigzag around her in a blur of plastic bags and ringing mobiles, thinking how weird it was. Nothing had changed, and yet everything had changed.

She and Spencer had separated. She'd moved out. She'd left their flat in Wandsworth, their coupley routine, her life as she knew it. For so long she'd trundled along in her relationship and, for all its faults, it was comforting, and steady, and safe. But now? Maybe Rhian was right, maybe this break would get their relationship back on track, resolve their differences, erase her doubts.

Or maybe it wouldn't.

Grace knew she was taking a big gamble. Who knew what would happen? There were no certainties, no guarantees, no way of knowing how the story would end. Only one thing was for certain: her life wasn't on hold any more.

The thought triggered an unexpected wave of liberation, excitement and freedom, and drawing in a lungful of inner-city air Grace gazed around her. There was a whole world out there. Thousands of people. Millions of strangers. Despite the sweltering heat her arms prickled up in goosebumps. And she felt something else.

Scared shitless.

Chapter Nineteen

She wasn't the only one.

The previous day, in the pine-panelled bathroom of a fourteenth-floor high-rise flat in Streatham, Maggie had made a discovery that was going to change her life for ever.

It had just gone eight o'clock. *Coronation Street* had just finished and she could hear the title music blaring from the living room where Sonny lay flat out on the Chesterfield. Losing his hearing, but refusing to admit it, he'd turned the volume up so loud it made her Capodimonte figurines vibrate on the mantelshelf.

Daaaaa-da-da-da-da-daaaa . . .

Maggie's heart thudded in time to the familiar theme tune. A bead of sweat had broken out on her forehead. She was getting ready for the golf club annual Harvest Festival raffle and in the middle of 'putting her face on' she paused to steady herself on the edge of the Victoriana sink bowl. Pull yourself together, girl, she silently scolded, hastily sharpening a black kohl pencil and lining her eyes. Her hand trembled. She tutted, wiping away the smudge with a piece of toilet paper, before turning to her mascara. Head down, mouth open, she applied two coats then finally unscrewed her lipstick and drew two brick-red arcs. There. Finished. She smiled at her reflection, rubbing the smear of lipstick off her teeth with her forefinger. As good as new.

Or was she?

Her mind flitted back to only a few hours earlier. Having taken the afternoon off work she'd been flaked out on her balcony, listening to the radio and enjoying a cigarette, thinking about what to wear that evening and reminding herself to set the video for the movie on Channel 4. It had been very hot. So hot she could see her legs mottling up in the heat, a tan line appearing round the edge of her bikini. Maggie was immensely proud of the fact that she could still wear a bikini. Not many women her age were still the same dress size as they'd been as a teenager, but she kept herself in trim through an iron will. Not to mention a thirty-a-day habit, she mused, stubbing out her cigarette and squeezing white wiggly SPF15 patterns all over her naked bits and rubbing vigorously.

Afterwards she must have dozed off, because it was half-six by the time she woke up, sticky and sweaty and in desperate need of a shower. Being a stickler for punctuality, she always gave herself an hour to get ready and so, putting in a couple of frozen pizzas, she left Sonny on the sofa and disappeared into the bathroom. Standing underneath the steaming jets of water washing her hair, she thought about the evening ahead. She was looking forward to catching up with her friends, not to mention wearing that new skirt she'd bought at the market, she mused as she climbed out then cleaned the condensation off the mirrored cabinets and towelled herself dry. It was the same routine as always: a squirt of perfume, a dusting of talc, a slick of deodorant.

And then she felt it.

People talk about time standing still and she'd always pooh-poohed their melodrama. Time didn't stand still. It marched along with a regular beat, not stopping for anyone or anything. But she'd been proven wrong. It did. Everything around her came to a standstill. Everything inside her froze. Her stomach curled itself up into a ball, her mouth went dry, her whole life seemed to hold its breath.

It was hard and smooth like a small frozen pea. Small and insignificant, tiny and harmless. Yet more terrifying than she could have ever imagined. Snatching her fingers away she grabbed her clothes from the airing cupboard and dressed on autopilot, going through the motions, seeking sanctuary in the normality, the everyday customs. First her knickers, then her bra, fastening it by her bellybutton, twizzling it around to adjust the straps. If she ignored it, it would go away, disappear. She'd made a mistake, it was nothing.

But now, staring at herself in the mirror, the fear sprang back. All those stories she'd read about famous people, all those boxes of pink ribbons she'd seen on shop counters, all those times she'd checked before and nothing had been there. Furtively slipping her hand underneath her blouse she brushed against the delicate lace of her bra, touched the warm smoothness of her skin. Her fingers returned to it automatically. Funny, how only a few minutes ago it hadn't been there, and now it was as if it had been there for ever.

'Mags?' A hand rapped softly on the bathroom door.

Maggie smiled at Sonny's old-fashioned politeness. They'd been childhood sweethearts, together for nearly forty years, and yet he still knocked before entering. 'It's open,' she replied, quickly pulling herself together and tugging the towel off her head. Shaking her head, she ran her fingers through her long swathe of chestnut hair.

Sonny smiled when he saw her. 'Who's the lucky fella?'

Maggie clucked good-naturedly and reached for her silver charm bracelet in the soap dish. She dangled it across her wrist, trying to fasten it. She must have done it a million times but now it was as if she was wearing oven gloves. She tried again. She noticed her hand was trembling.

'Here, let me do that.' Stooping down, Sonny

tenderly pinched the delicate fastener between his finger and thumb, pulled back the lever and, with the precision of a surgeon, looped it through. 'There. All done,' he nodded, straightening up.

'Thanks, doll.' Maggie smiled.

But something in her smile caused Sonny to wrinkle his forehead, the once thick, soot-black curls now wisps of grey that he insisted on combing over, falling into his eyes. With the flat of his hand he quickly brushed them back before she noticed and nagged him again to have it cut. 'Are you all right, sweetheart?'

Seeing the concern in his baggy eyes, Maggie hesitated. All these years together and they'd never had any secrets. Kind, sweet, gorgeous Sonny. He was going bald, he'd lost most of his real teeth, and he'd grown a little paunch, but he was still the same boy who'd walked her all the way home in the pouring rain, holding his teddy boy jacket above her head. Five miles he'd walked like that. His arms stretched over her head, his shirt wringing wet and sticking to his whippet-thin stomach, his breath white against the freezing air. He'd ended up in bed for two weeks with the flu. And all because he'd wanted to protect her, make sure she got home safe.

'Me? Oh, I'm as right as rain,' she said breezily, leaning over and kissing him on the lips.

The timer on the cooker shrilled.

'Saved by the bell,' he winked, patting her bottom before trotting down the hallway. 'Mmm, those pizzas smell grand.'

Watching him disappear into the small galley kitchen, Maggie felt suddenly very alone.

She couldn't tell him. Couldn't tell him that this time he couldn't protect her. Fear growled deep inside.

This time it would take more than his jacket to keep her safe.

Chapter Twenty

Sitting in the window of Prêt à Manger with a ridiculously overpriced carton of orange juice, a leaky biro and her mobile, Grace stared at the double-page spread of ads littered with dozens of black crosses. Her eyes ached. Her spirits had slumped.

She'd spent the last two hours on the phone, but everything had been taken already. Cocooned in Spencer's comfortable flat, she'd forgotten what it was like out there in flat-hunting land. It was dog eat dog, tenant eat tenant. For the moment she was staying with Rhian. Normally Grace would have balked at ousting a three-year-old child from his nursery, but she was desperate and a box room decorated with Barbie wallpaper, glow-in-the-dark ceiling stickers and a Teletubbies mobile was not to be sniffed at. If only for a few days, until she'd sorted herself out, she'd promised, throwing her arms around Rhian and Jack, who'd giggled delightedly and offered her a piece of Lego.

Taking a breather from *'young, funky professional with gsh, must like garage, late-nights and washing up'* she turned to gaze absent-mindedly out of the window, at the droves of shoppers, mothers with pushchairs, a traffic warden giving someone a ticket. All trussed up in his jobsworth cap and military-style uniform, he was gleefully punching in the number plate of a white Citroën DS that was parked across the street on a double yellow outside Dixons, its hazards flashing futilely.

Grace couldn't help smiling. With its hulking great wide body that lay beached against the kerb like a cruise liner gone adrift, the car was hardly inconspicuous. You could spot it a mile away. And that was without the added bonus of the attention-attracting hazards. Did the owner really think that was going to let them off a ticket? The driver had to either be a complete idiot or totally arrogant, she decided, her interest aroused as she saw a pair of legs appear through the swing doors of Dixons and begin heading towards the Citroën. With their face and body hidden behind the largest cardboard box imaginable, she watched as the legs tried to negotiate the pavement while clutching what, according to the box, was a Sony plasma-screen TV. An arm appeared and dug something out of the jeans pockets. It was the keys to the car. It beeped twice, its alarm lights flashing.

This is going to be interesting, thought Grace, watching the driver's struggle to get the new purchase safely into the boot of the car. Half crouching, half squatting, he began carefully wedging, easing, wiggling, sliding the cardboard monster inside. Until finally, mission accomplished, the boot was slammed shut.

Which is when he saw the ticket.

And she saw his identity.

Jimi Malik! For Christsakes, what was he doing here? Wasn't he supposed to be in Canada? On another continent? Thousands of miles away? Wasn't he supposed to be getting married? With the kind of dread unique to someone who sees someone else they really don't want to see, Grace watched as he snatched up the ticket, tossed it into the gutter and then, defiantly leaving the car where it was, gave the traffic warden the finger before marching across the road.

Towards me. Sitting in the window Grace suddenly felt like a shop dummy. Quickly grabbing the copy of *Loot* she attempted to erect a paper barricade and shrank down low behind it. Hidden behind the small ads, she waited. She felt more than a little ridiculous. What the hell was she doing? He wasn't so bad, they'd got on perfectly well that night last week in the cab, they'd patched up old differences, had a bit of a laugh, *kissed*. Suddenly remembering, she just as suddenly blocked it out again. In a funny sort of way they'd parted as friends.

Long-distance friends. She screamed silently, then set about consoling herself that in a couple of minutes he'd have walked past. He wouldn't have noticed her. And she would be able to make a quick exit and slink off back to Rhian's.

'The bastard.'

A voice behind her ear made her jump. The paper tent collapsed like a house of cards as she swung round and came face to face with Jimi, swearing furiously under his breath. He stopped when he saw her.

'Grace.'

'Jimi,' she smiled, pretending to look surprised.

'You know, we've got to stop meeting like this,' he smiled, his features relaxing. He felt unexpectedly pleased.

'I know. What a funny coincidence,' she agreed.

Jimi grinned darkly. 'You can't fool me, I know I'm the last person you want to bump into,' he replied, putting his bunch of keys, mobile and wallet onto the ledge in front of her.

Grace squirmed with discomfort. She'd always been a crap liar. She was about to protest when he winked.

'Only joking,' he smiled, grabbing a sandwich from the chiller cabinet. Leaving the money on the counter he peeled off the plastic wrapper. Grace glanced at it. Egg mayo. Yuk. The worst filling ever invented. Why on earth would anyone eat a stinky old egg mayo sarnie when they could choose from all those lovely, delicious ones like goat's cheese and sundried tomato, Parma ham with avocado, or smoked salmon and cranberry?

It just went to show. The man had no taste whatsoever.

'Want a bite?' With his mouth full, Jimi proffered the sandwich.

'No thanks,' she said, shaking her head firmly. His jaunty friendliness annoyed her. Did he have to stand so close? In fact, did he have to stand anywhere near her at all? Couldn't he just go away and leave her in peace?

Apparently not.

Unfazed, he took another mammoth bite. 'So, how are you? The other night you seemed a bit . . .' he searched for an adjective that wouldn't offend '. . . emotional.'

'Oh yeah, I'm fine now,' she said brightly. 'Never better.' She smiled manically. *Too* manically.

'So what's with *Loot*?' He tilted his chin, motioning to the copy she was trying to hide under her elbow.

'Oh that?' Damn. Grace pretended to be surprised, as if she had no idea that a thick, mustard yellow paper was wedged underneath her right elbow. 'I . . . er . . . was just looking at cars.'

'Oh really? Let's have a look . . .'

'Well, actually . . .'

But it was too late. Before she could stop him, he'd whipped it up from underneath her like a magician doing his tablecloth trick and her elbow was left resting on the shelf, not knowing quite what had happened.

Seeing the pages, Jimi raised one eyebrow disbelievingly. 'So what kind of car are you after? One that's five minutes from the tube? One that's a hundred and fifty a week? One that's preferably gay?'

Her cheeks burned. 'Spencer and I have decided to have a break.'

'You mean you've left him.'

She scowled. 'No, it doesn't mean that.'

'Yes it does.' Pulling up a stool, Jimi sat down.

Without even asking, noted Grace, irritated.

'Everyone knows that having a break is just a

euphemism for saying it's over. Like saying someone's passed away when really they've dropped dead.'

Grace's jaw dropped. 'You're incredible. Tell me, how does it feel to be so cheerful?'

Jimi shrugged off her sarcasm. 'If it was just a break you'd still be wearing the ring.' He nodded his head in the direction of her left hand.

It was true. She wasn't wearing it any more. And trust him to have noticed, fumed Grace, immediately stuffing her hand firmly between her crossed thighs. Only that morning she'd taken it off and put it away in her carved wooden jewellery box. It had been a wrench. Without it she felt odd. Naked. Vulnerable. *Single*.

Jimi continued chewing. 'Yep, I thought so.'

Grace watched him nodding like some infernal plastic dog in the rear window of a car. 'Thought what?' she asked, tight-lipped.

'You've broken up. Nobody gives back the ring if they're just having a break.'

'I haven't given it back,' she snapped defensively. Well that's the truth, I haven't, have I? she thought, quickly justifying her answer to herself. 'And anyway, since when did you get to be such an expert on relationships?' she retorted hotly. 'Just because you happen to have conned some poor, unsuspecting woman to walk down the aisle with you, doesn't suddenly make you a love guru. Far from it. It just makes you lucky. Unbelievably, jaw-droppingly lucky. Which –' she raised one eyebrow and glared at him – 'is the last thing that can be said for your bride.'

There was silence.

Grace didn't know who was more amazed by her outburst, herself or Jimi. He stared at her in silence. She felt a glow of victory. Ha, that's shut you up, she thought, detecting a glimmer of discomfort. And then slowly it dawned. 'Hang on a minute, what are you doing buying a telly when you're moving to another continent?'

'Actually it's an integrated DVD and video with an optional plasma screen.' Jimi tried avoidance tactics.

But Grace was already working out the dates. 'Aren't you supposed to be in Canada right now?' She stared at him. 'Isn't today your wedding day?'

There was no getting out of it. 'Was,' he shrugged, bracing himself.

'You mean it's *off*?' gasped Grace, comprehension flashing across her face as she got what he was saying. Only she got it wrong. 'I just knew it! I just knew you wouldn't be able to go through with it. That's why I was so amazed when you said you were getting married. I couldn't believe it. I thought, Jimi Malik? A husband? *No way!* It's been thirteen years but people don't change that much.' Sitting back on her stool, Grace stared at Jimi, remembering his Ford Capri, the ever-changing stream of girls in his passenger seat. She tutted. 'Your poor fiancée. How could you? Jilting her days before the wedding.' Shaking her head, she fixed him with an accusing glare. 'Is breaking hearts some kind of a hobby of yours?'

'I really got to you, didn't I?' Jimi cocked his head on one side and eyed her with amusement.

Infuriated, Grace's mind began scrambling around for a string of insults. And then catching his smile, she stopped. Paused. And smiled back. God only knows why, but his grin always had been infectious. 'You're lucky I'm even speaking to you,' she said begrudgingly.

'So why are you?'

'You really want to know?'

'Yeah, I really want to know.'

Grace paused. 'Because any man who can dance to "Wuthering Heights" can't be all bad.' Her smile spread even wider as Jimi rolled his eyes at the memory and smiled ruefully.

'You know what? This is actually pretty disgusting,' he confessed, gesturing to his half-eaten sandwich. He stuffed it back into its wrapper. 'Do you fancy grabbing some proper lunch?'

She hesitated, and then realizing she had nothing better to do, nodded. 'As long as it's not a Big Mac without the burgers.'

'Oh Christ.' He hung his head in shame. 'I'd forgotten about that.'

'I don't think I'll ever forget the look on that poor assistant's face,' giggled Grace.

'Or yours,' he teased. 'It was just two soggy burger buns.'

'. . . and ketchup,' she snorted, wiping away a tear of laughter from her eye. 'Don't forget the ketchup.'

Their laughter caught them both by surprise and caused other customers in the café to look at them oddly. Jimi's loud, growling chortles came from deep in his belly, whereas Grace had a giggle that was not only embarrassingly shrill but, worst of all, punctuated with loud, rattling snorts.

Through creased-up eyes, Grace looked at Jimi. Nostrils flared, eyes screwed tight, mouth stretched wide to reveal the gold crowns on his back teeth, he always looked so ridiculous when he laughed. He wasn't one of those people who politely tittered: his face would twist into unflattering contortions like some kind of latex puppet.

'Oh, by the way . . .' Rubbing his hand across his shaved head, feeling the tiny, needle-like bristles prickling his palm, Jimi caught his breath and stared at Grace.

'Yeah?' Grace was busily gathering up her things as she gazed absent-mindedly out of the window.

'Just for the record. I didn't jilt Kylie.' Stuffing his hands in his pockets Jimi made his confession. 'She jilted me.'

Grace was taken aback.

Translating her silence, Jimi continued. 'It's OK, you don't have to say anything. I know what you're thinking. I deserve it. It's my own fault. She had a lucky escape.'

Grace shook her head. 'No, I'm not thinking that at all.'

Jimi felt an unexpected rush of grateful relief. 'You're not?'

'Nope,' she said matter-of-factly.

Smiling, she motioned out of the window. Where a white Citroën DS was dangling twenty feet in the air as it was winched onto the back of a tow-away truck.

'I'm thinking you need to learn how to park.'

Chapter Twenty-one

'The weirdest thing is cooking.'

They'd decamped to a nearby sushi restaurant as it was Jimi's favourite, although he didn't look as if he was particularly enjoying himself. Perched on a stool, his earlier black humour had evaporated and he was sipping sake, staring dolefully as his lunch trundled past him on the conveyor belt.

'You cook?' After carefully weighing up each dish, most of which contained unidentifiable moving objects, Grace had chosen a plateful of neatly arranged cucumber rolls. She glanced at him with surprise. She'd never put Jimi down as a domestic kind of a bloke.

'I have been known.' Tapping his chopsticks out of their paper wrapper, he split them in two. 'The other night I made fettuccini carbonara. When there was two of us I always knew exactly the right amount of dried pasta, but I ended up making way too much. It's still welded to the bottom of the colander.'

Tasting a pink sliver of ginger, Grace made supportively sympathetic noises. 'For me it's the bed.'

'Don't tell me. You had a side,' he interjected, pouncing on a piece of tuna sashimi like a hunter capturing its prey. 'That was something I discovered about going out with Kylie. A woman sleeps in your bed more than once and – ' he clicked his fingers ' – they've suddenly got a "side".'

Grace ignored his evident bitterness. 'No.' She shook her head, waggling her chopsticks as she did so. 'I had more of an edge. Spencer used to take up so much room I'd end up teetering on the far side of the mattress, hanging onto a corner of the duvet like an abseiler.' She scooped up a smear of the green horse-radish paste and began mixing it with soy sauce.

'Go easy on the wasabi, it's pretty strong,' he warned.

'I *have* eaten sushi before,' grumbled Grace, defiantly adding a bit more. Stirring determinedly, she thought about Spencer. 'At least I get all of the duvet and all of the bed,' she added, trying to sound positive when in fact she felt a stab of sadness. Over the last few days, every time she'd found herself missing Spencer she'd dredged up thoughts of her birthday. What a selfish bastard he'd been. How she'd made the right decision to break off their engagement. But now she was finding it harder and harder to cling onto her anger and it was fast being replaced by a growing ache.

'Well that's got to be a good thing, hasn't it?'

'Yeah. I suppose so.' She smeared a cucumber roll with paste and popped it into her mouth. Her mouth immediately began burning. She felt her eyes water. Oh fuck. Her experience of sushi extended to a takeout from Prêt-à-Manger, and this was a lot, lot stronger. She blinked furiously. She didn't want to lose face in front of sushi-king Jimi.

'Are you OK?'

'Never better,' she managed to gasp, taking a glug of water. 'As I was saying . . .' Her tongue felt as if it was on fire and she sucked gratefully on an ice cube. 'Now I get to stretch out like a starfish.'

'Exactly,' nodded Jimi. 'I don't know why couples are so pleased with themselves. That's one thing you don't have when you're in a relationship. Space.'

'You're right.' Grace felt cheered by the thought. 'I thought I'd hate sleeping alone, but you know what? I'm beginning to love it.' As her tongue started to return to normal she turned her attention back to the food on the conveyor belt and, feeling much braver, decided to chance an eel roll. 'What about you?'

'Me?' Jimi poured himself another glass of saki. 'Oh I can't sleep in the bed, it reminds me of Kylie.'

'So where are you sleeping?'

Doing shots with the saki, he downed it in one and slammed it on the counter. And dropping the bravado, he confessed glumly. 'On the sofa.'

'Have you spoken to Spencer?' It was a few days after their lunch at the sushi restaurant and Jimi was at home, sitting at his desk with his socked feet up on the glass surface, the phone in one hand, a cigarette in the other. Having started smoking again with a vengeance, he'd already got through a pack and it was only four in the afternoon.

'Twice.' Crushed up next to an old-age-pensioner on the number 328 bus on the way home from work, Grace wedged her mobile under her chin as she searched for some change for the conductor. 'The first time he called to tell me my contact lenses had arrived and he'd given them to his secretary to bike over, and the second time was to remind me about a dental appointment . . .' she broke off to untangle a pound coin from a flapjack wrapper in her pocket. 'He knows how useless I am with forgetting things. But not once did he bring up the subject of us, or talk about how he felt, or ask how I was feeling. It was as if he was talking to one of his clients, as if I didn't mean anything, as if leaving him hadn't affected his life one little bit.' Remembering his brisk tone on the phone she felt hurt, and not a little miffed, all over again. 'It was just business as usual.'

'How did you want him to be?' replied Jimi stiffly, trying to quell the jangle of emotions this conversation was stirring up. Over the past week he'd found it impossible to talk about anything without relating everything back to himself, and his own situation. 'An emotional wreck?'

'Why are you being so defensive? I'm not talking about you,' chided Grace.

'I'm not being defensive,' he retorted defensively.

'Yes you are. Every time I say anything about Spencer you take it personally. You're being neurotic.'

'Me? Neurotic? How can you say I'm being neurotic? I've never been neurotic!'

There was a pause as Grace placed the pound coin in the sandpapery palm of the conductor, and accepted her ticket. 'So what are you being now? Cool, calm and collected?'

Jimi fell quiet. She was right. He'd spent his whole life perfecting the art of being cool. Women used to complain that he had no feelings, that nothing got to him, and now look at him. *Everything* was getting to him. His hard-on had gone awol, he'd come down with a severe case of writer's block. What next?

He flicked his ash into his new glass ashtray. He'd been sitting at his desk all day, still grappling with the novel that was refusing to be written. Bored and frustrated he'd spent the last hour going through his list of phone-buddies – working from home he had a list of people he could call during the day so he didn't feel like a complete outcast from society, but today the world and his mother was on voicemail.

Drawing a complete blank he'd sat there staring at the blinking cursor on his laptop, until his mind had started wandering towards Kylie. Before he could stop himself he was rehearsing a couple of contenders for his opening line, letting his mind run away with nostalgia. And then, just as his fingers were dialling the code for Canada he'd brought himself up short. No you don't. No you bloody well don't. For Christsakes man, what are you thinking of? Where's your pride? Your dignity? Your sense?

Cutting off the call, Jimi had stared at the handset, brow furrowed, jaw set, emotions all over the goddamn place. I'm going mad, he thought miserably. Seriously, I think I'm going stark, staring mad. He lit up a cigarette, took a gloomy drag and stewed over recent events. He'd never felt like this before. He'd never loved and lost a woman before, or known what it was like to feel rejected, or missed someone and not been able to do anything about it, and he didn't know how to handle it. He couldn't talk to his mates about this, Clive apart, they'd all assumed he was over it and was back to being his old, happy, single self.

Except he hadn't.

And he wasn't.

Digging out his mobile he'd searched through the list of names until he'd found the one he was looking for and begun punching in the number on his land line. He might not be able to talk to Kylie, but he could talk about her to the one person who would understand what it was like to be suddenly single again.

'Grace?'

Luckily she'd picked up and spent the last twenty minutes being the proverbial shoulder.

'Yeah?' she said now.

'I'm sorry, I'm feeling a bit off.' He relented. 'I think there's a bug going round.' But not enough to lose face.

Yeah right, the love bug, thought Grace, but she didn't say it. Instead she edged along the seat for fear of being involuntarily embroiled in a threesome with the snogging couple sitting – and groping – next to her. 'Have you called Kylie?'

'Sort of.'

'What do you mean, sort of?'

There was a pause as Jimi released the lever on the side of his leather swivel chair, and reclined even further back. 'Well, does it count if you hang up before they answer?'

'Hi, it's me. I'm just calling up to give you my new number . . .' Surrounded by empty cardboard boxes, Grace sat cross-legged on the bare floorboards leaving a message on Jimi's voicemail. After scouring the rental ads in *Loot*, being sneered at by pinky-ringed estate agents when she naively informed them she was looking for a furnished short let for less than a grand a month, she'd almost given up hope when someone at Rhian's playgroup had mentioned a friend who was working abroad and wanted to rent out their flat.

It was only a studio but it was cheap, it was centrally located in Earls Court, and it gave her some much-needed space and time to try and get her head together.

'. . . 7895,' finished Grace, reading the number that was felt-tipped on the back of her hand. 'At least I think it's a 5,' she added, trying to decipher a smudged digit. She made a mental note to actually start writing things in the filofax she so diligently carried around with her and yet just as diligently ignored in favour of her hand. 'So if you want to give me a flat-warming ring, you know where I am,' she ended brightly.

Hanging up she glanced around the empty, silent, strange flat. The owner had obviously tried to recreate a rustic Mexican farmhouse and had ragrolled the walls a bright ochre, built a ladder that led up to the mezzanine level which doubled as a bedroom and hung Mexican lanterns, a wooden Day of the Dead skeleton, and a framed Maharachi band costume on the walls.

On one side stripped pine doors led off to a tiny multicoloured tiled kitchen, and an even tinier shower room, while on the other french windows opened out on to a pretty balcony. Even so, considered Grace, it didn't alter the fact that the flat was probably the same size as Spencer's living room.

Their living room.

Abruptly, Grace burst into tears.

Her sobs were interrupted by the jangling sound of the phone ringing. She wiped her runny nose on the back of her hand, inadvertently obliterating her phone number, and picked up.

'Hello?' she hiccuped quietly.

'Sorry, I didn't hear my mobile ring. I was on the

scooter.' On the other side of town in Soho Jimi unclipped his helmet and dismounted from a silver Vespa.

Grace fell immediately into the trap. 'What scooter?'

'Didn't I tell you?' replied Jimi innocently, knowing damn well that he hadn't. He'd only bought his shiny new toy that morning but he was determined to grab any opportunity he could to talk about it. 'I thought I'd get myself a little runaround, beat the parking militia,' he added, his credit card still stinging from having to pay for his Citroën to be released from the car pound. Sitting astride his scooter, he spotted a lurking warden. This was now out and out war, and like a cowboy to a Red Indian he threw him a look of 100-per-cent-proof superiority, and began stroking his wing mirrors, as if ready to go into battle.

'So when did you move in?' He tugged himself back.

'Yesterday.'

'And how is it?'

'If I was an estate agent I'd call it compact.'

'I wasn't talking about the flat.'

'Oh.' Wiping her damp cheek, Grace struggled to put on a cheery voice. 'It's fine.'

'You're lying.'

She sighed defeatedly. 'OK, it's awful. The whole thing's terrible. I'm a wreck. I bloody miss him. Is that good enough?'

'No, that's just natural,' replied Jimi sympathetically. He knew exactly how she felt. He missed Kylie.

'Well it sucks,' said Grace angrily. 'I miss Spencer, I miss my flat, I miss my home, I miss my life . . .' She stopped herself before she got upset and started crying again. 'Do you know something, Jimi?'

'What?'

'I'm thirty-one years old and this is going to be the first time I've ever lived by myself. Even if it's only for a little while,' she added hopefully, her voice trailing off as she contemplated her future. *Was* this only for a little while? Or was it going to be more permanent?

197

'And I think I'm going to hate it,' she decided glumly, looking around her.

'It'll be fine.'

'Will it?' She was asking about a lot more than the flat. Had she done the right thing, moving out? Maybe she'd been too hasty. Too demanding. Too unreasonable. Too impulsive. Maybe she should have waited a bit longer. But how long? Six months? A year? Five years? Until she was pushing forty? By moving out she'd given their relationship an ultimatum. Either it was going to sink or it was going to swim.

Unfortunately at the moment it felt as if it had sunk. Without a trace.

'He hasn't called, you know.'

Seeing as she told him on the hour, every hour, Jimi was only too aware of the fact. 'Give him time. He'll call,' he soothed her knowledgeably. Stuffing his helmet under his arm he walked into Bar Italia and ordered himself a macchiato. 'Take it from me, men like to do things in their own time. They don't like to be rushed.'

'Rushed? We've been together for four years.'

'And you've been apart for only two and a half weeks,' reminded Jimi. Try as he might not to, he was still counting the days. 'It's still early days.'

Grace didn't know whether to feel pleased or saddened. 'Christ, is that all? It feels like months,' she groaned, slumping on the arm of the sofa and surveying the heaps of clothes that were littered all over the floor. 'Why did nobody ever tell me this is what "having a break" was going to be like? It sounds so easy. I'm exhausted.'

Staring at the mess, she sighed deeply. Too many movies had left Grace with the notion that she was going to be wallowing in Chardonnay and Marlboro Lights, being passed Kleenex by sympathetic girlfriends, watching *Four Weddings and a Funeral* on a continuous loop, dancing to 'I Will Survive' and making drunken, weeping, regrettable, phone calls at 3 a.m.

Bullshit. It was nothing of the sort. Apart from phoning the odd girlfriend and spending a couple of evenings eating takeout at Rhian's, she'd barely had time to feel sorry for herself. She'd been too busy buying bubblewrap to pack up her breakables, borrowing suitcases to pack up all her clothes, redirecting mail and sending emails informing people of her new telephone number.

'And I'm not just talking emotionally. I'm talking physically.'

'Why, what have you been up to?' asked Jimi, thinking back to his earlier encounter with Sammy-Jo, and then trying not to. He was desperate to forget all about it, but it was proving annoyingly memorable. And for all the wrong reasons.

'Not what you're thinking,' she tutted, shaking her head. Even in a crisis Jimi had sex on the brain. 'You know, somebody should warn women.'

'About what?' Nabbing himself a table outside on the pavement, he pulled up a chair and sat down with his coffee to admire his scooter parked across the street.

'About what it's *really* like,' she said. Unable to stand it any longer she stood up and, grabbing a black plastic roll of binliners, ripped one off and began picking up items and stuffing them in. 'They need to be warned that separating from your bloke isn't about Hugh Grant films and Cadbury's Fingers. Oh no.' Gathering momentum she scooped up a pair of leather trousers – she'd loved them in the eighties and was waiting for them to come back into fashion – and held them up to her. Not only did the waist have pleats, it was so high she'd give Simon Powell a run for his armpits. She stuffed them in, determinedly. 'You don't have time to be emotional, you're too bloody busy being practical. The chances are it's not going to be *your* flat, because you moved into *their* flat, and so now even though it feels like *your* home, it's not. It's *their* home, and you have to move back out again . . .'

Her voice was growing louder as her melancholy mutated into anger. Sod missing Spencer, she was bloody furious with him. How could he do this to her? How come his life continued much the same as always, while hers was turned upside down, packed into binliners and relocated to Earls Court? It seemed so terribly unfair.

'And so it's about having to pack up all your things, working out the tube route to work, getting to know where your nearest Sainsbury's local is,' she complained, chucking in a bra that really shouldn't be allowed, and yet another pair of laddered opaque tights. What on earth had she thought she was going to do with them all? Make cheese? Rob a bank? Make pop socks?

'It's about boring details that, if my life was an episode of some glossy US sitcom, would have been cut out and neatly edited . . .' Huffing loudly, she pounced on a pair of cropped trousers that made her legs look like cricket stumps: 'It would have all been glossed over with a jaunty bit of voiceover and a Dido track until the next episode when I'd reappear with a new bloke, and a new pair of Manolos,' she spat, trying to shove everything into the black plastic. 'And I would have looked fabulous, like Sarah Jessica Parker.'

Realizing her binliner was so full it was dangerously close to bursting she stopped, pushed the waves of hair away from her face, and caught her reflection in the Mexican-tiled mirror. Out of breath, sweaty and make-up free, it was not a pretty sight. 'Instead of revolting.'

There was silence on the other end of the line.

Across town Jimi was sipping his coffee and flicking through *Metro*. His mobile was lying on the table in front of him; he'd put it there five minutes ago when Grace had started ranting. Now, noticing the tinny voice had stopped yelling out of his handset, he picked it up and held it to his ear. He heard a tentative voice.

'Jimi?'

Back in the Yucatan paradise in Earls Court, Grace was standing in the middle of a bomb site, a redundant phone in her hand. Had he hung up? She frowned, feeling more than a little embarrassed by her outburst.

'Are you still there?' she persisted.

There was the rattle of a coffee cup on its saucer, and then Jimi's voice. 'Grace, can I say something?'

'Feel free,' she said cagily.

There was a pause.

'I think you need to get out more.'

Chapter Twenty-two

The last fortnight hadn't been one of Rhian's best. In fact, as fortnights in her life went, this was pretty much up there with the fortnight in June 2000 that had begun in her bedroom, stuck fast in a pair of size-16 trousers that were refusing to budge past her knees, and had ended two weeks and a broken zip later in the Gap buying elasticized jogging bottoms.

Jack had gone down with chickenpox. And not just any old bog standard chickenpox that could be taken care of with a bit of camomile lotion and a few *Rosie and Jim* videos. Oh no, this had involved several panicky trips to the doctor's fearing meningitis before she'd got the thankful diagnosis, followed by ten days nursing a sick, scratching and exceedingly grumpy child.

It was exhausting, especially as once Jack had begun feeling better he had decided that the only thing he would eat was shepherd's pie – and not the one from the packet that she could just shove in the microwave for two minutes, but the one that took her half a day to make, soaking kidney beans overnight, frying mince and mashing potatoes till her fingers blistered. He might be only three, but Jack's taste buds were like those of a Michelin chef, and any attempt to fool him with Marks & Spencer's finest was met with a tantrum that not even Elton John could compete with.

Even worse, the demands didn't stop at food, they

stretched to entertainment. And for the first time in Jack's short, square-eyed life, he didn't beg to be allowed to watch TV, he wanted to be read stories.

Twenty-four hours a day.

'. . . And the glass slipper fitted her foot perfectly. So the handsome prince kissed Cinderella on the lips . . .' Lying cuddled up on Jack's bed, Rhian closed the dog-eared Ladybird book and looked down at the glossy black head nestled into the crook of her arm. '. . . and together they lived happily ever after.'

Jack wriggled contentedly. His chickenpox spots had faded to pale pink splodges and he was sleepy, but struggling to stay awake. Clutching a headless Barbie to his blue flannel chest, he gazed up at her innocently, with his huge amber eyes.

'Is Daddy your prince?'

Rhian felt a stab of sadness. Jack rarely mentioned his father, and didn't seem unduly upset that, since he'd moved to the States, his only form of contact was the odd letter or birthday card. But now, meeting his gaze she felt both guilty for his loss, and furiously protective of him. 'No,' she answered lightly, tucking him up tightly as she tried not to think about Phil.

But Jack wasn't to be put off. He frowned, his baby-plump face contorted into comical seriousness. 'Don't you have a prince, Mummy?'

'Ssshh, go to sleep,' whispered Rhian, gently brushing away the curls that fanned onto his forehead. Princes seemed to be a tad thin on the ground in central London, unlike inquisitive three-year-olds, she mused, thinking about her recent fling with Noel.

After that first date they'd seen each other a couple more times, but she doubted she was going to be seeing him again. She'd last heard from him a few days ago. It had been late and she'd been in bed, tossing and turning and trying to fall asleep. Having no success, she'd flicked on her lamp, picked up a magazine and put it back down again, flicked on the portable at the end of the bed, and flicked it back off again, and finally, in desperation, had turned on the radio. A familiar voice had reached out across the airwaves '. . . *Good evening, you're listening to Dr Cupid at* Do You Come Here Often?' Feeling a little burst of pleasure, she'd turned up the volume and snuggled down into her pillows.

Rhian had been a fan of the show ever since Jack was born. It had been the early hours of the morning and she'd been breastfeeding, trying to keep herself awake when she'd turned on the radio and accidentally tuned in. It had certainly woken her up. In fact she'd been so engrossed in Andy from Brighton's search for a Miss Right who also shared his passion for tandem skydiving that she'd stayed up long after Jack had fallen asleep, unable to bring herself to turn the radio off.

Eighteen months later when Phil had left it was that show which got her through the sleepless nights, and even now she'd listen once in a while. It was like the adult version of the bedtime story, and as ridiculous as it sounded, Dr Cupid was like an old friend. She didn't know what it was about him, or the letters that he read out or the listeners that called in, but she loved hearing about all the different people and their lives: it was as interesting as it was entertaining, and it always made her feel that she wasn't alone. That she wasn't the only one out there looking for a soulmate.

And one thing was for certain: Noel certainly wasn't her soulmate.

Rhian had known that from the very first moment she laid eyes on his pierced eyebrow and split-toe Nike running shoes. And she'd known from that first date that they weren't going to fall in love and he wasn't going to be anything serious, but then that was why she'd been attracted to him in the first place. Noel hadn't been offering her security, commitment *or* a future – but Rhian didn't want that – she wanted fun, lots of sex, and the chance to have some 'me' time.

Rhian was bored with being Rhian the jilted lover,

Rhian the single mother. She just wanted to be Rhian for a change. She wanted to ditch the emotional baggage, leave her worries behind, and have a good time. Like Noel. Noel lived in a shared flat in Chelsea but it might as well have been on another planet. One without responsibilities and filled only with one single purpose – the pursuit of pleasure. Whereas she was a single thirtysomething mother, in bed by midnight and up again at six, Noel was a footloose and fancy-free twentysomething, in bed by dawn and up again after lunch. He lived a different life, in a different world and for a while the two had collided. Well, sub-duvet anyway.

And so that night, after listening to the radio show for forty-five minutes, she'd finally fallen asleep – only to be woken at 4 a.m. by Noel on her answering machine, urging her to 'pick up, Foxy.' Face-down under the duvet with her hair stuck up on her pillow like a loo brush, face squished so hard into the mattress that it had taken on the imprint of the springs, she'd felt anything but foxy.

Half asleep. Delirious. *Pissed-off.*

She'd sat up. This was turning into something of a routine. Noel had done this a few times, and in the past she'd dived out of bed, slapped on some make-up, tugged on her silky teddy and lit all her aromatherapy candles in preparation. But that night, listening to him calling from the back of a cab on the way home from a club, wondering if he could 'drop by and have some fun', Rhian had translated his twenty-six-year-old bloke speak as 'fancy a shag?' and decided that no, quite frankly, she didn't. Not any more. And not like that anyway.

Because that's when it had dawned on her. She wasn't having fun any more, she was being taken for granted. And there's nothing remotely fun about that, she'd thought, reaching over to her answering machine, holding her finger down on the delete button and erasing his message. Sitting back on her pillows she'd felt a great sense of satisfaction. And wide awake. Drumming her fingers on the edge of her duvet, she'd yawned, fidgeted, hesitated, and then, making sure no-one was looking – not even herself – furtively opened her bedside drawer.

Rhian might have been escorted out of Anne Summers, but there'd been nothing stopping her visiting their website. Pulling out the Rabbit, still in its packaging, she'd eyed it with wonder. Well, just because Noel wasn't coming over didn't mean she couldn't have a little fun, did it?

Giggling to herself, she'd turned out the light.

The buzzer sounded.

'It's someone called Grace!' Hester the babysitter hollered loudly down the hallway. 'Says she's outside in the cab . . .'

Jack made a slight moan. Having lost his battle with sleep, his mouth had fallen slightly open and his eyelids were drooping and fluttering. Rhian looked down at him, marvelling at the thick, black eyelashes that brushed against his cheeks like feather boas. Gently disentangling herself from his sleepy hug, she placed *Cinderella* on the bedside table and turned off his twirly dinosaur lamp. The room fell into darkness but for a sliver of moonlight that had found its way under the blind. She paused, gazing at Jack, fast asleep under his duvet. Her heart tied itself up in a knot. 'You're my prince,' she whispered, kissing him softly on his cheek.

'. . . And she says if you don't hurry up you're going to be late for the party . . .' yelled Hester, her teenage monotone blasting through the flat and breaking the tender moment. As one of seven, she was used to making herself heard.

Glancing at the clock on the wall, Rhian noticed the time, freaked, and dashing out of Jack's bedroom, ran barefoot past the dreadlocked sixteen-year-old who was standing in the hallway holding the intercom and blowing acid green bubblegum balloons.

'Tell her I'll be two secs,' she instructed, diving into her own bedroom, where she yanked off her faithful leggings and T-shirt and tugged on a black shift dress. Her mobile rang. Ignoring it, she grabbed a black liquid eyeliner and expertly swept a smooth, wobble-free line along her lashes, slicked on some red lipstick and stepped back to see herself in her dressing table mirror. The face was OK. She smoothed her palm over her glossy bob. And the hair was looking good.

Which only left the body. Stooping low, she caught her boobs, waist and tummy reflected from three different angles. She pulled a face. It didn't matter which angle she chose, she still looked huge. Maybe she could cancel tonight. Pretend she wasn't feeling well. Say that the babysitter had to leave by nine.

The message alert sounded on her mobile. Picking it up, she clicked open the small digital envelope. A message popped up. It was from Grace.

'You look great. Now get your booty in the taxi.'

A smile spread slowly across Rhian's face. She had two choices: either she could pay off Hester, let Grace down and stay in and feel sorry for herself, or she could go out and try and have a good time. Either way her thighs would still be the same size in the morning.

For a moment she deliberated, and then, grabbing her handbag, she clattered into the hallway and stuck her head around the living-room door. 'I'll be home by midnight,' she said decisively.

There was no reaction from Hester, but Rhian allowed herself a wide grin. She and Cinderella had a lot more in common than she'd first thought, she reflected, pulling open the door to her flat and stepping into the stairwell. OK, so her prince might be only three years old and recovering from chickenpox, her glass slippers were gold slingbacks she'd unearthed at a jumble sale, and instead of a royal ball it was a house party in Islington, but so what?

Feeling an uncharacteristic burst of pure giddiness

zapping through her veins, Rhian began trotting merrily down three flights of stairs. It was about time she started looking at things a bit differently, she decided, and first off was being single. On the one hand she could see herself as being on the shelf. Or on the other, she reconsidered, clattering onto the pavement and waving madly at Grace, she was footloose and fancy free. And her minicab awaited.

Chapter Twenty-three

After forty-five minutes sitting bumper to bumper in traffic along the Marylebone Road, they eventually arrived at a large Victorian house with balloons tied to the front door and the sounds of music drifting from the first floor windows. Jumping out of the cab, Rhian bounded eagerly up the front steps, while Grace paid the driver and hesitated on the pavement. She was having second thoughts. It was a long time since she'd gone to a party without Spencer, especially to a party where she didn't know anyone, and she was fast beginning to wonder if she'd done the right thing accepting Rhian's invitation.

Walking into the unfamiliar hallway of a grand, Regency-style building, she felt a flutter of nerves in her stomach. 'Whose party is it?' she whispered.

'Amanda Bartley's,' replied Rhian. 'I haven't seen her since sixth-form college so I don't have a clue what she does now, but she tracked me down on Friends Reunited and sent me an email inviting me to her thirty-fifth.' Instructed by an officious Polish maid, she laid her poncho on the coat pile in the bedroom. 'But whatever she's doing, she seems to be doing rather well for herself,' she added, noting the expensive lamps, vast walk-in wardrobes and not one, but two pots of crème de la mer on the bedside table.

'What does she look like?' Grace wanted to recognize the host. She'd once gone to a party with Spencer and bitched about the awful décor to a real laugh called Melissa, only to discover the 'real laugh' was the owner. She'd stopped laughing pretty quickly after that.

'I'm not sure.' Rhian's memory of Amanda was somewhat hazy. 'All I can remember is that she had a terrible fringe and a crush on Nathan from Brother Beyond . . .'

Grace threw her a look.

'. . . at least I think she did. Or maybe that was Joanna Rose.' She shrugged apologetically, her attention distracted as a waitress wafted past with a tray of smoked salmon blinis. This was a first. A catered party. After imagining the usual warm Bacardi Breezers and a few bowls of New York Cheddar Kettle chips, things were starting to look up.

Grace tugged off her coat, and it was magically whisked away. She felt unexpectedly vulnerable.

'Ooh, gorgeous dress,' cooed Rhian, gazing with appreciation at Grace. A deep coppery hue, the dress was slinky, off the shoulder and very sexy. In comparison, her own black tunic felt completely boring. 'You look fantastic.'

'I don't feel fantastic,' said Grace, catching her reflection in the mirror and fiddling unsurely with her straps. It hadn't looked this skimpy when she'd tried it on in the shop. It was as if it had magically shrunk in the plastic carrier on the way home on the tube. 'Maybe I should have worn my jeans. I feel really overdressed.'

It was an unfortunate choice of words. 'In that outfit?' hooted Rhian, and then seeing her friend's expression, linked arms supportively. 'Look, I know this is hard, but try not to think about Spencer for one night. Believe me, you're not missing anything. He'll be in some bar with some of his lawyer cronies, drinking red wine and telling that boring old joke of his . . .' She looked at Grace and they exchanged smiles. It felt like Grace's first smile in ages. 'So look on the bright side.' Grabbing two much-needed glasses of champagne from a passing tray, she handed one to Grace. 'At least tonight will have a different punchline.'

When Rhian had mentioned her friend's thirty-fifth birthday party a few days ago and invited her along 'because you need cheering up', Grace had jumped at the invitation. Initially, after Jimi had told her she needed to get out more she'd been huffy and offended. What did he mean, get out more? She got out plenty. Every morning she caught the tube to work, spent the day in the office, and came back home again. Occasionally she varied this with trips to the gym, or Sainsbury's, or even Cullens if she was suffering from a late-night craving for a Tropical Solero. Until one night, over a week later she'd been sitting on the sheepskin rug in front of the telly, chipping off the frozen orange coating with her front teeth, when she realized he did have a point.

It was all very well moving out of Spencer's flat so they could have 'a break', but sitting in every night on the sofa watching Trinny and Susannah ridiculing some poor soul's passion for shellsuits wasn't going to resolve the problems in their relationship, give her the answers she was looking for, or conjure Spencer up on his bended knee on her doorstep. And it certainly wasn't going to help in the happiness stakes either. Shellsuits were, after all, deeply depressing at the best of times. But there was something else.

Call it arrogance, trust, or just faith, but she'd hoped that when faced with an ultimatum, Spencer would fight hard to save the relationship.

That he hadn't, had been a shock.

In the beginning it was the shock that had kept the tears and loneliness at bay. She'd broken the news to her friends and family, and for a few days it had all been dramatic, highly charged and very emotional, but now their shock was wearing off too, as was the frequency of their phone calls. Reality had set in.

211

Nothing was happening.

And now, like it or not, Grace was having to face up to the reality that she was on her own and there was no point staying in every night feeling sorry for herself. Be it temporary separation or a permanent split, she and Spencer were no longer a couple. Which meant she was, to all intents and purposes, single again.

And there was one problem.

Grace didn't want to be single again. Not that she hadn't loved being single in the past. In fact, it had been great in her twenties. She'd adored the merry-go-round of drinking, clubbing, copping off with random men in random bars around London. Everyone was doing it. It was fun, exciting, traditional, *the norm.*

But not now.

Now she wanted to be part of a couple.

May feminism strike her down, may every female author of every self-help book entitled *Single And Just Fabulous*, *All Men Are Shits* and *Sisters Are Doing It For Themselves And Finally Getting The Job Done* bind and gag her, but Grace couldn't help herself. Physically she might want to stop the clock and look like she was in her twenties – and she had a whole bathroom cabinet of anti-ageing creams and a botox brochure to prove it – but mentally she didn't want to act like she was in her twenties again.

But she wasn't the only one. It seemed that all around her twentysomethings were turning into thirtysomethings and settling down, having babies, eating organic. She only had to take a gander at the papers and see that even all the celebs were at it. Uma Thurman, Catherine Zeta-Jones, Cindy Crawford, *even Liz Hurley.*

She couldn't understand it. She'd grown up with these people and they'd moved on, and yet here she was, rapidly moving backwards. It was as if, thought Grace, the little car that was supposed to be taking her on the journey of life had unexpectedly got jammed in reverse. But then, as Rhian kept spouting, life was unpredictable, things didn't always go to plan, the universe was a wonderful, unpredictable and mysterious place.

Or, as Jimi had put it more bluntly: Shit happens.

'Mini tartlet?' demanded a waitress, thrusting a tray underneath their noses as they negotiated the giant fern in the hallway.

'No thanks, I've just eaten,' lied Rhian, smiling and patting her stomach so as to prove just how full it was. It growled emptily.

Rhian and Grace walked into the front room. It was a large, very traditional apartment. Space had been cleared by pushing back the two square white sofas against bookcases that lined an entire wall and appeared to be filled with lots of hardback political biographies and not a paperback chick-lit title, or *Time Out* city guide in sight. Opposite was a large, coal-effect fire with an imposing marble surround, three large windows with heavy drapes and pelmets – obviously somebody's mother had been hard at work at Peter Jones, noted Grace – while the expensive French oak floor filled with people drinking cocktails and politely grazing from the trays of nibbles that were doing the rounds.

Grace paused in the doorway, her eyes taking in the room in the time it took for her to take a sip from her glass. It was a reflex action. But it made her realize that being a single woman was a bit like riding a bike – scouting the room for attractive men at a party was something you never forgot – and for a moment she felt a rush of anticipation. It was the first time she'd allowed herself to see the benefits of her new status, but now, glammed up in a new dress, she felt confident, independent and, unexpectedly, just a little bit excited.

The party stretched before her filled with people she'd never seen before. She didn't know who she might meet, what she might talk about, and what might happen. It was like Rhian had said: she didn't know how the story ended any more. And whereas before, that thought had terrified her, filling her with dread and panic, now, totally out of the blue, the same thought hit her with a shot of adrenalin-fuelled freedom that surged through her veins.

The party itself seemed to be the usual mix of Moby on the stereo, the whiff of cigarette smoke, the buzz of smalltalk. Stirred by expectation, Grace followed Rhian into the thick of it and was revelling in the first taste of champagne when suddenly it dawned on her. While she was a single woman, so, by the looks of it, was every other person in the room.

'Where are all the men?' she hissed in confusion. Like the fizz of bubbles on her tongue, she felt the tingle of excitement quickly dispersing.

'What did I tell you?' Lighting up a cigarette, Rhian blew curls of smoke down her nostrils and gave her a righteous look. 'Welcome to the desert.'

For someone who'd been one half of a couple for as long as she could remember, it was a revelation. Hearing about it at second hand was one thing, but seeing first hand that it actually existed was something entirely different. Like an explorer who had just discovered a new world, Grace paused to take in this phenomenon. Stretching out before her were clusters of attractive females. Over the bookcase were the leather-trouser brigade chatting about polo and fiddling self-consciously with the gold necklaces they wore over their sleeveless turtle necks. Posturing and pouting by the stereo, comparing bellybutton jewellery and fake tan, were the Atomic Kitten wannabes sporting Mojo jeans and caramel highlights. Blondes or brunettes, skinny or buxom, ladettes or Sloanes, they had one thing in common. They were all single, all attractive.

And all female.

'I once read the statistic that an educated woman of

thirty has only a 20 per cent chance of ever marrying; and at forty she's got more chance of being murdered by a terrorist than finding a husband,' announced Rhian brightly, moving swiftly past a jug of puff pastry straws.

'You call this cheering me up?' groaned Grace, remembering Rhian's earlier promise. Rolling her eyes, Rhian offered her a cigarette as consolation.

Grace shook her head. 'No thanks, I think I'm going to need something stronger than nicotine to get through tonight,' she joked, trying to hide her disappointment as she realized that secretly she'd been rather looking forward to the novelty of having a bit of a flirt, of going to a party without Spencer or, for that matter, her engagement ring.

As she took a sip of champagne Grace glanced down at her bare fingers. Engagement rings were funny things: romantically they were a token of love, but in reality they were the modern-day chastity belt. Don't get her wrong, it wasn't as if she wanted to *sleep* with another man, but it would have been nice to at least *talk* to one. Unfortunately wearing an engagement ring had been like wearing a chaperone on her finger. A great big, glittering, £5,000 bouncer to frighten men off.

But now I'm able to talk to anyone I want, thought Grace, trying to revel in her new-found freedom and being hit by the ironic reality that actually she didn't *want* to talk to anyone. In fact the only person I want to speak to is Spencer, she realized sadly, overwhelmed by the desire to call him. She fought hard to resist. So many times these last few weeks she'd wanted to ring him, she'd even picked up the phone and started dialling, but she'd always hung up before it had connected. She couldn't ring him now. Even if the desire was so intense she could feel her eyes brimming with tears.

God, she missed him. She missed the strong arm around her shoulder, the wink across a crowded room, the smile that could make her legs turn to jelly. She missed their pet names and their in-jokes, his scrambled eggs on Sunday mornings and his fantastic shoulder massages. She missed snuggling up with him on the sofa watching crap TV, missed chatting to him while she soaked in the bath and he shaved in the sink. And most of all she missed sleeping with his warm body curled around hers, missed trusting and believing that he would never, ever let her go.

Feeling as if she was going to burst into tears, Grace sniffed briskly and gulped back the rest of her champagne. This was no good. She couldn't start crying at her first party. She was supposed to be having fun. She was *supposed* to be enjoying herself. Savouring the bittersweet bubbles, she felt more wretched than she'd ever felt before.

Glancing across at Rhian who was busy doling out cigarettes to the Atomic Kitten wannabes, she slipped quietly into the hallway and found herself in the kitchen. What was it with kitchens and parties? thought Grace, dabbing her watery eyes with a sheet of kitchen roll. Trying to regain her composure, she applied more lipgloss and drained the rest of her glass. The champagne seemed to have absolutely no effect. She still felt completely sober. Way too sober, she decided, tugging open the large fridge-freezer in search of something stronger. Champagne was delicious and celebratory and all that, but it only served to remind her of when Spencer had proposed. Now she was no longer a fiancée: she was single and at a party. The occasion demanded spirits.

A bottle of Absolut Citron eyeballed her from the freezer compartment. Pouncing on it, she located a tumbler in a cupboard and poured a generous amount into a glass. A vodka tonic maybe, she thought, looking around for some tonic. Or maybe not, she reconsidered, as it dawned on her that for once she wasn't going to have to spend the evening nervously watching Spencer getting drunk. Tonight it was her turn. Tonight *she* was going to get wildly, recklessly and liberatingly hammered.

In which case, sod the tonic, I'll make that a shooter, decided Grace. Buoyed up by the idea, she felt much better. Grabbing hold of the glass, she slugged back a large, defiant, empowering swig of Russia's finest.

Chapter Twenty-four

'Grab your coat. You've pulled.'

A male voice behind her caused the vodka to shoot up Grace's nose. Feeling as if her sinuses were on fire, she twirled around to see a freckled man in a pink Ralph Lauren shirt, his top lip curled up in what she could only guess to be a flirtatious smile. Oh Christ. Grace shuddered. Having second thoughts about her engagement ring, she wished she could be like Wonderwoman with her gold cuffs, and flash it at him to deflect his unwanted attentions.

'Excuse me?' she demanded, her voice unintentionally coming out all high-pitched and prudish. She felt her cheeks burn with a mixture of neat vodka and vanity. Why was it that any semblance of cool always eluded her when she needed it the most? She felt annoyingly flustered.

'If I said you had a beautiful body would you hold it against me?'

Rendered speechless by his appalling chat-up lines and his sheer nerve, Grace stared at him, bemused. Was this his idea of a joke? Was he being ironic?

Sadly, no.

'I'm Rupert,' he smirked, holding out his pudgy signet-ringed hand.

Obviously misinterpreting her blushes and speechlessness as flattered interest, he'd moved on to stage two. Introductions.

Well he could sod right off, thought Grace. She'd been looking forward to this party, she wasn't going to let some creep with a hairline that was so low it was in danger of joining up with his eyebrows hold her captive in the kitchen while he verbally wanked all over her.

'I'm Grace,' she smiled politely, noticing that instead of meeting her eye, he was staring at her tits. She shook his hand. It was moist.

'Amazing.' He winked, still holding her hand.

Oh Christ, stop, *please*. First the chat-up lines, and now that old chestnut, she groaned inwardly, looking for an escape route. But it was useless. With one hand up against the fridge, his fingers splayed like salamis, Rupert had formed a human barrier.

Swigging back the rest of her vodka with her free hand, Grace struggled to think of something to say. Anything. Anything at all. The weather maybe. Or that joke Stuart at work had told her. Her mind drew a complete blank. She couldn't even remember the punchline.

Luckily, or unluckily, depending on your point of view, Rupert had a punchline of his own. 'Let me guess.' Narrowing his eyes he pointed two fingers horizontally towards her and pulled an imaginary trigger with his thumb. '*Bang*. You're Aries.'

Grace was, quite literally, lost for words. God Almighty, this man was unbelievable. And there I was, wishing there were some men at the party, she thought, discovering just how true was the saying, 'Be careful what you wish for.'

'Impressive, huh?' he smiled modestly, mistaking Grace's mortification for sheer amazement. 'Star signs are a little hobby of mine,' he continued merrily. 'I work in the entertainment industry. Mixing with celebrities, hanging out with Robbie, doing lunch with Caprice . . .'

Grace stared as he shamelessly namedropped.

'. . . and it's always a good conversation opener.

Tends to put people at ease.' Sipping his champagne, he leaned closer as if to let her in on a secret. 'Robbie was very impressed. Now we're like that,' he winked, crossing his pudgy fingers and waggling them boastfully under her nose.

Grace recoiled. 'What a shame I'm Taurus,' she deadpanned.

'You must be on the cusp,' he retorted, without missing a beat. 'It's very common,' he consoled, taking his opportunity to pat her bare shoulder. 'Taurean passion combined with Arian endurance.' His small eyes glinted.

'Who needs Russell Grant, hey?' laughed Grace, trying to avoid his gaze. It was like that of a preying mantis.

Fortunately, a welcome diversion was caused by the sound of the front door opening and a sudden influx of male voices.

'Well, thanks for the horoscope.' Grace smiled, already mentally regaling Rhian with Rupert's one-liners. Being an astrological nut herself, she'd be bound to love the bit about the cusp. 'But I think I'll go and find a waitress and grab myself a glass of that champagne.' Draining her vodka, she waved her empty glass. 'If there's any left.'

'Well that's where you're in luck,' he winked, tapping the side of his fleshy nostril. Opening a cupboard door under the sink, he revealed a large bucket full of ice, and the gold tinfoil heads of Dom Perignon bottles buoyantly bobbing up and down. 'There's plenty.'

Now, under normal circumstances, discovering a secret stash of champagne at a party would have caused Grace to whoop with delight. But under normal circumstances I wouldn't be in the kitchen with some stranger who's visibly wearing a white vest underneath his shirt, she thought, watching Rupert grab a bottle and greedily unwrap the tinfoil. I'd have been with Spencer. And cracking open a bottle of champagne isn't the same if you're not sharing it with someone you care about, she thought sadly.

'By the way, what time is it?' chortled Rupert with satisfaction as the cork popped. Grabbing two champagne flutes he began pouring.

Hope rose like a helium balloon. 'Nine-thirty,' said Grace, glancing at her watch.

'Thanks.' He nodded and carried on pouring.

'Don't tell me.' Her mouth twitched mischievously. 'You've got to leave. Dinner with Robbie?'

'No.' Shaking his head, Rupert passed her a champagne flute and, clinking his against hers, gazed flirtingly into her eyes. 'I just want to know the exact moment we met so we can tell our children.'

Next door in the living room, Rhian wasn't having much better luck. Having spent the last fifteen minutes scouting the party for her old school chum, she'd failed to spot anyone vaguely recognizable. Too embarrassed to ask, and short of starting to hum that great Brother Beyond classic 'The Harder I Try' in the hope that the real Amanda would join in the chorus, she'd consoled herself with a cheese straw. Correction. Twenty-five cheese straws. Now, not only was she feeling like a big, puff-pastry pig, she was trying to work out how many meals she was going to have to skip to cancel out her misdemeanour.

Rhian seemed to spend her whole life adding, subtracting, multiplying and dividing foods on a points system. Rather proudly she refused to count calories, but had instead devised a whole different system. It worked on the principle of substitution. For example, one slice of pizza = coffee + milk + Candarel for breakfast and an apple + fat-free yoghurt for lunch. Added to this there was the size and variety of the pizza to take into account. Thin and crispy scored a different rating to deep-pan, which could send her whole food abacus into freefall, and quattro formaggio was a much higher rating than Neapolitan which actually allowed for an extra Cup-a-Soup. But then again, no amount of mental arithmetic could get away from the fact that she shouldn't be eating pizza in the first place.

'They're good, aren't they?'

A loud voice caused her to turn around and see a man, who looked to be in his sixties, nodding at her agreeably as he chewed on a cheese straw. Or perhaps that should be sucked, she corrected silently, faced with a perfect white smile that owed more to acrylic dentures and fixative than to any tooth bleaching.

Rhian felt her dream of being Cinderella and meeting a prince fade as reality struck. She wasn't in a fairytale, she was in the desert. And in the desert there were no thirtysomething, intelligent, handsome, single princes. Oh no, they'd all been snapped up a long time ago, she thought, feeling her eternal flame of optimism in severe danger of being snuffed out. And all that's left are twentysomethings like Noel or pensionable men like the one standing in front of me.

Flirting.

'I saw you standing by yourself. You looked rather lonely,' the stranger said, and continued masticating on his M&S cheese straw.

'Oh no, my friend's just popped to the loo,' Rhian heard herself lying, and was instantly racked with guilt for being so horribly ageist. That was terrible. So what if he was old enough to be her dad? So what if he had oversized earlobes and wrinkles where they joined his cheek? He's not flirting, he's just being friendly. Making smalltalk. It was a party, after all. As Rhian's cheerful optimism swiftly returned, she embraced it happily.

'My name's Rhian.' She held out her hand and smiled broadly.

'Marvin.' Shaking her hand he returned her smile, revealing the clumps of cheesy straw that had welded themselves to his unnaturally pale pink gums. 'Pleased to meet you.'

Rhian felt a rush of satisfaction. See. He was

probably a really nice old guy. He was probably Amanda's father. He'd probably introduce her to his wife any minute.

Finishing his cheese straw, Marvin dabbed his mouth with a paisley hanky that magically appeared from his sleeve, and, looking her directly in the eye, asked coyly, 'So, tell me. Are you single, Rhian?'

'So this is where you are. I wondered where you'd got to,' Rhian said as she appeared in the kitchen doorway.

Like a guardian angel, thought Grace, using her appearance as a diversion and extracting her hand from Rupert's then ducking underneath his arm in a kind of limbo manoeuvre.

Grace and Rhian smiled at each other. It was difficult to say who was more relieved.

'I should've known you'd be in the kitchen,' continued Rhian, innocently exchanging smiles with Rupert, completely unaware of Grace's strangulated expression. Compared to the OAP she'd just escaped from, Rupert looked positively gorgeous.

'Sorry, I was just leaving,' replied Grace hastily, linking arms with Rhian and trying to propel her out past the fridge-freezer.

'You're going?' protested Rupert, frowning petulantly.

Grace paused to look back. Her eye caught his salmon pink stomach trussed into a pair of chinos that were belted too tightly. A thought struck her. Was this the fate that awaited her if she didn't get back with Spencer? Men like Rupert?

''Fraid so,' replied Rhian, quickly cottoning on to Grace's feelings.

Fearing she'd read her mind, Grace glanced across at Rhian, but she was addressing Rupert. Having survived the split with Phil, Rhian had already undergone the initiation ceremony of the first party after a long relationship and she knew what a shock to the system it could be. Swiftly stepping in, she took control. If all else failed, she had a tried-and-tested way of getting rid of unwanted attention. Initially it had been said entirely innocently, but having seen its effect it was now her fail-safe method. Fixing Rupert with an apologetic expression she sighed loudly. 'You know what it's like. She can't keep the babysitter waiting.'

'Babysitter?' Rupert's jaw dropped.

'For the triplets,' smiled Rhian brightly.

'Triplets?' He was beginning to sound like a bad echo.

'Sorry, didn't I mention darling little Wayne, Shane and Dwayne,' tutted Grace, stifling a giggle. 'I was going to tell you, but we'd just been introduced and . . .'

'Don't worry, there's no husband to contend with,' winked Rhian, nudging him jovially in the stomach. 'The divorce came through when he was in prison.'

'Prison?' croaked Rupert.

'Fifteen years,' Rhian nodded, struggling to keep a straight face.

'. . . for manslaughter,' added Grace, unable to resist.

'Oh I wasn't,' he blustered. 'Worried. I mean.' Grabbing a flute of champagne, he drained it in one. 'I was actually in here to grab a glass of bubbly for the wife.' He laughed awkwardly, a glassy smile pinned to his face. 'Anyway, must be getting back. It was nice meeting you . . . er . . .'

'Grace,' prompted Grace, and then, revelling in his discomfort, couldn't help turning the knife. 'Amazing Grace, remember?' she said, smiling sweetly.

His ruddy cheeks paling under the halogen spotlights, Rupert clutched the flute to his chest and tried to pigeon-toe it out of the kitchen.

'Oh by the way . . .' Rhian stopped him in his tracks. He wasn't getting away so easily. 'Have you seen Amanda?'

'Amanda?' repeated Rupert. He looked baffled. 'Amanda who?'

'Amanda Bartley,' tutted Rhian. 'You *know*, she's the reason we're all here. It's Amanda's thirty-fifth,' she prompted, expecting a flicker of recognition.

Puckering up his squat forehead, Rupert peered suspiciously at her. 'You mean it's Russell Bonnington's fortieth.'

'Of course I don't,' gasped Rhian. 'I've never heard of Russell Bonnington. Why would I be invited to Russell Whatsisname's fortieth, for goodness sake?' She was beginning to lose her patience. 'Amanda and I were at college together, she emailed me and...' Rhian suddenly broke off. 'This is Queensbury Gardens, isn't it?'

'I thought you told the cabbie Queensbury Villas,' butted in Grace.

'Did I?' She shook her head. 'God I'm useless with addresses.' She laughed, and then her voice tailed off as she realized that both Rupert and Grace were staring at her.

'Oh dear,' she whispered, as it began to dawn on her.

'Oh yes,' nodded Grace, as it began to dawn on her too.

'Oh *really*?' gloated Rupert, as it dawned on him as well. His sheepish expression was quickly replaced by a self-satisfied smirk. 'How interesting. It appears I've found myself a couple of stowaways.' Now that the pendulum of power had swung back in his favour, he threw Grace a lingering look. 'Don't worry, I'll be merciful.'

Grace and Rhian exchanged looks.

'Remember the babysitter,' prompted Rhian.

'Oh yes,' said Grace. 'I mustn't keep her waiting.' And without saying another word they walked out of the kitchen, calmly collected their coats and, politely throwing Rupert a little backwards wave, disappeared out of the front door.

'Oh I get it,' called out Rupert. 'You're pulling my leg, aren't you? You couple of minxes,' he chuckled, expecting them to return at any moment.

The door slammed.

There was silence.

Followed by the sound of a loud, explosive, whooping snort and a burst of deep, velvety laughter that drifted up past the open window. Rupert rested his stomach on the stainless steel draining board, and peered out over the ledge.

Grace and Rhian, unable to hold it in any longer, had stumbled out onto the pavement. Illuminated by the orange glow of the street lamp, they were clinging together as they collapsed in an uncontrollable fit of giggles. Rhian's tiny mother-of-pearl clips danced in the light as she jigged up and down holding her aching ribs. Grace's naked cleavage was rising and heaving as she snorted with laughter, the flimsy material of her dress swirling over her creamy golden skin like chocolate sauce being poured over two perfectly round scoops of vanilla ice-cream that needed to be licked, and sucked, and devoured . . .

'Rupes!' a female voice hollered down the hallway.

Jolted from his lascivious reverie, Rupert realized that the little soldier in his chinos was standing stiffly to attention. 'Er, just coming, darling . . .' he stammered. It was Veronica, his wife. Immediately he felt his hard-on stand at ease and, with his cheeks blazing, he dutifully picked up her champagne. Damn. He'd meant to ask Grace what her favourite position was on extramarital affairs. Throwing one last, lustful glance backwards out of the window, he headed back into the party.

Chapter Twenty-five

'So what do you think?' said Jimi, turning to look at Grace.

'I think I've fallen in love,' murmured Grace, staring wistfully into what had to be the most gorgeous pair of chocolate brown eyes. 'What about you?'

Jimi paused, knitted his eyebrows together in deep thought, and then said gruffly in his flattest Mancunian burr. 'Nah, not my type.'

The following weekend, way too early in the morning, Grace had been woken by the piercing shrill of her mobile. It was Jimi in desperate need of a favour. Would she meet him at Battersea Dogs' Home?

'Why?' she'd groaned from the murky depths of her Union Jack duvet cover. It clashed nicely with the Mexican lanterns.

'Why do you think?' he'd laughed.

'What? You're getting a dog?' It took a while for Grace to fire on all cylinders.

'I've been toying with the idea for ages and so I thought, why not?' In actual fact, 'ages' was yesterday afternoon when, in an attempt to cure himself of his appalling case of writer's block, Jimi had scootered down to Notting Hill and planted himself outside a café on Westbourne Grove to do a spot of people watching.

Notting Hill was always great entertainment.

Yogalites, Socialites, Trustafarians, Wannabe-bohemians provided a real-life circus and sitting in his ringside seat with his strong latte Jimi had watched them all stream past, pouting, posing, prancing, preening. He and Kylie often used to sit there on a Saturday afternoon after they'd been to Portobello market, and for the first few minutes it had felt like old times. But then reality had kicked him in the stomach. It wasn't old times.

He was alone.

In a sea of couples.

There was the skinny brunette nuzzling her boyfriend's ear at the next table, a husband and wife cooing over their designer baby across the street, and right there, on the pavement in front of him, a girl who for a second had looked just like Kylie, lovingly entwined in an embrace.

His spirits had plunged. Oh shite. Normally he loved being the bachelor on the block, but now he just felt like a sad old man. Abandoning his coffee, he'd stood up and was about to get on his scooter and return home to his clean, trendy, lonely bachelor pad, when he'd spotted a Dalmatian tied to the lamppost opposite. 'Hey boy,' he'd sighed, reaching out to stroke its velvety head. Instantly he'd been swooped on by two very attractive females.

'Is that your dog? She's gorgeous,' they'd cooed as another female joined them. Then another. And another, until Jimi was surrounded. He'd always been popular with the opposite sex but even by his standards this was amazing. He'd never known such interest. He was a babe-magnet. Or rather the dog was, because as soon as the real owner arrived on the scene, his female fan club had quickly switched allegiance.

But it had got him thinking. Maybe getting a dog wasn't a bad idea. Maybe it was even a very good idea. In fact, why hadn't he thought of this earlier? They were the latest designer accessory. They were company. *Women loved them.* He could see himself now, walks in the park, throwing sticks, attracting the ladies.

'I've decided that from now on, it's just going to be one man and his dog,' announced Jimi decisively down the phone.

'Well in that case you don't need me,' said Grace. Suffering from a bad case of the booze blues she curled herself back up in the foetal position and prepared to snooze. There was silence. And then a curious whining started up at the other end of the line. 'What's that noise?' she asked, thinking it was interference on the line.

She should have known better.

'Oh nothing. Just a poor homeless stray at Battersea Dogs' Home,' said Jimi in a woeful tone. 'I thought it was going to be going to a new, warm, loving home, but now it's going to have to stay in its kennel, all lonely and sad and . . .'

'OK, you win,' sighed Grace defeatedly.

'I knew I could rely on you. I'll pick you up in twenty minutes, then.'

'*Twenty minutes?* Hang on . . .' But he'd already hung up.

And I'm going to have to get up, thought Grace. For a countdown of ten she lay in the warmth until, taking a deep breath, she forced herself to sit up. Only to completely forget she was sleeping on the mezzanine level, whack her head on the ceiling, and promptly crash back down again on her pillow.

'Six hundred pounds a month and every time I get out of bed I knock myself out,' grumbled Grace, rubbing her temples. 'It's not a studio, it's an assault course. If I'm not climbing up and down that bloody ladder, I'm crawling on all fours to reach the mattress.'

'Maybe you should take a leaf out of my book and sleep on the sofa,' suggested Jimi who still couldn't bring himself to sleep alone in his own bed. Reaching out he touched the purplish lump that was glowering at him from Grace's forehead. 'That bruise looks pretty bad.'

'Ouch, it is,' she yelped, throwing him a glare. And then realizing what he'd just said, she changed it to a look of sympathy. 'Are you still not sleeping in a bed?'

'Not mine anyway,' he winked.

She tutted with amusement. She'd walked right into that one.

'What about you? Pull anyone at that party you went to last weekend?'

Having spent the week before the party boasting to Jimi about what an amazing night she was going to have — thus making sure she was exploding the myth that she stayed in every night — Grace had spent the whole of the following week trying to avoid the subject as she was too embarrassed to admit the truth. 'Oh, I had to fight them off,' she said airily, fiddling self-consciously with the chunk of amber on her necklace. Well that was sort of true, she consoled herself, thinking of Rupert.

And then promptly trying not to.

She turned away and stared into the kennel. An adorable mongrel with big floppy ears and stumpy legs that were too short for its body wagged back. The nametag on the kennel read: FLOSSIE.

'Aww, how can you not love Flossie? She's beautiful.' Crouching down, Grace patted her wiry head.

'She's a mutt,' said Jimi dismissively. On the drive over he'd been daydreaming about his canine soon-to-be companion, feeling boyishly excited at the prospect of a towering Great Dane trotting next to him, or a pure-bred Weimaraner sitting regally on the front seat of his car, or even one of those magnificent salukis fetching sticks in the park. He looked at Grace. 'And anyway, I can't have a dog called Flossie. I mean, can you imagine? *Here, Flossie?*' At the sound of her name, the dog bounced up onto her hind legs, wagging her stubby tail appreciatively. 'I'd sound like a right idiot,' he grumbled, stepping backwards and digging his hands firmly into his combats.

'My God, I can't believe it. *You're a dog snob*,' exclaimed Grace, rounding on him.

'I am *not* a dog snob,' Jimi defended himself. 'I just want something a bit more . . .' Casting his eye over the kennels he spotted exactly what he was looking for. A few yards away a boxer was standing bolt upright, muscles bulging proudly from his hind legs, his ears cocked perfectly upright at a 90-degree angle, his short coat a glossy tan. He was staring stoically ahead like a statue. 'Like that,' announced Jimi. 'Now *that's* my dog.'

'But he looks so *boring*,' argued Grace, loyally turning to look at Flossie who promptly rolled over and began waving her legs in the air, proudly showing off the silvery-pink scar where she'd been spayed. 'Whereas Flossie's completely kooky, aren't you girl?' she cooed, slipping her fingers through the wire and tickling her soft, pink belly.

'Kooky!' snorted Jimi. 'I *don't want* kooky.' He eyed Flossie, who cocked her head on one side, raised a raggedy left ear, and eyed him back imploringly. He looked away hastily. He wasn't going to be won over by those big chocolate-drop eyes, the cute little wag of the tail, the paw up on his lap. He wasn't some big softie who got attached to a moth-eaten old stray. He knew exactly what he wanted. And it was right behind him. 'Nope, I certainly do not,' he said decisively. 'Not when you can have a handsome hound like that.' He gazed over at the boxer with admiration. 'Just look at him. He's a pure pedigree.'

'Don't listen to him, he's just been jilted,' Grace confided into Flossie's velvety ear as she watched him stride purposefully over to the boxer. 'He's anti-women at the moment.' Crouching down, she waited with Flossie to see the great 'one man and his dog moment'.

And then everything seemed to go into slow motion. There was Jimi, looking all cool and confident, making knowledgeable, clicking noises with his tongue and reaching out to stroke the magnificent beast to whom he would be master. And then there was the dog, opening its black, velvety mouth, baring its amazing set of white, pointy teeth, and, with one deft flick of its hackles, launching into the air like a missile.

Towards Jimi.

'*Yeeeeeoooooowwwwwww!*'

A blood-curdling scream ripped through the kennel. All at once the whole place erupted into a cacophony of barking, yapping, growling, howling.

'Jesus Christ, he just went for me. *He just tried to kill me.*'

'Oh my God, are you all right?' gasped Grace, staring at Jimi as he came sprinting towards her, the whites of his eyes bulging, his nostrils flaring, before promptly tripping over the laces of his Nikes and sprawling onto the floor in a heap.

He didn't move.

'Jimi? Are you OK? Did he bite you? *Are you bleeding?*' Grace jumped up with alarm. It was looking serious. She regretted her earlier humour. Panic set in. She began imagining severed fingers, chunks of flesh hanging off his face, micro-surgery to reattach ears. '*Jimi, will you answer me,*' she pleaded desperately.

There began a grizzly moaning. 'Ugghhh . . . aggghhhh . . . yeoowwww.'

Grace looked on with horror.

'. . . Oh fuck . . . Oh shitting hell . . . Oh fucking, shitting hell . . .' Then horrible gurgling noises.

Grace shrank back. Fearfully, she stared at Jimi who was writhing on the floor, flailing around and clutching at his face. Until just as suddenly as it had all begun, it stopped when Jimi realized that actually, there was hardly a scratch on him.

He sat up hurriedly. 'I'm fine, just took me a bit by surprise there,' he flustered, feeling like a complete wally. 'I think I might grab a coffee from the vending machine in reception. Coming?' he asked, rubbing his jaw, which was throbbing painfully.

Without waiting for an answer, he set off, limping. Maybe a dog wasn't such a good idea, he reconsidered, wincing at his twisted ankle. In fact, thinking about it, didn't he recently read an article about how goldfish were having a revival . . .

Five minutes later they were sitting on the wall outside, sipping plastic beakers of powdery Kenco and enjoying the patchy sunshine. It was still unnaturally mild, but the weather forecast had warned that this was to be the last day of good weather before it changed into the usual November gloom.

'Or so they said on the radio.' Grace shrugged, bouncing her legs against the wall, her Birkenstocks dangling from her copper nail-varnished toes. She looked at Jimi. He wasn't listening to her forecast, just staring into the middle distance with a faraway look on his face.

'What was that on the radio?' Absent-mindedly, he turned to her.

'Oh nothing.' Grace shook her head. 'Just a hurricane warning for West London. Apparently Kensal Green's going to be the worst hit. Mass destruction, tidal waves, global warming . . .' She shook her head again. 'Isn't that where you live?'

She waited for his reaction.

There was a pause. 'Er . . . yeah . . .' He nodded vaguely, tearing little patterns into the rim of his plastic cup.

Grace ran out of patience. 'What the hell is wrong with you?' she said, exasperated.

Jimi ripped a huge chunk from his cup, causing his coffee to slop over the edge. Sighing, he chucked it at the bin.

It missed.

'You know I mentioned a favour,' he began, looking at Grace, his eyebrows knitted together imploringly.

His expression made her suspicious. He looked like

233

Flossie. And Jimi would never normally look like Flossie, she reflected. He'd be the boxer. All proud, and arrogant, and cocksure. She eyed him warily. 'I thought this was the favour.'

'Not exactly . . .' He broke off, wondering how to put it. 'You see, I've got a bit of a problem.'

'What kind of a problem?' she asked. This could only mean one thing. Either he had to buy his mum a birthday present, or he needed some feminine advice about a medical condition. Men, Grace had learned, seemed to think women were all frustrated nurses.

Surprisingly, it was neither. 'Well, the thing is, the features editor from *Chic Traveller* called me up yesterday,' began Jimi. 'She wanted a bit of a chat, to bounce around a few ideas about this article I'm writing for them.' This wasn't so much a lie as what he liked to call the airbrushed version.

In actual fact, what had really happened was that the previous day, round about lunchtime, Jimi had been sitting with his feet up at his desk, playing patience on his laptop when his phone had rung. Expecting it to be Clive on his break, he'd dived on the handset and declared in a staccato voice, 'My name's Michael Caine. Not a lot of people know that.' It was a long-running joke between him and Clive, and one of those where you had to have been there. Unfortunately for him, the editor of *Chic Traveller* hadn't been there and, unamused, she'd barked down the earpiece, 'Could I please speak to Mr Malik?'

Scrambling his feet off the desk, he'd nearly capsized in his chair. 'Er, speaking.'

There'd been an odious pause. Jimi didn't have to be telepathic to see her recoiling from the handset. After a weighty silence she'd continued. 'Your article on New York?'

It was less of a question, and so much more of an accusation. 'Ah yes, I was meaning to call you.' This was a lie. Jimi had been putting off calling Tanya Stiff at *Chic Traveller* for the past few weeks, since Kylie had jilted him. He'd been commissioned to write a piece on 'The Big Apple', all easy-peasy stuff. He just had to spend a couple of nights there checking out the best bars, sampling the grooviest new cocktail, the wackiest club, and write up what it was like to spend a weekend on the other side of the Atlantic.

There was just one teensy problem. It wasn't supposed to be just any weekend. Or just any old holiday. It was supposed to be a honeymoon.

His honeymoon.

'You're due to fly out next Friday. We've arranged the hotel, the restaurants, the photographer in East Village is on standby, but we can't issue your flight tickets until we have your wife's name,' Tanya Stiff was ranting down his handset.

Jimi stared ahead. Oh fuck.

'Have you forgotten your wife's name already, Mr Malik?'

'Forgotten? Why, of course not.' He gave a hollow laugh. Sweat prickled his forehead. If he fucked this up he would never work for *Chic Traveller* again. There'd be no five-star trips to Barbados to check out the best spas in the Caribbean, no two-week jaunts to Arizona to report on ranches, no weekends in Cannes writing witty ripostes about the antics of the rich and famous.

In short, he would be saying farewell to his travel-writing career, not to mention half his income. Which meant that he was going to die a pauper, unless of course he ever managed to write his novel, and that was looking extremely unlikely. Jimi wasn't the world's literary expert, but he was pretty sure novels had to have a beginning, a middle, *and* an ending.

In short, this phone call was going to have the same effect on his career as a head-on collision at a hundred miles an hour, with no survivors, he thought, chewing the end of his Bic biro so hard the plastic crunched between his molars. He heard Tanya Stiff breathing heavily down the telephone. Actually no, on second thoughts that was him.

'Which is why,' explained Jimi, looking at Grace and gulping, 'I . . . er . . .' He paused, remembering that moment when he'd realized that if he wanted to get out of this alive, keep his career, his flat, his life and some kind of future, there was only one way out.

And he'd taken it.

'. . . I said her name was Grace Fairley.'

It took a second for Grace to register. 'You said I was your wife?'

Jimi gulped. 'Uh-huh.'

'That you're my husband?'

'Erm . . .' He fidgeted with excrucition. 'I guess so.'

'That we're *married*?' Grace shrieked. Jumping off the wall she waggled her arms around, spraying tiny flecks of coffee all over her white embroidered Indian top.

'*That we're going on honeymoon?*'

He looked remorseful.

'But you can't write this article, Jimi, it's a pack of lies.'

'It's called journalistic licence,' he tried to explain.

'It's called fraud,' she fired back.

'But what could I do?'

'What about telling her the truth?' she gasped.

'I couldn't.'

'Of course you could. You just didn't want to. You'd rather save your arse and land me in it instead,' Grace was shouting. 'You're just a selfish bastard, Jimi Malik.'

Round one over.

Now for round two.

'OK, so if that makes me selfish, I'm selfish!' Now Jimi was the one shouting. 'I'm selfish because my girl-friend jilted me and we didn't go on honeymoon. I'm selfish because I'm worried that if Tanya Stiff finds out, I'll lose all freelance work. I'm selfish because I've got writer's block, because I can't write this novel, because if I don't earn some money soon I won't be able to pay my mortgage. And I'm selfish because the only way I could think of solving all my problems was to say you were my wife.' He stopped as suddenly as he had started, took a deep breath, and looked at Grace. 'OK? *Satisfied?*'

He looked so desperate, and so horribly dejected, that Grace felt remorseful. 'Oh hell I'm sorry, Jimi.' Leaning over she squeezed his hand. 'It's just New York. I went there with Spencer . . .' Her mind flicked back four years. 'I just can't go back.' Grace shook her head apologetically. 'It would just be too weird,' she said and glanced at Jimi. 'You understand, don't you?'

There was a pause, and then Jimi smiled ruefully. 'Yeah, I understand.'

Scrunching up her plastic cup, Grace hopped down from the wall. 'C'mon, we better go back inside, tell them we're leaving empty-handed. Albeit with a few bumps and scratches,' she added teasingly.

'Yeah right,' said Jimi, and raising his sore buttocks off the wall, he followed her in through the swing doors.

'I'm afraid Jaws can be a bit frisky.' Chloe, the teenage kennel maid, gave Jimi a sympathetic look.

'Jaws?'

'The boxer,' she explained. 'It was his nickname and it sort of stuck.'

'Oh right,' said Jimi, looking embarrassed. 'Not my type anyway. A bit boring.'

He didn't meet Grace's glance.

'We like to call it set in his ways,' smiled Chloe, standing next to the open door of Jimi's Citroën. 'But I know what you mean.' She winked conspiratorially. 'Anyway, you made a perfect choice. I'm sure you two are going to have a long and happy life.'

Grace and Jimi looked at each other.

'She means the dog,' said Grace pointedly.

'I know,' sniffed Jimi. Taking the lead from the

kennel maid, he looked down at the short, floppy-eared mongrel that was sitting by his feet like a bundle of hair. Bending down, he picked her up. 'C'mon Flossie, let's go home,' he instructed, and then pulled a face as she planted a large doggy lick on the side of his face.

Grace laughed as Jimi patted the front seat. Obediently Flossie jumped up, sitting upright and looking out of the windscreen for all the world as if she'd done it a million times. Jimi climbed in next to her. 'Sure you don't want to come along?'

'Thanks, but my friend Maggie's in Spain and I promised I'd pop in and feed her fish. She doesn't live far from here.'

'I meant New York.'

Grace shook her head. 'No thanks.'

'Definitely?'

'One hundred per cent.' She folded her arms firmly. 'You can beg, you can bribe, you can say what you want, but you won't change my mind. Read my lips. I am not going to New York.'

Chapter Twenty-six

'I'm going to New York.'

'New York, *New York*?' exclaimed Rhian.

'So good they named it twice,' sang Grace, wedging the phone under her chin to continue packing her weekend bag. After enduring five days of being stalked by Jimi's desperate phone calls, begging text messages and grovelling answering-machine messages – in one day he'd managed to fill her entire tape with twenty-six – guilt and pity had gnawed away at her. She was being a terrible friend. She was being horribly selfish. She was going to have to deal with bad karma for the rest of her life.

But she'd still refused to go.

Until that morning in the office. She'd been on the phone when she'd heard call-waiting, innocently picked up, and been serenaded with an appalling, off-key rendition of Sinatra's 'New York, New York'. It had finally broken her. Unable to take any more she'd given in and agreed to go.

But if she was honest there was also another reason for her change of heart. She'd been dreading spending another weekend in London by herself. Weekdays she kept herself busy with work, meeting friends, the odd jaunt to the gym, but weekends were Couple Central and she usually found herself at a loose end and missing Spencer. Spending this weekend in New York with Jimi was going to be very weird, but she was secretly glad of the diversion. And – although she hated to say it for fear of sounding like her grandmother – the *company*.

'Are you going with Spencer?' demanded Rhian, putting her on speakerphone and walking across the bedroom. She had that awful, disorientated feeling of arriving late at the movies, stumbling into the darkened theatre and, having missed the first vital twenty minutes, struggling to understand what was going on.

'No of course not,' tutted Grace, rummaging in her sock drawer, trying to find a pair that matched. 'I'm going with an ex.'

Having sat down at her dressing table, Rhian had unscrewed a tub of Nivea and was daubing industrial-sized dollops of Nivea onto her T-Zone. 'Not Matt McAndrew?' she gasped, smearing with the intensity of a cross-Channel swimmer. 'Oh my Lord, he was gorgeous.'

'And a two-timing bastard,' reminded Grace drily. 'The last I heard he was married with a couple of kids.'

'Aren't they all,' sniffed Rhian, pushing up her sleeves and dipping each elbow in turn into the tub of Nivea.

'No, this is an ex from years ago, when I was eighteen and living in Manchester. *He was the first*,' added Grace, unable to resist putting on a cheesy American accent.

'Awww, that's so romantic,' beamed Rhian, perking up at the whiff of romance.

'Erm . . . well . . . not exactly,' corrected Grace. 'Jimi Malik stole my virginity, broke my heart and I never saw him again. Until a few weeks ago at Zagora's . . .' Spying a matching stripy sock wedged right at the back, she tugged it out triumphantly.

Three miles away on the other end of her purple see-through telephone, Rhian was finding this all very confusing. 'You never told me this.'

'Didn't I?' continued Grace absent-mindedly.

'No you didn't,' said Rhian, miffed that she'd been denied this nugget of gossip. 'Why, what happened?'

'Oh, it was on my birthday when Spencer drove off and left me. I ended up sharing a cab with him.'

'You got in a cab with the man who stole your cherry? I'd have punched his lights out.'

Grace couldn't imagine Rhian trying to punch anything. Her violent tendencies just about extended to vacuuming up spiders. 'Have you ever been in a minicab rank at midnight on a Friday?' she asked pointedly.

Massaging her elbows, Rhian gave a little shudder. Just walking past builders sent her into apoplexy. 'Fair point,' she agreed. 'I would have got in the cab. *Then* I'd have punched his lights out.'

'You're telling me you're taking this Grace person all the way to New York for the weekend and you don't want to sleep with her?' Cradling his chips in their newspaper crib, Clive picked up the bottle of vinegar and began drowning them in Sarsons. 'Not even a little bit?'

'No,' replied Jimi, hungrily reaching out for the piece of crispy, golden haddock the shop assistant was serving him over the Formica counter. Fresh out of the deep-fat fryer it was sizzling with tiny bubbles of grease. 'Not even a little bit.'

It was after last orders and Jimi and Clive were standing in Mike's fish and chip shop, bathed in fluorescent light, the pungent aroma of boiling hot beef dripping, moist newspaper and plenty of salt'n'vinegar. They were talking about Grace. Having spent the previous week badgering her, that morning Jimi had been on the brink of calling up Tanya Stiff, confessing his lie and murdering his career, when his phone had rung. It was Grace. She'd said yes.

It had been one of those 'man from Del Monte' moments. Jumping up from his chair he'd punched the air, yelled at the top of his lungs and rung Clive to invite him out for a celebratory beer. Not an interrogation he thought grumpily.

'So what's wrong with her?' Clive was still reeling from the shock of discovering that not only did Jimi have a female friend, but that he was taking her away for the weekend to do an article. He put down the vinegar and began liberally sprinkling on the salt.

'Why should there be something wrong with her?' Grabbing the salt cellar from Clive before he gave himself a coronary, Jimi hurried him on to the pavement outside, where Flossie was patiently waiting for them, head resting on her paws.

'Because if there wasn't, you'd want to sleep with her,' said Clive matter-of-factly.

'You make me sound like a tart.' Bending down, Jimi clipped on Flossie's leash and the three of them set off down the high street.

'That's because you *are* a tart,' retorted Clive good-humouredly. His joking hid a pang of envy. He'd just spent an evening in Q&A, a new bar that was apparently *the* place to see and be seen, but whereas Jimi had seamlessly blended in, immediately getting served, flirting with a bunch of hip, attractive females, he'd propped up the bar being ignored.

'Or I should say you were before you met Kylie,' corrected Clive, throwing a chip in the air for Flossie, who caught it with a snap of her jaws.

At the entrance to his flat, Jimi unlocked the door and flicked on the light. 'Grace only agreed to come with me to save my career. She's doing me a favour.' Letting Flossie race ahead up the stairs, he turned to Clive. 'Anyway, for your information, Grace has got a fiancée.'

'I thought you said she'd left him.'

'They're having a break.'

'That's just a way of softening the blow,' said Clive knowledgeably, waggling a soggy vinegar-soaked chip at him.

'No it's not,' retorted Jimi. Whereas before he'd been

the one saying that to Grace, now hearing Clive saying it he suddenly felt defensive. 'She just needs some time and space,' he explained, and then frowned. He'd been spending so much time with Grace, he was beginning to sound like her.

'So what about the poor guy she's supposed to be marrying? Doesn't he get a say in this?' argued Clive, finishing the last of his chips and scrunching the paper into a tight ball. 'I thought you of all people would be on his side.'

'It's not about sides.' Jimi felt decidedly uncomfortable with the way the conversation was progressing. 'It's not that black and white.' Oh shite. There he went again – sounding like Grace. But now he'd started there was no stopping him. 'This *poor guy* had two years to have his say. They were engaged for two whole years but he refused to set a date.' He felt a tinge of pride. *Set a date.* See, he was really getting the hang of all this wedding lingo.

'What did I tell you,' pounced Clive jubilantly. 'There must be something wrong with her.'

Jimi was beginning to lose his patience. 'Yes – I mean no, no there isn't.' He was infuriated. 'OK so she's clumsy, but that's more endearing than annoying, and I'd be the first one to admit she can be as stubborn as hell, but that's good, it shows she knows her own mind.' He began climbing the staircase to his loft. 'She's funny and intelligent – do you know what her favourite movie is? *The Italian Job.*' He looked over his shoulder at Clive who was following up the stairs. A look of respect and admiration passed between them.

'But don't get me wrong, I know what you're thinking. You're thinking I'm saying she's got a great personality because she looks like the back end of a bus,' admitted Jimi. 'But she's actually really pretty in a sort of small, dark . . .' he fished around for a word and then stole Grace's, well if he was going to sound like her why not go the whole hog? '. . . in a *kooky* kind of way.'

Unlocking his flat, he flicked on the dimmer switch. A series of cleverly positioned down-lights threw subtle lighting across the room. It had always been a big hit with the girls he brought back but now it seemed a bit redundant. 'I'm used to women in head-to-toe black, a pair of Gucci heels, a diamond Tiffany cross, not a pair of flip-flops with great big flowers stuck on them and a piece of amber tied around her neck as if she's just got back from Glastonbury. But now I think she looks really cool,' he added, smiling dreamily to himself. An image of Grace popped up in his mind and his stomach did a funny kind of flutter, his skin went tingly, and inside he felt a weird glowing.

And then he caught Clive's expression.

It brought him up short. 'Cool, but definitely not sexy, no, not at all,' he corrected, shaking his head determinedly. 'Nah, there's absolutely nothing going on between us. Absolutely not. She's just a mate.'

'*Just a mate?*' echoed Clive, his mouth twitching.

'Look, I don't want to sleep with her, OK?' insisted Jimi. But Clive looked unconvinced. 'I don't,' he declared. 'And you know why? Because we've *already* slept together.'

Clive's jaw dropped with astonishment. 'Forgive me, but how does this support your argument?'

'Well it's like that saying, isn't it?' stammered Jimi.

'What saying?' demanded Clive.

Feeling himself blushing scarlet, Jimi retorted hotly. 'Lightning doesn't strike twice.'

'On honeymoon?'

Having just been told the real reason for the trip, Rhian was aghast. '*You're going on honeymoon.*' She repeated it as if somehow that would make it seem less crazy. It didn't.

'Not really,' corrected Grace. 'We're just pretending.'

Rhian was beginning to wonder if her friend had taken leave of her senses as well as her fiancé. 'And I suppose he's going to want you to pretend to sleep with him, is he?' she challenged. 'That has to be about the best excuse I've heard to get a woman into bed. And believe me, I've heard a few.'

'Of course I'm not going to sleep with him,' argued Grace. 'And anyway, who says he wants to sleep with me anyway?'

On the other end of the line there was the sound of pages being flicked through. 'When men see an attractive woman, they fantasize about sex. When women see an attractive man, they fantasize about a relationship,' read Rhian, quoting from a magazine article. 'It's true. It's here in black and white.'

'I don't care what colour it's in,' retorted Grace. 'It's not true. I don't want to have a relationship with Jimi. Absolutely not. We've just got to have a few photos taken and pretend, you know, gazing into each other's eyes, looking all gooey.' Deliberating between a pair of white flares or embroidered suede trousers she chucked both in. 'I mean come on, how hard can it be? I've seen *Green Card*. It'll be a doddle.' She felt a flutter of excitement. To be honest, she was beginning to look forward to the trip. It was such a mad, crazy, wild thing to do, it secretly appealed to every impulsive bone in her body.

'So this guy is single?' Rhian was like a dog with a bone.

'Technically – yes,' said Grace, turning her attention to footwear. She was now rifling through her cupboards on hands and knees. 'Emotionally, no. I reckon he's still in love with his ex-fiancée, although he vehemently denies it.'

'Really? Some people,' said Rhian, without a hint of irony.

'The poor thing, he was jilted the morning after his stag night. They were at Zagora's on my birthday – do you remember?'

'You mean he was with the stag party who knocked the wine over Spencer?' Putting down the magazine and picking up the handset, Rhian climbed into bed and propped herself up against the pillows. In her flowery pyjamas she felt like Doris Day waiting for her Rock Hudson.

'Oh yeah, I forgot about that,' said Grace, remembering Spencer's furious face.

'Wow, that's got to be fate,' cooed Rhian.

'No it was just a coincidence,' corrected Grace pragmatically. 'And anyway, it wasn't actually Jimi who knocked the wine over Spencer, he was on the dance floor . . .'

'Whatever,' dismissed Rhian, being carried away on a delicious wave of superstition and not really listening. 'Anyway, from what I remember he was rather cute.'

Unearthing a hideous pair of silver stilettos, Grace frowned. 'You did?'

'And you don't?' Listening to her stomach grumbling, Rhian spotted a packet of Silk Cut on her bedside table and eyed them hungrily.

'Well, I hadn't thought about it really . . .' A flashback of the kiss in the minicab sent a tingle through Grace's body, right down to the soles of her feet. She wriggled her toes, remembering the sensation of his lips against hers, her heart racing, her mind reeling, her groin aching. 'He's just a friend,' she stated firmly.

'That you happened to have had sex with.'

'Thirteen years ago,' reminded Grace, relieved that the feeling had passed as quickly as it had appeared. 'I don't fancy him any more, and he doesn't fancy me. To be honest, it's a good thing we slept together so now we can be friends without the whole sex thing getting in the way.'

'Mmmm,' agreed Rhian disbelievingly. In her experience, sex always got in the way. Leaning over, she flicked on her radio-alarm clock.

'What's that noise?'

'Oh that – it's the radio.'

In the background Grace could hear the slick banter

of a DJ '. . . *so good evening listeners and welcome to tonight's show. We'll start with a letter from Nina in Battersea that I read out last week . . .*'

'Oh marvellous,' whooped Rhian, giving in to the temptation and lighting up a Silk Cut in celebration. Sod Doris Day, she thought, taking a drag. Smoking in bed. And a single mother. What would the *Daily Mail* say?

'What show?' Grace was intrigued.

'*Do You Come Here Often?*'

'Crikey, you and Rupert should get together,' she joked. She still hadn't been able to forget his terrible chat-up lines from the party.

'It's supposed to be ironic,' said Rhian huffily. 'People write letters, or ring up to try and mend their broken hearts or to get help in their search for Mr Right, or sort out their love lives. It's a bit like *Jim'll Fix It*, except you don't get a badge.'

'Oh I think I've listened to that show before . . .' Grace tailed off as her mind flicked back to the taxi she'd shared with Jimi. It seemed there was to be no getting away from it.

'It's riveting. Turn it on if you don't believe me,' interrupted Rhian.

'I don't have a radio,' she stalled.

'What about your Walkman?'

A few birthdays ago Spencer had bought Grace a state-of-the-art, jogproof CD/radio to encourage her to take up running. So far she'd only ever worn it on the tube. Appeasing Rhian she unearthed it from underneath her clothes and stuck one earpiece in her ear.

'What frequency?'

'Ssssshhhh,' cut in Rhian. 'You're making me miss it.'

'But I can't find it,' grumbled Grace, furiously twiddling the dial past a medley of Blue, Westlife, Oasis . . . until . . .

'. . . *last week I told you about Nina who's thirty-five and single,*' the DJ was chuntering away '. . . *and we've*

*been inundated with calls. First on the line was John,
he's thirty-six and a fireman . . .'*

'Mmm,' Grace and Rhian both made favourable
noises.

'. . . *and he wanted to take Nina away for the weekend to his log cabin in Scotland, so they can snuggle
up in front of an open fire . . .'*

'Awww,' they sighed in unison.

'. . . *and then there was Gavin who wanted to wine
and dine her, and Russell who sent a text saying, "B
Mine." A man of few words, hey?'* The DJ gave a tinkly
laugh.

'I'd go for the fireman,' said Rhian decisively.

'Me too,' agreed Grace. 'I mean, you can't turn down
a fireman, can you?'

'Uhmmmm, I don't know, Gavin did sound rather
nice,' mused Rhian, changing her mind.

'Sshh, stop talking,' hissed Grace, now completely
hooked.

'*But before I let you know who she chose to mend
her broken heart, here's everyone's heartstopper, Frank
Sinatra and "Someday . . ."*'

'I need some music.' A few miles away in Kensal
Green, Jimi flicked on his stereo. Frank Sinatra filled
the living room.

'I need a spliff,' groaned Clive, dropping onto the
sofa and digging out his Rizlas and tobacco.

'. . . *so listeners, back to Nina in Battersea. Well,
after a long and difficult choice, she's decided that
John the fireman is the one for her. And we've got her
on the line to tell us why. Hi, Nina? . . .'*

As the song faded out and the DJ's voice struck up,
Jimi's forehead split into deep furrows. He squinted at
the frequency. Hang on a minute, this wasn't Virgin.
'Have you been messing with this stereo?' He glared
accusingly at Clive.

'Hey, never touched it,' he protested, waving a white
Rizla flag.

'. . . *Hi, Dr Cupid,*' a female voice boomed loudly across the airwaves.

'*Hiya, welcome to the show, Nina. So come on, what made you realize John was the one for you? Is it true women can't resist a man in uniform?*'

There was a loud hoot of laughter. '*True, true, but that's not the reason I chose John. I chose him because as soon as I heard his voice on the radio last week I knew we'd hit it off. He just sounded such a cool guy.*'

'What on earth is this load of bollocksy claptrap?' Jimi was now glaring accusingly at the stereo.

'Actually it's not that bad,' piped up Clive, taking a long, luxurious drag. 'The nurses have it on at work and I've caught it a couple of times.' He took another drag and passed the spliff. 'Last week they had this letter from a bloke called Derek who was in love with his girlfriend's mother,' he shook his head. 'It was a really sad love triangle . . .'

Jimi inhaled the joint. 'How strong is this bloody stuff?' He looked at Clive in disbelief.

'*Well, well, well, Nina, that's fantastic. So c'mon, let the listeners into a secret. Did John keep his promise and whisk you away to his log cabin in Scotland? And better still, did you snuggle in front of the fire . . .*'

'A log cabin in Scotland? Snuggling up to the fire? Do you think women really go for all that stuff?' Jimi looked at Clive, who was lying outstretched on the cushions, a sentimental smile on his face.

'*. . . We did a little more than snuggle,*' giggled Nina mischievously.

'*Hahaha, that's just great, Nina. I'm glad to hear you're sounding so much happier.*'

'*Oh I am, I am, I haven't been this happy for ages. Thanks, Dr Cupid.*'

'*Hey, don't mention it, that's what I'm here for! So, remember, listeners, if you've got problems of the heart, write me a letter*' – an irritating jingle began playing – '*or you can call us here at* Do You Come Here Often? . . .'

Jimi reached for the dial and turned off the radio in disgust.

'Hey I was enjoying that . . .' complained Clive.

'That's what worries me,' groaned Jimi, running his thumb along his alphabeticized CD cases. 'I mean, c'mon. What kind of person rings up a national radio station to try and meet someone? You'd have to be desperate – ' he shook his head in disbelief – 'or a sad git.'

'Or someone who just happens to be going on his own honeymoon with an ex because he's been jilted,' muttered Clive, his eyes closed.

With his back to him, Jimi could feel Clive's smile burning a hole through his shoulderblades. 'Yeah right.' He forced a hollow laugh, and plopping a disc into his CD drive, he thankfully pressed play.

Chapter Twenty-seven

A rakish wolf whistle streaked across the gentle evening hum of chirping crickets.

'Aye Señorita, you look fantastico.'

'Why *gracias* Señor Sonny, so do you.'

Blushing like a schoolgirl in her sundress, Maggie paused to complete a little twirl as she walked barefoot down the terracotta-tiled steps of the Spanish villa. Their Spanish villa.

They'd flown out to Málaga a week ago, hired a rentacar and begun their drive north-west. After blasting up the motorway they'd turned off and headed into the hills, screeching and braking up steep and dangerously windy roads for what seemed like hours. Finally, when Sonny's frayed nerves couldn't take any more of Maggie's driving and her treacherous habit of pointing out a lovely bit of scenery just as they were reaching a hairpin curve, they'd glimpsed it.

A higgledy-piggledy cluster of whitewashed houses and a tall, proud church spire clinging precariously to the very edge of the hillside. This was the vibrant, bustling village of Jerez de la Frontera. A picture postcard slice of cobbled streets, old women dressed in black, and colourful Mediterranean markets.

It was to be their new home.

'This is the life, hey?' Below on the terrace, swamped with an abundance of geraniums, bougainvillaea and dozens of brightly patterned plates pinned to the walls, Sonny was waiting for her. Freshly showered and doused in aftershave, his wisps of grey hair appearing almost white against his dark suntan, he looked like a negative from a photograph. He was holding a bottle of ice-cold Cava. They were flying back to London in the morning to organize the move – Maggie had to work out her notice, he had to hand over the barber's shop to its new owner, and they both had to say farewell to their friends in Streatham. But although they might not yet have officially started their new life, he had the keys to it in his pocket, and he wanted to celebrate.

'It sure is, doll,' smiled Maggie, sliding her arm around the waist of his freshly pressed Hawaiian shirt. He was a whole head taller than her and standing on her bare tiptoes she kissed him lightly on his mouth, tutting as his whiskers tickled. 'I thought you were going to have a shave.'

'I thought I'd go native,' grinned Sonny, pulling her closer and, stooping down, nuzzling his face against hers.

'Hey, gerrroff,' she complained. 'You'll mess up my make-up.' But Maggie was laughing as she pretended to swat him away, enjoying the feeling of his burly arms wrapping themselves around her bare shoulders so she couldn't escape.

Not that she wanted to. Sonny was everything Maggie had ever wanted. From the moment she'd laid eyes on him on the dance floor at Hammersmith Palais she'd known he was the one for her. He'd simply walked right up to her, held out his hand, and asked her to dance. It had been as simple as that.

'I mean, just take a look at the view, you can't put a price on that,' he said, gesturing with a tilt of his head. Below them stretched the sweeping valley. Dotted with olive groves, sprawling farms and a silver ribbon of river, it was bathed in the mango glow of the sunset. It was a world away from the grey concrete jungle that was the view from their high-rise flat in Streatham.

Turning to Maggie, he affectionately stroked her damp, newly washed hair. Sonny thought she had the most amazing hair. Most women cut their hair short when they grew older, but Maggie's fell over her shoulders in a mahogany curtain that skimmed the bottom of her waist in a straight, blunt line.

'Have you ever seen anything so bloody gorgeous?'

'Oi, I thought I was supposed to be the most bloody gorgeous thing you've ever seen,' teased Maggie.

'Did I say that?' Sonny frowned. 'Must have been all that sangria,' he said, raising an eyebrow jokingly.

'Or too much sun,' she chided, tapping his peeling nose with the end of her finger. She felt a warm rush of happiness. For years they'd dreamed of this moment, about giving up work and finding their place in the sun, and now they were actually living it. Inhaling the warm, balmy Mediterranean air, scented with lemon and honeysuckle, she snuggled into Sonny's sunburnt chest. She'd waited a long time for this moment. Nothing could spoil it.

Could it?

A lingering fear stirred deep within. A fear which had crept into her heart that evening in her bathroom six weeks ago and lodged there. It greeted her every morning she awoke, looked over her shoulder all day, and was there to say good night as she turned out the light. At first she'd tried to ignore the fear, dismiss it, pretend it wasn't there, but like the lump in her breast it wouldn't go away. Finally she'd plucked up courage and seen her GP, who'd duly examined her, told her not to worry, and then promptly sent her off to hospital 'for tests'. To be honest, as terrified as she was of the outcome, it had been something of a relief.

The breast cancer clinic had been filled with women of all ages, and she'd taken her place and realized she wasn't special, she wasn't different, and she wasn't the only one. Then her name had been called and there'd been no time for self-reflection because as soon as she'd shaken hands with the specialist it was as if a big wheel had been set in motion and she was plunged onto a steep learning curve. He'd used words she'd never heard before – fibroadenoma, lumpectomy, needle core biopsy – and some she had – mastectomy, chemotherapy, tumour – then before she knew it, she was moving from room to room, meeting a succession of people, undergoing a mammogram, ultrasound scan and fine needle aspiration. The procedures were uncomfortable, but relatively painless, and it all seemed to happen so quickly that before it had even begun to sink in she was back at home in time for *Neighbours*. Back to normality. It was almost as if it had never happened.

Almost.

A letter from the hospital had arrived the morning they'd left for Spain. Her future folded neatly in a small brown envelope that had slid incongruously through the black nylon brushes around her letterbox and fallen onto her welcome mat. It had been 9.06 a.m. Maggie knew the time exactly because they were leaving for the airport and she'd been working diligently through her regimental list of 'to do's – pulling out the plug of the kettle, turning the TV off standby, setting the light timers – when she'd seen it. Just lying there. Waiting to be opened.

But there hadn't been time. Breathing to the beat of punctuality, she'd quickly picked it up, popped it in her handbag along with her passport, and locked the front door behind her. She had a plane to catch, a house to buy, a future to get on with, she'd told herself, joining Sonny and the suitcases in the cab downstairs.

She would read it later.

Except later had never arrived.

The cork from the bottle of Cava made a loud pop.

''Fraid I couldn't find any glasses,' apologized Sonny, hastily pouring the frothy amber liquid into two cracked, old mugs and passing her one.

'Don't worry, it still tastes the same,' she said, hastily taking a sip to mask the taste of fear in her mouth.

'Hey, we haven't done the toast yet,' he grumbled.

Holding out his flowery mug, Sonny met her gaze. 'Here's to the rest of our lives.'

Maggie hesitated. Despite the Cava her mouth had gone very dry. 'To the rest of our lives,' she echoed, struggling to return his smile as she clanked her mug against his.

'So what time's the flight tomorrow?' Never able to sit still long, things were already whirling around in Sonny's brain. Getting back to the UK, organizing the removal people, finalizing a few details with the solicitors. The young couple who'd bought their flat were due to move in in a few weeks and he had to get things ready.

'Er . . . I think it's eight-thirty,' she said doubtfully.

Sonny looked shocked. 'Are you feeling all right?'

Maggie tensed. For weeks she'd kept her secret hidden from Sonny, she hadn't wanted to worry him. But had he found out? 'Yes, of course,' she shot back defensively. 'Why shouldn't I be?'

'Because I think that must be the first time in nearly thirty-seven years you don't know the exact time, down to the last second,' he said and smiled affectionately.

'Oh . . . yes . . . I know.' She felt her panic subsiding.

'It must be the sun.' Sonny grinned, running his sandpapery thumb down the side of her cheek.

Still agitated, she turned away. 'The tickets are upstairs in my handbag. I'll just check . . .' she began, turning to walk back into the villa, but Sonny stopped her.

'Don't be daft, I'll get them, Mags, you put your feet up.' He tugged out a sunlounger and promptly eased her into it. 'There you go, you've been running around all day. Just relax,' he murmured, topping up her mug. 'And get that down you.'

As his footsteps tapped quietly against the tiled staircase, Maggie closed her eyes, breathing in the warm air, feeling the thudding of her heart beginning to slow. She wriggled comfortably in the sunlounger, its canvas fabric still warm from the sun, and she brushed back the hair from her forehead. Sonny was right. She just needed to relax.

'Mags?'

On the verge of nodding off, Sonny's voice woke her. As her eyelids slowly broke apart she glimpsed his white-shirted figure through her eyelashes. He was walking towards her, his gold watch catching the last of the light, his sturdy calves stuffed into his socks which in turn were stuffed into his sandals. She was going to have to do something about that, she decided silently, opening her eyes fully and sitting upright.

Which is when she noticed what he was holding in his hand.

An envelope. *The envelope*. Every detail was magnified. The envelope's creased corner where it had been squashed in her bag, the black stamp that bore the name of the hospital, the blue smudged scribbles of her name and address.

Dragging her eyes upward, she met his gaze. His smile had gone and he looked quietly scared.

'It's from the hospital,' he rasped, his voice barely audible.

'I know, I didn't want to worry you . . .' she began trying to explain hurriedly.

But he didn't let her finish. 'Are you going to open it?'

She fell silent. There was no need for explanations. By the expression on his face, he knew. After bottling up her secret fear for so long, a tear trickled down her face. Nine times out of ten it would be a false alarm, but she was hopeful, not naïve. She was fifty-five years old. She smoked a pack of cigarettes a day. She'd found a lump in her breast. Nine out of ten still meant there was one left over. Was she the one? She stared with fear at the envelope. She didn't know what it said inside. She didn't want to know. Twisting a strand of hair around her finger, her voice trembled. 'I daren't. Will you do it?'

Sonny looked at Maggie. Crumpled up on the sun-lounger she looked like a small, frightened little kid. He walked over to her, kneeled at her bare feet and gently wiped away the tear that was spilling down her cheek. 'No, Mags, I won't,' he whispered. Placing the letter in her lap, he gently held out his hand. The same hand he'd offered her all those years ago when he'd asked her to dance. And as Maggie's fingers gently interlaced through his, he gazed at her with solid, unflinching determination.

'We're going to do this the way we've always done things. *Together*.'

Chapter Twenty-eight

The view from the Empire State was amazing.

Or at least it would be, cursed Grace, if she got a chance to look at it instead of the huge Nikon lens that was being shoved right in her face.

'Oh c'mon, you pair of adorable lovebirds. Heads just a little closer, flash those great big smiles, turn those bods some more towards the camera.' Brady, raving queen and New York photographer was enthusiastically barking out instructions while she and Jimi cuddled stiffly on the observation deck, cheesy smiles plastered on their faces, trying desperately to look like a couple of newlyweds.

'Oh purleasse, you guys. Think Joan Armatrading. Think love and affection. *Purleasse.*'

It was Friday afternoon and Grace and Jimi had been in New York a grand total of three hours. They'd been due to land at JFK at lunchtime, but unfortunately their plane had been delayed and they'd arrived late. Too late to check into their hotel room, according to the frazzled representative who'd met them in a state of nervous exhaustion, harping on about 'the schedule' and bundling them into a yellow cab. Immediately they'd been whisked uptown to meet the photographer and his assistant and despite being tired from the seven-hour flight and the time difference, had spent the whole afternoon trying to create suitably honeymoon-like poses in various New York hotspots.

It had been mortifyingly embarrassing. Apparently, it seemed honeymooners took leave of their senses and did shameful things such as giving each other piggy-backs in Times Square, biting from opposite ends of a hotdog on the corner of 42nd Street while adoringly wiping off dribbles of ketchup and mustard from each other's chins – and now this: a remake of *An Affair to Remember* with Grace in the role of Deborah Kerr, Jimi as Cary Grant, and the aerial view of Noo-Yawk City as the stunning backdrop.

At least that was the idea.

'C'mon you guys, show some affection,' whined Brady, frantically chewing gum and fiddling with his beret, which he'd positioned on his head at a jaunty angle. Being from the Bronx, it was his attempt to look arty and creative, in what he thought was a moody, Left Bank, *artiste* kind of way. Unfortunately, not being familiar with classic British comedy from the 1970s, Brady had unintentionally made himself look like Frank Spencer.

'Ooh, you Brits are so straight. Loosen up. Let your emotions grab a hold of you. You're madly and passionately in love, remember?' Swapping his lens for a whopping great telephoto number, he pointed it menacingly at them both like a submachine-gun. 'C'mon, work it baby, work it. I wanna see some action.'

'What is this – a porno movie?' hissed Grace under her breath. A crowd of curious tourists were beginning to gather. A couple of archetypal Japanese taking snapshots.

'Just think *OK!* magazine,' whispered Jimi through clenched teeth. He felt as ridiculous as Grace did, and he dearly wanted to tell Brady to shut the fuck up, rescue his ego, and throw himself on the mercy of a good New York barman and a whiskey sour. But he had too much at stake here to blow it now. If it meant grinning like a C-list soap star in a glossy at-home spread, then so be it, he thought, his jaw aching.

'You said a favour, not street cred suicide,' grumbled Grace, tugging at the brightly striped Dr Who scarf that Brady had thoughtfully wrapped around both their necks to symbolize togetherness and 'tying the knot'.

She felt as if she was being strangled.

'So when did you two first meet?' piped up the assistant, a pretty Oriental girl who was hovering around them struggling to hold a huge silver reflector.

'When we were teenagers,' said Jimi. 'At school.'

'Awww, childhood sweethearts,' she cooed, a romantic glow infusing her face.

Jimi and Grace smiled tightly as Brady's camera shutter rattled loudly.

'Was it love at first sight?'

Shifting uncomfortably, they both searched for a reply as the assistant waited expectantly. They didn't want to disappoint her and ruin her dreams of happy ever after.

'Er . . . whatever love means,' said Jimi finally. Well if it was good enough for His Royal Highness, it was good enough for him.

'Yeah, it was something like that,' agreed Grace, catching Jimi's eye. 'We definitely had strong feelings towards each other, didn't we, darling?'

Satisfied, the assistant beamed. 'It's so nice to meet two people like you. To see it can really work. It gives me hope that I can find someone.'

'Yeah, you and me both, honey.' Still getting over his recent break-up with his boyfriend, Brady nodded knowingly. 'It just goes to show that not all men are out there to break your goddamn heart.'

'Oh no,' agreed Grace, rather enjoying having a little dig at Jimi. 'Only the dysfunctional, emotionally incapable shitheads, and you have to steer clear of those.' She smiled, feeling Jimi wriggling with discomfort next to her.

But she should've known Jimi wasn't one to take a dig without getting his own back. 'And you certainly have,' he said, smiled and then wrapped his arms tighter around Grace's woollen shoulder. Fixing her with an amused smile he raised his eyebrows teasingly. 'You've got me now. Haven't you, chubbybum?'

Chubbybum? Grace threw him a murderous look while Brady and his assistant looked on, captivated by this intimate display. 'Yes I have,' she smiled. 'Teensy-weensy,' she added, wiggling her little finger playfully as Jimi coloured.

Throwing her a furious glare, he turned to his audience. 'Small hands,' he sniffed, hastily holding his hands up in explanation.

Or was it defeat? considered Grace, feeling the score a firm one-nil to her.

The photo shoot finally wrapped at five when the light began to fade and the sky darkened into a purplish bruise across the glittering Manhattan skyline. After having her close-up taken what felt like a thousand times, Grace foolishly assumed the ordeal was over and bid Brady a rather fond farewell as they clambered into separate cabs, kissing him on both cheeks while he hooted, 'See ya, wouldn't wanna be ya.'

It was funny how very annoying people can suddenly seem rather sweet when you're never going to see them again, she'd mused fondly, watching Brady fiddling with his beret and chewing noisily on his spearmint gum as he'd finished packing his silver cases into the trunk and slid into the back seat with his assistant. And then quickly changed her mind as his cab began pulling away and he wound down the window yelling that he'd meet them again tomorrow for the 'grand finale'.

'What did he mean, the grand finale?' demanded Grace, pulling off her grey woollen hat and gloves as she followed Jimi through the revolving doors into their hotel. She was impressed with their choice of accommodation. Situated downtown in the seriously trendy area of SoHo and surrounded by dozens of funky boutiques, groovy restaurants and the city's coolest bars, the SoHo Grand was like something out of the *Hip Hotel* guide. Probably because it was, she mused, noting the deconstructed entrance of the warehouse-type building, the suitably designer-clad doorman nodding discreetly and thinking how everything about the hotel, from the cutting-edge location to the young, creative-type guests flitting in and out, was so very Jimi.

And so *not* Spencer.

On her visit to New York with Spencer, she'd stayed at the grandly traditional Waldorf-Astoria. A world-renowned five-star, the huge hotel was located uptown and catered to a rich, professional, middle-class clientele. With its monogrammed carpets, old-school walnut furniture and formal brass chandeliers, it was supremely comfortable, but it had also felt just that little bit staid.

'He means the dinner.'

'What dinner?' she asked, climbing the steel staircase up to the lobby.

'The candlelit dinner for two,' explained Jimi, his eyebrows raised in a pained apology as he walked up to the reception desk.

'Oh Christ, can it get worse?' Feeling her feet throbbing in her suede ankle boots, Grace was fast beginning to regret agreeing to the whole charade. At first it had all seemed so amusing – putting on *faux* wedding rings at the check-in desk at Heathrow, conning the Virgin Airways stewardess into upgrading them, drinking champagne in their horizontal club-class seats. Now the joke was wearing thin and all she wanted was to get into her room, tug off her jeans, strip off her pancaked camera make-up, have a long soak in the bath, and climb into her bed. 'Mr and Mrs Malik, welcome to the SoHo Grand,' greeted the concierge, pouring out complimentary glasses of champagne. 'Your bags have already been taken to your room. I trust you'll find everything you need in the honeymoon suite.'

'The honeymoon suite?' repeated Grace brightly. Too brightly.

'Yes, it comes complete with a king-size bed, a couples hot tub, and we've taken the liberty of ordering you a basket of chocolate-coated strawberries, some massage oil and a selection of romantic CDs and videos.' The concierge was beaming. Honeymooners, it would seem, had the same effect on people as newborn babies. Everyone smiled wistfully, cooing and clucking. Luckily, as yet, nobody had pinched her cheek and gone goo-goo.

Probably because I've already gone gaga, thought Grace, feeling like an idiot. This was a complete shock. How come she'd had no idea they were staying in the honeymoon suite? It could be, she decided, because Jimi had spent the last week in London assuring her the sleeping arrangements were 'sorted'. Smiling sweetly, she attempted to remedy matters. 'I'm sorry, but there must be some kind of mistake . . .'

'Mistake?' In his muted Prada uniform, the concierge looked puzzled. 'No, there's no mistake.'

That was it. She'd had enough. Grabbing hold of Jimi's arm, Grace yanked him to one side. 'I thought you said we had twin beds,' she hissed, expecting some kind of explanation, a solution, *a way out*.

Instead he just looked sheepish, shrugged, and said simply, 'I lied.'

Suddenly all her breezy protestations to Rhian about how it was going to be like *Green Card*, how it was going to be a doddle, how of course there was nothing to worry about, came back and bit Grace right on the arse.

Her face froze. '*Lied?*' she repeated incredulously. And was promptly incredulous that she was incredulous. How could she not have suspected? How could she have trusted him to be honest? This, remember, was a man who'd slept with her, asked her to go around the world with him, and promised to call. Lying was, quite obviously, child's play.

'I didn't think you'd agree to come if I told you the truth,' he whispered, turning away from the prying eyes of the concierge who was up on tiptoes, desperately trying to eavesdrop. 'And how could I tell them we wanted twin beds on our honeymoon?' Jimi was trying to calm a volatile situation. Visions of Tanya Stiff on the phone, calling him a lying little cunt and promising he'd never eat lunch in this town again, terrified him. The woman hadn't got an ounce of sympathy in her scrawny body. She wouldn't give a damn about his wedding being called off, all she cared about was the story she'd commissioned.

'C'mon Grace, please calm down.' He'd taken to pleading.

But Grace wasn't to be calmed. Grace was tired, she had a blister on her big toe, a throbbing headache from too many in-flight Bloody Marys, and she was furious. Jimi may have ditched the orange Capri and 1988 haircut, but he hadn't ditched his arrogant self-belief that every woman was willing – *correction*: desperate – to jump into bed with him.

'Calm down? *You want me to calm down?*' she was yelling.

Jimi had turned ashen and was flapping his hands, trying to shush her. Which, as any woman knows, will do exactly the opposite.

'You're damn right I wouldn't have come with you,' she scoffed loudly. 'Because there is no way I'm sleeping with you, Jimi Malik . . .'

'I didn't exactly mean . . .' he tried interrupting.

Bad move.

'Oh! I think it's pretty *obvious* what you *meant*,' she exclaimed sarcastically. '*But you can forget it.*' Folding her arms, she threw him a contemptuous glare. 'I wouldn't have sex with you if you were the last man on earth.'

The concierge was craning his neck forward, trying to hear what was going on. He smiled to himself. A lovers' tiff. Aww. How romantic.

How bloody arrogant. Jimi reeled, feeling angrily indignant. 'Christ, what do you think this is? Some elaborate ruse to try and have sex with you?' he hissed, the vein that ran down the middle of his forehead pounding furiously. 'Don't flatter yourself, Grace. I might have been jilted, but what do you think I am? *Desperate?*'

Oh dear.

Only when the words had spat from his lips, and Jimi saw Grace's face crumple and her expression of anger morph into hurt, did he realize he might have gone a little OTT on the protesting.

'Oh shite . . . I didn't mean . . . I meant . . .'

'It's OK.' She cut him off brusquely. 'There's no need for further explanations. I think you've made yourself perfectly clear.' Tossing her hair, Grace struggled to pick up what was left of her ego, that was lying bruised and battered on the marble floor of the hotel lobby. She felt like an idiot – an unattractive idiot.

As far as she was concerned, it was perfectly understandable, sensible and downright obvious that she wouldn't want to sleep with Jimi. After all, as handsome, and as funny and as good a friend as he was, he was also a legendary womanizer, a heartbreaker, and a player. Jimi had sex on the brain and by his own admission he'd *slept* with a lot of women and wanted to *sleep* with lots of women, and so in theory, being a woman herself, wouldn't that mean he would want to sleep with her? And if he didn't – why the fuck not?

What the hell was wrong with her?

Struggling to regain her composure, Grace looked at Jimi. Due to this rather complicated reasoning, she'd now found herself in the bizarre situation of having gone full circle and wanting to pin Jimi to that reception desk and demand why he *didn't* want to sleep with her.

'Here you are – champagne, to toast the happy couple.' Sensing a gap in the lovers' tiff, the concierge passed them both a flute of Dom Perignon.

Grace hesitated. She was in half a mind to throw the champagne in Jimi's face, tell him to sod his honeymoon, and get on the first plane back to London.

Back to her rented studio.

Back to her hand-washing, Saturday night in on the sofa, and the leftovers of last night's tuna and sweetcorn pasta.

Oh what the hell.

Faced with the reality of getting through another weekend in couplesville, Grace did a U-turn. She'd endured a turbulent flight across the Atlantic. She'd spent the afternoon in all sorts of hideous romantic poses. Having to spend two nights with Jimi in the honeymoon suite was the least of her worries. She should think herself lucky. At least it wasn't a bloody lifetime.

'Thank you,' she smiled.

Sensing a ceasefire, Jimi held out an olive branch in the shape of his champagne flute. Chinking it against hers, he smiled stiffly. It was an apology and a thank-you rolled into one. 'To us,' he toasted.

'To us,' echoed Grace, smiling broadly.

Feeling a wave of relief that he'd been forgiven and everything was back to normal, Jimi slipped his arm around her waist for the benefit of their audience behind the reception as they began walking towards the elevators.

'Thanks, Grace.' As the lift doors slid open he stepped inside and turned to her, his confident grin firmly back in place. 'You were amazing.'

'Thanks,' she replied, savouring the taste of vintage champagne in her mouth. 'And you're on the sofa.'

Chapter Twenty-nine

'Jimi, what exactly are you doing in there? Grouting the tiles?'

It was the next morning and Grace's bladder was ready to burst. Clad in her complimentary Frette Robe and white foam slippers, she was jigging up and down outside the bathroom door, legs crossed, buttocks clenched, pelvic floor squeezed, *waiting*.

She'd been waiting for over an hour.

The night before, she and Jimi had ordered room service, attempted to watch *When Harry Met Sally* – one of their 'romantic' videos – and both crashed early. As arranged, she'd got the bed, and he'd got the sofa. Fortunately he'd been too knackered to put up a fight, and he'd gone quietly, flopping onto the cushions and – Grace had been amazed to see after four years with the kung fu snorer himself, Spencer – sleeping without the slightest noise or tiniest stir.

Jetlag had woken her up at the ungódly hour of 7 a.m., and finding the sofa empty, she'd followed the blankets and sheets strewn in a trail across the room and tracked Jimi to the bathroom, a locked door, and a medley of taps running, aerosols squirting, unidentified electrical appliances buzzing. An hour later and Jimi still hadn't emerged, her bladder had swollen to the size of a space hopper, and irritation had turned into desperation. And so, with one thing, and one thing only on her mind, she'd now been reduced to stalking the door.

'Are you still alive?' she hissed, visions of Elvis face down in his fried banana and peanut butter sandwich flashing before her. Grace was perplexed. Wasn't it women, not men, who were supposed to be guilty of hogging the bathroom? Spencer's routine had been briskly efficient – two minutes to shower, two to shave, and five to sit on the loo with his trousers around his brogues, reading the *FT* and flicking through estate agents' brochures. What was it about the male psyche that desired to linger on the loo seat? Was it the cave syndrome? Were men's bowels just lazier? Or was this evidence that, contrary to wide-spread belief, men could actually multi-task? A theory brought on by the time she'd mistakenly barged into the bathroom and discovered Spencer sitting on the bog, not only on the phone renewing his car insurance, but writing out cheques for his credit cards.

If this was the case, Jimi could have done his whole year's tax returns in the time he'd spent in there, cursed Grace, rapping on the door with her knuckles.

'For Godsakes will you answer me? What the hell are you doing in there?' she repeated, only this time she was yelling and hopping from one foot to another in a tribal war dance. There was no answer. But it's not as if I need one, is it? she thought furiously. Because Grace knew exactly what Jimi was doing in there.

Getting his own back.

If only she knew.

On the other side of the bathroom door Jimi had broken out in a sweat. Armed with a selection of instruments and appliances, he was embroiled in the lengthy and painful operation he had to perform each and every morning under locked, bathroom conditions.

Human Topiary.

Brushing away the beads of panic on his forehead, he grabbed the shaving foam and began liberally squirting. Due to his Indian heritage Jimi had, to put it

mildly, rather a lot of body hair, and during the nig
it grew like a lawn, and every morning, like a lawn, it
needed mowing.

Stripped naked to the waist, he stared at his reflection in the mirror. Jeez, just look at me, he cursed
silently. It's the American-fucking-werewolf. Con-
tinuing to squirt until he was head to navel in white
foam body armour, he dived for his razor and
launched into Operation Wolfman. *Scrape-scrape-
rinse. Scrape-scrape-rinse.* The water in the sink began
turning black with bristles with blobs of shaving foam
floating on top like soggy icebergs. Women had no
idea. For them it was just a couple of armpits, a pair of
shins and a few strokes of a Bic razor once a week. For
him there was no end.

There was nasal hair to be weeded, ear hair to be
tweezed, eyebrows to be plucked and trimmed, side-
burns to be clipped, chin and cheeks to be shaved, his
throat to be pruned, and his collarbone to be cut and
layered so that his chest hair didn't stop in a great big
furry collar around his neck. The daily ritual was as
exhausting as it was relentless, he raged, replacing the
blade on his razor which had blunted with the weight
of all that hair. *Scrape-scrape-rinse. Scrape-scrape-
rinse.* It was like painting the Humber bridge. As soon
as he'd finished he practically had to start all over
again.

And then there was his back.

Grabbing the shower attachment, Jimi began hosing
himself down, spraying water everywhere so that
rivulets ran down the tiles and began to form puddles
on the floor. It was so unfair. Turning thirty had been
the trigger for the hair to start receding from his
temples. At first it had been barely discernible. But,
follicle by follicle, it had begun slowly disappearing,
retreating in two little arcs that would no doubt meet
up on his fortieth birthday and present him with a gift:
a little Les Dennis island of hair at the front of his
head. It had been distressing. So distressing that he'd

immediately marched into his barber's and demanded they shave it all off. A number three buzzcut and ten minutes later it was all gone. A receding hairline had become a trendy skinhead. And the problem was solved.

Only for another to sprout. Except this time it was hair appearing, rather than disappearing. It had started with one rogue hair on his left shoulder. He'd plucked it out, thought no more about it, but a week later he'd noticed it had reappeared – and this time it had brought along a friend. And another, and another, spreading like an illegal rave across his shoulders and down his spine. Until in the space of a few short months his once smooth, nut brown skin was covered in a thick, curly pelt.

He'd been appalled. Overnight he'd grown himself a hairy back. Which matched his chest, he'd realized, twirling around and around in front of his bathroom mirror like a deranged maniac. He couldn't believe it. No longer was he the Jimi Malik women knew and fancied, he was black mohair jumper. It was Kafkaesque. It was sexually repellent.

It had to go.

It had taken twelve months of dislocating his shoulder, trying to get a razor halfway down his shoulders, until Kylie had discovered his terrible secret – via a rather nasty case of stubble burn on her nipples after a night spent spooning – and he'd been introduced to waxing. It had changed his life. Now, once every six weeks, he made the religious pilgrimage to a discreet little salon in the West End, endured half an hour of eye-watering torture, and like a sheep that's been shorn emerged a new man. A man with a weight, quite literally, lifted off his shoulders.

If only my eyebrows were so easy, fumed Jimi, glaring at the wiry monstrosities that grew like clematis across his brow. Listening to Grace yelling outside the bathroom door, he hastily finished plucking a path through the middle.

270

'Won't be a sec,' he placated, lunging for his electric beard trimmer. The trimmer came with three attachments: the first gave a close, smooth shave, the second left behind a designer stubble, and the third was for clipping beards. Or, thought Jimi, hastily grabbing it, perfect for straggly eyebrows.

'Just having a quick shave . . .' And turning on his Remington trimmer, he began attacking them with gusto.

'Oh, I don't know, I think it makes you look kind of . . .' Waggling her ice-cream cornet as she searched for the word, Grace's voice trailed off. Oh God, she couldn't do it. It was impossible. She couldn't keep a straight face any longer. Struggling to suppress her giggles, she glanced across at Jimi. It had to be the funniest thing. Where once there had been two eyebrows, all that was left were just two bald, empty spaces. 'Surprised,' she managed to gasp, before collapsing into loud snorts of laughter.

Jimi frowned, puckering up his naked forehead. 'Please. Don't hold back on my account,' he protested sarcastically, tugging his black beanie hat low down over his eyes as he walked along next to her. He was still reeling from the embarrassment of picking up the wrong attachment for his beard trimmer. He couldn't believe how stupid he'd been. How instead of merely clipping, he'd shaved the whole lot off. Completely. *Buzzzzzz* and they were gone.

Now, instead of looking halfway normal, he looked, as Grace had so kindly and thoughtfully put it, permanently startled.

'Don't feel you have to spare my feelings,' he added stiffly.

'Don't worry,' she squeaked, hugging her aching ribs and wiping the tears that were streaming from her eyes. 'I won't.'

It was a glorious, autumnal Saturday afternoon and they were taking a walk through Battery Park, eating ice-creams and dodging the joggers, powerwalkers and real-life cosy couples that were strewn across the grass like fallen leaves. All eye-gazing, arm-entwining, joke-sharing, they threatened to send Grace into sad, nostalgic overdrive but, luckily for her – and unluckily for Jimi – his eyebrows had caused so much of a stir she hadn't noticed them.

They'd been the running gag all day long. After Jimi had finally, and quite literally, plucked up the courage to leave the bathroom, and Grace had finished laughing so hard she'd nearly peed herself, they'd left the hotel and spent the morning trawling SoHo's plethora of vintage clothes shops and second-hand record stores. Not to mention Pink Pussycat boutique, one of the most outrageous sex shops in Greenwich Village where the real eye-opener hadn't been the merchandise but Jimi, who, instead of being blasé about the whole thing, had shuffled nervously around the merchandise, looking scandalized.

Grace had made up for his blushes by treating him to lunch at Kelly & Pings, a frantic, noisy, steamy Thai canteen where the food was cooked in front of them in industrial-sized woks – wonton soups, ramen noodles, green chicken curry – and eaten from huge, steaming bowls. Afterwards they'd ridden the subway – getting lost in the back streets of the Bronx, gatecrashing a gospel church in Harlem – and taken a slow, winding walk down to the waterfront where they'd ignored the huge queues of tourists buying $15 tickets to board a sightseeing cruise, and joined the rest of the native New Yorkers on the Staten Island ferry and sailed past the Statue of Liberty for free.

Grace had never expected to have so much fun. Fears that she would spend the entire weekend pining for Spencer and being haunted by nostalgic memories had miraculously failed to materialize. It was as if she was in a completely different city. This wasn't the New York she'd visited with Spencer. The glitzy, glossy, well-heeled Upper Manhattan that had provided a backdrop for all their classic tourist activities: taking in a Broadway show, dining in the best restaurants, shopping on Fifth Avenue, looking at art at the Metropolitan.

This was a completely different city. Instead of galleries and Broadway shows, Jimi had showed her the joys of people watching in East Village, which was fun, and free, and far more fascinating. They'd refuelled at various bustling cafés on strong 'cawfee' – Jimi's choice – and potent cocktails at some of the area's grooviest bars – Grace, and her ever-present *Time Out Guide to New York*'s choice. Until finally, he'd wrestled away her guidebook, chucked it in a trashcan, and they'd walked and walked and walked until her feet ached.

And she'd laughed.

She'd laughed until her sides hurt. But the source of hilarity wasn't just Jimi's brush with his beard-trimmer, it was Jimi himself. His bleakly comic sense of humour, his appalling map-reading, his tendency to strike up a conversation with everyone he met, from the waiter to the homeless guy on the subway. His obsession with Michael Caine, 'not a lot of people know that', his peculiar habit of sticking his little finger up in the air at a right angle when he drank a beer, the comic-serious way in which he'd spent ages deliberating over his food and then asked if they could add a little more lemongrass, take away some of the galangal, chop up dried chillies, substitute egg for tofu, until the exasperated Thai chef had asked him if he wanted to get behind the counter and cook it himself. Which he nearly had done, until Grace had pointed out that Americans could also do irony.

'So what do you want to do now?' asked Jimi, changing the subject away from his dratted eyebrows.

Grace gave it some thought while biting off the end of her waffle cone and proceeding to suck the vanilla ice-cream through the bottom. It made a loud, slurping, snorting sound.

Jimi paused from licking his scoop of mango sorbet to watch her in amazement. '*What is that?*'

'What?'

'That —' he motioned to the bottom of her cornet, which was dripping creamy blobs onto the footpath.

'Oh, that . . .' Blushing, Grace realized what she was doing. It was a childhood habit. When she'd first met Spencer he'd caught her doing it with a strawberry Cornetto, and had been so appalled she'd never done it in anyone's presence again. But being with Jimi she felt so comfortable, she'd completely forgotten. 'Oh God, sorry, it's revolting isn't it,' she apologized, hurriedly wrapping the napkin around the bottom to catch the melting ice-cream.

'No.' He shook his head. 'It's not revolting. It's just you.'

'Me?' Grace eyed him suspiciously. 'Is this a good thing?'

He laughed. 'Yeah it's a good thing,' he said, grinning so wide she could see the two gold crowns on his back molars. Leaning forwards he reached out to wipe the dribble of ice-cream off her chin. His thumb brushed her lip.

What the hell?

It was such a simple gesture, such a small thing, so trivial, and yet it was as if someone had just plugged him into the mains. His heart thwacked inside his ribcage. The laugh died in his throat. His skin prickled hot and cold. His eyes focused on Grace. She was staring at him, the gap between her eyebrows puckered in confusion, her lips slightly apart in surprise.

Now either she's feeling what I'm feeling, or she's looking at me and thinking I'm some kind of fucking idiot, thought Jimi, battling to work out what had just happened back there.

'You've gone pale. Are you feeling OK?'

It was the latter.

'Uh-huh,' he nodded, feeling confused, foolish, disconcerted. 'Just a bit of jetlag,' he blurted. He felt a rush of relief. That was it. Of course. It was just jetlag. Nothing more.

'I thought you said you never got jetlag?'

He stalled. No, that was right. He didn't. 'Erm . . . well . . . I don't . . . but there's a first time for everything.' Confusion whirled. 'But I do owe you a present,' he smiled, trying to change the subject.

'You do?' Grace's eyes lit up.

'Yeah, for doing me this favour and saving my ass,' he drawled. Crap Noo-Yawk accent, but what the hell. It was all he could do to speak, let alone do impersonations. 'Think of it as a sort of wedding present.'

'You mean like a toaster?' She grinned.

'Actually I was thinking more along the lines of some lovely china . . .'

'Is that so?' Her eyes twinkled. 'I was thinking more along the lines of a new outfit . . .'

'Hmmm, well only if it matches the place settings.'

Laughing, Grace punched him. 'It's the grand finale tonight and if I'm going to be in *Chic Traveller*, I'm going to need something very posh.'

'*Ow* . . .' he yelped loudly. 'Didn't I ever tell you I bruise like a peach?'

She punched him again.

'OK, OK, it's a deal,' laughed Jimi, flagging down a yellow cab. It swerved towards them, and he went to open the door. 'Where to?'

'Where do you think?' she said jokingly. Chucking her now defunct ice-cream in the trashcan, Grace walked over to him, licking the sticky-sweet vanilla splodges from her fingers. Ducking under his arm she slid onto the back seat. 'Barney's, of course.'

Jimi puffed out his cheeks and exhaled sharply. 'Why do I have the feeling my credit card is about to go into meltdown?' he groaned, clambering in beside her.

'Credit card? Don't you mean *credit cards*?' quipped Grace, throwing him one of her looks.

Jimi smiled. But it was more from relief than anything else. Thank Christ. Whatever weird feeling he'd had back there had disappeared. There was no need to worry. Things were most definitely back to normal again.

Settling back into the seat, he unpeeled the tinfoil wrapper from a stick of chewing gum, curled it into his mouth and gazed out of the window. New York began whizzing past. Sights, sounds, smells. He paid no attention. Instead he chewed thoughtfully, the frustrated novelist mulling over what had just happened. It was very weird. How could he describe it? A funny turn? A weird spasm? A bolt from the blue?

Rubbing the bristles of his eyebrows he flicked through his mental thesaurus. And then, unexpectedly, the fog of his writer's block lifted for the first time in weeks. Only instead of feeling elated, he felt a sudden sense of dread. He'd thought of another way to describe it.

Cupid's arrow.

Chapter Thirty

The door of the Churchill Arms swung briskly open and a tall, attractive man wearing casual designer clothes and with a black nylon laptop case slung over his broad shoulder strode confidently towards the bar. The pub was still reasonably empty – the Saturday afternoon rush of tourists had drifted off to nearby Covent Garden and Shaftesbury Avenue to take in a show, while the regular evening crowd hadn't yet started arriving – and the leather soles of his brogues striking the varnished floorboards made an assured beat against the low hum of conversation.

A few people looked up. The woman waiting for her friend eyed him appreciatively, while a group of thirtysomething alpha males paused momentarily from discussing Arsenal's latest match to suss out their competition. Finding themselves wanting, one of them made a derogatory remark, and they dragged on their cigarettes and sniggered insecurely into their Buds.

Behind the polished mahogany bar, the barman neatly folded the *Daily Mail*'s *Weekend* supplement in half and began walking past the rows of optics. Reaching the well-stocked wine racks, his hand instinctively reached for a particular bottle of Chilean Merlot and, without waiting to be asked, he uncorked it, balanced a fresh glass on the counter, and began generously filling it with red wine.

Without saying a word, Spencer pulled up a

barstool. Placing his nylon case on the bar, he eased himself onto the leather seat and reached for the wine glass. Gently cradling the bowl, his little finger brushing lightly against the stem, he gave an easy flick of his wrist and rocked it towards his lips, relishing the taste of the warm, burgundy liquid flooding his mouth.

This was a well-rehearsed routine.

During the week, between seven and eight in the evening, work events permitting, Spencer would switch off his computer, leave his office and walk next door to leave memos on his secretary's desk before making his way to the lift at the end of the corridor. He worked on the third floor and so usually had to wait a couple of seconds for one to arrive – time to check his reflection in the metal button panel – before travelling downstairs to reception where he would nod to the porter at the front desk, walk out through the revolving doors, and cross the busy side street for a quick drink before heading home.

But now it was the weekend, and whereas usually he'd have played a game of tennis, taken a drive up to Hampstead and jogged around the heath, or enjoyed lunch in a pub along the river, he'd spent today at the office catching up on his work, going over his cases, making sure he met a few deadlines. He'd left the office as usual, crossed the busy side street, and entered the pub to have a quick drink before heading home. Just because it was a Saturday, tonight was no different. Tonight was the same as every other night. And tonight he'd be going back to an empty flat. Again.

Slugging back another large mouthful, Spencer eased off his jacket and pushed up the sleeves of his jumper. It was no good pretending any more, he missed Grace. Ever since she'd walked out four weeks ago he'd been trying to convince himself that this was just a lovers' tiff, an ill-advised attempt to shock him, a melodramatic way of making a point – and he'd refused to react on principle. Not even when she'd given him back the ring, or packed her suitcase, or disappeared to Rhian's.

Spencer had never given in to an ultimatum, and he wasn't about to start now. Instead his knee-jerk reaction had been anger, indignation and annoyance that she was doing this to him. OK, hands up, so he'd had a few too many drinks and behaved like an idiot on her birthday, but he'd tried to apologize. It was a one-off, it would never happen again, and he was sorry, really sorry. As for the issue of the wedding, had Grace really expected him to drop everything in the middle of an important case and jet off to Las Vegas?

But as the protestations had whirled fast and loud around Spencer's mind, a part of him, deep down inside, had stuck up its hand and confessed that it was scared and upset. That he was making excuses. That he was in the wrong. That if he didn't do something he was going to lose the best thing that had ever happened to him.

He'd refused to listen.

Instead he'd plunged his energies into the case at work. He'd left early and run that extra mile around the common and spent an extra hour in the pub. He'd told himself he had no choice, that being emotional was simply not an option. He was thirty-nine years old, he was a partner in a law firm, he was a man who boasted a 100 per cent success rate and had never lost a case. He didn't have the luxury of being able to do confusion, or self-doubt, or grief. He couldn't run to his colleagues at the Queens tennis club and over a vigorous rally start pouring his heart out. He couldn't stand in front of a jury and break down in front of a packed courtroom. He worked in a profession where appearances were everything.

And it was taking its toll. Spencer felt as if he'd spent his whole life having to hold it together. He hadn't cried when he'd been sent to boarding school at just seven years old, he didn't react when his first wife had left, brandishing blame and furious tears, and when he'd sat next to his father's hospital bed and watched him waste away, he'd refused to break down. It felt like a sign of weakness. A sign that he'd failed. And that was something that terrified Spencer more than anything. Something that silenced the tiny voice inside of him. Something that made him get up every morning, and go to bed every night: the fear of failure.

And so, composed and controlled, he'd stood barefoot in the hallway as Grace had walked out of the flat, stuffed binliners of her belongings into a waiting minicab and climbed into the back seat. He'd packed all his emotions away, just as if he'd wrapped them in newspaper, and watching her he'd felt numb. Paralysed. She'd called it a break, but the outcome was still the same, she was still leaving.

And he had no idea if she was ever coming back.

Draining his glass, he put it down on the bar, only for it to be magically filled up again. He could feel the effects of the wine. It was already beginning to take the edge off, soften the corners a little, take the harshness out of reality.

'How's things?' ventured the barman.

In all the time Spencer had been going to that pub, they were the only two words Eddie the barman had ever said to him. It wasn't a question, he didn't really want to know. In fact he'd probably be appalled if Spencer told him. It was merely an acknowledgement to one of his regulars.

He responded accordingly. 'Fine, fine.' He nodded, swigging back another mouthful, and letting the warm liquid trickle down the back of his throat. What the hell was he talking about? He wasn't fine. He wasn't anywhere remotely near fine.

'Actually, no, I take that back. I'm not fine. My fiancée's moved out and I'm miserable and lonely and . . .' Draining his second glass of wine, he slammed it noisily down on the bar. '. . . and in need of another drink.'

Eddie's amiable expression dropped. That was rather more information than he'd been expecting. Gladly attending to his duties to cover his awkwardness, he hastily reached for the bottle and refilled the glass. His eyes flicked to Spencer. He was a regular, one of the lawyers who worked across the road. Every evening, Monday to Friday, for the past eight years he'd been coming in to the pub and Eddie had been serving him. But never in the whole eight years had he come in at the weekend.

He looked at him now. Hunched over the bar, his broad frame was gradually beginning to crumple, the broad shoulders sunk down into his cashmere jumper. Eddie's eyes moved to Spencer's face. Already it had lost its fair complexion and was beginning to blotch and redden with the alcohol. Eddie sighed. There was only ever one reason why men worked weekends, and it wasn't anything to do with deadlines.

'Do you love her?'

Taken aback, Spencer jerked his head up, and met Eddie's gaze. 'Yes . . .' He nodded. Of course he loved Grace. That was never in question. He sighed. 'But . . .'

'But what? You're too pig-headed to go after her?'

Spencer felt a prickle of annoyance. He didn't want a barman telling him what to do with his life. His pride opened his mouth to throw out some cutting remark, and then something seemed to take hold and sprout inside. It was uncomfortable to admit it, but it felt like a niggly seed of truth. He avoided it. 'Do you have a smoke?'

Eddie pulled out a gold packet of B&H from his top pocket and silently slid it across the bar. Flipping open the lid, Spencer took one and clamped it between his teeth.

Across the other side of the pub, the woman sitting in the corner paused from admiring the clothes her friend was proudly pulling out from a Whistles carrier bag, like a magician with a string of multicoloured hankies, and glanced over. She was surprised. The fanciable bloke at the bar was still alone. She watched, briefly, as he lit up his cigarette, the hollows of his cheeks accentuated as he took a long, firm drag, the strong line of his jaw flexing as he tilted his chin to blow a smoke ring, before looking away.

Spencer watched with satisfaction as a perfect grey circle floated up above the bar. As a teenager he'd seen Steve McQueen do it in a movie and been so impressed by how cool and in control he looked. Even now, twenty-some years later and I'm still trying to be him, he mused drily, taking a sip of wine. Absent-mindedly he flipped the thought around. Still trying to be someone I'm not.

Discontent stabbed. What had been a trivial recollection seemed suddenly to be a comment on his whole personality. He looked at Eddie who was mopping up a spillage on the bar.

'It's not that simple,' he tried to explain. He wanted to justify himself. He thought about the few times he'd called Grace, the heavy silences and the pregnant pauses where he'd meant to say something profound, and instead ended up talking about something as trivial as contact lenses.

Eddie stopped wiping and looked up. 'Yes it is.'

Spencer stared at him. A small, middle-aged man with a slight paunch pushing through his polyester shirt, a soggy grey dishcloth hanging limply from his hand. Suddenly Eddie the barman had turned into some kind of oracle.

He tried again. 'Listen, I know you're only trying to help, but believe me you don't know the half of it. You're looking at a divorce lawyer who's been divorced once, who's got a lot of pressure at work dealing with couples who once were so madly in love they didn't sign a pre-nup and now hate each other's guts so much they would quite happily kill each other for who gets the fucking microwave, who's got pressure from his fiancée Grace who got pissed off because they weren't planning a wedding and said she wanted a break . . .' Spencer broke off. He'd committed the ultimate sin. Too many personal details. The wine was loosening his tongue. He ran his fingernails roughly over his scalp and stared into the ruby depths of his glass. 'Look, let's just say my life's complicated.'

'Because you're making it complicated.' Eddie refused to be convinced by a noughties sob story. He eyed Spencer with interest. 'You think just because I serve drinks I don't know about life . . .'

Spencer fidgeted uncomfortably and dragged on his cigarette.

'. . . But I know more about life from working in this pub for the last thirty years, than you can ever learn from any university or degree course or library. I've listened to more problems, watched more relationships start and finish right here at this bar, witnessed more slices of people's lives, experienced more emotions, than you could ever imagine. I might be no psychiatrist, I might not have fancy letters after my name, but I get people. And I get you.' Leaning across the bar, he fixed Spencer with a keen gaze. 'I've been watching you for a long time.'

'You have?' Christ almighty. The oracle had now turned into Big Brother, thought Spencer, feeling slightly freaked and seeking reassurance in his red wine.

But now there was no stopping Eddie. 'And you know what I see?'

'A lawyer,' he joked, trying to bluff his way out of what was fast turning into a claustrophobic situation. But there was no way out. He was cornered.

'I see a frightened man.'

Spencer bristled, his ego putting up its fists in a knee-jerk reaction. Right, that was it. He wasn't going to sit here all night and put up with this psychobabble. 'Yeah well, thanks for the therapy session, but I think I'm going to make a move.' Tugging out his wallet he pulled out his credit card. 'This should cover the damage.'

Wordlessly Eddie took his American Express and swiped it in the machine. There was a pause, and then the familiar whirring as the transaction began and a receipt appeared. Tearing along the perforated edge, he passed it to Spencer. 'Do you miss her?' he asked.

Spencer ignored him. He wasn't going to answer any more of his intrusive questions. Unclipping his Mont Blanc pen from the pocket of his computer case, he went to sign, and then something made him relent. He looked up. 'Yeah.' He nodded. Then added with a lot more conviction, 'Yeah, I really miss her.'

'Do you want to be with her?'

This time Spencer noticed his tone was kind, not accusatory. He paused, allowing himself time to think about it. As a lawyer, answers had to be carefully thought out. Spontaneity might be attractive, but it was lethal. Careful consideration and strategic forethought, that's what his legal training had drummed into him and what had spilled over into all areas of his life. But surely that was a good thing? It didn't make an answer less certain. On the contrary, it made it more sure.

In contemplation, Spencer ran the edge of his thumb's clean, square-cut fingernail over his chin. Eventually he nodded. 'Absolutely.'

'So what's stopping you?'

He'd done so well up until now, but Spencer felt himself fall at the last hurdle. He could think of hundreds of reasons. He could blame Grace for being unreasonable, he could cite his refusal to be blackmailed into an ultimatum, he could say they argued too much or confess to having cold feet. He could explain he was terrifically busy at work, divulge how they'd agreed to do the extension on the flat first, point out how being a divorcee made it difficult for him to be married in church, or even argue that marriage was just a piece of paper anyway. He could say any of them, and any of them would sound convincing – they'd been so convincing he'd even convinced himself – but ultimately they were all just lousy excuses. He hesitated, took a deep breath, and finally, after all those years, he said it out loud.

'Fear. Fear of failing.'

Signing on the dotted line, he looked up and met Eddie's gaze.

It was as unflinching as his answer.

'But if you don't try, you've failed anyway.'

Chapter Thirty-one

Across the other side of London, not trying wasn't something Rhian's date could be accused of.

'So I'll call you next week and arrange another date?' Jeff – forty-five, divorced, and a cosmetic dentist – was flashing his Persil-white porcelain veneers at her from the back seat of the black cab.

'Another date?' Being forced to share a cab because she had less than a fiver in her purse, Rhian was sitting primly opposite on one of the flip-down seats. There was an awkward pause. They faced each other. Him: legs confidently splayed, arms outstretched along the back of the headrests, looking, Rhian thought, as if he was being crucified in his Drizabone mac. Her: fifteen-denier pull-ups tightly crossed at both knees and ankles, arms folded self-consciously in her cream-tasselled poncho, looking, mused Jeff, not only very foxy, but as if she was waiting for him to make a move.

He lunged.

She swerved.

'Well, speak to you next week,' she trilled, diving for the door handle, narrowly avoiding his farewell clinch and tumbling out onto the kerb. Waving as the cab pulled away, she dug her flat keys out of her clutch bag and climbed her front steps. Over my dead body, she thought grimly.

*   *   *

Rhian had just been on her first and last date with Jeff. It had been a fix-up. A friend-of-a-friend-of-a-friend had played matchmaker and, despite her reservations, loneliness, boredom and her inherent optimism that maybe, *just maybe*, this was the one had made her agree. And so, via a couple of text messages, they'd arranged to meet.

In hindsight, both those things should have rung warning bells. Rhian was an old-fashioned romantic at heart, and she wanted a man to at least take the time to ring her to ask her out for dinner, not send her a text saying 'R U Free 4 a bite on Sat?' But, consoling herself that hey, it could have been worse – it could have been via an email – she'd replied 'Yes.' And received a rapid, no-nonsense 'C U at PJ's at 7.'

Cue the second warning bell.

PJ's was a restaurant in Fulham. It had been there for as long as Rhian could remember, and for as long as she could remember she'd always avoided it. It was frequented by rugger-bugger types in insignia yachting jackets and ladies who lunched. To make matters worse, Jeff had been late. She'd waited, perched on a barstool, trying to make one hideously expensive Bailey's-with-ice last, in two minds whether or not to abandon the whole thing, go home, pay off Hester, and spend the evening in a different kind of PJs. Except the little 'what if' voice had piped up again. What if Cinderella had never gone to the ball? What if Helen Hunt had never looked at Jack Nicholson and realized this was as good as it gets? What if Jeff was the one?

Well if he is you might as well bloody shoot me, thought Rhian, letting herself into the flat and kicking off her black patent court shoes. She stuck her head into the living room. Hester and a gangly youth of about fifteen were bolt upright on her sofa watching TV. They were the picture of innocence. Well, almost. His flies were undone and Hester's T-shirt was on inside out, observed Rhian, feeling envious. Even her teenage babysitter was getting more action than she was.

Sparing their embarrassment, and hers, she quickly paid Hester and watched her scuttle out of the flat with her boyfriend, heard their giggles on the stairs, caught them kissing under the street lamp as she went to pull the curtains closed. She paused to watch as they began to walk down the street, one hand stuffed tightly in each other's back pocket, all wrapped up together in the flush of first love.

God it all seemed so simple back then, she thought, checking on Jack, who was fast asleep, before slipping on her marabou mules and padding into the kitchen to make herself a cup of tea. Reaching into the cupboard for the teabags her eye fell on a family pack of Penguins. They were for Jack as a treat, but after the evening with Jeff it's Mummy who needs a treat, she told herself, padding back into the living room. She flicked on the radio and, curling up on the sofa, dunked a Penguin in her tea and began a thorough post-mortem on her date.

It had been a nightmare.

Her Bailey's and ice had long since dissolved to cloudy water by the time Jeff had arrived, twenty minutes late with some excuse about bad traffic, and a terrible underbite. Not that she usually noticed, let alone cared, about a person's physical attributes. On the contrary, 'it's what's inside that counts' was one of Rhian's fundamental philosophies on life, except when applied to herself. But Jeff's underbite was, pardon the pun, jaw-droppingly bad. Bruce Forsyth bad. Jimmy Hill bad. Will Young bad. And him a cosmetic dentist, she'd thought, unable to take her eyes off it as he'd proceeded to fire questions at her.

Jeff, she concurred, was a man with a very busy lifestyle. So busy that he didn't like to waste valuable time getting to know someone the old-fashioned way, but preferred to skip the introductions, the polite chitchat and the initial smalltalk, and, in his own words 'cut to the chase'. Cutting to the chase involved asking a series of multiple-choice questions. *Speed Dating*.

'I find it's very successful,' he'd beamed, over his salmon fishcakes and fries. They'd dispensed with the starters. His decision. 'That way we can discover immediately if we're compatible.'

Fiddling with her chicken Caesar with no dressing, Rhian had doubted that very much. Immediately she'd chastised herself for jumping to conclusions. Maybe he was just shy, she'd decided, layering up dry pieces of cos lettuce and chicken on the prongs of her fork. Maybe this was his way of trying to break the ice. To be humorous. First impressions and all that.

'Bali or Val-d'Isère?'

'Pardon?'

'Which would you choose?' He was looking at her as if she should be instantly getting this.

'You know, imagine you're going on holiday. Bali or Val-d'Isère?'

'Oh . . . er . . .' Rhian stalled mid-mouthful. Neither was the answer she would have liked; she was more a *dolce vita* type, two weeks in a Tuscan villa, soaking up all that sunshine, architecture, fashion, *passion*. She broke off from her thoughts and looked at Jeff. He was staring at her, eyebrows raised, forehead furrowed. He glanced at his watch. A thought crossed her mind. Was he timing her? 'Erm, Bali?' she answered, dare she say it, hopefully?

'Damn,' he tutted, disappointed. Spearing another chunk of fishcake he shook his head. 'Wrong answer.'

'Why is it the wrong answer?'

'You prefer lazing on a beach, I prefer skiing,' he shrugged matter-of-factly. 'Completely different. Imagine the arguments we'd have, trying to choose a holiday together.'

We've barely exchanged first names and now he's thinking about going on holiday together? thought Rhian, agog. Well, he was right about one thing: he didn't like to waste any time, that was for sure. 'Oh well, never mind,' she smiled tightly, turning her attention back to the food.

'Don't worry, I've got another seven questions left.'

'You have?' Horror mixed with intrigue.

'Sure have.' He nodded and took a swig of his mineral water. They'd skipped the wine too. 'And don't worry, you're allowed three wrong answers.' He began sloshing the water around in his mouth as if it was Listerine.

'Lucky me,' she said brightly.

Missing her sarcasm, Jeff put down his glass, and eyed her intently.

'Cat or dog?'

Rhian desperately wanted to refuse to play this game, but Jeff was like some great big bully. 'Dog,' she answered contritely.

'Cat,' he said, sliding a photo out from his wallet. 'Tigger. A Persian Blue. She's my baby.' Not for the first time that evening was Rhian lost for words.

Predictably, Jeff wasn't. 'Cheese plate or sticky-toffee pudding?'

Still only halfway through her salad, Rhian's heart soared at the promise of dessert and some proper conversation. 'Actually, I've had my eye on the cheesecake . . .' she confessed. And then caught his eye. 'Oh, you mean . . .' With clunking disappointment, she realized she'd misunderstood.

'Erm . . .'

'C'mon, c'mon,' chivvied Jeff, clicking his fingers. 'Fastest answer, fastest answer.'

It fuelled her competitive streak. Rhian had never liked losing. Not even when she was a kid playing Connect Four. 'Sticky-toffee pudding,' she declared loudly. His questioning had gone from being vaguely amusing to a fight-to-the-death.

'Ditto.' Jeff looked triumphant.

Alarmingly, so did Rhian. Like a child that's been praised by its teacher, she visibly sat up straighter in her chair.

Now Jeff was on a roll. Stabbing a chip in a tub of ketchup, he began punching it in the air as he fired questions at her.

'Tea or coffee?'

'Wine or beer?'

'Gold or silver?'

Rhian fired the answers back. 'Tea. Wine. Gold.' And then hearing herself, suddenly got a grip. What on earth was she doing? This was absolutely ridiculous. 'Hang on just one minute.' Throwing down her napkin, she stared at him indignantly. 'I came here to have dinner. Instead I feel as if I'm being interviewed.'

'You are,' he said simply.

The waitress appeared to clear away their plates. In retrospect Rhian didn't know why she hadn't left the restaurant there and then, but a mixture of politeness, curiosity and pride made her stick it out. She ordered a cappuccino, while Jeff ordered a cup of hot water and asked for the bill.

'Favourite film?'

'I thought this was multiple choice,' she grumbled. But she still thought about it and answered honestly. '*Gone with the Wind.*'

He nodded favourably. 'Sexual position?'

'*Excuse me?*' Her voice rang out loud, even above the restaurant din.

'Oh c'mon, let's not be coy.' He began fiddling in his pocket.

Oh my God. Rhian's heart froze. What on earth was he going to produce? A *condom*? It was a peppermint teabag.

She didn't know whether to laugh or cry.

Holding its tag, Jeff began dunking it in his cup. 'What's there to be embarrassed about? We're both adults.'

'Maybe. But I think I'll pass on this one,' she said primly. And she wasn't just talking about the question.

'So how many men are you dating at the moment?' asked Jeff, picking up the bill from the silver tray that had been unceremoniously plonked on the table.

Was this a trick question? Rhian lit up a cigarette. They'd never got to the non-smoker or smoker question but it was obvious by the way Jeff crinkled up his nose like a Venetian blind which camp he fell into. 'None. Which is why I've come out for dinner with you,' she answered honestly.

'Oh.' Jeff seemed surprised. 'I'm actually seeing four other girls.'

'Four?' Shocked, Rhian aimed for derision, but missed and hit indignation.

'But only sleeping with three of them,' he smiled in justification, and turned his attention to the bill. He studied it carefully. Digging his mobile out of his pocket, he selected 'CALCULATOR' and began divvying it up. Rhian deliberately blew a chimney of smoke in his direction. 'What's wrong with the other one?' She couldn't resist. She'd gone to a huge effort for tonight. She'd booked a babysitter, squeezed herself into a black velvet dress and trailed all the way to Fulham on public transport – all with the promise of dinner with a man who just might be the one. And what had she got? No conversation. No wine. No flirting. Just eight questions and a lousy salad. That *she* had to pay for.

'Her favourite film was *Four Weddings and a Funeral*,' he confided, rolling his eyes.

'Is that a joke?' Rhian stared at him incredulously.

'Exactly,' snorted Jeff. 'That's what I said to her too.'

And right there and then Rhian's rose-tinted glasses smashed into a thousand smithereens. Throughout the entire date, she'd been struggling to keep them firmly in place, all during the past eighteen months since Phil had left she'd been trying to look on the bright side, focus on the positive, to see the glass as half full. In fact for pretty much the whole of Rhian's life, she'd been resolutely wearing those goddamn glasses come what may, determined never to lose sight of her dreams, her idealism, her hope. But now Jeff's answer had finally tugged them off, stomped all over them, and left her staring the stark reality in the face.

His face. Deflated, she looked at Jeff's self-satisfied expression. Is that what romance had been reduced to? Multiple-choice questions and an automatic dis-qualification for liking Richard Curtis films? Is this what the future held for women brought up on a child-hood of Cinderella and dashing white knights? Of teenage years spent watching Cary Grant films and dreaming of your own affair to remember? Of twenty-something fantasies of passionate weekends in Monte Carlo, diamond solitaires and Vera Wang wedding dresses?

Was this thirtysomething reality?

Rhian wasn't one to swear, but looking at Jeff her good manners abandoned her. Was this, she thought despairingly, fucking *it*?

Rendered speechless, she watched as Jeff opened his wallet, leafed through a wad of notes and, pulling out a twenty, continued hammering those nails into the coffin of good old-fashioned romance.

'I've paid for my fishcakes, the mineral water, and the service, but they forgot to charge me for the hot water.' He paused to look delighted by this. 'But yours comes to a little bit more, because you had the cappuccino, and the gin and tonic . . .' Deftly he punched his mobile. 'An extra £6.85 more, actually.'

Bang, bang, bang go those nails in that coffin, thought Rhian, dragging on her cigarette. Stubbing it defeatedly out in the ashtray, she unclipped the brass catch on her silk embroidered butterfly purse and began counting her change out onto the tray. As she did, her disappointment suddenly changed to anger. Hang on a second. Who did Jeff think he was? How dare he come in here with his revolting Drizabone mac, appalling underbite and failed marriage, *and interview her*?

'Actually, I have a question for you,' she said, glaring at him.

He looked surprised, and somewhat uncomfortable. 'You do?'

Standing up, she pulled on her coat, tightly knotted the belt, and fixed him with a stare.

'Arsehole or wanker?'

'Hmmmm.' Placing his forefinger on the tip of his nose in serious contemplation, Jeff hesitated. Finally, 'Wanker,' he answered confidently.

'Ditto.' Shaking back her hair, she threw him a withering smile. 'I couldn't have put it better myself.'

Chapter Thirty-two

To passers-by, it couldn't have appeared a more romantic scene. Saturday evening in fall. Central Park at dusk. A horse-drawn carriage. Two lovebirds snuggled together underneath a red mohair blanket.

'Boobs out, dicks in, smiles purrleeaasse.'

Except they weren't lovebirds, and it wasn't remotely romantic. This was the grand finale and, as the flash popped, Grace and Jimi cringed with embarrassment. Unlike Brady the photographer, who was cantering alongside on a horse like some paparazzo highwayman, gripping the reins with one hand, and with the other firing off pictures with his Nikon.

'This is gonna be totally awesome. It's like action, it's like spontaneous, it's like so totally fabulous it breaks my fucking heart. Jeez. I'm such a sucker for an *affaire du coeur*.' Letting go of the reins he threw his arm in the air and did the kind of flourish only ever seen in bad costume dramas. 'Hey honey, I said smile not snarl,' he barked loudly. 'And you *inamorato*, you're supposed to be nuts for this woman. Nuts, do you dig? I wanna see nuts!'

Grace winced. This was a man who appeared to have been born without the embarrassment gene. Pumped up with adrenalin and a boyhood dream of being in a spaghetti western, he'd come to the shoot prepared with his ten-gallon stetson and, she noted rather worryingly, a pair of suede fringed chaps. He'd transformed himself from Noo-Yawk city slicker into a dead ringer for the cowboy from the Village People.

'*Yeeeh-haaaa.*'

As Brady raced ahead to get a panoramic shot, Jimi untangled himself from underneath the suffocating mohair blanket, and looked across at Grace with a mixture of pity and sufferance. He'd noticed she'd gone very quiet.

'You must be freezing in that dress,' he said affectionately, tucking her up in the blanket like a toddler in its duvet.

'And who've I got to blame for that?' she admonished him good-naturedly, pulling up the collars of her leather coat.

She was still buzzing from their afternoon shopping spree in Barney's. Jimi was even more impulsive than she was and grabbing a Diane von Fürstenberg dress from the rail he'd bundled her into a cubicle. She'd been thrilled by his choice. Off-the-shoulder and asymmetrical in a golden, fairy-print silk, it was gathered all the way down one side, and softly flared at the knee. It was very sexy, very beautiful, and very beach in Barbados.

Goosebumps prickled on her bare legs. She steadfastly ignored them.

'Well it suited you,' shrugged Jimi modestly. For someone who prided himself on being so articulate, that had to be the understatement of the year. The dress more than suited her, it *transformed* her. Every man in the store had stopped to stare at the willowy, graceful, sexy woman who'd stepped out of the changing room in Barney's and twirled in front of him.

Devoid of her bobble hat, scruffy jeans and Ugg boots, Grace had been unrecognizable. He'd watched her, and watched them watching her, and felt suddenly proud of Grace. Of his friend. Who, despite being a female and with no disrespect to Clive, he'd recently come to look upon as his best friend. And then, unexpectedly, he'd felt something else.

Jealousy.

'It's Spencer, isn't it?' Jimi tried to get a grip. Christ, this whole honeymoon charade was getting to him. What had happened to his cynicism? Rationalism? Realism? Mentally picking himself up by the scruff of his Oswald Boateng collar, he shook himself hard. This was all just for Tanya Stiff's benefit. To save his career, his arse, his livelihood. It was a fantasy. A load of lies. Complete bollocks.

He glanced across at Grace. She still looked amazing. So amazing that if he wasn't careful, he was going to start believing his own hype.

Sitting next to him, Grace fidgeted uncomfortably. All weekend she'd tried not to think about Spencer and thanks to Jimi it had been surprisingly easy. But now, 'It just brings back memories . . .' she confessed. Her eyes searched the softly lit grass, the winding paths, the small humpbacked bridge dwarfed by the illuminated backdrop of high-rises. 'See that lake over there,' she motioned with her head. 'In winter it's frozen over and becomes an ice rink. That's where we skated,' she said quietly.

Seeing her pained expression, Jimi felt like the biggest, most selfish bastard ever. He also felt those stirrings of jealousy again. He stomped on them hard. 'Christ, I'm sorry, Grace. It's all my fault. I shouldn't have made you come to New York.'

'Don't be silly,' Grace broke from the memory. 'I've had a great time.' She brushed a rogue piece of hair behind her ear. 'The hotel's amazing, the Cosmo's have been first-class, and you've been . . .' she broke into smile 'a real eye-opener.'

They both groaned at the pun.

'It was just being here in the park . . .'

'I did suggest a helicopter ride instead but it seems Brady's got a fear of flying.'

'Even more reason to go for the helicopter,' quipped Grace.

They both laughed, the mood lifting.

'What about you?' Grace felt a stab of guilt. This might be difficult for her, but it could hardly be easy for Jimi. This was supposed to be his honeymoon, after all. He was supposed to be having a dirty weekend with the woman of his dreams, and instead he'd got her. And her terrible eyebrow gags. 'How are the Kylie pangs?'

Jimi shrugged it off. 'In a box, with the lid on.'

In other words, he probably hasn't thought about her once, thought Grace with a mixture of amazement and envy. For her, the last few weeks had been spent trying to understand, analyse and figure out Spencer, mentally regurgitating details of their relationship, believing that if she could only break this frustrating man code it would lead to some kind of enlightenment about *their* relationship, about *her* feelings, about *his* innermost thoughts.

Jimi on the other hand had spent the last few weeks chatting up women, getting drunk in bars, smoking spliffs and generally using every kind of diversion available to prevent him from thinking about Kylie. He didn't understand why she'd jilted him, and he didn't want to. He wanted to simply ignore it and hope it would go away.

A disconcerting thought struck.

Is that what Spencer was doing with her?

Two Stoli martinis later and they were snugly ensconced in Pastis, a replica of a Parisian brasserie plonked in the middle of the trendy meat-packing district. Thick loaves of crusty bread were stacked against the wall, intricate mosaic floor tiles and large antique mirrors attempted to recreate the ambience of the chic Left Bank, while chiselled waiters flitted around, serving trays of oysters and cocktails to a polished crowd.

In London, dressing up meant dressing down, but here it was a return to old-fashioned glamour, had thought Grace as she'd been shown to their table. The women were wearing more diamonds than J Lo could shake her rocks at, and the men were equally resplendent in their expensively cut suits. But then, in preparation for the grand finale, she and Jimi weren't doing too bad themselves.

'Don't we look chichi,' she whispered as they sat opposite each other at a small candlelit table. Having glammed up in her dress, she'd persuaded Jimi to keep her company by dragging himself out of his uniform of jeans and trainers, and donning his only suit – which just happened to be the one he'd bought for his wedding. 'Well, I might as well wear it,' he'd shrugged, slipping the deep aubergine jacket off its hotel hanger and tugging it on.

'If it's any consolation, my wedding dress is hanging up on the back of the bedroom door,' she'd confided, affectionately brushing a stray hair from his lapel. Usually whenever Grace was reminded of her dress hanging forlornly in its cellophane wrapper, she felt tearful and resentful, but looking at Jimi in his suit it had suddenly seemed tragically comic.

'Well, at least that's one thing we've got in common,' he'd joked, and they'd both burst out laughing.

'You scrub up well, Mr Malik,' grinned Grace, sliding the martini olive off its toothpick and popping it into her mouth.

'You don't look so bad yourself, Mrs Malik,' smiled Jimi, chinking his glass against hers. And then shook his head. 'Shit this is weird,' he sighed, hanging his head and running his thumb and forefinger over his eyebrows, which had already grown back.

'Fun weird,' corrected Grace. She was determined to take on board Jimi's approach to life. For the last few weeks she'd done nothing but think about Spencer: now it was time to think about herself for a change. And so, with the aid of two very strong cocktails on an empty stomach, she'd put all reminiscences of Spencer in 'a box, with the lid on' and was concentrating on enjoying the whole experience.

Jimi looked up. He gazed at her intently, his expression serious, his voice deliberate. 'I'm glad you agreed to come to New York.'

Grace ran her eyes over the familiar contours of his face. It was strange. Whereas once the memory of that face had instilled such hurt, anger and irritation, now it generated such feelings of warmth and security.

'Me too,' she nodded.

'Would madam care to order?' A shiny-faced French waiter began busily clucking around the table, laying cutlery, manoeuvring condiments, arranging napkins. With his pale, hairy forearms moving briskly between them, he fixed Grace with an irritated glare.

The ability to reverse roles and make the customer feel as if they should be deferring to them was a skill only waiters in expensive restaurants could pull off. Grace quickly scanned the menu. 'I'll have the steak, please,' she said, almost apologetically.

'And how would madam prefer that?' he asked, barely concealing a sneer. As a Parisian working in New York, used to the Americans' Neanderthal requests for their steak 'well done', he was prepared to have his country's culinary heritage insulted – yet again.

But Grace surprised him. 'Rare,' she said, and smiled, sensing a change in atmosphere as the waiter looked upon her with new respect. Unlike Jimi, she thought, as she caught his look of disapproval.

'You eat meat?'

'Don't you?' she asked equally incredulously. This was, after all, the same man who'd sat next to her on the Virgin flight and wolfed down his mid-movie snack of a turkey roll. And hers as well.

Ordering oysters to start and halibut to follow, Jimi passed his menu to the heel-clicking waiter, and then, turning to Grace, pretended to shudder. 'No way, I'm a vegetarian.'

'Who just happens to eat sushi, Thai chicken curry,

and wears a leather jacket,' she couldn't resist adding.

Looking defensive, Jimi ignored her. 'Red meat's bad for you. Didn't you read all the stuff in the papers about mad cows and foot-and-mouth?'

'Oh, and I suppose cigarettes and alcohol are full of vitamins, are they?'

Midway between taking a drag of cigarette and sipping his martini, Jimi slumped back in his chair and held up his hands in defeat. 'OK, you win,' he smiled good-naturedly. 'It's just that I can't remember the last time I was with a girl and she ordered steak.'

'That's because you go out with skinny model types who graze on rocket salads,' grinned Grace, firmly buttering a roll of bread. 'And dessert's a gram of coke.'

This time Jimi didn't say anything. She'd just described Kylie.

For the next hour food and drink flowed, as did the conversation. Over their entrée of oysters, they traded anecdotes about Manchester, each of them revelling in the enjoyment of being with someone who shared the same background, the same references, the same accent. Waiting for the main course to arrive they made half-hearted stabs at politics and religion before both confessing, as they puffed on a shared cigarette and ordered more Stoli martinis, that neither really had a clue. Another round of drinks was accompanied by an argument over whether the moon landings were faked or not – Jimi cynically insisting they were, Grace indignantly refuting it. And so it was with relief that by the time their main courses had arrived they moved swiftly and happily on to something much more interesting.

Sex.

'That's just it, it doesn't have to *mean* anything,' argued Jimi, waving his fork on which was impaled a juicy chunk of steak. One bottle of Sancerre, four Stoli martinis and a very dull-looking piece of halibut later, all fears of BSE and mad cows had gone out of the window and he was tucking into Grace's steak *au poivre*, served with a tall order of slender fries. 'Sometimes sex can be just about sex.' His mind threw up a mental photograph album of his past as if to prove a point.

'For you, maybe,' said Grace, scooping up mayonnaise on the end of a fry. 'But for me, sex is about being in love. About *making love*.' She chewed defensively. She could feel this discussion fast turning into a heated argument.

Jimi raised his eyebrows. 'You mean you've never had sex and thought, "wow, that was a great fuck."'

'I've had great fucks,' admonished Grace loudly.

Too loudly. Diners in the restaurant turned round to stare.

'But I've also been in love,' she hissed, averting her eyes from the curious stares and dipping her head down low over the table.

'Exactly,' replied Jimi knowledgeably.

And somewhat smugly, thought Grace.

In the background there was the sound of a horn section as the resident swing band struck up a rendition of 'Mr Bojangles'. People started moving from the bar across to the small dance floor.

'You're getting the two confused. Love doesn't have to have anything to do with good sex. In fact, often being in love just means emotions get in the way,' argued Jimi. He recalled Sammy-Jo and his absent erection. He ignored it. Having sex with one woman while being in love with another wasn't quite what he was referring to. 'Sex isn't a mental exercise, it's purely physical.'

'Oh spare me,' said Grace derisively. 'Lookee here, it's Don Juan.'

'And who are you? Mother Teresa?' retorted Jimi sarcastically.

'Just because I don't sleep around, doesn't mean I haven't had great sex.'

'Maybe not, but it means you've never had sex purely for sex's sake.'

302

'Whereas you have,' she said, unable to bite back the sarcasm.

'Of course,' he shrugged.

'And you think that gives you the right to smugly lecture me on what is and isn't good sex?' Grace was trying to keep this objective, but it was getting more and more personal.

Sitting back in his chair, Jimi eyed her challengingly. 'Tell me, have you ever had a one-night stand?'

Feeling a blush prickling up past her collarbones and into her cheeks, she pulled back her shoulder and eyed him defiantly. 'Once,' she replied. 'But it wasn't very good.'

'It is if it's with the right person,' he winked.

'*Exactly*,' she replied sarcastically.

'Oh, and what's *that* supposed to mean?' He sniffed, throwing down his napkin.

Grace immediately threw down hers. 'It means, Jimi Malik, it just so happened to be with *you*.'

All at once an awkward silence fell like a guillotine over the table.

Oh dear. Perhaps that had been a little below the belt, thought Grace, looking at Jimi whose neck was beginning to break out in blotches.

Picking up his wine glass, he used the time it took to drain it to pull himself together. 'Well, I haven't had many other complaints,' he joked, attempting to rescue the situation, not to mention his ego.

'And you think that makes you the expert?'

'Well you did call me Don Juan,' he laughed. And then stopped. Grace was glaring at him furiously.

'You wouldn't know good sex if it came up and jumped on you,' she said loudly.

'And you would?' he retorted indignantly. 'You, the woman who for the past six months has been having a sex life with her fiancé that consisted of once a month?'

Betrayal flashed across Grace's face. 'You smug bastard,' she hissed, finding her voice.

As the waiter came to remove their plates, he stared at them open-mouthed.

'We have a very open relationship,' quipped Jimi, ordering a couple of brandies to appease him.

But it didn't appease Grace. 'How could you? I told you that in strictest confidence,' she continued, deeply regretting she'd ever divulged this piece of information to Jimi. 'And anyway, it's quality, not quantity,' she added primly.

'What? I haven't had quality?' He looked affronted. 'I've had quality,' he protested.

'Rubbish,' she refuted. 'You've had shags, and fucks and bonks and flings. And that's not quality, that's just a sad imitation. You might be some stud in bed, but it's all a performance. It's not just about that –' she motioned to his crotch. 'It's about this –' she pointed to his head. 'And this –' she leaned across the table and pressed the flat of her hand against his heart. 'You don't know what it's like to really make love, because, you know what?' Her voice rose, and she leaned back in her chair, her chest heaving, catching her breath. '*I don't think you've ever been in love.*'

No sooner had the words flown out of her mouth than Grace wanted to stuff them back in again. Oh Christ, me and my stupid lousy temper, she cursed silently. Why can't I think before I speak? But it was too late. The words were out there – suspended above Jimi's head in some great big cartoon bubble.

She watched as his face crumpled.

'Oh Jimi, I'm sorry. I've got a stupid temper, I didn't mean . . .' she said as she reached out for his hand across the table.

'No, maybe you're right,' he interrupted her, his mind throwing up images of Kylie, dredging up memories of his initial devastation when she'd jilted him, and the gradual realization once the shock had worn off that it was only his vanity that had been bruised, not his heart that had been broken. 'I don't think I have.'

Until now.

Staring at Grace's delicate pale fingers, stretched starfish wide over his own, Jimi slowly raised his eyes. And it was at that moment, at exactly five minutes to nine East Coast time, in the middle of a crowded Manhattan restaurant, surrounded by the eclectic din of stroppy French waiters, clattering cutlery, chattering diners and a forties swing band, across a white linen tablecloth smeared with ketchup and mayonnaise, and littered with white floury crumbs of French bread and specks of cigarette ash, that Jimi Malik took one look at Grace and, for the first time in his life, fell totally, utterly, and helplessly in love.

Oh shite.

Chapter Thirty-three

Curled up on the sofa, Rhian let out a sudden snort, and woke herself up with a start.

'Uh . . .' She snapped her eyes open, feeling a little disorientated. She must have dropped off. It was dark. What time was it? Sitting up sleepily, she squinted at her watch. It had stopped. Probably needs a new battery, she thought, shaking it and holding it up to her ear.

The only sound she could hear was the radio. Turned down low in the background, she recognized the faint murmuring of Dr Cupid's voice. She couldn't hear what he was saying, but it told her it was late. Probably nearly one, she thought, easing herself off the sofa and walking into her bedroom, the kitten heels of her marabou slippers softly clicking on the floor.

Yawning, Rhian sat down at her dressing table, grabbed a cottonwool ball and doused it with baby oil. Rubbing her heavily kohled eyes, she thought about Jeff. Why on earth did I even bother going on that stupid date? I mean, really, what was the point? With mascara smudged around her eyes like Ling-Ling the Chinese panda, Rhian spoke crossly to her reflection.

And then, quite unexpectedly, she burst into loud throaty laughter.

'Bali or Val-d'Isère,' she squeaked, clasping her face in her hands. 'Cheese plate or . . . or . . .' she could barely get her words out for laughing '. . . *sticky-toffee*

pudding,' she yelped, her body shaking uncontrollably. Now, unable to see anything but the
funny side of the evening, she was shrieking with
hysterics. 'And he had a cat called Tigger . . .' She
snorted loudly '. . . and he carried teabags in his inside
pocket . . . and they were *peppermint* . . .' Hugging her
aching ribs, she dissolved into another fit of giggles. It
was just too funny. It was like a black comedy. It was
so tragic, it was hilarious, simply hilarious.

Thankfully, when her stomach was aching so much
it was actually painful, her laughter began to subside.
Sighing and wheezing, she reached for a tissue and
began to wipe away the mascara tears running down
her face. She hadn't laughed so hard in ages and it felt
good. Very, very good. A wide smile spread across her
face and looking up at her reflection she took a deep
breath. 'Rhian Octavia Jones, what are you *like*?' she
gasped, shaking her head and grinning. 'I mean, c'mon
girl, it's all very well talking about paths crossing, and
fate, and destiny and waiting for your soulmate, but you
can't spend your life waiting for him, going on dates
with men like Jeff . . . Dear Lord, *can you imagine*?'

At the very idea, Rhian groaned loudly. 'And what if
this soulmate of yours never shows up? What if he's
out there looking for you right this minute but he's lost
your address, or can't read a map, or he's taken a
wrong turning? *What if he can't find you?*' Blowing
her nose loudly, she threw her tissue in the wicker
basket. She stared at herself. An idea stirred. Flipped
over. Took hold.

She knew exactly what she was going to do.

Experiencing a rush of determination, she lifted the
embroidered lid off a wooden box that sat on her
dressing table and selected a piece of notepaper from
inside. Scented with lavender, she kept it along with
an old fountain pen of her grandmother's as she
thought it was all very romantic and very Jane Austen,
although in reality she'd never actually written anything more than a shopping list.

Until now.

Because Grace's right, decided Rhian. I'm going to stop relying on the universe, stop wishing the stars would hurry up and work their magic and that Venus would get its finger out. I'm going to throw away all those magazines, stop reading my horoscope, stop waiting for *un colpo di fulmine* – that great big Italian thunderbolt – to strike me while I blindly go about my life.

Bugger leaving things to chance, I'm going to get proactive. My soulmate is out there somewhere, and if he can't find me, then there's nothing else for it.

I'm going to find *him*.

Dipping the gold nib in a pot of lilac ink, her large curly handwriting flowed over the page. And with hope, optimism and steely determination, she began her letter.

'Dearest Doctor Cupid . . .'

Chapter Thirty-four

You could have cut the atmosphere with a knife.

Actually, on second thoughts forget the knife, you'd have needed a heavy-duty JCB to get through the wall of silence that separated Grace and Jimi as they stood two trolleys apart at the baggage carousel at Heathrow airport. It was a grey, drizzly, typically British Monday morning and having just endured a terrifyingly turbulent night-flight from JFK, they were both relieved to be home. Staring doggedly at the suitcases rattling past on the conveyor belt, they were so jet-lagged, hungover and shaken up, they could barely stand, let alone hold a conversation.

Or so they were both trying to convince themselves.

Because if either of them was being honest, it wasn't the turbulence that was to blame for why they were feeling so shaken up, or why they weren't speaking, or why they were avoiding each other's eyes.

It was all down to what had happened on that last night in New York.

'Is it the oysters?'

In the awkward aftermath of their somewhat heated debate about sex, they'd remained sitting at their table in Pastis, fidgeting with their cutlery, staring into space, until after a few minutes Grace had noticed, rather worryingly, that Jimi had turned ashen and adopted a peculiar glazed expression.

'Oysters?' Zoning back in, Jimi had tried to speak, but it was as if his tongue had turned into some strange rubbery object that flailed around in his mouth making it impossible to articulate. So this is what they mean when they say 'struck dumb', he thought, staring blankly at Grace.

'Jimi?' Still feeling terrible about her earlier accusation that he'd never been in love, Grace squeezed his hand, trying to get some kind of response. His silence was unnerving. Either he was preparing to retaliate with an equally venomous attack. Or, she reconsidered, moving back slightly in her seat, he was about to throw up.

He did neither.

Unexpectedly he scraped back his chair, stood up and held out his hand. 'Shall we dance?' he asked.

Taken aback, it was now Grace's turn to stare blankly. What on earth had got into Jimi? He was behaving very weirdly. Was he drunk? she mused, her confusion turning to delight as she followed his eyes to the small dance floor filled with couples, smiling and laughing, twirling and dipping.

A large grin spread across her face, and tugging her napkin off her lap, she stood up. 'I'm warning you now, I have two left feet,' she confessed, accepting Jimi's hand.

'Good job I've got two right ones, then, isn't it?' he quipped, using flippancy to hide the fact that his legs felt as if they'd turned to jelly. His brow prickled with sweat. His stomach churned. He clenched his teeth together so tightly that he felt the muscle in his jaw go into spasm and begin to twitch. This was ridiculous.

This was *Grace*.

They were buddies. She squeezed her blackheads in front of him, he farted in front of her, she'd confessed to plucking ingrowing hairs from her bikini line and embarrassing sexual fantasies about Ross from *Friends*, he'd shared the secret of his hairy back and his recent, and very humiliating, encounter with

310

Sammy-Jo. Even the bit about the King Kong vibrator. At which Grace had keeled over with laughter, hid her face under a cushion, and hadn't resurfaced for at least ten minutes.

Memories, reasons, disagreements. Past conversations, shared moments, furious arguments, layer upon layer they built up in his mind like a huge lasagne. He looked at Grace, saw her smiling at him, and quickly hiding his true feelings he switched on his characteristic grin. And to a bawdy fanfare of trumpets, he threaded his fingers firmly through hers and led her onto the dance floor.

Oh dear.

As soon as the sole of Grace's new Kurt Geiger mule hit the parquet flooring, she suddenly realized what she'd let herself in for.

Jimi was a good dancer.

Like, a really, really good dancer. Like the kind of dancer you see in a club that makes you want to pick up your handbag, get your coat and take your pathetic excuse for a gyration home to your bedroom mirror where no-one can see you. Except everyone can see me, she silently groaned, as Jimi twirled her for the umpteenth time and she ended up getting tangled up inside the crook of his arm, her ankles bending over sideways as she tried to right herself. Wrapping his arm tightly around her waist, Jimi smiled warmly.

She smiled back gratefully. Not only had the guy got rhythm, he'd got a sense of humour as well.

'You know, my friend Rhian was right,' began Grace, doing what crap dancers always do when they're feeling self-conscious, and striking up a conversation to divert the attention from her appalling footwork and complete lack of rhythm. 'She's single and she's always saying that for women in their thirties there simply aren't any nice men left.'

Grace was having to shout above the music, but a few trumpets weren't going to stop her now she'd started. 'But if you're single and male it's a different

311

story. Just look around you, you're spoilt for choice. You should think yourself lucky.' Treading on Jimi's foot, she smiled up at him apologetically. It was a heavy-handed way to cheer him up, to apologize for her earlier bluntness, but it did happen to be true. The place was full of women and, as far as she could tell, there was only one single guy in the place other than Jimi, and he was a gay photographer.

The camera flashed. Grace screwed up her face with embarrassment, as Brady pointed the camera at her and fired off a series of frames. Having failed to get the number of the barman, a disillusioned Brady was intent on getting his final few shots, before he went home and took up his new career as a Trappist monk.

Grace wished he'd hurry up. Being a bad dancer was bad enough, but to have it captured for ever in *Chic Traveller* was something else.

'Yeah, and why is that?' asked Jimi as he twirled her around.

'Because while I'm stuck in the desert, you're in a permanent oasis. There are hundreds of women for you to fall in love with,' she argued, catching sight of one such woman. Poised seductively at the bar, eyelashes down, lipglossed lips slightly apart, the pretty redhead was staring very obviously at Jimi.

'Come on guys, it's my last shot, let's getta close-up.' Brady dived towards them, brandishing a zoom lens.

'Hundreds,' repeated Grace, her voice trailing off as Jimi's hand inched across her waist to the small of her back. She was supposed to be cheering him up, but instead a tiny part of her deep down felt oddly protective. Instinctively she threw the redhead a territorial look. Or was that possessive?

As soon as the question sprung up in her mind, it was as if it had been there for ever. All at once Grace felt the oddest sensation. It was as if someone had come along with a great big remote control and adjusted the picture, turning down the music, zooming in for a close-up. Jimi was all she was aware of.

The pressure of his chest against hers, the small triangle of skin where his collar was unbuttoned, the faded smell of aftershave and cigarettes.

'One kiss and then I'm outta here.' Far, far away in the background, Brady's muffled words sounded like a distant voiceover.

Jimi pulled her closer. 'But what good are hundreds of women?' he asked quietly, his face so close she felt his breath on her cheek as he spoke. Tilting her chin with his finger, he shrugged apologetically. 'When I only want the one?'

And then, before she knew what was happening, he was kissing her. And she was kissing him. And they were standing in the middle of the dance floor, wrapped around each other like two teenagers in a slow dance. And in the distant background was the sound of Brady squealing frantically from the sidelines like a cheerleader, 'OK guys . . . that's it . . . you can stop now . . . I said cut . . . cut . . . Goddamn *cuuuuttttt.*'

In baggage reclaim there was a dull humming noise as the carousel abruptly started up, followed by the first few suitcases thumping noisily down the chute. Spotting his holdall, Jimi dived through the gaggle that had gathered territorially around the conveyor belt and lunged at the handle. Like a cowboy wrestling a heifer to the ground, he threw himself on its black leather back and hoisted it, biceps bulging, onto his trolley. As he did, a small box of matches fell out of his pocket. Bending down to pick it up, he saw they were from the restaurant. His mind flicked back to Saturday night. Pastis. Kissing Grace.

At the memory Jimi's heart hiccuped. Actually, it wasn't so much a kiss, more one of those moments in a movie where the camera circles endlessly and the theme tune strikes up. Until finally they'd broken apart, opened their eyes, and the soundtrack that had been playing in his head had stopped dead as Grace had blurted 'I need the loo' and vanished.

313

By the time she'd returned he'd pulled himself together, settled the bill and was cracking some joke or other with Brady as if everything was perfectly normal. It had been an Oscar-winning performance. Beneath the easy smile and confident swagger he'd been all over the place. On the one hand he could still tantalizingly taste Grace's lipgloss on his mouth, yet on the other he'd just seen her run away from him with a look of sheer horror plastered across her face.

She didn't mention it again, and of course he didn't either, and so they'd pretended to ignore it by entering a very bizarre situation of acting as if nothing had happened, saying their goodbyes to Brady, catching a cab back to their hotel, making smalltalk on the back seat. And apart from a few self-conscious silences, it *was* as if it had never happened. Almost, but not completely, for when Grace's thigh had brushed next to his he'd felt a tingle of something that wasn't static electricity, and when she'd firmly tucked her coat around her and glanced agitatedly out of the window, he'd half hoped, half suspected she'd felt it too.

Which just goes to show how wrong you can be, thought Jimi, sneaking a look at Grace across the luggage carousel. Because when he'd asked her to join him for a nightcap in the hotel bar she'd made up some excuse about feeling sleepy and gone straight back to the room. It was almost as if she couldn't run away from me fast enough, he'd thought as he'd walked dejectedly into the dimly lit bar, slid onto an empty barstool and, feeling like a complete loser, ordered himself a whiskey sour.

A large one.

Leaning on her airport trolley Grace was struggling to keep up her act of sleepy uninterest. It was impossible. On the pretence of stifling a yawn, she couldn't resist sneaking a look at Jimi through her fingers. It was just so weird, she thought, watching him staring thoughtfully at a box of matches before sliding them into his pocket. He still looked the same – khaki T-shirt with a Bloody Mary stain, Diesel jeans with the hole in the knee, unlaced acid-green Pumas – yet he looked completely different.

Or is it because I'm looking at him completely differently? thought Grace, a hot, guilty flush flooding her body. Is it because . . . She broke off, momentarily distracted by his bottom, which she'd never noticed before, and which she didn't seem able to take her eyes off. Unexpectedly, she had an urge to slip her fingers into the faded denim pockets of his jeans, to wrap her arms around his neck, to breathe in that warm, musky smell of his, to kiss him . . .

Even now, back at Heathrow, she couldn't believe what had happened on the dance floor in New York. It had been the alcohol's fault. All those Stoli martinis had confused all those neurotransmitters or whatever, and she'd ended up lusting after Jimi because she was missing Spencer. Simple. Except it hadn't felt simple. It had felt embarrassing, confusing, *and incredibly thrilling*.

On the cab ride back to the hotel it had been as if every nerve ending had been on full alert. Every gesture, every breath, every pause magnified into some great big significance, and when he'd suggested a nightcap the possibilities had circled dizzyingly around them both. Tingling with excitement, she'd looked at Jimi. At the thin silvery scar above his ear where his hair refused to grow, the easy, intimate, familiar smile, the dark triangle of skin that was revealed where his shirt collar gaped open. He'd looked so adorable. He'd looked so endearing. *He'd looked so fucking sexy*.

'No thanks, I'm tired. I think I'll go straight to bed.' Yanking on a mental handbrake, she'd forced her desires to screech to a halt. Life was complicated enough without making it even more messy. 'Good night, Jimi. See you in the morning.' Throwing him a little wave, she'd left him in the lobby and walked towards the elevators. She'd had to fight with herself every step of the way.

'Well, I guess this is it, the honeymoon's over.' Having swept unchallenged through customs and into the packed arrivals hall Jimi was doing his best to lighten the atmosphere with a rather sad attempt at a joke. He smiled apologetically at Grace.

'Yep, I guess so.' Grace smiled awkwardly.

There was an excruciating pause.

'Erm . . . so . . . do you want a lift back to London? Clive offered to pick me up, well, not so much offered, I had to twist his arm and . . .' Jimi could hear himself blathering but was powerless to stop.

'No, it's fine,' cut in Grace, shaking her head. 'I thought I'd catch the Heathrow Express.'

'Oh . . . right.' Jimi felt curiously deflated. He'd loved spending the weekend with Grace and now he didn't want her to go. He missed her already. 'Yep, of course.' He nodded, rubbing his temples agitatedly.

Watching him, Grace wavered. He looked so sweet, and awkward, and gorgeous. *Christ almighty, there she went again.* She caught herself. Thoughts like that were going to get her into trouble.

It was thoughts like that which had been running through her head as she'd stood in the elevator at the SoHo Grand, watching the floors lighting up as she headed back to their room. She'd tried ignoring them, blocking them out by thinking about getting in the bath, putting on her pyjamas, eating those delicious chocolate truffles the maid left on her pillow and watching *Love Story* on video. What more could a girl want?

Only when the doors had pinged open, she'd put one foot in the corridor and stopped. She couldn't do it. She didn't want to do it. She *wasn't going to do it*. Sod Ryan O'Neil. Sod Ali McGraw, even if she did look absolutely amazing in that little pleated kilt and bobble hat. And sod sitting in the room, she'd thought, impulsively stepping back inside the elevator and hitting the down button.

It had been complete madness. She'd known she was being crazy. Jimi was her friend, he was her ex, and he was also a complete tart when it came to women. Yet despite knowing all the reasons why she shouldn't be even contemplating what she was doing, before she knew it she'd been stepping into the lobby. And hurrying towards the bar, her stilettos clattering on the marble floor, her heart drumrolling behind her push-up bra as she thought about what might happen, what she wanted to happen.

Pausing at the entrance to the bar, she'd spotted Jimi immediately. He was sitting with his back to her at the bar, but he wasn't alone. Next to him was a pretty blonde. Deep in conversation, their heads bent low, it had been pretty obvious by their body language that Jimi was chatting her up. He certainly hadn't wasted any time, she'd thought, feeling unexpectedly jealous. And so bloody foolish. How could she? After all this time and she'd nearly fallen for it. Again.

For a moment she'd stood there, all the suspense, anticipation, excitement and hopefulness trickling away as she'd watched them together. And then turning away before he could notice her, she sadly headed back to their room.

'Are you sure you don't want a lift?'

Jimi's voice interrupted her thoughts. 'I've already bought my ticket,' she lied hastily before she did anything stupid. After that night at the restaurant I don't trust myself anymore, she thought, looking at Jimi, who was staring at her with the kind of intensity that made her flesh go all goosepimply.

The mood was broken by the sound of Jimi's mobile ringing. Still programmed to the theme tune of *Rhubarb and Custard*, which he seemed to be having a real problem changing, it began to play jauntily while he frantically patted his pockets, searching for it and cursing under his breath. Finally he found it. 'Hello? Oh hi Clive . . .'

Taking it as her cue, Grace grabbed the handle of her trolley. 'I'll call you,' she said, throwing him a wave.

'Wait . . .' Jimi motioned to Grace.

But she was eager to leave. Bobbing forwards she quickly kissed him on the cheek. 'Oh by the way, I nearly forgot,' she whispered, fumbling momentarily before pressing something into his hand and hurrying away.

'Hang on, Clive . . . I mean Grace,' he flustered as she began quickly weaving her way through the crowds. 'I'll call you!' he shouted after her. 'And thanks,' he added quietly, putting a hand gingerly up to his throbbing temple.

God, he felt rough. He'd only ever intended to have one whiskey sour. Or at least that had been the idea as he'd sat by himself that night at the hotel bar, dragging miserably on a Marlboro. Just the one and then he'd been going to head back to the hotel room and crash on the sofa, by which time hopefully Grace would already be asleep. He'd been slugging back the last mouthful, about to ask for the bill when someone had sat down in the seat next to him, ordered a vodka tonic, and said, 'I don't suppose I could steal a smoke, could I?'

Looking up he'd recognized the waitress who'd served him earlier. Petite, with short vanilla blond hair and freckles that looked as if they'd been crayoned on, she was gaminely pretty. 'Help yourself,' he nodded, flicking open the packet and holding it out to her. Usually he would have jumped at the opportunity to chat up a pretty New Yorker, but now the desire had mysteriously disappeared.

'Don't worry, I'm not hitting on you,' she'd laughed, striking a match and placing the cigarette daintily between her china doll teeth.

'Do I look worried?' he'd smiled, but it was friendly, not flirty. It had been a first.

'Nope.' Shaking her head, she'd narrowed her eyes

and surveyed him as if she was trying to work him out, like an exhibit in a gallery. 'You look like you're in love,' she'd said after a moment.

'Excuse me?' he'd said, taken aback.

She'd laughed at his shocked expression. 'So c'mon, what's her name?'

For a moment he'd toyed with the idea of pretending he didn't know what she was talking about, but there was something oddly comforting about confiding in a stranger. The anonymity. The impartiality. The knowledge that he would never see this person again. He'd motioned to the barman. 'I'll have the same again.' And turning to the waitress he'd begun. 'Her name's Grace . . .'

'*Thanks? Thanks for what? What have I done?*' Confused, Clive was bleating at the other end of the line.

Jimi snapped back to the arrivals hall. 'No, not you, you daft bastard,' he snorted. 'I'm talking to Grace.' He looked up and caught a last glimpse of her bobble hat as swarms of people welled up behind her and she vanished. 'At least I was . . .' he murmured, suddenly conscious of something in his hand. He unfurled his fingers. Resting on the creases of his outstretched palm was the cheap gold band he'd bought at a tacky jeweller's in the high street. It was Grace's fake wedding ring. Staring at it Jimi felt a thud of disappointment. And there was nothing at all fake about that.

Chapter Thirty-five

On the Apple Mac computer, the starburst screensaver was busily twirling and metamorphosing, the kaleidoscope patterns exploding brightly and hypnotically against the black outer-space background.

It could have saved itself all the effort.

Nobody was paying any attention. Least of all Grace, who was sitting inches away from it slouched at her desk, fingers resting on the keyboard, eyes gazing blankly out of the window.

It was nearly five-thirty and all day she'd been cooped up in the office trying to catch up on the backlog of work. It was two days since she'd flown back from New York and discovered her in-tray had mushroomed into a pile marked 'urgent' but now, with the day drawing to a close and Janine's Glade plug-ins giving off a sickly sweet scent of 'desert rose', combined with the last dredges of jetlag, her concentration had slipped and her mind had wandered back across the Atlantic.

It was hard to believe she'd actually been there. Plunged back into the grey normality of her life in London, New York seemed like a surreal memory, a collection of crazy, fun, happy images that lay scattered in her mind like Brady's Polaroids. The weekend had been one long masquerade – two newly-weds madly in love and on their honeymoon – and she'd got so caught up in the hype she'd almost started to believe it. Why else would she have kissed Jimi on the dance floor? Why else would she have gone back down in the lift? She was just thankful she'd spotted him chatting up that blonde at the bar before it was too late and she'd made a complete fool of herself.

Grace hadn't seen Jimi since she'd left him at the airport and caught the tube back to her flat. At first, racked with all those weird feelings of hurt, anger and guilty embarrassment she'd intended to avoid Jimi, to not call him – at least for a few days – but after only a couple of hours she'd started to miss him and so she'd been relieved when he'd called and cracked his latest joke. 'Heard about the new pill? Fifty per cent valium, 50 per cent Viagra. If you don't get a fuck, you don't give a fuck.' It had been a good way to break the ice, and as Grace burst into laughter, any awkwardness had vanished and they were back to being friends again, just as if nothing had happened.

A pigeon landed fluttering onto the window ledge, its loud cooing breaking into Grace's daydream and snapping her eyes back into focus. As it flew away again she found herself looking out through the vertical slats of the blind, across the red brick rooftops towards Hyde Park. A sulky gloom hung over the city, trees rose brittle and skeletal against the pebble-coloured sky. Even the shiny, gold-painted Albert Memorial looked dull and muted.

Grace smiled to herself. According to every novel she'd ever read, the weather always mirrored the character's mood. Traditionally, it was gloriously sunny when they were cheerful, and bucketed down when they were miserable. Which is probably a good reason why I'm not a character in a novel, she thought, because she certainly didn't feel gloomy or grey. On the contrary, the good mood that had descended upon her in New York still lingered like the cosy warmth of a hot water bottle.

It was ironic, really: she'd gone to New York to do Jimi a favour, yet it was *he* that had done *her* the

321

favour. It was as if somehow, something inside Grace had changed. She felt different, she looked different, thanks to the haircut she'd treated herself to on that last day in New York. Glossy and dark, with a long, shaggy fringe, she'd spent the last forty-eight hours glued to every passing wing mirror and shop window, checking out her reflection. It was a terrible cliché, she'd thought as she stopped in front of the mirror of a passport photo booth in the underground on her way to work that morning, but although it might be just a new hairstyle, it actually made her *feel* like a new person.

So new in fact that after she'd got back from the airport, it wasn't until she'd dutifully unpacked her bag, made herself a mug of tea, and was prostrate on the sofa, enjoying the luxury of taking Monday off work, that she'd realized she'd forgotten to check her messages. Her forgetfulness had been momentous. Since her break with Spencer, the first thing Grace did when she got back to her rented studio was to look for the light on her answering machine. If it wasn't flashing, her spirits would plummet. If it was, she'd dive on it, sending keys, bag, groceries flying as she pressed the magic button, heart thumping, hope stretched tight like an elastic band.

That Monday there'd been three messages, all from her mother. Mrs Fairley had taken to calling her on a daily basis since she'd moved out of Spencer's or, as her mother preferred to call it, 'taken leave of her senses'. As far as she was concerned, how could a wealthy, middle-class lawyer with a limed-oak kitchen and a full head of hair not be Mr Right? The small matter of his refusal to set a date had been pooh-poohed away with a 'Your father was just the same.' Which didn't exactly instil confidence in Grace, considering they'd been divorced for the past ten years.

Pressing the delete button that morning, Grace had watched the digital display turn back to zero. She'd be lying not to admit to a sting of disappointment as the elastic band of hope had snapped and she'd realized there was no message from Spencer – but this time it only hurt for a few moments, the time it took to pick up a Polaroid of Jimi that was lying on the breakfast bar. Maybe Jimi was right. Maybe all Spencer needed was time. Maybe he would ring in a few weeks and say everything she wanted to hear. Peering at the picture of Jimi on the top of the Empire State, a daft grin plastered all over his face, she'd smiled fondly. To be honest, she was beginning to forget what that was.

'Ahem . . .' There was the sound of someone loudly, and very obviously, clearing their throat.

Startled, Grace swung round on her chair to see Janine hovering next to the photocopier, grasping a large cellophane bouquet in her solid fingers. She looked extremely uncomfortable.

'Attention, everybody. I want to make an important announcement.' The usual office hum of clicking mice, tapping keyboards, phone conversations and jokey banter fell whisperingly silent. Satisfied that she had a captive audience, Janine paused to look across at Maggie, who was dutifully affecting surprise and astonishment. 'Margaret, if you'd be so kind as to share the podium,' she intoned in her most authoritative voice.

Grace smiled, a mix of fondness and sadness. This was Maggie's retirement speech. After fifteen years at Big Fish Designs, she was leaving to start her new life in the sun, to swap her days photocopying reports and drinking coffee, for drinking sangria and collecting hand-painted Spanish plates for her villa.

She watched Maggie blushing furiously as she stood up from the greenhouse of spider plants and ferns that was her desk. Wearing a pair of tight cream jodhpurs and a white embroidered gypsy top that showed off her cappuccino tan, she padded across the office. Despite the cold weather, she was still wearing sandals, her tanned toes set off by bright, letterbox-red nail polish. Out of the corner of her eye, she glanced at Grace and rolled her eyes sardonically.

'Now, as you all know, Margaret is a valued member of staff,' began Janine, launching into her pre-scripted speech with all the determination and obvious rehearsal of an actor accepting a lifetime achievement award. '. . . who's been with us for more years than some of us care to remember . . .' Cue fake laughter from Janine.

Grace cringed. Here was a woman who, for as long as anyone could remember, had made no secret of the fact that she couldn't abide Maggie and yet here she was, playing the sycophant, gushing about how she was a 'shining star' – yes, she really did use those words – and how she'd be sorely missed. Until thankfully, after what felt like for ever her speech came to a welcome end, the bouquet and vouchers were presented, and the sparkling wine was duly dispersed into plastic beakers.

'Cheers, doll.' Accepting a top-up from Grace, Maggie smiled gratefully. Although she'd never admit it – to herself or anyone else – Janine's speech had actually made her feel rather emotional, and the subsequent round of good lucks and fond farewells was threatening to trigger a few tears. She sniffed brusquely, and focused on Grace. 'So c'mon, spill the beans. How was your weekend?'

'Fine,' said Grace. Since she'd got back from New York and Maggie had returned from Spain she'd been so busy, they'd barely had a moment to catch up. 'No, it was more than fine, it was good,' she corrected. 'Great, in fact.' She smiled.

Sipping her wine, Maggie's eyes widened. 'How great?'

Grace laughed. 'Jimi's just a friend,' she protested, feeling unexpectedly embarrassed at the implication.

Maggie looked unconvinced. 'Is that so?' she replied,

coral-lipsticked mouth pursed in a seaside postcard pout. 'So he's got nothing to do with why you've spent the last two days staring out of the window?'

This time it was Grace's turn to blush furiously. 'I was thinking about Spencer,' she remonstrated. Well, partly, she realized, feeling guilty.

Maggie's expression softened as she looked at Grace sitting hunched on the edge of her desk in a pair of dusky pink cords and a fluffy mohair sweater. Sometimes she looked much younger than her thirty-one years. 'Have you spoken to him?' she asked hopefully. Ever since Grace had told her she'd moved out of Spencer's, she'd listened silently and supportively to the whole saga.

Grace shook her head. 'No. I haven't called him, and he hasn't called me. Well, not since my contact lenses arrived,' smiled Grace, in a feeble attempt at humour. 'But enough about me, what about you?' she said, quickly changing the subject. 'How's the new Casa Maggie?'

'Fabulous,' enthused Maggie. Her mind flicked through her mental photo album: golden sunshine, their new home, the smells, sights and tastes of Southern Spain. And then there was another image. Curled up on the sunlounger with Sonny crouching at her bare feet, her hands shaking as she'd carefully peeled back the sealed edge of the envelope. Passing the letter to Sonny, his eyes silently skimming its neatly typed contents, his voice wavering as he read aloud the words.

'Before we all dash off I just want to say *bon voyage* and all that.'

Jolted back to London, the clamour of the office, the sweet taste of sparkling wine, Maggie swung round to see Janine cutting a swathe through the clusters of people, a barely concealed smile of pure jubilation on her face as she held out her hand. 'It's not going to be the same without you.'

Lighting up a cigarette, Maggie took a drag. 'Thanks,

325

doll, the feeling's mutual,' she said, and shaking her hand, promptly blew a jet of smoke into her face. It was her final parting shot and one that sent Janine scowling and spluttering towards the photocopier.

One by one, people began pulling on coats and scarves and drifting over to say their goodbyes, giving hugs, cracking jokes. Maggie was like mum to the whole office, and everyone was sad to see her go.

'Are you walking to the tube?' asked Grace, tugging on her coat. Since Maggie had sold her beloved Panda, they'd taken to walking together to the station after work.

'No, I'm off to meet Sonny,' replied Maggie, as she scooped her cream leather jacket and handbag from her desk and pulled out her lipstick. Owing to years of practice, she expertly reapplied without a mirror, and then rubbed her lips together.

'Ooh, lucky you, off to celebrate,' smiled Grace. 'Anywhere nice?'

Maggie hesitated. 'Not really,' she said and smiled tightly.

Mistakenly taking her refusal to elaborate for modesty, Grace held open the swing doors for her and they began to descend the stairs – Maggie always steadfastly refused to take the lift due in part to claustrophobia and vanity: steps, according to Maggie, were a bottom's best friend – and walked through the foyer onto the street.

Outside it was beginning to spot with rain. Standing on the pavement, Grace fastened her coat against the icy wind that was wrapping her legs like an over-excited Labrador. 'Well, I guess this is it.' Smiling, she leaned across to give Maggie a hug. She felt suddenly quite emotional.

'Hey, less of that. I've only retired. I haven't died, you know,' scolded Maggie, her arms laden with the thoughtful, but extremely cumbersome, bouquet. A few shoppers hurrying by glanced up from underneath their umbrellas, throwing the kind of affectionately

326

wistful looks that bouquets always inspire. The polythene crackled noisily as she returned Grace's hug. 'You'll have to come out and visit. Get yourself a bit of colour in those cheeks of yours.'

'You just try and stop me,' laughed Grace.

They were both getting wet with the drizzle, and spotting a cab approaching with its yellow light on, Maggie flung out an arm to hail it. As it pulled over to the kerb, Grace heard the muffled beeping of her mobile in her pocket.

'Bye.' She threw Maggie a wave, watched her climbing inside and waited for her to slam shut the heavy taxi door, before digging her Nokia out of her pocket. She glanced at the display – 'One Message Received' – and clicked on the small envelope. Without warning, her stomach did the most almighty backflip.

It was from Spencer.

From the dry warmth of the cab, Maggie tugged down the window. 'Bye, doll,' she yoo-hooed, her chunky silver bracelets clanking as she stuck out her arm and began waving at Grace. But she couldn't catch her attention. Bent over her mobile, Grace didn't look up, and as the cab pulled out into the throng of rush-hour traffic Maggie gave up and flopped back against the vinyl seat, resting the bouquet on her lap.

'Where to, luv?' Turning down his radio, the driver glanced appreciatively at the very attractive older woman in his rearview.

Maggie faltered.

And only then did the smile she'd been clinging onto ever since that moment in her bathroom, ever since she'd opened the letter in Spain from the hospital, ever since she'd woken up that morning knowing she had an appointment with her specialist to discuss the results of her tests, fall away like a mask. Taking a deep breath, she summoned up every last drop of courage and said quietly, but firmly,

'St Mary's hospital.'

Chapter Thirty-six

'So what did it say?' Selecting a rather scary-looking carving knife, Rhian plonked herself down at the kitchen table and began ferociously decapitating a pumpkin.

Without saying a word, Grace thrust her mobile under Rhian's nose.

Pausing from repeatedly stabbing the orange flesh, Rhian shrank back to squint at the display. 'WE NEED TO TALK,' she read aloud.

She looked up at Grace. Their eyes met. Two sets of eyebrows were raised. 'That's it?' asked Rhian incredulously. Having received Grace's gabbled phone call from High Street Kensington a few hours earlier, breathlessly telling her Spencer had just been in touch and could she come over that evening for discussion, advice and opinion, she'd assumed there was going to be a lot more to dissect, analyse and ruminate upon than '*Four stingy words?*' gasped Rhian.

' "I love you" is only three,' pointed out Grace. 'And look at the millions of connotations that had.'

Rhian looked at Grace. The hope was visible in her face. It worried her. She didn't want to see her getting even more hurt. 'But it's not "I love you", is it?' she corrected gently.

Grace stiffened defensively. 'You know what Spencer's like, he's a man of few words.'

Rhian was amazed. How was it that after the way

he'd behaved, after getting hammered and abandoning her on her birthday, after asking her to marry him and then refusing to make a commitment, after just sitting back and letting her move out, and after being a selfish bastard and steadfastly ignoring her for weeks, all Spencer had to do was send a text message – correction: a text *command* – and somehow he'd redeemed himself? She looked at Grace. Female loyalty was staggering.

'And so when are "we" talking?' Squashing her anger, she resolutely hacked off the pumpkin's scalp and, glancing across at Grace, dangled it between thumb and forefinger. Not that she was being symbolic or anything.

'Not until after next weekend. He's going away on business tomorrow . . .' Grace broke off to sit down. She was still reeling from Spencer's message. It had come completely out of the blue. Just when she'd finally stopped thinking about him 24/7, he'd thrust himself back into her mind, switched on the spotlight, and demanded her full attention.

If the truth be told, her reaction had been one of pure relief. The waiting game was over. He hadn't forgotten about her, or moved on without her, or found someone else. She'd sat tight, stood her ground, and given him time. And Jimi had been right. He'd made the first move. 'We need to talk' might only be four words, but to Grace they spoke reams.

'. . . and he doesn't get back until a week on Monday,' she finished, looking at Rhian. 'Or so he said,' she added.

Pulling out the cutlery drawer, Rhian retrieved two dessert spoons and passed one to Grace. 'And you don't believe him?'

Watching as Rhian began determinedly scooping out the pulpy insides, Grace wrinkled up her nose as she thought about it. Texting him back, her mind had gone into overdrive with possibilities: he missed her, he wanted to see her, he was sorry, he couldn't live without her. But then he'd rung, and their subsequent telephone conversation had left her feeling oddly flat and disappointed. 'He just seemed a bit cool . . . You'd think by the way he was that it was me who'd made the first move,' she complained.

'All relationships are mini power struggles,' observed Rhian. 'Sometimes you're in control, sometimes they're in control. It goes up and down like a see-saw. He's just trying to get some of the power back. You know what Spencer's like. He's a control freak.' She pulled a face, and then quickly added, 'But only sometimes.'

'And only with the TV remote,' smiled Grace.

Rhian laughed.

Digging her spoon into the pumpkin, Grace began to scoop. 'I wonder what he's going to say,' she mused quietly.

'What do you want him to say?'

'Isn't that obvious? I thought you'd know.'

Tucking her hair behind her ears, Rhian turned to face Grace. 'What I *do* know is you've had it tough recently, and I do know you've missed Spencer. But I also know you can idealize someone. Time has a funny way of airbrushing relationships, removing all the things that were wrong so when you look back it looks much better than it really was.' She smiled ruefully. She was talking about herself as much as Grace. 'I should know, I did it with Phil.'

'Did?' Grace picked up on the past tense.

Rhian nodded decisively. 'Yeah, but not any more. It's time to stop remembering Phil as this perfect man, to stop thinking our relationship was perfect, because it wasn't. There were good times, but there were some pretty dreadful ones as well . . .'

Grace looked at Rhian. She didn't know what had happened over the weekend to cause it, but it was as if the cloak of sadness and regret she'd worn like a security blanket had been thrown away, and underneath was the confident, happy, secure Rhian she used to know.

'I've been guilty of feeling sorry for myself, feeling as if I didn't have any control, as if I was the loser in all this. But all the time I was looking at it completely the wrong way round. I was forgetting one thing. And it was the most important thing.' Her serious expression broke into a smile, a look of delight spilling over her face like happy paint. '*Jack.*'

Grace couldn't help smiling. Rhian's was contagious. People often talked about smiles that lit up faces, but Rhian's really did have a luminous quality. It made her glow from the inside out.

'And as for you . . .' Snapping the conversation right back on track, like a train that had momentarily derailed, Rhian pointed her knife in mock-menace. 'Whatever you and Spencer end up talking about, however you might feel, don't forget one thing – *you* left *him*, remember . . .'

There was silence as Grace absorbed what Rhian was saying. She knew she was right, just as she knew that all that stuff about remembering Phil as this perfect man was a thinly veiled warning not to build Spencer up into one. She knew he wasn't, but right now she didn't care. She didn't care if he *was* the wrong man, all she cared about was that she missed him, she wanted to see him, and she loved him. Rhian might be ready to move on, but she'd had more than eighteen months to reach that conclusion. She'd only had weeks, however endless they might have felt, and right now she was perfectly happy wallowing in Spencer's text message and the promise of a fairytale ending.

'What exactly are we making?' she asked, steering the conversation firmly away from her and back towards Rhian.

'A Hallowe'en lantern,' replied Rhian as if it was obvious.

'But Hallowe'en was three weeks ago,' said Grace, looking at her friend who was covered in splatters of orange flesh.

'I know, I'm a terrible mother,' Rhian groaned, clasping her forehead and smearing a tangerine trail. 'I forgot,' she sighed heavily, looking woebegone. 'But I don't think Jack's realized. So I thought we'd have a sort of belated one,' she added hopefully. Hoisting a value-bag of tealights from underneath the sink, she placed one in the pumpkin's belly and lit it with a match. The cock-eyed pumpkin grimaced back. It looked like Rhian felt.

Watching this display, Grace felt terribly selfish. There'd she been, going on about Jimi, flying off to New York, talking about Spencer, and all the time Rhian was sat at home doing her damnedest to be a good mother, shouldering responsibilities that she couldn't even imagine, and never getting any credit. Rhian was always such a good listener, always supportive, always at the end of the phone, it was easy to forget she had her own problems too. Grace squeezed her sticky fingers supportively.

'I'm sure Jack's going to love it,' she said encouragingly.

'Do you think so?'

'C'mon, how could he not?' protested Grace, 'It's a work of art,' she said and smiled. So did Rhian. The atmosphere lifted. 'By the way, I meant to ask you earlier but I got sidetracked.' She gestured to her mobile. 'Are you free next Sunday night?'

Putting her forefinger to her lips, Rhian cocked her head to one side, pretending to think deeply. 'Ooh, hang on . . . let me check my diary and see if I've got a free window,' she cooed.

Grace smiled. 'Jimi's got tickets for the new rink that's opening up at Somerset House. Apparently there's a huge Christmas tree and mulled wine and carol singers . . .' She knew Rhian would love all that. She was the only person over five years old that still got so excited at the thought of Christmas that she bought herself an Advent calendar. Although she insisted it was for Jack she didn't fool anyone.

'And we wondered if you wanted to come along . . .' She hesitated, thinking of how she could work this in without looking completely heavy-handedly match-making. Sod it. She came clean. 'Jimi's invited Clive.'

Tinkling sounds of 'White Christmas', visions of Bing Crosby, and herself in a fur hat and muffler had been pirouetting through Rhian's mind, but at the mention of Clive, they suddenly crashed. 'Oh no.' Shrinking back, she held up a sticky palm. 'I'm not doing another fix-up. Not after Jeff.'

Grace had heard all about Jeff. In fact yesterday she and Rhian had spent the entire evening on the phone in hysterics. 'But Clive's the right side of forty and he's a doctor,' she cajoled, nudging Rhian in the ribs. 'And you know how sexy they are in their white coats and stethoscope. Just think *ER*.'

'I'm sure he's lovely. Adorable, even. But you're not going to fix me up. I'm going to do it my own way.'

'And what's that? Destiny? Star gazing. *Paths crossing?*' said Grace, wide-eyed.

'Not necessarily,' murmured Rhian, fidgeting uncomfortably.

Grace eyed her curiously. She was being very cagey. 'Is there something you're not telling me? Are you up to something?'

'*Me?*' Rhian looked shocked. Too shocked. It was like the actions of a pantomime dame. Clutching her chest, which had started to blotch into raspberry red patches, she stared at her. 'No. Nothing,' she protested.

Grace was suspicious. Everybody knew that when a woman said 'nothing' there was very obviously some-thing. 'Is it Noel? Are you seeing him again?' she demanded.

Rhian looked piqued. 'Don't be ridiculous,' she said, scraping back her chair to stand up, and busying her-self by clearing up the kitchen.

Grace watched her agitatedly squirting the sink with a jet of Fairy Liquid and turning on the taps full blast. This was a classic avoidance tactic. Whereas some people steered their way around awkward situations by watching TV, going to the gym, having a drink down the pub, Rhian relentlessly cleaned – her bottles of Jif, aerosols of Pledge and four-pack of sponge scourers acting as camouflage.

'*Rhian*,' Grace cajoled.

'Tsk . . .' she tutted. 'This stupid watch . . .' Noticing it had stopped again, she was banging it with a soapy rubber finger. She looked up at Grace. 'What time is it?'

Yet another avoidance tactic, thought Grace, glancing at the digital clock on her mobile. 'Nearly midnight.'

'*Midnight?*' Two spots of colour burned high on Rhian's cheeks. Immediately she yanked her hands out of the washing-up bowl, scattering foam. 'It can't be. *Already?*'

'Er, yeah.' Grace was startled by her reaction. It was late, but these past few weeks she and Rhian often stayed up yakking into the early hours. 'Why? What's happening at midnight that's so important?' asked Grace. And then smiled. 'Don't tell me. You're going to turn into a pumpkin,' she quipped, unable to resist.

The Cinderella gag didn't even raise a smile. 'Oh nothing . . . nothing.' Flustered, Rhian shook her head, and launched into an exaggerated yawn. 'I'm just exhausted. I'm going to have to go to bed.'

'What? *Right now?*'

'Immediately. Before I collapse.' Rhian nodded vigorously. Snatching up Grace's leather coat that was slung over the back of the chair, she ushered her into the hallway and shoed her out of the flat. 'Bye. I'll call you tomorrow,' she gabbled, thrusting her coat, hat and gloves at her and promptly closing the door.

Abandoned in the communal stairwell, Grace reeled. What on earth was going on? Clomping down the tired stair carpet she tugged open the front door and stepped out onto the pavement. She looked over her shoulder and peered up at the flat, at the crack of light filtering through the heavy velvet curtains. For a few minutes she watched and waited, but nothing happened. She gave up. Turning away, she spotted the yellow light of a cab rattling towards her and sticking out her hand she flagged it down.

Chapter Thirty-seven

'. . . *So listeners, on to our next love letter, this time it's a woman from Paddington who's looking for someone special to mend her broken heart, but first a song to get you into the mood from our man himself, Luthor Vandross . . .*'

It was past midnight. Dark and drizzly. Across the length and breadth of the capital, traffic-choked roads were eerily empty, thronging high streets had turned into hostels for the homeless, and tucked snugly away in a million bedrooms, under a million duvets, millions of Londoners were sleeping, snoring, dreaming.

Most, but not all.

In the slow lane of the A40 Clive was driving home from his shift in his knackered old camper van with his radio turned up loud and hissy, while on a gold velvet sofa in a high-rise in Streatham Maggie and Sonny were enjoying a cuddle and a nightcap as Luthor Vandross singing 'Endless Love' played in the background. Above Baltic Travel in Paddington, behind a pair of velvet curtains, Rhian was pacing up and down her flat, waiting for the telephone to ring. Different people, different places, different lives. And one connection. A radio. An FHM frequency. And the fact that they were all listening to the same show.

Except there was a difference.

Rhian was about to be on it.

Having managed to get rid of Grace five minutes ago with that dreadful excuse about being exhausted, she'd dashed to the living room, flicked on the radio and lit up a cigarette. *Deep breaths. Deep breaths. Deep breaths.* Muttering to herself, she paced backwards and forwards in her marabou slippers and faded Snoopy nightshirt, one eye on the telephone, waiting for it to ring. Ash dripped onto the sheepskin rug. For the first time ever in her life, she let it.

She'd been in a state of high alert all day. The phone call had come just after lunch. It was Helen, the producer of *Do You Come Here Often?* ringing to inform her that her letter had arrived and caused such a stir in the offices, they'd brought it forward and would be reading it out on the show tonight, when she would be live on air.

Live on air. Rhian had nearly fainted. Struggling to keep it together, she'd yes'd and no'd and listened, as everything went in one ear and promptly out the other. Until finally, Helen, who'd been all bouncy and efficient and was no doubt the kind who wore Airmax trainers and combats, had said goodbye adding, 'Just one last thing. The best of luck, Cindy.'

Cindy?

For a split second Rhian didn't have a clue what she was talking about. Numb from the speed at which everything seemed to be happening, it was only after she'd replaced the handset that she'd remembered. And like Alice in Wonderland, had suddenly experienced the sensation of falling deeper and deeper into a hole.

It had been last Saturday. 3 a.m. She'd begun sitting propped up in bed, surrounded by scrunched-up scented lavender balls of paper, about to sign her finished letter. 'Yours . . .' She'd paused, fountain pen poised above the paper. Now this was the tricky bit: did she use her real name, or did she use a pseudonym like George Eliot, or Acton Bell or . . .

Her eye had fallen on her bedside table and Jack's

337

dog-eared Ladybird book. *Cinderella*. Picking it up, she'd flicked through the pages, the illustrations of the glass slipper, the handsome prince, the happy ending. She'd been hit by a flash of inspiration. Of course. I'll call myself Cinderella, she'd thought, before swiftly reconsidering. Well, not exactly, otherwise they'll think I'm a fruit-loop. I'll be Cinders instead, or no, hang on, she'd decided, merrily signing her name and feeling very Miss Marple, I'll be Cindy.

The shrill ringing of the phone startled Rhian and she jumped, clutched her chest, and then answered it.

As the song was faded out, the DJ struck up.

'*Hi this is Dr Cupid and have I got some late-night-lovin' for you. The author of tonight's love letter is a woman whose life was shattered when her partner walked out on her and their son.*'

Above Baltic Travel, Rhian stopped pacing. Clutching the telephone, she felt her heart stop.

'*Hi, Cindy, are you there?*'

This was it. She was on. Nervously vacuuming her throat, she took a deep breath.

'. . . Er . . . yes . . . hello.'

Chapter Thirty-eight

The following week London woke up to discover that although its streets might not be paved in gold, they were covered in three inches of pure white snow. It was an early Christmas present, and one that the Met Office had been unprepared for. Ditto the transport system, which took one look at icy pavements and frozen roads and ground to an abrupt standstill. Yet, despite all the disruption, the *Evening Standard* headlines screaming 'Commuter chaos', and the schools and offices that had to be closed, the city, with its dusting of snowflakes like sieved icing sugar, had never before seemed so beautiful.

Like a magical winter wonderland, thought Jimi, drawing in icy lungfuls of city air as he scootered happily along the fairy-lit Embankment, the satisfying noise of his two-stroke engine *put-putting* as he deftly weaved in and out of the evening gridlock with the grace and precision of Beckham on the pitch. Nipping in behind the Audi, ducking and diving to the left of the taxi, squeezing past the National Express coach, he revved the accelerator and set off joyfully down the home straight.

Jimi was in an extraordinarily good mood. That afternoon he'd received a phone call from Tanya Stiff at *Chic Traveller* saying how much she'd adored his article, how fabulous the photographs were, and how did he fancy an all-expenses trip next year to Uluru –

otherwise known as Ayers Rock – to write a travel piece? Silently punching the air, his face contorted into Munch's *Scream*, he'd intimated his interest. *Interest?* Dream-come-fucking-true, more like. Finally he'd be able to fulfil his teenage ambition of riding around it on a Harley-Davidson. He'd never got there at eighteen, but thirteen years later he was finally going to make it.

Swiftly moving through the gears, he zipped into a parking space, turned off the engine and dismounted. Tugging off his helmet, he set off walking, his feet making a satisfying scrunching noise on the impacted snow that covered the pavement, his breath creating ghostly clouds against the evening's darkness.

But that wasn't the only reason for the grin that was plastered across his face like a ventriloquist's dummy's. His good mood hadn't just sprung upon him, it had been hanging around like some kind of annoyingly cheery relative ever since he'd got back from New York. His usual cynicism had been hijacked by a cheery optimism – only the other night he'd watched *Pop Idol* all the way through without making one Simon Cowell-type comment: his hypochondria – which in recent weeks had manifested itself as a suspected brain tumour, heart murmur and pneumonia – had been stolen and replaced by a disconcerting feeling of well-being: and, most mysteriously of all, his writer's block had completely disappeared.

And what – or should I say who – is responsible for this transformation? thought Jimi, taking a run at a patch of bottle ice on the pavement with giddy, childish exuberance. Whose fault is it that I've turned into some positive, robust, grinning idiot? Bending his knees and sticking out his arms like an aeroplane he executed a perfect skid in his trainers. There was only one answer. *Grace*. That's who. From that moment in the restaurant in New York he'd known he was in serious trouble. Or, to put it another way, he'd gone and fallen in love. *And it was a nightmare.*

Apologies to all those romantics out there, but Jimi wasn't one of them. He didn't want to be in a good mood. And he didn't *want* to be in love. Love was a four-letter word. It wreaked havoc. It caused untold misery and human suffering. It turned normally sane people into gibbering wrecks who listened to Atomic Kitten records and *sang along*, who took leave of their senses and paid good money for padded pink satin cards and would forgo coherent speech for cooing baby talk. He'd seen it among his friends, hell, he'd even experienced a brush of it first-hand – much to his chagrin and embarrassment. Who could forget that kiss outside Heathrow airport? But thankfully he'd escaped pretty much unscathed.

But this time I might not be so lucky, reflected Jimi, trying to frown at the idea and discovering that his facial muscles were frozen, botox-like, into a permanent grin. Already he'd found himself under the influence. Catching himself humming a Blue record yesterday in the shower, smiling at strangers in the post office, reading his horoscope – a crime in itself, but made ten times worse by then *reading hers*. It was alarming. For years he'd routinely worn his cynicism, his pessimism and his neuroticism like a suit of armour, and without it he felt suddenly vulnerable. Foolish. Out of control.

It had all taken Jimi by surprise. It didn't seem to make sense. His feelings for Kylie hadn't been anything like as intense as this, or as powerful, or as exhilarating. At the time he'd assumed, to use the words of Suggs, 'it must be love' but now he realized he'd been mistaken. It had been nice, but like Diet Coke, it wasn't the real thing. But at least he could *understand* his feelings for Kylie. After all, what man wouldn't have had feelings for Kylie? She was twenty-one, she had skin that looked as if it had been dipped in melted caramel and she giggled, a delicate, gurgly, laugh, at every single one of his jokes.

But Grace? Grace was everything he wasn't. She

loved olives, he hated them. She adored Top Shop, he had to have designer. She listened to Capital, he listened to Virgin. And she could be very annoying. In fact nobody could annoy him like Grace. She could infuriate the hell out of him. She had the ability to penetrate right under his skin and stir him up like a whirling dervish. On the other hand, she also had a knack for making him laugh, real belly laughs that made his eyes water and his stomach ache. He didn't know what it was, but Grace just got him. He could be sitting with her at some dreadful café in Heathrow airport, or talking to her on the phone as he lay sprawled on the sofa with Flossie, or texting her as he sat stuck in traffic, and she gave him a lift that no line of Charlie, bottle of champagne or all-expenses trip to Oz could ever give him.

And they weren't even sleeping together!

Good or bad, Jimi felt as if he was on an emotional rollercoaster rather than his usual even keel. No longer was he sailing through life, he was *living* it. And one thing was for certain: he might feel a lot of things, but one thing he never felt was boredom.

But hang on just one minute.

Let's not get carried away here, thought Jimi, pulling himself up short. The fact of the matter was, he hadn't chosen to be in love. There'd been no choice involved. The whole thing was sudden and inconvenient and uninvited. Love had just turned up like a gatecrasher at a party and now he couldn't get rid of it. And, what was even more frustrating, he couldn't even get annoyed about it. That was all part of the power of love. It wouldn't *let* you be pissed off about it. You couldn't get angry with it. You just ended up smiling like a loon and having all these happy, glowing, cosy feelings.

Bryan Ferry was absolutely right, decided Jimi as he reached the entrance to Somerset House. Love is the drug, and he might as well have swallowed an E for all he could do about it. It was all he could do to stop himself running around hugging everyone. As the thought struck, he stuck his hands firmly and deeply into the pockets of his fur-trimmed parka and gazed at the magnificent building which loomed before him, bathed in Christmas lights. But surely it was mind over matter. You didn't just 'fall' in love. *You had to jump.*

And I'm not jumping. No sireee, thought Jimi huffily. Tonight he was meeting Grace and it was going to be the same as it always was. Just good friends. Nothing more, nothing less. Jutting out his jaw, pulling back his shoulders, puffing out his chest he scoffed to himself, feeling the old, confident, independent Jimi returning. What was he worrying about? For a minute there he'd been scared he was teetering on the edge, about to fall, but there was absolutely nothing to worry about. He was simply going to turn his back and walk away. Tall. Proud. Determined.

'Jimi.'

Waiting by the ticket booth, he looked up to see Grace running towards him, tufts of her dark hair sticking out from underneath her stripy bobble hat. Rushing up to him, eyes shining, cheeks glowing, nose running, she gave him a big bear hug. 'Sorry I'm late,' she said, smiling apologetically.

Engulfed in her scent, the warmth of her breath on his cheek, Jimi merely grinned as his heart set off running. And, like something out of *Butch Cassidy and the Sundance Kid*, hurled itself right off the edge.

In other words, he jumped.

Across the other side of the city, far away from the frosty, fairy-lit River Thames and inside a 100-watt-lit, central-heated bedroom, Rhian was picking her way through the assault course of rainbow-coloured Lego bricks as she tried to get ready.

'Ooh, that's lovely,' she cooed, smiling at Jack who was lying on the floor in his Barbie pyjamas, building

. . . well, she wasn't sure what he was building. It looked like a deconstructed Rubik's cube, 'What is it, muffin?'

Muffin stared intently at his construction, his three-year-old face contorted into seriousness like a scientist looking at his invention. After looking pensive for a few moments, he cocked his head to one side and answered solemnly, 'Santa Claus.'

Watching his tousled head bent over his creation, Rhian felt a little burst of pride. 'That's amazing. Aren't you clever?' she praised, bobbing down to give him a cuddle. Only three years old and her boy was into abstract art. Smiling fondly, she stood back up and, deftly unpinning the scattering of Carmen rollers from her hair, ran her fingers through the soft curls.

Rhian was on a high. Over the last few days she'd gone from Rhian-the-single-mum to Cindy-the-*femme-fatale*, and she was revelling in all the attention. Her life, which had been trundling along through its daily routine, had suddenly taken an unexpected turn after her radio début last week, which had triggered a sequence of events that were as thrilling as they were terrifying.

At first her reaction after being 'live-on-air' had been one of deep regret. Had she gone absolutely, stark staring mad? What on earth would people think if they found out her secret? What, she'd thought, feeling all at once terribly provincial, would the neighbours think? But despite a few first-day nerves, jumping as the mail arrived, stiffening as the phone rang, everything seemed to be exactly as normal. There were no strange deliveries, no weird phone calls, no sniggers in the street, no pointed fingers in Sainsbury's, and after a couple of days she'd begun to forget all about it.

Until last weekend, when she'd staggered out of bed, padded bleary-eyed downstairs to the communal hallway to see if she had any post, and discovered a pile wedged in the letterbox. All addressed to 'Cindy c/o Do You Come Here Often?' it had been forwarded by the radio station. Heart thumping, self-respect teetering, she'd roughly wrestled it from its brass clutches, desperate to remove it before her neighbours discovered they had a lonely-heart in their midst, before scuttling gratefully back upstairs.

That had been only the beginning. First post, second post, special delivery, registered packages – the letters just kept coming and coming until, at the last count, she'd received a grand total of one hundred and twenty-one. Rhian had never felt so popular. It was like having her own fan club and, for a woman who in her entire lifetime had received less than half a dozen Valentine's cards, the novelty had been thrilling.

It had soon faded.

There'd been 'Depressed from Woking', who'd written on the back of a quotation from his life insurance company, 'Bearded from Marble Arch', who'd sent her a touching poem and told her all about his allotment in a suspiciously shaky – read geriatric – handwriting; and finally, 'Roger from Ickenham', who'd thoughtfully included a photograph of himself – *wearing a black PVC gimp costume*. Admittedly there'd also been lots of nice, normal, polite letters from lots of nice, normal, polite men. Just not any she'd wanted to go out with.

But instead of feeling defeated, Rhian had been imbued with a new sense of self-belief. If she could bare her soul to millions on the radio, she could do anything. She could change anything she wanted in her life. All she had to do was be brave enough to take that first step. Well, actually three steps. The first had been to fill four large black binliners with her stash of glossy magazines – she could do without being made to feel like a big fat, frumpy failure because she didn't have a yoga-honed figure, the latest Balenciaga shoulder bag, and a reservation at Nobu, thank you very much – the second had been to dig out her old swimming cossie and enrol in an aqua-aerobics class at her local swimming baths. And the third was to take the first tentative steps to restarting her career. With Jack now at nursery there was nothing stopping her and so, with the help of Grace, she'd printed up some new business cards to send to dozens of fashion editors.

It had been just after she'd finished addressing the last one to the achingly trendy *Hip-Style* that she'd noticed Jack was doodling over an envelope. *And it was still sealed.* Coaxing it from Jack with the lure of a piece of flapjack, she'd looked at it and immediately warmed to the handwriting on the address. It wasn't flowery, or spiky, or sloppy, it was all solid, square letters and a little flick on the 'g's. Rhian was no calligraphy expert, but somehow she felt the author of the handwriting was kind, considerate, full of integrity – but not dull – because that little flick showed a sense of humour, an eccentricity, a uniqueness. His letter had been nice too. Neither slushy nor cocky, it was just very straightforward. He'd heard her on the radio, would she like to meet for a drink on Sunday night?

Rhian felt a delicious flutter of nerves. It was seven-thirty. Less than an hour until her date with Michael. After reading his letter, she'd texted him a reply. Despite every criticism she'd hurled at texting for killing the art of conversation, when faced with the prospect of sweaty-palmed dialling and an awkward phone conversation, she'd completely changed her opinion. It was a godsend. Probably one of man's best inventions, she'd decided, watching the little envelope winging itself away on the screen of her mobile.

Clipping on her beaded jet earrings, she felt a tingle of excitement. She bent her knees and tried to see herself in the dressing-table mirror, only to gasp with frustration. It was impossible: even wriggling herself into Cirque du Soleil contortions she couldn't fit herself into the mirrored pane. For a moment she hesitated, and then before she could change her mind, she reached behind the wardrobe and tugged out the full-length mirror. Covered in dust, it had been sitting there undisturbed for the past eighteen months, ever since she'd shoved it there in a fit of disgust at her body. She wiped it with an old T-shirt, rested it against the wall and then, taking a huge breath, stepped back.

A pretty dark-haired woman in a 1950s black and white polka-dot dress stared back at her. Rhian was imbued with a warm glow. It was like seeing an old friend again. She smiled delightedly. Her reflection smiled back. It was good to see her again. She'd missed her. Boy, how she'd missed her, she thought, feeling a little fountain of love well up inside. Grabbing her fur stole and fastening it with a diamanté brooch, she twirled and grinned unashamedly at herself in the mirror.

'How does Mummy look? Pretty damn hot, eh?' she laughed, turning around and looking for affirmation from Jack. Splayed out on the floor in his pyjamas he was waiting for Hester to arrive so she could read him a bedtime story. Hester, according to Jack, was much better at this than Mummy who, he'd informed her as she'd earlier rattled through *The Lazy Giant*, 'missed bits'.

As Rhian twirled, Jack watched like a beauty-pageant judge. Clapping his pudgy hands, he giggled happily, and then, in what later Rhian came to assume had been a show of approval – a three-year-old's version of holding up score cards – promptly stuck a piece of Lego up his left nostril.

'Jack, don't do that.' Crouching down next to him she attempted to snatch away his fingers. But it was too late. The fingers reappeared, but the Lego did not. Not one to panic unduly, Rhian had a go at retrieving it herself. Unfortunately, not having yet grown the great hooter of his father, his nostrils were so tiny she didn't have much luck. It might have gone in, but it certainly wasn't going to come out without a fight, she thought, feeling a tremor of alarm.

By now Jack was beginning to realize that perhaps

he shouldn't have done that and was looking at her, trembly-lipped.

'Hey muffin, don't worry. Mummy will fix it,' she cooed comfortingly, trying to hide the red-hot panic that was blasting through her veins. Fast running out of options, she made him blow his nose into her hand. There was a snort, a rattle, and a stringy jet of snot landed on her palm.

But still no sign of the Lego.

Her smile faded. As did Jack, who started bawling his head off. Damn, blast and goddamn it, Rhian cursed inwardly. It was stuck. Like big-time stuck. Like, thought Rhian, beginning to feel quite hysterical, there was no-way-that-motherfucker-was-coming-out-of-there, stuck. As the truth hit, fear gripped like a vice. Terrifying thoughts multiplied with ferocious speed. What if it slipped further? What if it blocked his airway? What if it stopped him breathing? What if . . .

As an unthinkably morbid thought hit, Rhian knew this could only mean one thing. Swigging back her Bach's flower remedy, she threw the diamanté strap of her handbag over her shoulder and scooped up a sobbing Jack.

Casualty.

Chapter Thirty-nine

The scene that greeted Grace and Jimi as they walked into the courtyard of Somerset House was like something straight off a BBC Christmas trailer. Filled with hundreds of skaters, the floodlit ice rink was presided over by a towering Christmas tree, glittering and sparkling with thousands of silver fairy lights, while around the edges burned huge ten-foot-high torches that threw orange flames into the winter darkness. For the less energetic a bustling café provided hot mulled wine, mince pies and ringside seats from which to watch young and old alike twirling, wobbling, weaving and falling over to the tune of the Christmas carols that were being piped over the outdoor speakers.

Goddamn it, even the most bah-humbug Scrooge couldn't fail to be moved.

Even Jimi.

'So Rhian couldn't make it tonight?' Standing in the queue for the skates, he edged forward, scooter helmet in one hand, Pumas in the other. He felt really chuffed he'd arranged tonight. Since getting back from New York he'd been dying to see Grace again, but he hadn't wanted to suggest anything too intimate like dinner, or too impersonal like the movies. This, he reflected, gazing up at the Christmas tree with uncharacteristic fondness, was just perfect.

'Rhian? Er no . . .' Handing over her boots to the dreadlocked assistant, Grace took her skates. ''Fraid

349

not,' she said and smiled uncomfortably. It was a sore point. Despite several phone calls and different reasoning tactics, Rhian had flatly refused to be fixed up with Clive, saying she wanted an early night. Grace didn't believe a word of it. After her bizarre behaviour the other evening, she was convinced she was secretly seeing Noel again. Not that she was going to admit that to Jimi, however. He was hardly the king of tact, and she didn't want him telling Clive and hurting his feelings. Even if she had never met him.

'It's such a shame. She really, really wanted to. I mean, she was really looking forward to meeting Clive but . . .' Grace hesitated, her mind grappling for an excuse that at *least* sounded plausible '. . . but she couldn't get a babysitter.' Perfect. Realistic but at the same time *sympathetic*. Plonking herself down on one of the benches, she began tugging on her skates. Job well done, she looked across at Jimi and passed the baton. 'What about Clive?'

'Oh Clive? Working late.' Jimi shrugged, refusing to meet her eye. Sitting down next to her he hunched over and began lacing his skates. He didn't know why he felt so guilty. He was telling the truth. That *was* the reason Clive had given him when he'd cancelled a few days ago, only when he'd said it the muscle in his eye had started twitching uncontrollably. Clive had never been able to lie convincingly, mused Jimi, feeling certain he was up to something and it definitely wasn't working late. To be honest, he had a sneaking suspicion he'd finally gone and got himself a date. But then again . . .

'He felt really bad about letting Rhian down like that, but you know how it is.' Tying a double knot, Jimi looked up at Grace. He didn't want to ruin Clive's chances with this Rhian girl, just in case he was wrong, or his date didn't work out. It was always good to keep a reserve on the bench. 'He's a Casualty doctor, so you can imagine the pressure he's under. Long shifts, emergencies . . .' He hesitated, deliberating over

350

how thick to lay it on. Luckily for Clive, women adored doctors, along with firemen and, Jimi thought, judging from first-hand experience, dog-owners. But still, if Rhian was half as nice as Grace, he'd better lay it on with a trowel. It was the least he could do. '*Saving lives*,' he added, eyes suitably downcast.

'Wow.' Grace nodded dumbly. Her babysitting excuse seemed horribly feeble. 'Oh Christ, tell him not to worry about tonight. Of course Rhian will understand. I mean, who wouldn't?'

Forget being a novelist, I should become a spin doctor, thought Jimi, as he witnessed Grace's initial look of disbelief transform into total admiration. Talk about a PR job well done. Flaky Clive was now transformed into Saint Clive. 'So I guess it's just the two of us,' he smiled, apologetically.

'Yeah.' Standing up, Grace wobbled newborn-foal-like as she tried to keep balance. 'I guess so,' she smiled.

A look passed between them.

Jimi's heart drumrolled. For an instant he could have sworn she was implying something, and then just as quickly realized he was misreading the signals. Foolishness prickled. He exhaled sharply. Christ almighty. This just-good-friends routine was proving much harder than he'd ever imagined. If I'm not careful I'm going to end up making a bloody idiot of myself, he thought, tying his fleece around his waist for a professional speed-skater look and standing up. His ankles promptly bent at right angles and he narrowly missed falling flat on his face. 'Well, if it was good enough for Torvill and Dean . . .' he joked, trying to regain his balance. And he wasn't just talking physically.

But Grace didn't seem to notice. Laughing behind a mittened hand, she linked an arm through his and inch by inch they set off tottering nervously towards the ice.

* * *

Rushing up the corridor, white coat tails flapping, size ten Converse slapping along the linoleum, hair stuck up in weird mohican style, Clive was not a happy bunny.

Rewind a few minutes. Freshly steaming from his shower, he'd been humming off-key to the Sugababes on the radio, attempting to tame his fringe with Shockwaves gel and dabbing all the usual bits of his anatomy with aftershave, not to mention some others because . . . well, just, you never know, he'd thought, shaking the bottle onto the palm of his hand and baptizing his nether regions in Gucci's Envy for good luck.

The aftershave was a recent, and very extravagant purchase. Tonight was a big occasion. In fact it was more than big, it was huge – momentous – a *miracle*. Hold the front page. Clive Eddington was going out to dinner with a member of the opposite sex. It was official. He had a date.

'Fuck-a-doodle-do.' He grinned jubilantly, congratulating his reflection in the mirror. Before peering closer and beginning a thorough dental inspection. Food between teeth was one of the worst turn-offs. That and bad breath, he thought absent-mindedly, trying to floss with his fingernail.

Panic seized.

Bad breath? Jesus Christ. He'd had a Kentucky for lunch. A whole bucket of deep-fried chicken wings. Gulping back a mouthful of Listerine he began gargling. It was the fourth time he'd gargled in half an hour. His tonsils would be gleaming. And ready to be tickled, he joked to himself, spitting out into the sink and reaching for his T-shirt. Pulling it from its dry-cleaned wrapping, he tugged it over his head, smoothing out any little crinkles on his chest. *REM: Green World Tour 1988*. It was his favourite tour T-shirt. His most prized piece of clothing. Along with his beloved Converse and his trusty suede jacket.

Which he'd just been throwing on in final

preparation when, like an alarm clock rudely awaking a glorious wet dream, he'd heard an electronic beep. His high spirits had gone into freefall. No. Please. Not now.

Not tonight.

It was his pager. He was being called to A&E. Clive glared at it hatefully, listening to it beeping away from the pocket of his white coat hanging on the back of the door of the staff locker room. For a moment he ignored it, scowled at it like an angry parent, before, inevitably surrendering, he grabbed his doctor's coat and dashed into the corridor.

And slap, bang into Sister O'Donoghue.

'Oh c'mon, give me a break, I was supposed to be out of here forty-five minutes ago,' he protested to her as she marched alongside him in her sturdy no-nonsense Doc Martens, like some kind of army corporal. 'I've got a table booked for eight . . .' he began.

But was cut short. 'I'm sorry, Dr Eddington, it's just that this patient's been waiting over an hour . . .'

'And I've been waiting for over a year for a date,' he interrupted, spotting his reflection and trying to flatten down his hair. 'Finally I get one and –' He clicked his fingers in the air to symbolize a puff of smoke '– there go my chances.'

'You'll go to bed feeling good about yourself,' she smiled cheerily, waving the clipboard on which were attached the patient's notes.

'But I'll be going to bed alone,' he sulked.

'*Oh I see,*' she said scornfully, her shoulders visibly stiffening. 'So you were presuming this date of yours was going to be an easy lay, were you?'

'Of course I wasn't thinking anything of the sort,' said Clive, flustered. 'I respect women,' he hissed, his cheeks reddening. 'I was just . . .' his voice tailed off under the intense lesbian scrutiny of Sister O'Donoghue. He could feel himself getting very hot under the collar.

And, if he wasn't careful, into very hot water.

'You were saying?' She raised one very thick, black eyebrow.

How on earth does she do that? It makes her look just like Jack Nicholson in *The Shining*, thought Clive, feeling his resistance fast diminishing. 'But . . .' Reaching the row of curtained-off cubicles, he turned to look at her. She was looking back at him unblinkingly. His own eyes were twitching uncontrollably as if he'd got a bit of grit in them. He tried staring her out, but the woman was terrifying. She reminded him of his old nanny. At the memory of Nanny Bunting, he caved in, and irritably marched across to the cubicle.

'You'll be needing your notes, doctor,' she reminded him, holding out the clipboard and throwing him a triumphant smile. He snatched it out of her hand and, throwing her a look of pure fury, went to tug back the cubicle's curtain.

Cradling a whimpering Jack on her knee, Rhian was chewing her fingernails with such ferocity her thumb had begun to bleed. Ignoring it, she continued chewing.

She was a woman on the edge of a nervous breakdown.

This had to be one of the worst nights of her entire life, she'd decided as she rushed out of her flat and began dashing along pavements with Jack in his pushchair. Her car was parked miles away and she'd decided it would be quicker on foot. So she was sprinting to the hospital. She didn't know if you could get fined for speeding with a McClaren buggy, but she could certainly get done for dangerous driving. Mounting pavements, vaulting kerbs, zigzagging through tourists being offloaded from white double-decker coaches, she'd pushed people out of the way screaming 'Emergency, Emergency!' like some kind of deranged lunatic, while Jack had joined in by bawling his head off, his little body shaking and trembling, his podgy fingers stuck firmly up his nostril. Along with the Lego.

Dressed up like an extra from *West Side Story*, Rhian had attracted curious glances. Disapproving glances no doubt, she'd thought, hanging a sharp left by the post office and careering down the ramp towards A&E. They're looking at me as if I'm a bad mother, and I am. I'm a terrible mother. I'm not qualified for this job. I don't know what I'm doing. I have a three-year-old son who wears Barbie pyjamas, celebrates Hallowe'en in November and has a Lego brick wedged up his nose. And why? Because I wasn't paying attention. I was too busy getting ready for a date. With a man. A man who I just might want to have sex with. Oh, Mary Mother of Christ.

Rhian's dormant Catholicism had erupted like a volcano and begun spewing hot, molten guilt. I'm a selfish, wicked, shameful mother. Good mothers don't think about sex. They think about *Pingu*, and recipes for organic pumpkin soup, and school catchment areas. It's a Sunday night. Right now, good mothers across London are in their respectable homes, in their respectable velour tracksuits, doing respectable things like making pastry or sewing nametags into PE kits. A sob had risen up in Rhian's throat, and her eyes started welling up. Not dolled up in a prom dress, a pair of hold-ups and a fur stole, brazenly charging through the streets with a hysterical and no doubt psychologically scarred child.

With streams of tears spilling down her cheeks she'd run full pelt into Casualty, expecting a team of doctors to whisk Jack away in a full emergency-code-red kind of way. Except this was the NHS, not *Holby City*, and so instead of running alongside a trolley, holding Jack's hand and telling him everything was going to be OK, Rhian had been forced to sit on a plastic chair in the packed waiting room and wait her turn with all the other emergencies, until there was a doctor available.

Which there hasn't been for nearly an hour and a half, thought Rhian, abandoning her right hand which was now sore and bitten to the quick, and beginning to

355

chew her left. Even though the nice Irish nurse who'd moved her into the cubicle had told her there'd be one along to see her in a minute. She sighed angrily, rehearsing the furious words she was going to say to that doctor when she saw him until, distracted by the sound of a commotion outside her cubicle, she cocked her head to listen. It was a man and a woman and it sounded as if they were having a humdinger of a row. He was awfully well spoken, she had a strong Irish accent. Their voices were raised. Almost shouting.

Then silence.

The curtain of the cubicle was sharply pulled back. Startled, Rhian looked up ready to launch into an angry diatribe and saw a tall, attractive, Titian-haired Adonis staring right at her. At precisely the same moment Clive strode into the cubicle and saw a stunningly beautiful, voluptuous, ruby-lipped Venus staring right at him. Their eyes met. Their hearts stopped. Their paths crossed. And it happened.

Just like every cliché, every superstition, every horoscope and every romantic hopes.

Love at first sight.

356

Chapter Forty

Arms behind her back, knees bent, body swaying side to side, Grace swished happily around the ice rink. Cheeks pink with the frosty air, eyes shining brightly, blades rhythmically striking the ice, she felt invigorated, uplifted, revitalized.

Happy.

She had left Jimi wobbling by the edge, all male bravado and indignant protestation: 'I'm perfectly fine, just a few teething problems with the skates,' he'd assured her, promptly falling flat on his arse. 'You go ahead, I'll catch you up in a minute.' Nervously she'd joined the revolving wheel of skaters. It was four years since she'd skated in Central Park, and she was afraid she might have forgotten how, that she might stumble, that she might not feel the same buzz. But within seconds her feet had automatically found their rhythm, her body had regained its balance, and she'd slipped effortlessly back into it.

As if it was yesterday, thought Grace, feeling the cold air rush past, her fringe fluttering against her forehead. A thought hit her. Would it, she wondered, be the same tomorrow, when she met Spencer?

Grace had spent the past week and a half in a state of nervous anticipation. Since the 'we need to talk' text, she'd experienced tunnel vision. It was all she'd been able to think about. Would it be awkward? Effortless?

Comforting? Upsetting? What was he going to say? How was she going to feel? What was going to happen? Hour upon hour, Grace had tried to imagine, predict, prepare herself for their . . . their what? Meeting? Talk? *Date?* She didn't know what to call it. The boundaries of their relationship had shifted so radically, she was confused about everything. It was just her and Spencer, talking over a drink in a pub. It was no big deal.

It was so much *more* than a big deal.

What had once been a casual, everyday occurrence had now taken on such huge importance it felt like a superpower summit. Like a nervous actress, she'd rehearsed everything she wanted to say, had obsessed about what she would wear, deliberated about how she was going to act. She hadn't seen Spencer for nearly two months – *two whole months* – and she'd been counting down the days, the hours, the minutes, feeling like a giddy schoolgirl going on a first date.

At the prospect Grace felt excited, yet at the same time strangely calm. Deep down inside she couldn't help thinking that 'we need to talk' was just Spencer's way of saying 'let's get back together', couldn't help feeling the story was going to end as all good stories did – *happily ever after.* But what Grace seemed to have forgotten was how the story had started. Happily blinkered by anticipation, she'd forgotten all about 'once upon a time' and wasn't thinking about the reasons *why* she hadn't seen Spencer, *how* this had all started, *what* the bigger picture was – and she was too gloriously caught up in the moment to care.

Spotting Jimi ahead, she waved happily. After weeks of anguishing over decisions about Spencer, their relationship, the rest of her life, the only decision she was anguishing over right now was what to wear.

'I'm thinking about my Diane von Fürstenberg dress.' Skating up to Jimi who was hanging onto the safety barriers as if his life depended on it, she spun round in a circle, creating an ice halo around him.

She faced him, breathless and grinning. 'For tomorrow night,' she explained.

Jimi's earlier good mood evaporated. Struggling to stand upright, while his feet flew out beneath him, he tried to keep his dignity intact. It was difficult. He looked like a dork, and he knew it. 'The one I bought you in New York?' Glaring at her with a miffed expression which he tried, and no doubt probably failed, to disguise, he retorted sulkily, 'I thought you said you were just going to the pub?'

Jimi suddenly felt extremely jealous. When Grace had told him she was going to meet Spencer, he'd presumed it was an amicable, let's-be-adult-about-this chitchat over a glass of wine and some pub grub. But now, faced with her obvious excitement, he realized he'd been horribly mistaken. Whereas he'd been translating Spencer's 'We need to talk' (he too, like every other friend, colleague and family member, had been forwarded the message for detailed analysis) as meaning that Spencer wanted to draw a line under their relationship, Grace – judging by her glowing expression – had been translating it as something completely different.

'We are, but I want to wow him,' she confided.

And I want to punch his lights out, thought Jimi. And then quickly pulled himself together. We're friends, he told himself sternly. Good friends. Friends who offer support, guidance, advice. And friendship. 'Look, Grace,' he began, wondering how much he was saying this for her, and how much he was hoping it for him, '. . . I don't think you should get your hopes up.'

With the speed of a circus clown, Grace's smile flipped upside down into a frown. 'What do you mean?' she demanded.

'It's just a text message. Not a *fait accompli*.' As he said it, Jimi balked. A *fait accompli*. What am I saying? I sound like a complete prat, and judging by the way Grace is staring at me, that's exactly what she's thinking, he thought miserably.

But Grace wasn't thinking that at all. Like most people in the midst of a relationship crisis, she was thinking only of herself and Spencer. Jimi, for the moment, had ceased to exist. 'Don't you think he wants me back?' she asked, alarm rising.

'Do you want him back?' asked Jimi pointedly, turning the question around.

She brushed it off. 'I'm not talking about me, I'm talking about him,' she said impatiently.

Jimi looked at her. At the way her forehead had puckered just above her nose. At the way her soft, round cheeks had turned blush pink like two Gala apples. At the way she was wearing odd gloves, one stripy mohair, one black leather, as if it was the most normal thing in the whole world.

How could any man not want her back?

How could any man let her go in the first place?

With his heart pulled as if by opposing tug-o'-war teams, Jimi knew he had a choice. The selfish half of him wanted to say no, to do everything in his power to ruin Spencer's chances, to turn her against him. The guy sounded like a dickhead. He didn't deserve Grace. But the other noble, decent, compassionate half of him that loved Grace to bits, that would do anything to make her happy, just couldn't do it. Couldn't hurt her like that. The guy might be a dickhead, but he was her dickhead.

So, for what was probably the first time in his life, Jimi put someone else's feelings before his own, and made the ultimate sacrifice. *Himself.*

'Wear the dress. You'll look stunning in it.'

'There you go.'

It was music to Rhian's ears. The sound of a piece of Lego rattling in the petri dish.

'It's a little trick of mine. I find olive oil always works.' Armed with a bottle of Extra Virgin and a pair of tweezers, Clive successfully removed the obstruction, and glanced up at Rhian.

There was a quick squawk from Jack, but it was more surprise than pain. His nose was a little red, but it was back to its normal shape and, all smiles, he immediately shoved a pudgy finger up to check.

'Thank you.' Delighted that her son was still in one piece, and feeling that perhaps she wasn't such a bad mother after all, Rhian glanced self-consciously at this very handsome doctor who had not only saved her son from near-death, but was the reason her chest had gone all red and blotchy and she felt strangely breathless. She'd felt like that ever since he'd swept into the cubicle, all angsty and impatient, and watched him melt into the kindest, sweetest, most considerate man she'd ever met. And she'd felt something else. It was the weirdest feeling. Dr Eddington was a complete stranger and yet, thought Rhian, she couldn't help feeling she already knew him.

But how? thought Clive, looking at the gorgeous woman before him and thinking exactly the same thing. Dark curls tumbling over her forehead, she was hugging her son, who was nodding off in the sheepskin rug lining of his pushchair, exhausted after the evening's drama. Talk about Madonna and child, he thought, gazing at them with the kind of adoration normally reserved for paintings at the National Gallery.

Glancing up from underneath her eyelashes, Rhian caught him staring at her and felt ridiculously nervous. 'Well, I better be off then,' she flustered, standing up and beginning to gather her things. This was another of Rhian's inbuilt avoidance techniques. When she couldn't clean, she gathered like a squirrel. Her fur stole, her handbag, the piece of discarded Lego.

'A souvenir,' she stammered, catching his eye as she plucked it from the petri dish and blushing furiously. 'Something to remember tonight by.' She laughed, her embarrassment turning up the volume so that her laugh was even louder and more throaty than ever.

And the sexiest laugh I've ever heard, thought Clive, catching himself lusting and clearing his throat self-consciously. 'Er . . . yes, indeed.' He cringed inwardly. *Indeed*. Who on earth said *indeed*? Gripped by nerves, his speech had reverted fifteen years to his days at Eton.

Rhian had begun to gabble. 'I'm sure you've got lots more people to see,' she was saying. 'Lots and lots of people . . .'

Clive shook his head. 'Actually, no,' he confided, lowering his voice, as he knew Sister O'Donoghue had a habit of lurking outside cubicles. 'You're my last patient.' Or at least she is now, he thought to himself determinedly.

Rhian's heart leaped. 'I am?'

The tension in the atmosphere tightened another notch. A great big gap that both waited expectantly for the other to fill. Only neither did. Pausing by the olive green folds of the curtain, Rhian began fiddling with the strap of her handbag, fastening and unfastening the little brass buckle as if it was the most fascinating thing in the whole world.

Hovering at the end of the trolley, Clive remained hypnotized by her delicately pale fingers, her gloriously alabaster smooth arms, the sheen of her neck, the small shadow cast by the spotlight underneath her earlobe . . . He swallowed hard.

'Is there anyone you'd like me to call, to come and pick you up?' He hesitated, edging closer and closer. He had to ask, to find out, to put an end to this desperate hope he could feel welling up inside. 'Your husband, maybe? Or boyfriend?'

Rhian jerked her head up. Her lips parted to speak.

Clive's heart seemed to slow right down. Please God. For once in your life. Give me a break. Please.

'I'm not married,' she smiled shyly. 'And I don't have a boyfriend.'

Clive could have got down on his knees and kissed the vomit-stained linoleum of the hospital floor.

'You're not? I mean . . . you don't?' His voice came out like a helium squeak.

'No, it's just me and Jack and the Lego,' she added, still fiddling with the strap. Was this conversation as blatant and ambiguous and thick with possibility as it felt? Or was she getting it all wrong and imagining something that wasn't there? *Hoping* for something that wasn't there?

As the idea took hold she grabbed hold of the handles of the pushchair, did a hasty three-point-turn and said 'Well, cheerio.' Her cheeks blazed. Giving a little wave, she charged through the curtain and began trotting hurriedly up the corridor before she could embarrass herself any further.

For a moment Clive watched her polka-dot figure disappearing towards the exit, and then with the kind of split-second, gut-instinct decision that makes you do all kinds of mad things without thinking about them, he followed her. Actually, it was more like raced. Ignoring the stares of the nursing staff he hurried to catch up with her, dodging instrument trays, weaving around trolleys, the soles of his pumps squeaking loudly on the lino, like tyres burning rubber on a racetrack. Until finally at the bend ahead, and in the pretence of opening the fire doors for her, he threw himself in front of the pushchair and skidded to a halt.

'*Oh my goodness . . .*' Nearly knocking him down, Rhian was startled to see the fire doors swing open and slam against the wall as this vision in white appeared in front of her. Breathless. Anxious. Speechless. She stopped and, looking up, met a pair of big spearmint green eyes that were staring at her with an intensity that would normally have made her look away. Only this time she *couldn't* look away.

'So . . . er . . . if you don't have a husband . . .' stammered Clive, swallowing furiously, '. . . but if you don't have a boyfriend . . . and . . . er . . . unless you're a lesbian, in which case you'd have a girlfriend . . .' he blurted hastily, and then laughed awkwardly, his face

flushing vermilion as he fiddled with his hair. 'I . . . er
. . . we . . . suppose that means . . . maybe . . . -
perhaps . . .'

Every bone in Rhian's body suddenly did a Mexican
wave in celebration. Never had she felt so delighted to
be so wrong. She hadn't been misreading the signals.
On the contrary, there was most definitely something
there. And, she realized with a thrust of determination, it was up to her to bloody well grab it with
both hands.

'I'm single.' The words rushed out. Unambiguous.
Bold. Obvious.

Released from his torturous attempt at a chat-up
line, Clive gazed at her unblinkingly.

'*Really?*'

'Really.' She nodded, aware that for the first time in
a long time she was absolutely delighted to be single.
Pushing her hair away from her face she tried to
placate the nerves that were holding her body
to ransom. 'I was supposed to be going on a date
tonight but Jack had his accident and now −' glancing
at her watch, she smiled, half regretfully, half hopefully. 'I guess I'm too late.'

Her confession jogged Clive's memory. Looking
down at his fob watch he saw it was nine-thirty. Guilt
hammered at him. Christ almighty. He'd stood up his
date. He'd left her sitting in the restaurant by herself.
He'd probably blown his chances with her for ever.
Raising his eyes he looked at Rhian, and in an instant
all the little voices inside fell silent. Somehow it
didn't seem to matter any more. Smiling sheepishly,
he nodded. 'Me too.'

They gazed at each other. The atmosphere was
gloriously awkward.

'I don't suppose . . .' he began.

'I'd love to . . .' finished Rhian.

There was a pause as they both broke into relieved
smiles, until Clive's chivalrous gene rose to the surface
like a bubble. And popped. 'My dinner date will think

364

I'm terribly rude . . . I should call . . .' He made a telephone signal with his thumb and little finger.

'And leave a message.' Rhian was nodding vigorously.

'Apologizing . . .' he continued, digging out his mobile.

'Profusely . . .' she agreed, hastily rummaging for hers.

Standing on opposite sides of the corridor, a fire extinguisher on one side, a 'No mobile phones' sign on the other, they both began furiously dialling.

'Voicemail,' whispered Rhian, hearing the answering machine pick up and a message beginning to play.

'Same here,' mouthed back Clive listening to the recorded voice, '. . . *and if you want to rerecord this message, press one at any time* . . .' 'Hi there, Cindy,' he stammered into his mobile.

Cindy? Listening in to his conversation, Rhian was startled. What a coincidence. 'Er hello, Michael,' she began hurriedly.

Michael? Overhearing the name, Clive felt a flush of embarrassment. Desperate to avoid awkward questions he hadn't told a soul about his date. After all, could you imagine people's reactions if they knew the truth? That he'd written a letter to a radio show? Even worse, he'd signed it Michael, in honour of his hero, Michael Caine.

'. . . it's Cindy here,' Rhian was whispering into her phone.

At the same time Clive was mumbling into his, 'er, this is Michael . . .'

Now hang on just one minute. They both fell silent. Confusion was fast turning into realization. It couldn't be. There was just no way. Now that would just be too much of a coincidence.

Unless of course it was fate.

The stillness of the corridor was broken by the sound of Clive gasping incredulously, 'You're my date? *You're Cindy?*' Screwing up his face in a mixture of shock and amusement, he stared at Rhian. With a wide smile breaking over her face, she was looking prettier than ever.

'Actually it's my pseudonym,' she confessed shyly. 'My real name's Rhian.'

The revelation was a double whammy. 'Not Grace's friend?' Clive stood, open-mouthed. Crikey, it was all getting too much.

Rhian puckered her forehead in confusion. Her dark eyes flashed with curiosity. 'How do you know?'

'Because I'm Clive. Jimi's friend.'

Rhian had to wait a second as the revelations sank in. This had to be the most amazing piece of good fortune ever. It was cosmic. It was karma. *It was serendipity.*

'I didn't sign the letter with my real name because I felt a bit . . .'

'Embarrassed?' ventured Rhian, widening her eyes and nodding in that been there, done that, bought the T-shirt way.

'I prefer to call it shy,' smiled Clive ruefully.

It was like that party game of pass-the-parcel, removing layer upon layer of paper until finally there they were — Rhian and Clive, untangled, unwrapped, uncomplicated. In years to come, the story of how they met would become legendary, to be retold time and time again by different people, at different dinner parties, in different cities across the world, as proof that destiny really does exist.

But for now Rhian and Clive were reeling from its novelty as they began walking down the corridor, talking about Grace and Jimi trying to fix them up and how they'd both refused, the radio show, why Rhian had called in, why Clive had felt compelled to reply.

'Not that I usually listen to it,' he began, and then, catching Rhian's disbelieving expression, broke into a wide smile. 'But that night I'm glad I did. I heard you and . . .' he shook his head at the memory. 'I've never written a letter to a radio show before.'

'Neither have I,' she confided, smiling at his confession.

As they stepped into the lift, Clive bent down to help her with the pushchair, tipping it expertly onto its back wheels and manoeuvring it over the gap so as not to wake Jack. Rhian watched him, feeling more comfortable than she'd felt in ages. He fitted. Perfectly. Just like that glass slipper, she mused happily, as the lift doors opened and they stepped out into the foyer.

Talking and laughing they made their way across the brightly lit reception area towards the automatic doors. Engrossed in that first intoxicating rush, they were oblivious to a balding, middle-aged man walking towards them. Clutching a bunch of fuchsia tulips and a bag of grapes, he hesitated, unsure where he was going. He didn't like hospitals. They gave him the willies. And damn confusing places they were too, he thought, squinting myopically up at the list of wards on the wall. Spotting a doctor striding towards him, he cleared his throat nervously.

'Excuse me, son.'

Clive stopped and looked across to see a middle-aged man. Hugging a plant in one hand, with the other he was flattening the feathery piece of grey hair down across his scalp, all the while shuffling uncomfortably. He looked anxious and afraid.

Clive smiled warmly. 'Feeling a bit lost?'

'Er, yes.' The man visibly relaxed. 'I was looking for the Queen Elizabeth The Queen Mother building,' he explained, and then did what people always do when they're nervous and provided more information than was necessary. 'I'm Sonny . . . here to see Maggie – Maggie Chapman. She's got breast cancer and she's had to have an operation,' he added, completely confident that as she was the most important person in the world to him, she would surely be the most important to everyone else. And not just one of the millions of patients that passed through these doors. 'They said she could have visitors,' he began in his defence.

'And I'm sure she'll be delighted to see you,' replied Clive, trying to put him at ease. He knew that expression. Hundreds of worried boyfriends, partners, husbands and sons wore the same one as they passed through the sliding doors of the hospital. 'If you ask at the information desk they'll find her for you,' he said, pointing him in the right direction.

'Thank you.'

They exchanged smiles, Clive, Sonny and Rhian: she had the vague feeling they'd met somewhere before but for the life of her couldn't work out why this balding middle-aged man with twinkling jet eyes seemed so familiar, before they began walking in opposite directions. Sonny hurrying towards the lifts to be reunited with the woman he'd shared his life with, Clive, Rhian and a sleeping Jack walking outside together for the first time.

As the automatic doors slid closed behind them, Clive gingerly put his arm around Rhian's shoulders. Feeling the warmth of his body against hers, she let her head rest against the crook of his armpit, and breathing in the warm, musky scent of his suede jacket, made a mental note to always remember this moment. To wrap it up and put it away carefully in her mind for safe keeping. They were right at the very beginning, they had no history, no pet names, no holiday snapshots together. They were, she realized, leaning a little closer as they walked along the pavement, a bit like a blank canvas. A delighted smile, the spitting image of Jack's, broke across her face. Imagine the fun they were going to have colouring it in.

Chapter Forty-one

'. . . of course NASA landed on the moon,' reasoned Grace, warming her hands on her plastic beaker of mulled wine. 'Millions of people watched it live on TV.'

Jimi laughed derisively. 'Rubbish. It never happened. They filmed it in a studio.' He shifted in his plastic ringside seat, his bruised buttocks throbbing painfully. 'The whole thing was just an elaborate set. One great big con.'

Having spent the last half an hour skating – or in Jimi's case flat on his backside on the ice – they'd taken a break and were sitting at the side of the rink, watching the steady stream of skaters.

And still arguing.

'Look, you might as well give up,' retorted Grace. 'You're never going to convince me. We've been quarrelling about this for weeks and you *still* can't come up with any concrete evidence to prove it was conspiracy.' The fresh, frosty air combined with the warm, perfumed wine was making her feel light-headed and giddyingly competitive. She took another sip for good measure, enjoying the buzz of alcohol spreading through her body.

'What makes you think you're so right?' Winding a strand of her fringe around her finger, she eyed him challengingly.

'Oh c'mon, it's *obvious* from the photographs. The

shadows are all over the place, there's no stars in the sky –' as he spoke he was ticking the points off on his fingers for extra emphasis. *'And . . .'* he paused dramatically '. . . don't you think it's strange that not one of the Apollo team have ever written their auto-biography or memoirs of "How I landed on the moon"?'

They stared at each other. This argument was proving irresolvable. Jimi refused to be convinced, and Grace refused to disbelieve. Neither of them showed any signs of backing down.

'I'll tell you why they haven't,' continued Jimi, feeling victory within his grasp. *'Because they didn't.'* There. Done. In the bag. Sitting back in his chair, arms folded, he looked triumphant.

Grace glared at him. How could anyone take such delight in trying to disprove one of the most inspiring events of the twentieth century? The man was astonishing. He wasn't just a sceptic. He was the prophet of doom. Clutching her mulled wine to her chest and shaking her head, she said passionately, *'Don't you believe in anything?'*

Her question caught Jimi off guard. He looked up, and as their eyes met all thoughts of astronauts, moon landings and conspiracy theories flew right out of his mind. Of course he believed in something.

He believed in her.

So why don't you bloody well tell her? barked a voice in his head. Forget about your ego. Forget about making a fool of yourself. Forget about getting hurt. Bare your soul and tell her how you feel. Tell her that you can't stop thinking about her. *Tell her that you love her.*

With his heart and head knocking seven bells out of each other, Jimi glanced across at Grace, who'd taken his silence to be his answer and was now gazing absent-mindedly out across the ice rink. Un-expectedly, he felt very scared. He wasn't used to being out of control, it was unnerving, but he had a choice: either go with it, or fight it. Draining the last of his mulled wine in a pathetic attempt to find Dutch courage, he made his choice. To be quite frank, he thought, looking at Grace and feeling his heart somersault – there wasn't one.

Grace had barely noticed that Jimi had fallen silent. Lost in contemplation, her eyes were fluttering across the rush of brightly coloured hats and scarves and gloves whizzing by. Her butterfly gaze landed momentarily on the small child with his mum, his rosy-cheeks flushed with excitement; the trio of teenage girls wearing too much make-up, all linked up and circling the ice looking for talent; the slalom skater, bent low, hands clasped behind his back, weaving in and out of the crowds and showing off his technique.

She smiled happily to herself, sipping the last of her mulled wine and breathing in its sweet, pungent aroma. Tonight felt special. It was only the beginning of December but the evening had a Christmas Eve quality to it. Anticipation. Speculation. Excitement. The plethora of anxieties, doubts and confusions that had plagued her these past weeks – these past months – looked as if they might be disentangled, worked out, and finally resolved. The promise of tomorrow lay waiting like a wrapped present.

A snowflake landed on her woollen glove. Melting quickly into the pink mohair, it was followed by another, and another. Grace felt a rush of delight. *It was snowing.* Feeling a childish burst of excitement, she watched the flurry of snowflakes whirling onto the ice rink. For a moment it was almost as if her snowglobe had come to life. New York. Ice-skating in Central Park. Her and Spencer. Together. In love.

She felt a tingle up her spine. It was a sign. It just had to be. Draining the last of her mulled wine, she drew in a lungful of crisp, winter air and stared dreamily at the ice-rink.

And then she saw them.

On the far side of the rink a couple were smiling and laughing, dappled with coloured lights and shadows. She caught sight of them for the briefest of seconds, as if in the shutter of a paparazzi camera, before they vanished again into the crowds of skaters. And like the snowglobe, Grace's life suddenly flipped upside down.

'You're wrong. I do believe in something . . .' Clearing his throat nervously, Jimi had begun speaking, his voice low and uncertain. 'I believe in you . . .' Studying Grace's face, the soft hue of her cheek lit by the Christmas tree, his cerebral thesaurus flicked through hundreds of different, clever, witty, new ways of saying how he felt. Until it dawned on him: the original was always better than the remakes.

'I'm in love with you.'

There. Finally. He'd said it.

In the background, seemingly miles away, as if down a long, dark tunnel, Grace heard Jimi's voice, but she couldn't hear what he was saying. She wasn't aware of anything but the crowds parting, the couple hugging, her heart racing. She recognized the woman immediately. It was Tamsin. Only the man wasn't Matt.

Wide-eyed with bewilderment, she turned to Jimi, who was waiting expectantly. Mentally exhausted, having fought his inner demons and found the courage to confess his true feelings, he was expecting some kind of response. Embarrassment. A rebuffal. *Maybe even a kiss.* But what he wasn't expecting was for Grace to gasp in a voice that was barely audible.

'It's Spencer.'

Chapter Forty-two

'I just can't believe it.'

Grace must have uttered those words a hundred times, but that didn't stop her repeating them for the hundred-and-first. Slumped motionlessly on the tan suede sofa in Jimi's loft, a lit but unsmoked cigarette dangling between her fingers, she stared vacantly into space. She was still anaesthetized from the shock of seeing Spencer and Tamsin.

Together.

Grace's stomach lurched at the memory. Of the moment of impact when an emotional locomotive had smashed into her head-on, hurtling through her body laden with a tumult of emotions – jealousy, possessiveness, insecurity, anger, horror, panic, devastation – and then, *whoosh*, had gone, leaving her dazed and reeling. Curiously dry-eyed, she wasn't crying, or shouting, or wailing, or raging. She wasn't doing any of the traditional, *EastEnders*-type stuff, she wasn't angrily stomping up and down and calling Spencer a two-faced bastard and Tamsin a sneaky little bitch, she wasn't getting pissed on vodka Red Bull and copping off with some unsuitable random male. And she wasn't even sobbing tragically into a box of man-sized Kleenex about how much she loved Spencer and – breaking off to blow her snotty, sniffy, swollen nose – wailing *how could he do this to her*?

But that was just it. Grace wasn't doing anything.

A chimney of ash broke off from the end of her cigarette, sprinkling grey powder onto the polished oak floorboards and, for the hundred-and-second time, she murmured numbly, her lips hardly moving, 'I just can't believe it.'

Neither could Jimi.

It had all happened so bloody quickly. One minute it had been all snowy and romantic in a *It's a Wonderful Life* kind of a way – cosying up with their mulled wine, Grace looking all dreamy and gorgeous, him confessing he'd fallen in love with her. And the next that intoxicating, perfect moment was history and Grace had turned ashen, mumbled something about Spencer and fled the ice rink.

Right. OK. Probably not exactly the best response.

For a couple of seconds Jimi had remained in his plastic seat, crushed by disappointment. The reel of videotape he'd been playing in his mind, of Grace turning and smiling up at him, wiping the dark, floppy strands of fringe from her eyes, leaning in towards him, the tickle of mohair as she threw her gloved hands around his neck, the cold tip of her nose as it brushed against his, her warm tongue searching his mouth . . .

Suddenly went blank as someone pressed the eject button.

That someone being Spencer.

Up until then, Jimi hadn't given Spencer that much thought. Apart from the basics – lawyer, late thirties, blond (and no doubt hairless) – he didn't know that much about him, and he didn't much want to. He'd never been able to understand the female fascination with exes. Kylie had made a hobby of quizzing him about his former lovers. Demanding age, height, weight, number of forehead lines, amount of cellulite and, most importantly of all, what kind of shoes they wore, she continuously and untiringly squirrelled away information. Blokes, however, were the complete opposite. They didn't want to know about an ex-boyfriend's passion for early Ska, the depth of their frown lines, or that their favourite footwear was Timberland boating shoes. In fact the less information the better.

Only he no longer had a choice, because suddenly Spencer had been there. In the flesh. Or rather a nasty quilted jacket, Jimi had thought sniffily as he'd jumped up from his seat and set about running after Grace. Talk about timing. Trust Spencer to choose that precise moment to show up. And with another woman. No wonder Grace had freaked out.

Well, not so much freaked out as gone eerily quiet, thought Jimi, unearthing an old bottle of port still in its Christmas wrapping paper at the back of the kitchen cupboard, and grabbing what was left of an ice-cold six-pack of beers in the fridge. Having caught up with Grace outside the ice rink he'd expected a furious out-burst, or a jealous rage, or an explosion of tears, but instead she'd mutely put on his spare crash helmet, ridden silently back to his flat, and without saying a word, curled up on the sofa.

Where she was still sitting in silence, noted Jimi, padding barefoot back into the living room. He was hit by the graveyard hush. There was none of the usual banter, no weird compilation CD she'd selected play-ing on the stereo, no crappy home improvement programme that she loved blaring from the TV. Even Flossie was lying corpse-like on the floor, her usual thumping tail lying like an abandoned brush on the floorboards.

Grabbing the stereo remote he flicked on the radio for a bit of background noise. He felt horribly awkward. He wasn't good at silences, they unnerved him. He never understood it when couples went on about being able to enjoy a 'comfortable silence'. What on earth was so enjoyable about silence, for Christsakes? thought Jimi, plonking himself down on the leather beanbag opposite Grace, unplugging the cork from the bottle of port, and filling a pair of wine glasses with large, treacly glugs.

Jimi was at a complete loss. He wasn't sure how to handle this. His instinct was to throw his arms around Grace and give her a great big hug, to tell her how much he loved her, to tell her Spencer wasn't worth it, but the fear of sounding flippant stopped him. Whatever he thought about Spencer, four years with someone was a long time, it was longer than many marriages, and he didn't want to trivialize their relationship – or her feelings – regardless of what his own might be. Because right now Grace needed him. She needed his friendship, his black sense of humour, and his Aunt Phyllis's ten-year-old port. What she certainly didn't need right now was him complicating matters by declaring his undying love.

So in retrospect it's probably a good thing she didn't hear me, decided Jimi, looking at Grace and proffering a glass of port in one hand, and a can of Fosters in the other. Curled up in her faded jeans and fluffy, cream mohair jumper, she looked so small and vulnerable you would never have believed this was the same woman who could burp 'The Frog Chorus', wolf-whistle back at a rowdy gang of tattooed scaffolders, or had the balls to stand up to a racist thug when she was only eighteen years old. At the memory, his heart melted.

''Fraid that's the choice,' he said smiling apologetically.

'*Bastard.*'

Her fists clenched into white-knuckled balls, Grace met Jimi's gaze with a look of pure, 100-per-cent proof fury.

Startled, he spilled the port. 'What?'

'Spencer,' she spat in explanation. Jerking forward to grind the filter of her cigarette into the ashtray, she weighed up the drinks in Jimi's hands, and then took both. Tugging off the ring-pull she took a fizzing swig of lager, knocked back the port chaser, and threw herself back against the sofa. 'How *could* he, the bastard?'

Fucking brilliant. Witnessing her angry outburst, Jimi felt a wave of pure joy. Anger was good. In fact anger was bloody great. It was normal and healthy and totally understandable. If I spotted Kylie with another bloke I'd have been furious too, he thought, running through the scenario in his head and waiting to feel an influx of anger and jealousy. Only to discover that actually, now he came to think about it, he didn't feel angry or jealous at all. Just indifferent.

'How could he say we need to talk?' screeched Grace, interrupting his thoughts. 'Talk about what, for fuck's sake? *His new fucking girlfriend?*'

Jimi stared at Grace. He'd never seen her look so angry before. Eyes flashing, fists tightly curled, her jaw set defiantly, she was perched on the edge of the sofa. Looking, he thought adoringly, absolutely magnificent.

'How could he have led me on like that?' demanded Grace, glaring at Jimi.

'Erm, well maybe . . .' he began, refilling her glass.

But she wasn't listening. She didn't want an answer, just an audience. 'How could he have been so dishonest?'

Jimi didn't even try to reason. Pointing out that perhaps Grace had got completely carried away and misinterpreted what Spencer was doing – something, he thought as an aside, women seemed to have a habit of doing – probably wouldn't have gone down too well at that moment.

'How could he have found someone else so soon? I thought he loved me, and he's just replaced me like . . . like an old toothbrush . . .' Grace wailed.

Grace was angry, not just at Spencer, but at herself. How could she have been so naïve? So blind. So fucking stupid. All this time she'd convinced herself it was just a break, when in reality they were breaking up. There were no 'ifs' and 'maybes' any more, there was to be no reconciliation, no resolving, no trying to work things out. She and Spencer were over. The moment she'd seen him with Tamsin their relationship had been wrenched for ever out of the future and thrown roughly into the past.

And he's already moved on, she thought sadly, grabbing hold of her refilled glass and taking a slug. She felt as if she'd been kicked, hard, flat in the stomach.

'It's as if I didn't mean anything,' she whimpered into her port, a lone tear breaking free and trickling down her blotchy cheek. She brushed it away roughly. This was pathetic. She was being pathetic. Fuck him. Fuck her. Fuck the both of them with knobs on. Filled with indignant pride, Grace tipped what was left of the glass of port down her throat. And promptly burst into a messy, pathetic, blotchy ball of tears.

Now hang on a minute. Jimi tensed with alarm. What had happened to the anger? Where was the raging jealousy, the seething possessiveness, the battered but furious pride? Those were emotions he could deal with, *but this*? This was veering dangerously into weepy insecurity, for which he was utterly ill equipped.

Feeling the panic gurgling in the pit of his stomach, he drained his can of lager and waded in anyway. 'Of course you meant something,' he consoled, topping up her glass again for want of something to do. His hands felt like a pair of ornaments that he didn't know where to put. 'But I thought you told me you left him.' Getting no answer, he watched the tears leaking silently down her face, before trying again to reason. 'You said you wanted a break.'

It had the desired effect.

'Only because I loved him,' spluttered Grace, sobs rising up in her throat, her eyes blurring with salty tears. She was swamped by a feeling of loss: not just Spencer, but the loss of control. This was happening to her and there was nothing she could do about it. The choice had been taken out of her hands. She felt powerless. She felt like a victim.

She felt wronged.

'I only left because I wanted him to make a commitment.' Not strictly true, but hey, there was nothing like seeing your boyfriend with another woman to put a different slant on things. Sprawled drunk and snoring on their sofa Spencer had felt like Mr Wrong; in the arms of Tamsin, he'd transformed himself into Mr Perfect.

'You left him to make him commit?'

Sniffing loudly, Grace nodded miserably and wiped her damp cheek with the cuff of her jumper. 'Yes.'

'Bloody hell,' muttered Jimi, feeling bewildered. Flopping back onto the beanbag he stared up at the fan whirring silently on his ceiling, trying to digest this piece of information. 'And women wonder why men don't understand them.'

Two hours, one and a half packets of full-strength Marlboro, a six-pack of Fosters and one very nearly empty bottle of Aunty Phyllis's port later, Grace and Jimi were lying tip to toe on the sofa with Flossie wedged into the gap between their knees like a draught excluder.

'God I feel like such a cliché,' Grace was moaning, a wine glass in one hand, a Marlboro Light in the other.

'Awww fuck it,' hiccuped Jimi, reaching over to give her a refill. Intelligent reasoning having gone out of the window after beer number three.

'Yeah, fuck him,' agreed Grace, relating everything back to Spencer. She took a gulp of port. And then another thought struck. 'Do you think she is?'

'Do I think who is?'

'*Tamsin,*' she retorted hotly, as if it was obvious. 'Do you think she's fucking Spencer?'

Hearing herself say it, Grace felt bizarrely detached. As if she was discussing a couple of celebrities she'd never met before.

'Erm, I dunno . . .' Jimi shrugged, feeling distinctly weird. Grace always referred to sex in a loving, romantic, soft-focus kind of a way. To witness her talking about it in a physical, feral, carnal way was a shock. It was also, he realized, an incredible turn-on.

'But then again he's probably too busy asking her opinion on his cufflinks to have sex,' snorted Grace. She looked at Jimi, who was staring at her in lustful confusion.

Shite, there she went again, talking about sex. In his boxer shorts Jimi felt something stir. *Oh no*. Not now. *Please God not now*. Alarmed, he fidgeted self-consciously, trying to hide the bulge in his jeans. He couldn't help it, he was a red-blooded male, he hadn't had a shag for God knows how long, and now, not only was he lying on the sofa with a woman he adored, but she kept harping on about . . .

'*Sex*,' repeated Grace loudly. 'That's all Tamsin used to talk about.'

'Maybe you're jumping to conclusions, maybe they're just friends,' he suggested. Anything to get her off the subject before my balls turn blue, thought Jimi desperately.

'He was hugging her,' she protested.

'I hug you,' he pointed out. He realized he was digging his own grave by defending Spencer but if it made Grace feel better, and it got rid of the bloody erection that so far he'd managed to conceal underneath Flossie's stumpy tail, then he'd keep on shovelling. 'I hugged you tonight.'

'But that was different, that was platonic,' Grace insisted, resting the glass on her collarbone and peering at him over the rim. 'Believe me, a woman can tell the difference.'

Oh yeah? Looking at Grace at the opposite end of the sofa, Jimi resisted the urge to jump over there, grab hold of her and rip off that woolly jumper of hers. To remove every last garment until she was just lying there, completely and utterly naked . . .

He gulped as his button-fly threatened to burst.

'Tamsin's a man-eater. Men go mad for her,' she

declared. Grace's mind was one-track, but it was on a completely different track to Jimi's.

'Men go mad for you,' he argued, swiftly blotting out his sexual fantasy.

Grace snorted drunkenly. 'Don't be stupid. No they don't.'

'Yes they do. I saw them in Barney's in New York, when you were trying on dresses. All the men were drooling.'

'Is that a line from your novel?' she mocked, flinging a cushion at him.

Deflecting it with his hand, he yelped defensively. 'Hey, I'm serious.'

But Grace wasn't having any of it. Downing a large syrupy gulp of port she eyed him accusingly. 'In that case why didn't you ever call me back?'

Her words caused the laughter to die in Jimi's throat. He gazed at Grace, his witty one-liners vanishing as he tried to think of something to say. But nothing was good enough.

'Two weeks I sat by that phone, you bastard,' she added quietly.

She was smiling ruefully, but the hurt was still audible and Jimi was flooded with regret. He suddenly felt very sad. If only he could change things, go back, make that phone call ... He caught himself. He couldn't change the past, but he could tell her the truth. 'Grace ... I ...'

'*It's Dr Cupid!*' Grace whooped loudly and waved her wine glass at the stereo as if it was the remote. 'Turn it up.'

'Uh?' About to make his confession, Jimi took a second to register what on earth she was talking about. He rolled sideways, peering at the luminous glow of the frequency, his forehead ruched in bleary confusion. 'Oh God, not this again,' he began as it dawned on him that Clive had been messing with the radio. Again.

'*Jim-eee*,' Grace pleaded, her voice slurring.

'OK, OK,' he groaned, giving in and increasing the volume.

'*Tonight our letter is from Martin whose soulmate recently left him for her lesbian lover . . .*'

Jimi snorted loudly. 'You've got to be joking . . .' he began, before being silenced with a glare from Grace.

'*. . . and he's now looking for a new lady to share his life with. In his letter he describes his ideal woman as being Charlotte, from Sex in the City . . .*'

'Men always go for women like Charlotte,' nodded Grace, unaware that her cigarette had long since gone out and attempting to drag on the tab end.

'Which one's Charlotte?'

'The pretty, dark-haired one.'

'Nah, bullshit,' dismissed Jimi, flopping back against Flossie who growled, disgruntled, as he crushed her under his weight.

'It's not bullshit, it's true,' protested Grace.

Shaking his head in disbelief, Jimi lit up a cigarette and stared thoughtfully at the glowing embers. 'You really have no idea about men, have you?' he murmured quietly.

It was actually meant as a compliment, but in her port-saturated mind Grace misinterpreted it as a criticism. The cheeky sod. There he went again, having another dig at her, making out she was some kind of frigid prude.

Infuriated, she rounded on him crossly. 'Yes I do, actually. I know lots of men. I've had lots of experience with men.' She tried self-righteously raising herself up on her elbows, but was hit by the spins and collapsed back against the armrest. 'And I know that men fancy women like Charlotte, all swingy hair, and perfect smiles, and girly dresses.' Tilting her chin, she peered down at her own attire. Old jeans that had faded at the knees, a big baggy jumper, two odd socks, and that wasn't even mentioning her knotty hair and blotchy face. It was hardly what you'd call a polished look.

'You don't know what you're talking about,' insisted

Jimi. 'I'm a bloke and I've watched *Sex and the City* –
once or twice,' he lied hastily. Well, he didn't want
Grace knowing he'd recently watched every episode in
a failed attempt to have at least some understanding of
what made women tick. And it appeared to be shoes.
'But I don't fancy whatever-her-name-is one little bit.'

'So who do you fancy?' she demanded accusingly.
Poor Jimi. Unable to vent her emotions on Spencer,
she was directing them at Jimi, who'd suddenly gone
from a shoulder to cry on to one great big hairy
punchbag.

Jimi felt as if he was going to burst. *You.* I fancy you,
you bloody idiot, he thought, gazing at her with utter
frustration. The incredible, wonderful, gorgeous
woman sitting at the other end of my sofa, the woman
I just spent my honeymoon with in New York, the
woman who's got just about the most appalling taste in
music of anyone I've ever known. And the woman
who, quite simply, doesn't seem to have one sodding
clue how I feel about her.

His burst of unrequited love was interrupted by Dr
Cupid: '. . . *but there's just one other thing. Martin's
soulmate would need to share his love for David
Essex . . .*'

'Argghhh,' groaned Jimi, pressing his lager can
against his forehead, relishing the cold metal against
his flushed skin.

'Hey, stop being such a spoilsport,' rebuked Grace.

'*So tonight, just for that special someone who's out
there somewhere, Martin has asked us to play a very
special song . . .*'

'Awww, I think it's kind of romantic.'

'You mean insane,' scoffed Jimi. 'The guy's a fruit-
cake, you'd have to be to dedicate a song to someone
you've never even met. Correction: *that special someone*,' he drawled, mimicking Dr Cupid.

'Has anyone ever told you you're a cynical bastard,
Jimi Malik?' teased Grace, looking directly into his
eyes.

Holding her gaze, Jimi returned the compliment. 'Has anyone ever told you you're gorgeous, Grace Fairley?'

And in that instant something passed between them, a spark ready to be ignited or quickly snuffed out. Deep inside, Grace felt a stirring so intense it was almost carnal. The hairs on her arms prickled. Her heart pounded like heavy rain on a window pane. Her groin ached. All she was aware of was Jimi, the pressure of his body against hers, the faded smell of his aftershave, the faint sound of his breath. All she could think about was Jimi Malik, self-confessed gigolo, king of one-night stands, and guaranteed bloody good shag.

And suddenly sex was out there. The air crackled with it. Nothing was said, nothing needed to be said. Right at that moment Grace knew she had a choice. Either she could be sensible, call a cab, go back to her rented studio in Earls Court and drink three pints of water, or she could be utterly stupid and go to bed with Jimi.

As the opening chords of David Essex crooning 'A Winter's Tale' began to resonate around the room, Grace wriggled her mobile out of the back pocket of her jeans and began scrolling down the numbers until she found Cosmic Cabs, the minicab company she always used. With her thumb poised, ready to call, she hesitated, then turned off her phone. Being sensible was never that much fun anyway.

Chapter Forty-three

Rhian woke up with the smile from the night before still spread across her face. And the smile had a name: *Dr Clive Eddington.*

After leaving the hospital they'd gone to a little Italian restaurant around the corner. Not that either of them had been hungry. Too busy looking at each other to look at the menus, they'd had to send the waitress away twice before Clive eventually ordered two of the house specials, without even bothering to ask what they were. It didn't matter. They could have been dining in the best three-Michelin-starred restaurant in London, eating the finest *foie gras*, feasting on the freshest lobster and drinking vintage Cristal. And they wouldn't have noticed.

Together in their own hermetically sealed bubble, they were oblivious to everything around them. For the other diners it was sickening. Couples who had long since run out of things to say to each other gazed with wistful envy at the attractive, dark-haired woman and her tall, russet-haired male companion who sat tucked away in the corner with an angelic little boy who was fast asleep in his pushchair, their conversation flowing as effortlessly as the contents of the bottle of Chianti in its traditional straw basket.

Over two great big steaming plates of creamy tagliatelli carbonara, Rhian and Clive chattered nonstop about everything and anything. From her relationship with Phil, to her love for Jack, to her desire to restart her career as a make-up artist, across to Clive's passion for being a doctor, to his love of his old VW camper van, to his dream of surfing the big waves in Hawaii. Backwards and forwards, questions and answers, revelling in shared interests, marvelling at weird coincidences, and hooting with laughter at their glaring differences.

Between them stretched a wooden table with a red and white checked tablecloth, but it proved a useless barrier. They were drawn to each other. Her small hands inadvertently clashing with his large freckled ones as she'd gone to dip her ciabatta in the small bowl of olive oil, his corduroy knees rubbing against her stockinged ones, their eyes bumping together like badly driven dodgem cars.

And the time flew by. It was only when the manager started blowing out candles and pulling down the blinds that they realized it was time to leave. Usually in Rhian's experience this was where it got awkward. The point when phone numbers were exchanged, promises to call were made and both parties hovered next to each other on the pavement, gauging whether or not it was a case of politely kissing on the cheek, or nose-bumping on the lips.

But with Clive there were no hesitations or uneasy silences. It was as if they'd known each other for ever, and it felt the most natural thing in the world to catch a cab back to hers, tuck Jack into bed, crack open another bottle of wine, and for Rhian to lead him by the hand into her bedroom. So natural that when he began to undress her with the light still on, she hadn't dived for the light switch and bellyflopped under her patchwork quilt. Instead she stood proud and erect in her gold satin stilettos while he slowly undressed her. Until finally when she was completely naked he carefully stroked her dark hair away from her face, tilted her chin between his thumb and forefinger, and told her she was beautiful.

And then, only then, did he slowly, gently, and lovingly, kiss her.

Reliving the delicious memory, Rhian uncurled her fists, which she kept hugged to her chest while she slept, and with eyes still firmly closed, stretched out an arm and slid it across the mattress towards Clive's hard, rangy body.

It wasn't there.

Filled with alarm, she snapped her eyes open. On the other side of the bed was an empty space where Clive should have been. The pillow bore an indentation where his head had lain, a few stray red hairs lay on the broiderie anglaise pillowcase and the faded smell of his aftershave clung to the sheets. Which are still warm, she thought, running the palm of her hand over the mattress like an iron.

Automatically, Rhian felt a knot of fear. *He'd gone.* Legged it. Waited until she was still fast asleep and then done a runner. Age-old insecurities began multiplying, until in the space of a few seconds she'd got herself into such a right old state she didn't notice that Clive's knackered Converse were still lying crumpled on the floor, or that his suede jacket was hanging over the back of the chair where he'd left it, or that his watch, with its old brown leather strap, was still curled up like a piece of orange peel next to the radio on her bedside table.

It was Leo Sayer that did it. Not in the flesh of course, but his voice belting out 'You Make Me Feel Like Dancing'. It was her favourite song. It was her favourite CD. And, she thought, perching on the side of her bed and wriggling her toes into her slippers, it was coming from the direction of the kitchen.

Unhooking her faded, snaggy towelling dressing gown from behind the door, Rhian was about to put it on when hanging underneath she spied the cream satin one she'd bought for that first date with Noel a couple of months ago. She paused. Goodness, I'd forgotten all about that, she thought, catching the soft sheen of the fabric. It seemed so long ago, Noel seemed so long ago, that thinking about herself then was like thinking about a different person. Probably because I was, she realized, hanging her towelling faithful back on its hook, slipping the slinky material over her naked body, and tiptoeing into the hallway.

Yep, the music was definitely coming from the kitchen, she decided. Unable to resist humming along, she pattered along the narrow, fairy-lit corridor that ran the length of her flat. At the far end she noticed the kitchen door had been firmly closed, the rubber door jam having been kicked to one side. Filled with anticipation she curled her fingers around the handle and, with a soft click, pushed open the door.

'Sorry, did we wake you?' Clive looked up when she walked in.

Rhian paused in the shaft of sunlight that was pouring in from the window, to take in the scene before her. In the middle of her kitchen stood her little fold-down camping table covered with a tablecloth – and not just any tablecloth, she noted with appreciation, but her favourite one with bits of lace around the edges. Upon it sat her portable stereo, her Princess Di teapot, and, she thought, inhaling the delicious smell of burnt Hovis, a full rack of toast.

But what Rhian noticed most of all was Clive. Sitting next to Jack, a colouring book open between them, he made a very peculiar sight. Wedged across his tousled red hair was a pair of bubblegum pink Barbie earmuffs, knotted tightly around his neck was a matching pink scarf, and squeezed halfway down his fingers were the gloves that completed the set.

Rhian stifled a giggle. Jack's favourite game was dressing up Mummy's friends in his favourite Barbie accessories, but usually the friends were female. On this occasion Mummy's friend was a man. And he looked utterly ridiculous.

'Hey, good morning.' Clive smiled as she walked in

388

and gave a little wave, not seeming to notice the pink woollen glove flapping on the end of his hand.

'Hi.' Rhian smiled back, her mouth twitching with amusement. 'Feeling a little cold this morning?' she asked, desperately trying not to laugh.

'Cold?' he asked looking bewildered. And then glancing down he remembered what he was wearing, and blushed scarlet. 'Oh ... I ... erm ...' Embarrassed, he began hastily tugging off his Barbie gloves and scarf. He looked at Rhian. Tears of laughter were running down her cheeks.

He broke into a huge grin. 'I don't think pink's my colour,' he laughed, shaking his head.

'No, I don't think it is,' squeaked Rhian, tapping her head to remind him of his earmuffs.

'Oh ... yeah ...' He tugged them off, running his fingers through his dishevelled hair. 'I think this might have been a ruse by your son.'

'I think it probably was.' She laughed, looking across at Jack who was bent over the double-page spread of a giant caterpillar, furiously felt-tipping the body in green. Sensing Clive had stopped, he reached out a pudgy hand and tugging his sleeve urged bossily, 'Clive, you have to do the eyes. If you don't, he won't be able to see the worms and Mummy says he's a very hungry caterpillar ...'

Rhian felt extraordinarily relaxed. This was the first time she'd ever allowed a man to stay over at the flat when Jack was there. It was the first time she'd thought anyone was special enough. It was the first time she'd *wanted* anyone to be introduced to her son. She'd been nervous about how they'd react to each other, but watching them together, she felt reassured.

'This little chap woke up early and you were still sleeping so I thought I'd fix him some breakfast, just some Weetabix and a glass of milk ...' Clive's voice trailed off nervously as his eyes met Rhian's. He'd fallen head over heels for this woman, he didn't want her to think he was being presumptuous or overstepping the mark where her son was concerned. 'I hope that's OK . . .'

'That's fine. Everything's fine,' she murmured, grinning at the understatement as she reached out and began tousling Jack's mop of curly hair. 'Hey muffin, how are you this morning?'

'Fine. Everything's fine,' he parroted, cocking his head from side to side. Still not looking up, he happily continued kicking his bare legs backwards and forwards against the rung of his stool.

Rhian and Clive exchanged bemused looks as she pulled a chair and sat down next to Jack. Giving him a hug, she nuzzled her nose into his neck, inhaling his warm, baby smell.

'Fancy a cuppa?'

'Ooh I'd love one.'

As Clive poured out a cup of Earl Grey – into her favourite mug, she noted, feeling deliciously superstitious – she eyed up the toast in the white porcelain rack.

Clive poured in the milk and passed her the cup. 'I hope you're not one of those women who skips breakfast under the misguided notion that it keeps them slim,' he smiled teasingly.

Rhian feigned a look of surprise.

'When in actual fact breakfast is one of the most important meals of the day as it gets your metabolism going. Otherwise your body thinks it's starving and starts hoarding fat . . .' He broke off. 'Sorry, listen to me. The doctor talking,' he stammered nervously. 'Not that you need a lecture from me on losing weight. You've got an amazing body,' he added shyly.

Rhian felt her cheeks blush, and promptly plucked a piece of toast from the rack. 'Butter and jam?' asked Clive holding aloft a pack of Lurpak that had lain abandoned in the back of the fridge for yonks and some of that delicious raspberry jam Rhian had bought from the deli on the corner but had always felt too racked with guilt to open.

390

'Yes please,' she smiled, feeling gloriously ravenous.

Rhian watched as he took the toast from her fingers and began slathering it with thick white swirls of unsalted butter, followed by a generous layer of bright pink raspberry jam. Noticing the way the muscle in his forearm was flexing, she allowed her eyes to wander up the bare expanse of skin to his biceps that bore the mark of a childhood measles jab. She caught herself, amused by the awareness that she was actually getting turned on by watching him buttering a slice of toast. Goodness, I have got it bad, she smiled to herself, as he held out the slice across the table and she leaned forward to take a bite. He reached towards her and brushed the crumbs from her cheek with his thumb. Her lips parted. Their eyes locked.

It was deeply erotic.

'The caterpillar wants toast,' piped up Jack, breaking the moment with the perfect timing that only children ever have. 'He's hungry,' he bleated indignantly.

'That's because he's a hungry caterpillar,' chorused Rhian and Clive, sharing what felt like a parental smile and bursting out laughing. Jack joined in, his tinkly belly chuckles running over theirs like a gurgling descant.

God only knows how long they would have stayed like that. It was one of those moments when giggles appear for no reason. Rhian's deep-throated guffaws inspired Clive's lazy laughter, which in turn fuelled Jack, who immediately saw this as an opportunity to start getting all silly and began felt-tipping the table.

At which point the phone began ringing.

'There's only one person who calls me at this time in the morning,' groaned Rhian, rubbing her aching belly and rolling her eyes skywards as she reached for the handset. 'Nana,' she smiled, looking at Jack, who promptly stuck his tongue out and pulled a face. The same face he pulled every time Nana Jones came to visit and insisted on smothering him in powdery, perfume kisses.

Slurping a mouthful of tea, she picked up. 'Hi, Mum . . .' she drawled lazily, and then the smile slid from her face. 'Oh sorry, I thought . . . *oh hello.*' Eyes widening, a blotchy rash immediately sprung up across her neck. Jerking up from her stool she began to pace up and down the kitchen, her heels click-clacking against the lino.

'No of course it's not too early . . . yes of course I'd love to . . .' She was nodding ferociously, her chest falling and rising, her fingers fiddling agitatedly with the tie from her dressing gown. 'Mmmm . . . absolutely . . . mmm . . . mmm.'

Clive watched with raging curiosity. Who was she talking to? Perhaps it was Phil, he pondered, remembering how she'd told him all about what happened last night. Or maybe not, he thought, changing his mind as he saw her smiling widely, her cheeks flushing with excitement. 'That's great . . . thanks ever so much . . .' Waving her arms around wildly she was gesticulating to Clive.

But I haven't a clue what she's trying to tell me, he thought, resigning himself to just grinning back inanely. Rhian's smile of feverish excitement was infectious.

'OK, so I'll see you there . . . oh and thanks again.'

Rhian hung up.

For a moment she stood in a daze in the middle of the kitchen and stared at Clive and Jack.

They stared back. 'Well?' coaxed Clive, bewildered.

Catching her breath, Rhian seemed to take for ever to find her tongue. 'That was the fashion editor of *Hip-Style*. I've just been commissioned for a shoot,' she gasped in disbelief.

'Wow that's great,' enthused Clive, although in reality he wasn't really sure what 'commissioned for a shoot' exactly entailed. But whatever it was, it was obviously pretty good, he decided.

Luckily she was only too happy to elaborate. In fact there was no stopping her. 'The magazine's doing a fashion shoot down at Regent's Park Zoo this morning and the make-up artist that they originally booked has just called in sick, and the fashion editor remembered receiving my card that I sent her last week and, would you believe it, but she'd put it in her wallet and so she dug it out this morning and . . . well . . .' Rhian's voice had been getting higher and higher and suddenly she stopped and took a deep breath. '*I've got my first job,*' she squeaked.

And then insecurity knocked.

'Oh my goodness, it's been years since I had a shoot, I'm so out of practice. What if I can't cope? What if my neighbour can't mind Jack after nursery? What if I don't know what I'm doing? What if I make a complete fool of myself?'

'You'll be fine. I promise,' he reassured her, reaching out and sliding an arm around her silky waist. 'Trust me, I'm a doctor.'

Her panic subsided and a smile broke across Rhian's face. 'I'll just jump in the shower,' she whispered, kissing him on the cheek. She lunged towards the doorway, and then suddenly remembering she stopped, swivelled around on her heels, and stuffed her sticky, half-eaten slice of toast and mug of tea into Clive's hands. Earl Grey promptly sploshed over the rim onto Jack's hungry caterpillar. 'Oops sorry . . .' she grinned at Clive and Jack, who stared at her in bemusement as she disappeared into the bathroom in a frenzied whirl of cream satin.

Chapter Forty-four

The delicious aroma of freshly brewed coffee wafted into Grace's nostrils. Lavazza espresso. Italian, roasted and gloriously pungent, it seeped underneath the duvet, filtering into the dark, musky warmth. Eyes closed, head nestled into a feather pillow, limbs curled in sleepy hibernation, she stirred groggily.

'Uhhhh.'

Like a wounded animal, she let out a piteous moan. Her head couldn't have moved more than a few millimetres, but all at once it was as if the Sex Pistols had re-formed and were doing a comeback gig inside her head. All thrashing guitars, thundering drums, and Sid Vicious in his steel-toecapped Doc Marten boots stomping behind her eyelids.

'Uhhhh,' she whimpered quietly, her body shuddering with what had to be the worst hangover she'd ever, *ever* inflicted upon herself.

Grace felt as if she was regaining consciousness from a head-on collision. Her whole body was sore and aching, her eyes felt bruised and swollen, her head was painfully thumping, and her stomach was churning and gurgling. And boy did she feel sick. The bile rose in her throat and she felt as if she wanted to vomit. She tried swallowing, only to discover her tongue was welded to the roof of her mouth.

At least I presume it's my tongue, mused Grace, although in reality it feels like a dried, rancid piece of flesh. It tastes like that too, she thought, a sweaty flush of nausea erupting from the pit of her stomach and pinning her to the plum-coloured sheet.

Plum-coloured sheet?

Easing open one puffy eyelid, she peered between the crook of her shoulder and armpit, at the triangular gap of fitted sheet beneath her. All her bedlinen came courtesy of her mother, and Mrs Fairley didn't do coloured bedlinen, she did whites and ivories and calico and perhaps the odd duvet cover in pink gingham or an Oxford stripe in pale blue. All 100 per cent cotton. And all with matching pillowcases.

Even in her death-like state, there was no mistaking this was deepest, darkest, purplest plum. This was also, by the looks of it, expensive Irish linen. And what's more, thought Grace, her eyes moving sideways like a painting in a haunted house, barely daring to look for fear of what she might see, *the pillowcases don't match.*

Oh fuck.

A hot, searing stab of panic burned like battery acid through her veins. Which could only mean one thing: she wasn't in her own bed. She was in somebody else's.

Fuck, fuck, *fuck.*

Peeling her eyes off the sheet, Grace was terrified of what she was about to see. It was like the time she'd rammed her mother's new Renault Clio into a lamp-post and had sat glued to the steering wheel, staring straight ahead. As if refusing to look would make it all go away. Only this time she hadn't just dented a bumper, smashed a headlight and scratched some paintwork, thought Grace, her heart thudding with horror. She'd woken up in Jimi's flat, she'd woken up in Jimi's bed. And, she realized, lifting up the duvet and peering underneath, *she'd woken up naked.*

Sweaty panic flooded her body. This can't be happening, this just simply can't be happening. How? Why? What on earth? As fragments of last night began piecing together like some mad, drunken jigsaw, Grace winced as a picture began to form: skating at Somerset House, seeing Spencer with Tamsin, lying on Jimi's sofa crying, drinking all his Aunt Phyllis's port – at that bit she paused to fight off nausea – and then? Her eyes flicked across the ruffles of the duvet, past the leather bedstead, down onto the polished floorboards. And there, in full, pearlescent, latex glory was the damning, irrefutable evidence that was her answer. Not one, not two, but three condoms.

And then she remembered.

She'd had sex with Jimi.

'So how do you like your coffee?'

As the last piece of the jigsaw clicked into place, Jimi appeared in the doorway wearing nothing but a pair of fly-buttoned boxer shorts and a huge grin.

A huge, self-satisfied, triumphant, post-shag grin, thought Grace, wincing.

Oh. My. God.

Faced with the vision of his hairy chest, the thickly etched eagle tattoo on his biceps, his muscular thighs and the sheer, sexual nakedness of him, her stomach churned. That was way too much naked flesh. And this is way too much to take on board, she thought, experiencing a flashback of them both naked and tangled up in the bed sheets, Jimi doing something with his tongue that was as indescribable as it had been amazing . . .

A hot flush of guilty pleasure erupted through her body and urgently grabbing the edge of the duvet, she yanked it up under her chin so it covered her naked breasts like a shield. Raising the beatbox that was her skull off the pillow she smiled cheerily, as if she was totally cool with the situation. And not, as was the reality, totally freaking out.

'Er, milk and two sugars please,' she gabbled, self-consciously brushing her knotted hair out of her eyes. The duvet slipped. She grabbed it near-hysterically, letting out a high-pitched peep of jittery laughter. Her cheeks burned with shame and mortification. God almighty she wasn't used to this. She felt so incredibly awkward, so embarrassed, so – Grace caught her breath as another flashback reared its grunting, panting, orgasmic head – so ridiculously coy. Unlike Jimi, she noted, looking at him casually propped up against the doorframe, legs crossed, arms folded. Having obviously had plenty of experience of all this one-night-stand malarkey, he seemed totally unfazed by it all.

'OK, coming right up.' He grinned. Whistling softly to himself, he turned on his bare heels and padded jauntily back into the kitchen.

Halle-bloody-lujah.

Infused with a burst of pure, undiluted happiness, Jimi was walking on air. Whistling cheerily, he tugged open the fridge, grabbed the carton of half-and-half, and doing his honky-tonky Huggy Bear strut, sashayed over to his espresso machine and poured creamy glugs into two latte glasses. Christ it felt good to be alive. He felt invincible. Empowered. Amazing. Even the mother of all hangovers couldn't pierce the happiness bubble that was enveloping him.

Reaching over to the sash window, he yanked it open, leaned out, closed his eyes and took a deep, gusty, lungful of fresh, frosty air. Boy that was good, he mused, relishing the invigorating feeling as it blasted out the cobwebs and wrapped his naked flesh in hundreds of delicious, shivery goosebumps. He opened his eyes and looked down on the Monday rush hour below, cars pumping exhaust fumes at the lights, people in thick winter coats hurrying along the pavement towards the tube, and suddenly had an irresistible urge to yell in his broad Mancunian Robin Williams, 'Good mawning, Kensal Rise.'

Jimi was euphoric. He and Grace had made love. Yep, that was right. They hadn't slept together, or shagged, or fucked, or bonked, they had, without

397

question, *made love*. Jimi had never felt so delighted to discover he'd been so wrong. Grace was right. Making love *was* different to sex. There was no comparison. Sex was a cheap imitation, like sparkling wine instead of Moët, flying economy instead of first, wearing high street instead of designer. It served a purpose and did the job, but it wasn't a patch on the real thing. But of course you only discovered the difference if you were lucky enough to experience the real thing. And now I have.

Bloody hell. Ducking back inside, he steadied himself on the edge of the fridge-freezer and recalled last night. A night which, thought Jimi, his whole body trembling with the memory, was quite simply the most amazing experience of my entire life. *Bloody, bloody, bloody hell.* In danger of being overcome with sentimentality, he reached hastily for the sugar shaker and liberally sprinkled fountains of brown crystals into the glasses. Then he grabbed a teaspoon and began stirring with determined concentration. But it was too late.

Lunging for the kitchen roll he ripped off a sheet. It was nothing. Just a bit of hay fever. OK, so it was December, but what with the global warming and everything . . . And sniffing tersely, Jimi Malik, master of cynicism, champion of no-strings-attached sex and general, testosterone-fuelled, thirtysomething male, found himself standing in the middle of his kitchen, furiously dabbing his eyes as they began to fill up with tears.

Oh God, what have I done? This is a mistake. Like, a really, huge, monumental, whopping great big mistake.

And now I can't escape.

Suffocating with embarrassment, Grace was lying stiffly in Jimi's vast leather bed. She wanted nothing more than to dive out from under the duvet, yank on her clothes and spring out the front door. But shock, guilt, shame and disbelief had frozen her, like a rabbit in headlights. Completely rigid against the buckskin headboard, she listened to the hissing sounds of the espresso machine, the gurgling, gushing, snorting noise of the milk being frothed, the clink of the teaspoon against the cup as the sugar was stirred.

It was purgatory. Normally she loved being in Jimi's funky, minimalist loft. Loved its comfortable and familiar surroundings, loved hanging out there and watching DVDs on his plasma telly, arguing over which takeout to order from the stash of leaflets in the cutlery drawer, trying to thrash each other at Connect Four. But now everything about it felt horribly claustrophobic. Every noise was magnified a hundred times, the aroma of coffee which had been so delicious a few seconds earlier was now so strong it was oppressive, and every second was stretching into an eternity.

She pulled herself up sternly. Grace Rosemary Fairley, you're being ridiculous. You're making a great big fuss. You're a modern, thirtysomething adult in the twenty-first century. So what if you've slept with Jimi? So what if you've had a one-night stand. *So bloody what?* It doesn't actually mean anything. I mean, it's not as if you *made love* or anything emotional like that. A faint huff of scornful laughter tickled the back of her throat. This is Jimi, remember. And Jimi doesn't make love, he has fucks and flings and shags and bonks. What was it he'd said in the restaurant in New York? Grace paused to press play on her cerebral tape recorder. The recording of their conversation whirred into life, and Jimi's voice struck up, loud and certain.

'. . . *that's just it, sex doesn't have to mean anything . . . sometimes sex can be just about sex . . . love doesn't have to have anything to do with it, it's purely physical . . .*'

Exactly, thought Grace. It was purely physical, nothing more. She felt a wave of relief, followed by an unexpected backlash of disappointment. It caught her by surprise. Where on earth did that come from? It wasn't as if last night had meant anything to her. Last night she'd been pissed, shocked, upset, confused. She loved Spencer, fancied Spencer, missed Spencer – Jimi had just been in the wrong place at the wrong time. And I ended up sleeping with the wrong man, concluded Grace, with absolute certainty. After all, it's not as if I feel anything other than friendship towards Jimi, is it? It's not as if I'm attracted to him, or fancy him, *or am in love with him*.

Is it?

Awww bless, just look at her, she's fallen back to sleep.

Reappearing with two tall, skinny glasses of steaming coffee, Jimi's heart flipped over like a pancake at the vision awaiting him in his king-size bed. Hair all ruffled and tousled, bare freckled shoulders peeping out from under the duvet, eyes closed and slightly puffy, Grace had to be the most adorable thing he'd ever seen.

Padding across the bedroom, he inadvertently trod on Flossie's tail. She yelped loudly and Grace opened her eyes.

'There you go.' Feeling like a man who'd won the lottery, he smiled at her in wonderment as he passed her a coffee.

'Ummm . . . er . . . thanks.' She smiled tensely. Why was Jimi staring at her in such a funny way? Hooking her fingers around the shiny chrome handle of the glass she averted her gaze, but out of the corner of her eye she could see the expression on his face. He looked weird. As if he was in some kind of dreamy, cultish trance.

Putting it down to a hangover – well, he had drunk as much as she had – Grace raised the glass to her lips and took a grateful sip of hot, milky coffee. And then nearly choked as Jimi promptly placed his cup next to the bed, climbed back under the duvet and – Oh – My – God – *snuggled up*. Feeling his soft, fuzzy chest rubbing against her back, the sturdy warmth of his arm curling around her waist, the prickly stubble of his chin as he nuzzled the nape of her neck, she jerked across the bed. A mouthful of hot latte shot down her throat, scalding her oesophagus and she burst into a fit of coughing.

'Hey are you all right?'

'Arrghh . . . yeah . . . fine, fine.' Doubled up, she was struggling with the complicated juggling act of keeping hold of the duvet, not spilling her coffee, and saving herself from asphyxiation.

'Sorry, it's my fault. It's probably too hot, you need to let it cool down,' apologized Jimi, his voice loaded with concern. 'Here, let me take it from you.' Easing the handle from her fingers, he rolled back across his side of the bed and put the glass next to his.

Released from the pressure of his naked body, Grace felt a rush of relief. Swiftly followed by near-hysteria as he began giving her a back rub. *Arrgghhhh*. Feeling the touch of his fingertips on her naked skin caused her to cough even harder and spluttering loudly she bent double over the duvet while Jimi continued rhythmically rubbing the dip between her shoulderblades.

It was startlingly erotic.

Mmmmm. With the gentleness and a sensitiveness of a trained masseur, he ran his hands over her skin, making a strange sort of billing and cooing noise as he traced the individual vertebrae that ran all the way down her spine to the two little indentations at the top of her buttocks . . .

She jerked away hastily. 'I should go.'

'*Go?*' repeated Jimi, his happiness bubble promptly bursting. The burgeoning erection in his boxer shorts collapsed with disappointment. After last night, he'd sort of assumed they'd be going for a repeat performance.

'Er . . . yeah, it's getting pretty late . . .' Half wiggling, half sliding out from underneath the duvet, Grace began the tricky manoeuvre of trying to keep hold of the duvet while picking up her knickers with her big toe – an exercise which Daniel Day-Lewis might have been able to perform with great dexterity in *My Left Foot*, but which in reality was bloody impossible.

Finally, after a few seconds, she managed to hook them over her foot, albeit inside-out, and squatting over the floorboards began kicking out her legs like a Russian Cossack dancer, while tugging them up, one leg at a time, with only one hand. Thankfully she'd had years of practice – putting on a bikini underneath a beach towel had never been easy – and at least this time there was no sand to contend with.

This time there was just Jimi.

'Late? But it's only just gone seven.' As he spoke, Jimi was suddenly aware that he sounded alarmingly similar to Sammy-Jo. And that the tables, he realized with a sad sense of irony, had been horribly turned. 'I thought you said you didn't have to be at the office until ten today,' he added sulkily.

'Er . . . yes but I've got an appointment before work,' jabbered Grace, clutching the duvet to her chest as she tried to fasten her bra. She was hit with a sense of the ridiculous. God knows why she was performing this prudish display. A few hours ago she'd been lying naked and spreadeagled on his bed with Jimi licking her all over. And she meant, *all over*.

'What kind of appointment?' asked Jimi in a very small voice. Insecurity began to mushroom. For the first time in his life he felt foolish and vulnerable. He felt, he realized with an anxious rumble in his stomach, like all those girls he'd slept with in the past and then left at the crack of dawn with some excuse about having to let in the gas-man. It was all coming back to haunt him. He'd got a taste of his own medicine. And, he thought miserably, he really didn't like it.

'Erm . . .' Grace's mind thrashed around wildly, every atom of hesitation seeming like an eternity, until . . . 'The dentist,' she gasped, then cringed inwardly at the implausibility. She continued regardless. 'It's an emergency, I've got this terrible toothache . . .' Immediately she grabbed her jaw and screwed up her face in what she hoped was a suitably agonizing expression. 'They think it's probably some kind of septic ulcer and that I'm going to need an urgent root canal with injections and drills and needles and everything . . .'

'I can give you a lift,' quickly offered Jimi, making to get out of bed.

'No . . .' said Grace loudly. Way, way, too loudly. 'I mean, it's OK, don't worry. It's much quicker on the tube.'

But Jimi's ardour wasn't going to be put off. 'What about tonight? Are you doing anything? I thought maybe we could go see that new Brazilian film . . .'

Tonight? Grace felt a jolt as she was reminded. 'I can't.' She shook her head. 'I mean . . .' she faltered, then blurted, 'I'm meeting Spencer.'

Jimi looked incredulous. 'You're still going to meet him?'

Am I? Grace hesitated. 'Why shouldn't I?' she asked defensively, but it was more a question to herself than to Jimi.

'Well I just thought, you know . . . after last night . . .' he added delicately. Jimi was referring to seeing Spencer with Tamsin at the ice rink, but he didn't want to come right out and say it.

Which was a shame as Grace completely took him the wrong way and assumed he was alluding to the fact that they'd spent the night together. Indignation bubbled. How bloody arrogant. Did he really think that just because she'd had sex with him she'd forget all about Spencer? That he was so amazing in bed she'd undergone some kind of evangelical enlightenment? OK, so admittedly the sex had been good – oh all right, let's be honest, it had been totally unbelievable, thought Grace, a shiver running deliciously up her spine. He'd been so confident, so unselfish, so enthusiastic. So unlike Spencer, who always seemed self-conscious with his sexuality and had a set routine he didn't like to vary. But it didn't change anything. Nothing. Not one little bit.

She looked at Jimi. She was talking bollocks.

It had changed everything.

Sex had *ruined* everything. Overnight their friendship had changed irrevocably. The platonic hugs, casual affection, impartial advice and comfortable comradeship were gone for ever. Now everything was awkward, feelings were in danger of being hurt, neither of them was being honest.

With themselves, or each other.

'He said we need to talk, and after last night I think we've got a lot to talk about,' she said primly.

'Oh, right . . .' Watching Grace hopping around the room, tugging on her clothes, making excuses, trying to run away from him as fast as she could, Jimi knew he'd made a mistake. A stupid, foolish mistake. Last night hadn't meant anything to Grace. She didn't love him, she wasn't *in love* with him. He'd just been convenient, a one-night stand, a way of getting her own back at Spencer. Rejection stabbed at him. He felt violated. Hurt. *Used.*

'Of course . . .' Jimi nodded. Once so close, he could already feel a distance between them.

Backing out of the bedroom door, Grace met Jimi's eye and out of the blue, and thirteen years later, she realized they were right back where they'd started. Only this time they weren't eighteen years old and in the woods, they were thirty-one and in Jimi's flat. And not only that, Grace thought, but the shoe was now, quite unexpectedly, on the other foot. Her mouth twitched at the idea of revenge. But that's just silly, she chided herself. Jimi and I are adults now and it was all such a long time ago it would be childish, and pathetic and immature.

But her eighteen-year-old self that had sat by that

phone stirred deep within, and all the hurt and the anger and the crushing disappointment came flooding back as if it was yesterday. Scooping up her leather jacket she went to leave, but at the last minute she turned back round to look at Jimi and, unable to resist, made a promise that she knew she wouldn't keep.

'*I'll call you.*'

Chapter Forty-five

There is something bizarrely exhilarating about walking home the morning after the night before. It doesn't matter that you've got the worst hangover known to man, that you're wearing yesterday's clothes, or that with your tangled bed-hair, smudged eyeliner and nasty case of stubble rash it's obvious to everyone you pass that you've spent the night shagging your brains out.

Because that's exactly what makes it so thrilling. You feel alive – even if, quite frankly, you feel like death. It's an affirmation that even though you're in your thirties, you contribute to a monthly pension plan, eat five portions of vegetables a day and body brush religiously, you've still got it in you to walk on the wild side and be just that little bit reckless.

Or in my case a drunken idiot, thought Grace, trying to avoid the curious gazes of a cosy, cappuccino couple who were staring at her from the window of a coffee shop, like a couple of spectators in ringside seats. Tugging her scarf up like a neck brace, she stared resolutely at her feet. She felt like a harlot. A dirty stop-out. A complete mess. And, she realized as she took a deep breath of smoggy, inner-city air, *more invigorated than she'd felt in years.*

Grace continued hurrying towards the tube, along the traffic-choked Harrow Road, past the profusion of Sudanese, Thai and Indian restaurants, the boarded-up shops covered in tatty billboard posters and graffiti, and a barber's shop called Mario's complete with a window of faded black and white photographs of men with seventies mullets and Tom Selleck moustaches.

On any other day Grace would have paused to stare, to smile in amusement, to make a mental note to point out the picture of the outrageous poodle perm to Jimi next time they walked back to his place. Only this time Grace didn't notice. An awful lot had happened in the last twenty-four hours, and just like that snowglobe she was shaken up, her emotions whirling around like snowflakes, making it impossible to see the clearer picture.

Grace's plan was to go home, ring in sick, and spend the rest of the day in bed. *Her bed*. Exhausted, confused and suffering the mother of all hangovers, she wanted to sleep for a week. Only life has a habit of throwing surprises at you, a bit like a knife-thrower in a circus. And on that sunny, clear-skied December morning, Grace might as well have been dressed in leotard and tights and pinned spreadeagled to a wooden board at the side of the busy main road.

The first knife was thrown the moment she turned on her mobile. Within seconds it rang. 'Private number' flashed up. She answered.

'Hi, Babes . . .'

It was Spencer.

With his distinctive voice still resonating in her ear, the phone promptly slipped out of her fingers like a bar of wet soap. She attempted to grab it, her heart pounding loudly as it clattered onto the pavement, narrowly missing being trodden underfoot by a workman in paint-splattered overalls reading the front page of the *Mirror*. Diving on the cracked plastic case with the relief of a mother being reunited with her child, she rammed it tightly to her ear. Despite its bashed appearance, it was working.

'Grace? Are you still there?'

'Yeah . . .' she panted, thrown completely off

407

balance from the sensation of being catapulted from Planet Jimi to Planet Spencer. She ducked into the doorway of a boarded-up shop. She couldn't walk *and* talk. 'I'm still here,' she stammered.

'Are you ignoring me?' he challenged, the lawyer within him coming straight to the point.

'Ignoring you?' repeated Grace, doing what people always do when they're at a loss what to say and merely repeating the question.

'I tried calling you last night.'

Last night. Grace's brain suddenly split down the middle like an old sixties movie. On one side Spencer and Tamsin were hugging on the ice rink, on the other she and Jimi were lying naked in bed together.

'Oh, umm . . .' Hastily switching off the memory, she dragged her attention back to the phone conversation. It wasn't easy. She was struggling to stay adrift in a sea of confusion, guilt, relief and, she realized, a whacking great sense of indignant anger. Why on earth was she feeling so guilty? It was Spencer who'd been unfaithful first, Spencer who'd fed her a pack of lies about being away on business until today, which is why he couldn't see her until later that evening. How convenient for him. She remembered his text: *We need to talk.* Damn bloody right we do, she thought grimly.

'My phone was turned off.'

'*Turned off?*' The very idea of turning off his mobile was unthinkable to Spencer, who was constantly connected to his earpiece. So much so that Grace had often mistakenly thought he was chatting to her, only to discover he was actually having a telephone conversation with some legal eagle in Brussels.

'I thought you were away on business, anyway,' continued Grace tersely. Hearing herself she regretted her tone of voice. She wanted to sound cool and nonchalant, as if she'd been so preoccupied with her new and amazing life that she hadn't given him or his business trip a second thought. And not, as was the case, that she'd been obsessing about it all week.

'We finalized the deal early. I flew back yesterday.'

Having expected to catch him out, Grace was surprised. 'Well, I was busy . . .' she continued defensively, trying to rescue a bit of dignity. More images fluttered through her mind. Curled up with Jimi in a tangle of limbs, laughing as he blew raspberries on her stomach. She zoned back in to find Spencer was still talking.

'. . . I was calling about tonight. To make sure you could still make it.'

Automatically, Grace's mind flicked forward a few hours – blow-drying her hair, applying her make-up, catching a cab, walking into the pub, kissing Spencer awkwardly on the cheek, ordering a glass of wine and making excruciating smalltalk until finally he plucked up the courage to tell her this wasn't a break, it was over and he was seeing someone else.

Why not save herself all the bother?

'Look, about tonight. I already know what you're going to say. I know it's over. I know about Tamsin,' she blurted.

'*Tamsin?*' Spencer sounded bewildered. 'What's she got to do with anything?' he demanded brusquely.

'You don't have to pretend, Spencer. I saw you together,. At the ice rink.' An image of Tamsin giggling cut like a knife. 'And to be honest, I think you should be a bit more discreet if you're going to have an affair with a married woman,' she snapped, jealousy and hurt making her sound like some kind of pathetically prim Miss Jean Brodie.

'*An affair?*' snorted Spencer loudly down the line.

'Yes. You heard. An affair,' repeated Grace, trying to blink back the film of tears that was rapidly forming over her eyes. Feeling utterly wretched, she chewed her lip and waited for him to say something.

There was silence.

And then, quite unexpectedly, Spencer threw the second knife of surprise. He exploded into laughter. Rich, bellowing, resounding laughter. 'Babes . . .' he urged, pausing for breath. 'I can explain everything.'

The Tabernacle was something of a living legend. A five-minute walk from Earls Court station, it had been a popular hangout since the sixties and in its heyday had graced endless album covers and been the backdrop for countless fashion shoots. But like an ageing movie star who has lost her looks, it had long since been forgotten by the cutting-edge crowd and was now a much-loved haven for students and backpackers.

'That'll be six quid, love.'

As the cabbie pulled up outside and switched off his meter, Grace finished smoothing down her hair, applying lipgloss and concealer – the two items she always carried like army rations – and dug out a crumpled tenner from the pocket of her jeans. Paying the driver, she waited for change, taking the opportunity to bob down and check her reflection in his wing mirror. Of all the times she'd imagined seeing Spencer, of all the outfits she'd planned to wear, all the grooming, blow-drying, moisturizing she'd wanted to do, here she was, about to see him for the first time in months, and she was still wearing yesterday's knickers.

'Thanks.' Smiling, she took the change from the driver's large, sandpapery hand. Stuffing the pound coins into her back pocket, she paused for a moment, lost in reflection as she remembered the last time she'd had coffee in a café with Spencer. It had been the morning after her birthday, the morning she'd decided to leave. Her spirits dipped and she glanced at her watch. She was late. Spencer would probably already be inside. Her heart skipped as she remembered their earlier phone conversation. 'It's not what you think,' he'd urged, his voice thick with concern. 'Meet me, just for ten minutes, just for a coffee, and I can explain.' A proud part of her had thought about refusing, about sticking to plan A and dragging herself home to bed, but you don't love someone for four years to say no.

And, thought Grace, feeling a rush of nervous excitement as she pushed open the door and stepped inside, she didn't want to anyway.

Walking into the Tabernacle was like being transported to the Tyrolean Alps, all apple strudel, cigarette smoke and hearty laughter. Spencer was sitting in the far corner, underneath a large pair of bleached antlers and a signed photo of Jimi Hendrix. Hunched over his *FT*, freshly showered, clean shaven and starched-collared, he looked very out of place amongst the dishevelled, dreadlocked Ozzy travellers who lay sprawled around him, smoking roll-ups and laughing raucously as they tucked into full English breakfasts.

Grace paused by the entrance. She'd spent the entire cab journey trying to imagine how she was going to feel when she first saw him again, trying to prepare herself for the influx of emotions. Would she feel upset, angry, guilty, weird? So much had happened, would he seem like a stranger? Would he have changed?

Would she have changed?

Engrossed in his paper, Spencer reached for his croissant. Slicing it into two perfect halves, he carefully unwrapped the butter portion, meticulously covering every inch of pastry with a thin layer and finishing with a neat topcoat of strawberry jam, before finally taking a careful bite. Watching him chewing methodically, scrutinizing the share index with the concentration of a man with £50,000 invested, Grace was struck by just how deliberate Spencer was, how everything was always so carefully considered and thought out, how nothing was ever spontaneous or impulsive. He was the antithesis of Jimi, who'd squeeze the butter portion until it splurged out one end, ripping up chunks of croissant to wipe it up and then dunking them in the jam like soldiers into a boiled egg. All the time talking with his mouth full and waving his arms around, dropping greasy splodges of croissant and flecks of raspberry jam all down his T-shirt.

'Oh ... hi ...' Feeling her gaze upon him, Spencer looked up. He stood up awkwardly, banging his knees under the table, his tie swinging across and dipping into his coffee.

Grace was surprised to see he appeared more nervous than she was. 'Hi.' She walked towards him and hesitated, unexpectedly self-conscious.

The conversation stalled. Briefly, Grace regretted her decision to come. Maybe it was a bad idea. Maybe they'd simply run out of things to say to each other. Maybe whatever they'd had together was gone. Maybe there really was no going back.

'You look great,' he said, pushing his glasses up his nose with his finger, a warm, easy smile crinkling up his blue eyes like the folds in velvet.

Or was there?

Feeling her anger vanish, she returned his smile. 'You don't look so bad yourself,' she said, then forced a laugh, her heart thumping against her chest so loudly she could have sworn he would hear it. He looked so unfamiliar, and yet so familiar. He also, thought Grace despite herself, looked absolutely gorgeous.

She sat down on the bench opposite.

'What do you want? Coffee? Croissant?'

Grace looked at him. He was being all polite, as if this was one of his breakfast meetings, moving the menu, clearing away his paper.

'How about an explanation?' she interrupted quietly. After everything that had happened, he at least owed her that.

Collapsing back onto the bench, Spencer took off his glasses and furrowed his forehead. It was now or never. His shoulders rose as he took a deep breath, and let it slowly exhale. 'All my life I've had this big fear, a fear of failing ...'

His voice low and deliberate, he began speaking. It all came out. About his first marriage, with its innocent hopes and expensive Claridges reception, and the subsequent anger, disappointment and hurt of

412

the divorce. About how eighteen months later he'd met Grace, how he'd fallen in love with her and asked her to marry him, and how he'd immediately panicked with fear that it would all go wrong again. He talked about the last few months spent throwing himself into his work, ignoring his emotions, stubbornly refusing to think about what had happened. Until that evening in the pub, when it had taken a barman called Eddie to give him the wake-up call he'd been waiting for. And the courage to pick up the phone and call her.

And then he told her about Tamsin, and how she'd called him yesterday morning saying she needed to talk about something important, and how her suggestion they met at Somerset House instead of one of their usual haunts, coupled with her strict instructions 'not to tell Matt', had led him to assume she was planning some kind of surprise. Being in PR, Tamsin was always planning something; be it for Matt's birthday, or their anniversary, or just for no reason other than she wanted an excuse to go out and buy a new pair of Jimmy Choos.

Only when he'd arrived at the ice rink he'd discovered it was none of the above. Tamsin wasn't there to talk parties, she was there to break a different kind of news. 'I'm going to divorce Matt for adultery,' she'd announced as they stepped onto the ice. Neatly tucking a glossy curtain of blond hair behind her ear with the perfect poise of a woman trained in PR, she'd fixed him with a look of ice-cold calm. 'And I need a divorce lawyer, I need the best divorce lawyer. And that's you. He can fuck who the hell he likes, but he's not fucking with me,' she'd declared furiously, her demeanour slipping as she'd thought of Matt having sex with his, quite frankly, dumpy assistant.

'Christ, I'm sorry.' Taken aback, Spencer had tried to console her.

But it wasn't necessary. 'Don't be. I'm not. I'm just sorry I married him in the first place.' She'd sighed heavily, sticking her manicured fingers firmly into her

413

fur muffler. 'And that I wore that stupid Vera Wang dress. Six grand or not, it never fitted properly.' A look of pure irritation clouded her perfect features.

'Look, if there's anything I can do, not just as a lawyer but as a friend . . .'

Pouting, she'd dipped her head and looked at him from under her eyelashes. 'Just being here, that's enough, I really appreciate you coming tonight.' Even in grief, Tamsin couldn't resist flirting. She'd heard Grace had moved out and a successful partner in a law firm was so much more her than the owner of an organic café. 'Actually, there is one thing . . .' she'd said, waiting for a flurry of whooping skaters to pass them.

'Yes?'

Shaking back her hair, she'd looked at Spencer beseechingly. 'I need a hug.'

For a moment Spencer had hesitated. He wasn't the most tactile of people. He'd never been the type to walk down the street holding Grace's hand, or throw his arms around his mother in a loving son embrace, or ruffle the hair of his colleagues' children when they visited the office.

But maybe that was part of the problem, he'd thought later, after saying goodbye to Tamsin in the NCP carpark and watching her accelerate out of the exit in her shiny, silver Audi TT. Maybe if he'd been more open, more affectionate, less uptight, things would have turned out differently with Grace. Which was why, in the middle of the ice rink, in full view of all those hundreds of strangers, he'd ignored his gaucheness, put his arms around Tamsin and given her a supportive, encouraging, platonic hug.

'After all, it was no big deal. What's a hug?' finished Spencer, looking tentatively at Grace trying to gauge her reaction.

It was one of silent shock. Listening to him talking, Grace's initial response had been one of sympathy, relief, pleasure. Followed by a bombshell of guilt and shame for doubting him with Tamsin, for betraying him with Jimi and for jumping, quite dramatically and rather spectacularly, to the wrong conclusions.

'I'm sorry, Babes.'

Reaching across the table, he wrapped his fingers around hers. 'I've been such an idiot. I'm sorry about everything. Really, I am.'

Grace stared at his hands. This was a man with whom she'd shared a home, holidays, memories, a history. A man with whom she'd planned to fill photo albums, a church, a nursery, a future. Looking up, she met his gaze. And in that moment, the last few months, New York, Jimi, last night, were all magically erased and she was back in her old life. Back with Spencer. Back together again.

'Me too,' she murmured quietly.

Chapter Forty-six

Revelling in her morning sojourn in the park, Flossie was scampering ahead on her retractable lead, delighted to be indulging in her favourite hobby of sniffing the scent of every single tree trunk, bench leg and wastepaper bin as if she were a woman in the perfume hall of Selfridges. Before finally choosing the ones she liked the best by squatting on her hind legs and, in what was a canine version of swiping her MasterCard, peeing on them.

Meanwhile Jimi followed mournfully behind. Tramping across the grass, his shoulders slunk deep inside his black crombie, a black woollen hat pulled down low over his forehead, and with his eyes hidden behind a pair of black Fendi shades, he was plunged in the depths of depression.

'. . . I mean, I just can't believe it,' he bleated down his mobile. Slumping onto a wooden bench, he stared dolefully into the middle distance and sighed heavily. 'She just used me for sex.'

'This is the reason you're calling me at eight-thirty in the morning?' gasped Clive incredulously. 'This is the *something terrible*?'

Having just arrived back at his flat in a cloud of post-orgasmic bliss, Clive had idly pressed play on his answer phone and heard a strangled voice blasting into his tiny living-room. '*Shite almighty, it's me, Jimi. Where the fuck are you? I need to*

416

talk to you! Something terrible's happened.'

His heart had skipped a beat. Dreadful images of car crashes, appalling accidents, family deaths and Jimi lying mugged and fatally injured somewhere in the East End, flashed across his mind as he dived on the telephone and, with trembling fingers, dialled his mobile.

Only to discover (with a twinge of the anticlimax) that Jimi wasn't hurt, he wasn't in danger, and he wasn't about to kick the bucket. In fact the only thing wrong with Jimi, Clive realized, holding the handset away from his ear while Jimi gushed on and on about Grace, about how they'd spent the night together, about how she'd legged it at the crack of dawn, was that he'd fallen totally, completely, and barkingly *In Love.*

'I mean, I can't believe it. We made love,' he was whining piteously.

Clive had to stifle a snort of laughter. Hearing Jimi talking about 'making love' was like hearing Vinnie Jones talking about embroidery.

'It's not funny,' snapped Jimi.

'I'm not laughing,' protested Clive, stuffing his fist in his mouth and jack-knifing across the sofa.

'*Uggghhhhhheeoowwww.*' Groaning loudly, Jimi put his head in his hands and stared fixedly ahead. He was so absorbed in the grief-stricken depths of his gloom that he didn't see a perky-nippled jogger staring over at him, breathing in strenuously as she bounced past, hoping he'd notice her.

He didn't. Proof, if any was needed, that he'd got it bad.

'I don't know what's wrong with me. I feel awful,' he moaned dully. Like an alcoholic reaching for the bottle, Jimi embraced his hypochondria. 'I think I'm coming down with a brain tumour.'

'I'm sure you're fine,' Clive reassured him impatiently.

But Jimi wasn't listening. Determined to be a martyr

to his suffering, he continued revelling in his depression. 'Did I tell you I saw that programme about the woman with a tumour that was so big they had to put it in a wheelbarrow? And when they cut it open it had hair and teeth and everything.'

Clive ignored him. 'Why don't you call her?' he suggested pragmatically.

Why didn't I call her thirteen years ago? thought Jimi, spiralling downwards into mawkish regret. Gloomily he looked to Flossie for a bit of canine comfort. 'At least we've got each other,' he cooed, clicking his tongue and patting his knee. She promptly responded by squatting down in front of him, and with a loud grunt, depositing a large, steaming turd at his feet. Jimi gazed at it dolefully. Great. Just great. The perfect cherry on my cake of life, he sighed, tugging a plastic bag out of his pocket. Sticking his hand inside he scooped it up, feeling the warm squidginess through the plastic.

'Why don't you just be honest and tell her how you feel?' Interpreting his silence as acquiescence, Clive continued, 'What have you got to lose?'

'I've already tried that,' Jimi told him, thinking back to his disastrous declaration of love at the ice rink. 'Not the biggest success, I have to say.'

'Why don't you try again?'

'Why don't I just put a gun to my head and pull the trigger.' If he was going to be melancholic, he might as well go the whole hog and be suicidal.

'Nah, too messy,' replied Clive drily. He'd known Jimi too long to react to his neuroticism. 'If you're going to do it, it's got to be pills. Oh, and alcohol. Lots and lots of alcohol.'

On the other end of the line Jimi smiled ruefully. There were only two people who never let him get away with his shit: Clive and Grace. Reminded of her, he was hit over the head with a shovelful of longing. 'So anyway, what happened to you last night?' he asked, standing up so quickly he got a

418

headrush. Or is it a sign that I really *do* have a brain tumour? he thought, filled with a sudden panic. He began stomping across the grass towards the exit, dragging Flossie behind him and carrying his plastic bag of dog-shit. Life, he decided, could not get any worse.

'Me?' Clive hesitated as he thought of Rhian in her cream satin dressing gown. His stomach fizzed appreciatively. Oh what the hell, why keep it a secret. 'Nothing much. I just happened to meet the woman I'm going to spend the rest of my life with,' he said matter-of-factly. Or at least he meant to say it matter-of-factly, but it was impossible to stop his voice from dripping with delight.

'Wonderful,' said Jimi blithely. 'I hope you'll both be very happy.'

'You sound bitter.'

'That's me. Bitter and twisted.' Depositing his carrier bag in the dustbin, he left the park by the Albert Memorial.

There was an ominous pause.

Usually Clive would bite his tongue and ignore Jimi's selfish cynicism, but that morning something snapped. Today he was in a good mood. Today something wonderful had happened. And today nobody – not even Jimi – was going to spoil it. '*Once*,' he snapped loudly, his voice coming out high and offended. 'Just this once I wanted you to be happy for me. Happy that I happen to have met a woman, a woman who I actually like – correction: *adore* – and who, by some miracle, appears to like me. Whereas I've had to be happy for you hundreds of times. Probably thousands. I've had to listen to you talk about every single woman you've ever met. I've had to be enthusiastic when you've talked about their fabulous bottoms, I've had to appear interested when you've gone on and on about their amazing designer wardrobe, *I've even had to give you my lucky condom . . .*' he declared indignantly, drawing another huge breath. 'And what have you done for me? Hmmm? *Hmmm?*'

Marching down past the Natural History Museum, Jimi was lost for words, stunned that Clive, polite, self-effacing, loyal Clive was shouting – literally *yelling* – at him down the phone.

'Nothing. You've done nothing except make some horrid, snidey, selfish little comment . . .' Clive fell silent, his ribcage heaving up and down, his breath loud and panting, his hands trembling on the handset. He felt like a child that has stood up to a bully. But as his adrenalin began ebbing away he felt a stab of worry. Christ, I've really gone and done it now, he thought, preparing for an angry outburst from Jimi.

And getting the exact opposite.

'Oh shite, I'm sorry, mate.'

In a dishevelled flat, on the top floor of a large Edwardian house in Ealing, Clive collapsed back onto his blue corduroy sofa. He was, quite literally, gobsmacked.

'Ignore me,' pleaded Jimi, apologizing profusely. 'You're right, and I'm wrong . . .'

At this point Clive held the handset away from his ear and pulled a funny face that involved making his eyes spookily wide and dropping his jaw wide open.

'I'm an idiot. I've *been* a fucking idiot, and it's not fair to take it out on you. I love Grace, and I've fucked up. I fucked up thirteen years ago. You don't get second chances in life and I know that. Everything's always been so easy, nothing's ever affected me like this. I mean Kylie jilting me wasn't exactly a blast but it wasn't like this, I didn't feel like this. If I'm honest, she did us both a favour, we would never have worked. We didn't want to spend the rest of our lives together, we just wanted to piss our parents off . . .'

Jimi broke off, hearing the words that came tumbling out of his mouth. It was the first time he'd ever vocalized his reasons for wanting to marry Kylie, probably because he'd never really admitted them to himself before. But now he'd said it out loud he knew it was true. In his own way he'd loved Kylie but he'd wanted to get married for all the wrong reasons. It was his last act of rebellion. A way of getting his father's attention, of proving to him that he'd finally grown up and was now a man. To show him that he could marry who the hell he liked, that she didn't have to be Muslim, she didn't have to come from a good family, and she didn't have to have his blessing. His father would have been angry, upset, disappointed, but so what? He couldn't do anything about it. Marrying Kylie would have proved that he no longer had a hold on him.

Jimi was shocked. He was shocked by his confession, shocked by his true feelings, and shocked by the realization that in actual fact, the opposite was true. Because even after all this time, after all these years of being estranged, his father was still very much part of his life, he was still influenced by him, and he still mattered. Whether he liked it or not.

'You see, that's my whole fucking problem. I didn't really want Kylie and she didn't really want me,' confessed Jimi quietly, shaking his head. 'I'm used to getting what I want . . . but I can't have Grace. And why should I? I mean, just look at me. I'm a jilted fiancé, I've got writer's block, I turn into the American fucking werewolf overnight. What is there to love about me?'

'Oh I don't know, you're not that bad,' joked Clive, trying to cheer him up. Having told Jimi what he thought, he was now feeling dreadfully responsible for his friend's obvious torment.

'*Yes I am*. I'm a fucking disaster, Clive. I'm selfish, I'm arrogant, I'm stubborn, I'm neurotic . . .' Jimi paused to glance at his reflection in a shop window. For the first time since puberty, he hadn't bothered with any hair removal that morning. He hadn't shaved his beard, or weeded his eyebrows, or attacked his nasal hair. '. . . and I look like shit,' he wailed, taking off his Fendi wraparounds and staring at the strange hirsute creature staring back at him. *Thirty-one years old and I've turned into a fucking yeti.*

'Maybe you should come over, we could go for a coffee,' suggested Clive, attempting to defuse the situation.

'I don't need a coffee. I need to see Grace,' said Jimi determinedly. 'I need to tell her that thirteen years ago I made a mistake.'

'Actually I'm not sure if that's wise . . .' Clive began backtracking massively.

'No, you were right. I'm going to be completely honest. I'm going to tell her how I feel.'

For the first time in his life, Clive desperately didn't want to be right. He didn't like all this being right business. It carried with it a huge amount of responsibility. People could get hurt. He wanted to be wrong instead. Ridiculously wrong. Naïvely wrong. Flippantly, foolishly, fabulously wrong. So wrong that nobody listened to a blind word he said. In fact, what had he been complaining about all these years? Being wrong was bloody brilliant.

'I mean, like you said, what have I got to lose?'

Clive listened in silence, deeply regretting his words of advice.

But it was too late. Having confronted his demons, got it all off his chest, and made up his mind, Jimi was beginning to feel a lot better. 'Thanks mate, for everything. I'll call you later.'

'*Later?*' Panic seized Clive. He could feel himself beginning to flap, 'Why, where are you going?'

'Where do you think?' laughed Jimi, taking big strides along the pavement and looking sideways at Flossie, who was having to scamper alongside to keep up. 'Grace's.'

Clive gave a strangled yelp, but the line had gone dead. Oh dear. Oh dear, oh dear oh dear. What had he done? Why had he interfered? He'd probably made matters much worse. Perhaps he should call him back and try to stop him, or maybe he should leave him to get on with it. Torn, Clive felt a huge sense of responsibility. If it all worked out he'd be a hero, *but if it all went wrong . . .* For a moment he sat rigidly on the sofa staring at the white plastic handset, worry setting like cement on his furrowed brow, not knowing what to do. And then it came to him. Frantically he began dialling. He was going to have to call in the troops.

He was going to have to call Rhian.

After talking for nearly an hour Spencer looked at his watch with dismay. 'Work,' he'd said, then shrugged apologetically. Without waiting for the bill, he left a tenner wedged under his coffee cup and together they walked outside into the sunshine, bright and brittle after the dark, smoky warmth of the Tabernacle.

Hit by the raucous noise of the traffic, the scores of people zigzagging around them, Grace experienced the sensation of walking out of a cinema, the moment when fantasy slips away and it's back to reality. Back to a life without airbrushing, a fabulous soundtrack and a guaranteed happy ending.

Inside the darkened café she and Spencer had been isolated in their own little world, in the moment, but now they were faced with reality, with the prickly issues of their relationship, their broken engagement, *what had happened between her and Jimi.* Grace stopped herself. Nothing had happened. It had just been sex, it didn't mean anything, he didn't mean anything to her, she didn't mean anything to him.

'I wish I could have stayed longer but I'm needed in the office.' Standing in the middle of the busy pavement, Spencer turned to face her and continued apologizing. 'A very big client of mine is due his decree nisi today and if I'm not there, heads will roll. Mine included.'

'Is this the *very big client* you've been so secretive

about for months?' asked Grace, grabbing onto the topic to stop her mind from wandering.

'The very same one,' Spencer confirmed, sliding his arm protectively around her waist.

'Oh c'mon, tell me who it is, it must be some big celebrity,' said Grace, pretending not to notice the familiar security of his forearm curling around her back, his fingers clasping her mohair waist tightly. Just the way he always used to.

'I can't, that's breaking client confidentiality.'

'Not just this once?' she persevered, inhaling the nostalgic scent of his antiperspirant and aftershave.

'You probably won't have even heard of him,' Spencer was protesting. Slipping his keys out of his breast pocket, he pressed the alarm. The Jeep Cherokee flashed and beeped.

'Try me.'

'You drive a hard bargain,' he laughed, leaning forward to kiss her.

Grace was silenced as he pressed his lips against hers. It was a warm, firm, Spencer type of kiss. It felt remarkably comfortable. Too comfortable, thought Grace, feeling a vague twinge of disappointment. She brushed it off. He was in a hurry, she had a hangover. What was she expecting? Fireworks? That was the stuff of novels, not real life, she scoffed silently. A flashback of kissing Jimi exploded like a skyrocket in her head, showering her with tiny, glittering stars, causing her to hold her breath, making her lips tingle, *proving her wrong*.

'But you've got to promise not to tell a soul.'

Spencer had broken away and was climbing into his jeep, slamming the door closed behind him and buzzing down the electric window. He leaned out. 'Not even Rhian,' he added pointedly.

'I promise,' she stammered, trying to block out the memory of those fireworks, but they were etched on her mind as if she'd looked at the sun.

'Well he's a DJ. He goes by the name of Dr Cupid

and has some ridiculous lonely hearts show . . .'

'*Do You Come Here Often?*' finished Grace without missing a beat.

Spencer looked surprised. 'You've listened to it?'

'Once or twice.' Grace was catapulted back to Jimi's flat, to them lying together on his sofa, listening to the radio, talking, laughing, *making love*. 'He's a Jim'll Fix-It of the heart,' she said, dragging herself back and quoting the show's cheesy trailer verbatim.

'Well I'm afraid he hasn't done such a good job on his own heart. Or his wife's. They've just gone through a very bitter divorce. Irreconcilable differences.'

'*Dr Cupid's divorced?*' gasped Grace in disbelief. 'Wow. I'm gutted,' she laughed, part nerves, part irony.

'So will his 500,000 listeners be. Why do you think it's hush-hush?' said Spencer, putting his finger to her lips.

It was just a gesture, as insignificant as it was fleeting, but Grace felt as if she was being reprimanded like a silly child. Over the last few months she'd grown used to saying, and doing, and laughing as loud as she liked. Jimi used to fondly call her as 'daft as a brush' but now, seeing Spencer's serious expression, she didn't feel daft. Just immature.

Turning the key in the ignition, Spencer checked the digital clock on his display. 'I'll pick you up at seven tonight. I want to take you out for dinner. Somewhere special.' He held her gaze, the silence thick with innuendo. And then clearing his throat self-consciously, he added quietly, 'It hasn't been the same without you, Grace.'

She smiled appreciatively at his compliment, his apology, his declaration that he loved her, his acknowledgement that they were back together again. But watching as he pulled out into the traffic, she couldn't stop the small, indignant voice inside from piping up, 'Did you really think it would be?'

Turning into Old Brompton Road, Jimi took a deep breath of air. Wow, he felt so much better. He'd made a decision, he was going to tell her, lay it on the line, be totally honest. Like Clive had said. What had he got to lose?

'C'mon girl,' he tugged on Flossie's lead. 'Let's go and see Grace.' Flossie barked happily, and wagged her stumpy tail in delighted approval as they rounded the corner.

And stopped. Dead.

The smile slid from Jimi's face. Flossie's tail collapsed and she began whining. Because there, a hundred yards away, was Grace. Only she wasn't alone. Standing with his arm around her on the pavement was Spencer. Frozen, Jimi watched Spencer climb into his jeep. He couldn't hear what they were saying, but he didn't have to. The way they were smiling and looking at each other said one thing, and one thing only – they were back together.

Like a stone hitting the water, sadness hit Jimi and sank deep inside him. For a glorious moment he'd allowed himself to believe anything was possible, but now he knew it was too late. He'd lost her. 'C'mon Flossie, let's go home.' Tugging on her lead, he turned away, and it was then that he realized the saddest thing of all.

He hadn't lost Grace. Because she'd never been his to lose in the first place.

Chapter Forty-seven

Inside the brown paper bag was an extremely large bunch of Muscadet grapes. Big swollen clusters of faded purple berries, they were exuding their wonderfully soft, musky perfume. '*Ahhh . . .*' Sticking her nose inside the bag, Maggie inhaled deeply, before popping the biggest, plumpest one she could find into her mouth. It burst, exploding sweetly scented juice and hard, nutty little seeds over her tongue. Mmmm, delicious. Bleedin' delicious, she thought, looking up at Sonny, who was hovering over her, concern etched into his craggy face.

'I thought the idea was you're supposed to feed them to me,' she complained, throwing him a rakish smile.

His face ironed out with thankful relief. Maggie was fine, she was going to be fine. After everything she'd gone through, she'd come out of it with her sense of humour intact. Even if the rest of her wasn't.

Maggie was lying propped up on a pale-blue mound of pillows in St Mary's hospital in Paddington. She'd had a mastectomy, three lymph nodes removed and armpit clearance. And, considering the ordeal she'd just been through, she was in remarkably good spirits.

Maggie was feeling lucky to be alive. After her initial tests, the subsequent results and the appointment with her specialist, her worst fears had been confirmed. The lump was cancer. She'd absorbed the news with a

427

calmness that had astonished both Sonny and the professionals. She hadn't broken down in tears, she hadn't felt sorry for herself, she hadn't plunged into a morbid depression.

Instead she'd spent the days leading up to her admission to hospital in a non-stop, busy whirl of preparing and freezing a week's worth of meals for Sonny, refilling the little china bowls dotted around the flat with fresh pot-pourri, shopping for new nightdresses 'in preparation for visitors', and organizing change of address cards ready for their move to Spain.

In fact she was so rushed off her feet that it was only the night before her operation that she finally stepped off the mad, frantic carousel and allowed herself to think about what had happened, about her diagnosis, about how she was going to feel afterwards. She'd been sitting on the bed, listening to the radio and packing her overnight case – neatly folding her nightie, slotting her sheepskin slippers down the sides, squashing in her bulging toiletry bag – when she'd leaned over to her reproduction French dressing table and pulled open the drawer.

It was filled to the brim with underwear, stuffed full of multicoloured scraps of lace that doubled for thongs – that she was well into her fifties and still able to wear G-strings was one of Maggie's proudest achievements – and dozens of bras in black velvet, ivory satin, pink embroidered cotton, and sheer Lycra leopard-print. Reaching hesitatingly into the rainbow depths, she randomly picked one out. Black Chantilly lace dotted with tiny pink rosebuds, two tiny satin ribbons sewn onto each strap. She ran her fingertips along the lace cups, tracing the intricate pattern like a person reading braille, only this spelled out only one word: 'femininity'.

Which is when it hit. It was like going through the clothes of someone who'd died, because she was never going to be that person again. The person with two perfect healthy breasts. Breasts that had been kissed by

Sonny, that had suckled her children when they were babies, that were part of her. And now one of them was going to be removed, cut off, gone for ever. A large tear burst through her mascaraed lashes and spilled down her cheek. For a brief moment she'd remained sitting there, aware only of her own grief, the thudding of her heart, the sound of her breath, until she vaguely became aware of a song playing on the radio. It was Gloria Gaynor and she was belting out the old classic, 'I Will Survive'.

Maggie felt the hairs on the back of her neck prickle. She'd heard that song a million times, danced around her handbag to it plenty of them, but never had the lyrics seemed so fitting. *She would survive.* She would beat this disease. She would get better. And she would live to dance around her patent leather handbag for years to come. She was more than just a pair of breasts. And there's more to life than a bloody lace balconette bra, she thought suddenly, rejecting her sentimentality and stuffing it roughly back into the drawer. Flicking the brass clasps closed on her tartan suitcase, she reached across to the box of tissues that sat on her dressing table and, glancing at her reflection, resolutely wiped her cheek. From now on, there were going to be no more tears.

Standing in the foyer, Grace waited for the people to spill out of the lift, before stepping inside and pressing the button to the eighth floor. Hit by the pungent smell of antiseptic and bleach, she was overcome with a sense of dread. Together with an almost indignant disbelief. *She couldn't believe it.* She didn't want to believe it. In fact, initially she'd thought she'd misheard Rhian when she'd told her the news. But then that wasn't surprising, considering that she'd been in the middle of getting ready for her dinner with Spencer when she'd phoned for 'a chat'.

Only what transpired was less of a chat, and more an outpouring of mind-boggling confessions and jaw-dropping revelations. What was that about life throwing surprises at you like a knife-thrower? Before Grace had barely had the chance to say hi, Rhian was chucking surprises at her left, right and centre, pinning her open-mouthed against the fridge-freezer, her phone in one hand, her mascara wand in the other.

'. . . so I wrote a letter to Dr Cupid and guess what? I was on the show live on air . . . *Thwack* . . . and after receiving over a hundred letters I arranged to go on a date with one of the men who replied but then Jack had an accident and I had to go to Casualty . . . *Thwack* . . . And I met Clive the doctor, Jimi's friend, and by a magical twist of fate he was my date and so we went out for dinner and then we spent the night together and, well, I can't believe it but I think I've found my soulmate . . . *Thwack. Thwack. Thwack.* Which is so amazing, but not actually the reason I'm calling you tonight, because in fact I was supposed to call you this morning but I was on a shoot . . . *Thwack* . . . and I didn't get Clive's message until it was too late, though to be honest it's all a bit gabbled and doesn't sound that important. Just something about Jimi calling him up and saying he wanted to see you because he'd made a mistake . . .'

Grace had flinched as her heart pitched sharply, before quickly struggling to pull it back up again. So Jimi thought last night was a mistake? So what? So did she, she'd thought indignantly. Then Rhian had thrown her last and final surprise.

'. . . Oh and by the way, I nearly forgot. I'm sure I saw the husband of that friend of yours last night, the woman who used to give you a lift to work. Maggie, I think her name was. I didn't recognize him at first, but I'm pretty certain it was him. He was at St Mary's and was going to visit her. You never mentioned she had breast cancer . . .'

With a heavy heart, Grace stepped out of the lift and

pushed open the swing doors that led into the ward. Her eyes flicked past the front desk, past the harassed nurse on the telephone, past the rows of screens erected around the beds. She hesitated. After getting no answer on Maggie's home number, she'd raced to the hospital. She wasn't planning to stay long, she wasn't even sure if she'd get to see Maggie, if she'd be well enough, if she'd want visitors, but she needed to see how she was, to make sure she was OK, to say sorry for being a completely crap friend.

Maggie's illness had come as a terrible shock to Grace. It had also brought her up short. All the time Maggie had been having to cope with something like this, and what had she been doing? Getting upset about a stupid wedding, obsessing about pathetic arguments, worrying about being thirty-one and single again. All stupid, trivial stuff. At the memory she felt ashamed. It took something like this to put everything in perspective, she thought grimly, her heels quietly clicking against the linoleum as tentatively she walked along the row of beds. Something like this to make her realize what was truly important in life.

And then something made her stop in her tracks. Something completely unexpected. It was the sound of laughter. But not the polite, quiet, tittery kind – this was bawdy and brassy, and really, *really* filthy.

'Ooh, a bit higher, no . . . no . . . a bit lower . . .'

Grace recognized the voice. '*Mags?*'

'*Grace?*'

Peeping round the edge of the curtain she was treated to the sight of a fully made-up Maggie lying on the bed wearing red satin pyjamas and a fair amount of plastic tubing, and Sonny bending over her dangling a bunch of grapes. Down both their faces were streaming tears of mirth. Having prepared herself for a distressing scene of tears and illness, Grace was caught off guard. This was not, she thought in delighted astonishment, what she'd been expecting.

They pulled apart hurriedly, like a couple of guilty

teenagers that had just been caught necking, and Sonny abruptly sat down.

'Hello, doll, how are you?' gasped Maggie, a wide smile breaking over her tanned, but tired face.

'Forget me,' admonished Grace. 'How are you?'

'Oh, you know . . .' she went to shrug, and then winced. 'Thought I'd get myself a boob job,' she quipped ruefully.

Despite the obvious irony, Maggie's self-deprecating humour couldn't help but bring a smile to everyone's face.

'Would you like a chair?' asked Sonny, beginning to ease his portly frame out of the regulation NHS plastic chair.

'No . . . please, I won't stay long. I just heard and I wanted to pop by and see how you are,' Grace began to explain. 'I got a phone call from my friend Rhian, you met her at the barbecue I had last year – pretty, dark hair, had a bit too much fruit punch and sang Leo Sayer's 'You Make Me Feel Like Dancing' all night . . .' Seeing that this was going to turn into a very long story, Grace interrupted herself before anyone else could. 'Well anyway, I'm here now,' she added. And then smiling at Maggie, she scolded affectionately. 'You should've told me, you know.'

'I know, I know.' Maggie nodded, picking an imaginary piece of dust from her red satin sleeve. 'But I didn't want a fuss.'

'Don't you believe a word of it,' muttered Sonny, winking at Grace.

'Ooh, you cheeky pillock,' tutted Maggie in-dignantly. 'And this from a man who makes a song and dance when he's got a bit of athlete's foot.'

For a moment both women looked at Sonny, who'd turned the same colour as Maggie's pyjamas, before they all started laughing. It was difficult not to, thought Grace, dabbing her eye and trying not to smudge her make-up, Maggie and Sonny were like a comedy double act.

'So did you make that appointment at the hairdresser's for me?' As her laughter subsided, Maggie stroked Sonny's hairy forearm that rested protectively on the side of the bed.

'Aye, ten o'clock Thursday.' He nodded obediently, and then his face crumpled. Sonny was finding this a lot harder than Maggie.

'*You're* going to the hairdresser's?' asked Grace, listening to this conversation with disbelief. Maggie's hair was her pride and joy and in all the time Grace had known her she'd only allowed Sonny to cut it.

'Chemo starts next week so I thought I'd get it cut off before it falls out,' she said matter-of-factly.

'Oh Mags, I'm sorry . . .' stammered Grace, both appalled by her lack of tact and amazed by Maggie's bravery.

But Maggie didn't want sympathy. 'Don't be, I'm not.' She shook her head decisively. 'I should have cut the bloody lot off years ago. I would've done as well if Sonny hadn't always begged me not to.' She winked sideways at Grace as she spoke.

Surreptitiously finishing off the rest of the grapes, Sonny inadvertently inhaled a seed. 'Me?' he spluttered, rising to the bait, before catching Maggie's teasing smile and flushing with good-natured embarrassment.

'. . . but it will be much better for when we're in Spain anyway. It's far too hot there for all that hair. So, what do you think? A Dame Judi Dench crop, or one of those boy band buzz-cuts?'

'Oh, definitely a Dame Judi,' advised Grace, blown away by her friend's attitude to her illness.

'Sonny?' Maggie looked across at him, head cocked to one side, magenta lips pouted provocatively.

'I'll settle for a Maggie Chapman,' he said quietly, tenderly interlacing his fingers through hers.

And that's when it hit Grace. It was such a small gesture, but it spoke volumes. She was on a hospital ward, with a couple, one of whom was suffering from a life-threatening illness. Yet cocooned inside their tented green cubicle the overriding feeling wasn't one of fear, or sadness, or pain, it was one of love.

Because these two people really, really love each other, thought Grace, glancing across at Sonny, who was gazing at Maggie with the kind of unquestionable devotion that to describe would seem saccharine and sentimental, but to witness was genuinely beautiful. It shone so brightly it cast a shadow over her own relationship. What they had together was a world apart from what she and Spencer had. They didn't have doubts, or fears, or hesitations. There were no 'what ifs' or 'maybes' or nagging doubts. These were two people who were just meant to be together.

It was as simple as that.

'How long have you two been together?' she was prompted to ask, brushing thoughts of her own relationship aside.

'Thirty-seven years,' they answered in stereo, the pride audible in their voices.

'And she still refuses to let me make an honest woman of her,' grumbled Sonny, looking put-out.

'What do I want with a piece of paper?' she protested.

'What about a nice diamond ring?' he said persuasively.

'Bleedin' hell, Sonny Mancini, you're a tight old sod,' said Maggie indignantly. 'Nearly forty years and two sons and you mean I've got to marry you before you'll buy me a diamond ring?' As Maggie swatted him playfully, they both laughed ruefully.

A look of amazement flashed across Grace's face. 'You mean . . . are you telling me . . . *you two aren't married*?'

'Of course not,' scoffed Maggie, looking genuinely surprised. 'Why? Whatever gave you that idea?'

'I just . . . uhmmm . . . I don't know,' murmured Grace. Because she didn't know. Maggie had never said she was married, she'd always just presumed.

'I did ask her,' interrupted Sonny, feeling as if his chivalry was being called into question.

'Last week, when he thought I was going to snuff it,' retorted Maggie bluntly.

'*Mags!*' he gasped, affronted.

'*Sonneee*,' she mimicked, widening her eyes and throwing Sonny a teasing smile.

Shaking his head, he smiled good-humouredly. But he couldn't help gripping her hand even tighter. Maggie's fighting spirit might be the reason to be resolutely cracking jokes, but he'd been so terrified of losing her that fear still clung to him like wet clothes in a swimming pool.

'OK, so there's probably a bit of truth in there,' he confessed begrudgingly. Leaning towards Grace he confided quietly, 'And like the lady says, "If it ain't broke, why fix it?"'

'Actually, I said, "If we've got something this good, why change it,"' corrected Maggie loudly.

'Well, same thing,' conceded Sonny.

Listening to their conversation Grace had fallen quiet. She was thinking about Spencer, her delight when he'd proposed, her hurt when he'd refused to set a date. For two whole years his apparent lack of commitment had caused a host of doubts, resentments, insecurities and fears. But now she wasn't so sure. Perhaps marriage really was just a piece of paper, perhaps it was only an outdated tradition, perhaps it didn't really change anything, it just celebrated what was there already. And, thought Grace, as the realization hit. *Perhaps she'd known that all along.*

'Don't you believe in marriage?' she asked curiously.

'It's not that we don't believe in it, it's just that we never really saw the point.' Maggie shrugged, looking at Sonny, who nodded in agreement. 'It was the sixties and it was all free love and flower power, and Sonny and I, well, we were terrible hippies. If you could've seen us . . .' Maggie broke off as she reflected with a giggle. 'Do you remember those flared dungarees you used to wear, with that Afghan coat of yours?' She looked at Sonny and they both grimaced at the memory. 'And then afterwards ... well, it just never seemed that important as we grew older, did it?'

Sonny shook his wispy head, smoothing down the hair with his huge shovel of a hand. 'I'm not knocking anyone who's hitched, but I've always thought marriage is for people who've run out of things to say, gives them something to talk about for the rest of their lives.'

'Or at least till the divorce,' interrupted Maggie wickedly. 'Like I always say, if you want to wear a nice dress and have a party and a lovely holiday, you can do all that without having to go and marry the bugger.' She hooted with laughter, and then winced as her stitches pulled.

'And this is when she's just come round from the anaesthetic,' grumbled Sonny to Grace as he fussed with Maggie's blankets. 'Can you imagine what she's like when she's not undergoing life-saving operations?'

Beaming as if this was the greatest compliment, Maggie looked across at Grace. She hesitated, but something in Grace's eyes compelled her to speak. 'Marriage isn't a magic wand, you know,' she added quietly. 'It's what's inside the heart that counts. That's the magic.'

Grace listened in silence. For all her eccentricity and bawdy humour, Maggie could be astonishingly intuitive. 'You're very lucky,' she said and smiled wistfully.

But Maggie pooh-poohed her. 'It's got nothing to do with luck,' she said firmly, squeezing Sonny's hand with an uncharacteristic gesture of sentimentality. 'It's about being with the right man.'

'But how do you know if he is the right man?' she urged quietly, waiting, expecting some great, big, complicated explanation.

Looking at Grace's aggrieved expression, Maggie smiled fondly. And gave her an answer that was simply two words:

'You'll know.'

436

Chapter Forty-eight

It was almost an orchestral arrangement. Bowie's 'Life On Mars' was crooning loudly out of the speakers, the incessant rain was beating a drum roll on the windscreen, the whining *whirrrrr-squeak-whirrrr-squeak* of the wipers was providing the string section. And then there was Jimi, who'd taken on the role of conductor and was sitting in the driver's seat, one hand lazily resting on the hub of the steering wheel, the other rhythmically waving a Marlboro Light around like a baton.

It was Sunday evening and outside it was pitch black, pissing down, and bone-numbingly freezing. So freezing that even despite the blasts of warm air being pumped out of the under-floor heaters and his thick woollen coat and hat, Jimi was still rigid with cold. He shivered, tugging his collars up, and concentrated on the road ahead, watching the rows of bay-windowed semis receding behind him in his rearview mirror as he drove past the cricket pitch, St John's church, the primary school and the park, with its graffiti-covered toilets and benches filled with gangs of bored fourteen-year-olds, sharing cigarettes and drinking cider.

Indicating left at the roundabout, he stuffed the Citroën into second, and began to climb slowly up the steep hill, the engine making a painful whining sound above the noise of the stereo. Perched bolt upright next to him on the passenger seat was Flossie, her greying snout wedged into the chink in the window, her stumpy tail wagging animatedly as she sniffed a medley of new and exciting smells.

Eventually, at the top by the bus terminus, Jimi spotted the road sign he was looking for. Turning into a small cul-de-sac he slowed down and his eyes scanned the houses dotted neatly around manicured lawns. They were so familiar, yet so unfamiliar. It seemed like only yesterday since he'd walked past them with his schoolbag thrown over his shoulder. There was Mrs Bennett at number 43, the Hayleys at number 25, that old woman he could never remember the name of, who used to feed him Cadbury's Roses at number 19. And then there was number 11.

Pulling up outside he turned off the engine and flicked off the CD player. Silence descended. Real silence, not the silence he'd grown used to in London which was still filled with echoes from distant taxis and rumbling tubes, but total suburban nothingness. The kind of nothingness that drives teenagers into poster-covered bedrooms to dream of the day they can escape into the big, wide, boisterous world.

And that's exactly what I did, thought Jimi, his mind flicking backwards. He'd escaped to London and a whole new life. A life of shiny espresso makers, cool left-hand-drive cars and designer lofts, a life filled with the hippest bars, the prettiest girls, the latest fashions. He'd fulfilled his dream of becoming a journalist, he'd turned freelance, he'd got an agent, he was writing his first novel – how fucking cool was that?

Frankly, not very.

Because the sad thing was, Jimi had discovered that none of it made him happy. Sitting by himself on his designer sofa, drinking designer coffee, in his designer loft might look *über*-cool and aspirational in a magazine photograph, but in reality it was actually pretty damn boring. Being invited to a trendy new launch party, or hanging out with friends in the pub, isn't much fun when you feel lonely, even when you're in a crowd. And writing a groundbreaking novel isn't all it's cracked up to be during those periods of writer's block when all you do all day is bid on ebay.

And never even make the reserve.

Rubbing his bleary eyes, Jimi stared out of the windscreen, absent-mindedly watching the splatters of rain trickling down the glass. He'd had one hell of a long day. After the shock of seeing Grace kissing Spencer, he'd walked back to his flat, his mind in a blur, his heart in bits and pieces. He loved Grace, really, truly and damn well bloody loved the woman. This wasn't like how he'd felt about Kylie, this wasn't like Clive's unexpectedly good impression of Prince Charles. There was no 'whatever "in love" means' any more, because now he *knew* what being in love meant. It meant Grace. And only Grace. Without Grace everything just felt worthless, and meaningless, and empty.

But there was nothing he could do about it. Grace and Spencer were back together. She'd moved on. She was getting on with the rest of her life. Just as Clive was getting on with the rest of his. What was that saying? Today is the first day of the rest of your life? Well now it was time to get on with the rest of his. He was thirty-one years old. It was about time he grew up and faced up to things. He didn't want to be the archetypal playboy any more, he didn't want his life to revolve around guest lists and girls and having a good time, and he didn't want to have to prove anything any more.

Because on that slow, painful, revealing walk back to Kensal Rise, Jimi had taken a long, hard look at himself and, to be quite frank, he hadn't liked what he'd seen. He needed to start making some changes. *Big changes.* Which is why, arriving back at his flat, he'd jumped in the car with Flossie and his laptop and driven two hundred miles up to Manchester.

With a soft click he opened the car door and,

stepped into the frosty night, began walking down the familiar gravel driveway. He could hear the soles of his shoes crunching loudly in the silence and his heart thudding loudly in his ears, until eventually he reached the wooden door, with its stained-glass insert. He curled his fingers around the shiny brass knocker. Because it was time, he decided, taking a gulp of cold Northern air, that he finally made his peace.

In the floral living room, a bald-headed Indian man put down his paper and walked into the hallway to answer the front door. Probably carol singers, he thought amiably, sliding back the latch and tugging it open.

'Hello?' The door swung open.

For a brief instant Jimi hesitated, his courage deserting him. Then swallowing nervously, he finally spoke.

'Hello, Dad.'

Outside the hospital, Spencer was waiting for Grace in the jeep. With the engine still running, the fumes from its exhaust were sending white swirling clouds into the inky darkness and Grace gazed at them as she pushed through the revolving doors. Her mind was racing.

Seeing Maggie had both gladdened and disturbed her. Her positivity, humour and steely determination to beat her illness had been inspiring, as had the love and affection between her and Sonny. But their relationship had also turned the spotlight on her own, dredging up nagging doubts. Rewinding the conversation in her mind, she listened again to Maggie. '*It's got nothing to do with luck, it's about being with the right man.*'

Stepping outside into the icy night she began to walk towards the jeep. Against the background of inner-city noise she heard the muffled sounds of the stereo reverberating from inside, and as she approached it grew louder and louder. She shivered, abruptly reminded of when Spencer used to arrive home drunk at 2 a.m. and play opera on full volume. She quickly banished her thoughts. He didn't get drunk any more, he'd promised he was going to stop drinking that morning in the café, months ago. That was all in the past.

And this is the future, she told herself, hugging her coat tightly to her chest as she hurried along the pavement. Now up close she noticed the whole chassis of the jeep was vibrating to the thundering bass line, and she recognized the music. She should've guessed.

Coldplay.

Chris Martin's voice greeted her as she tugged open the door, but for an instant Spencer didn't notice her. Engulfed in the deafening music he had eased himself back in the driver's seat, his carefully gelled hair lolled against the headrest, eyes half closed, obliviously singing along to the lyrics. She noticed he was wearing one of her favourite shirts, pale blue and unbuttoned at the collar to reveal that perfect triangle of skin at his throat; noticed the lapis lazuli cufflinks as he lifted up his hand; *noticed that he was smoking.*

A seed of worry sprouted. He only ever smoked when he'd been drinking.

'Wow, you look amazing.'

Glancing upwards from the embers of his cigarette, she met Spencer's gaze. He was smiling approvingly at her, and normally she would have blushed at his compliment, would have felt a warm glow of attractiveness infusing her body, would have silenced all those nagging doubts and reassured herself that he was her Mr Right: his smile would have made her realize how much he loved her, how much she loved him. But as she looked into his bloodshot eyes, all she felt was a familiar sinking dread. All the signs were there.

'Have you been drinking?' She tried to make it sound like a joke, a flippant reply to his flattery. But she was deadly serious.

'I had a glass of wine down at the squash club.' Turning down the volume, Spencer stubbed his cigarette in the small ashtray on the dash.

'But I thought you said you were going to stop . . .'

'Getting drunk, yeah I have. I can't handle the hang-overs like I used to,' he laughed, and then catching her worried expression, shook his head. 'Don't worry, this was just the one,' he reassured her, smiling warmly.

And woozily, thought Grace, suddenly remembering all those old feelings she'd conveniently forgotten. The reality hit like a blast of cold air. Was this how it was always going to be? Was she going to spend the rest of her life worrying if it was just the one?

'Hurry up, you're going to freeze in that dress.' He patted the passenger seat. 'I don't know if you realized, but you can see everything through that material,' he noted disapprovingly as she climbed in beside him.

'Really?' said Grace, affecting a tone of surprise when really she knew full well the delicate chiffon was diaphanously transparent. It was one of the reasons she loved it.

As she climbed in beside him he brushed his lips against her cheek. 'Mmm, you smell good,' he murmured appreciatively.

'Thanks,' she smiled, but in her stomach she could feel a flutter of nerves. Unexpectedly self-conscious, she began fiddling with the hem of her dress.

'So, how's your friend?'

'Oh good. She's good,' smiled Grace, the tape record-ing in her mind began playing. '. . . *it's about being with the right man . . .*'

'That's a relief,' continued Spencer.

Inside Grace's head the tape was still running and she heard her own voice, '*But how will I know?*'

'I mean, that's great . . .' His voice trailed off and taking off his tortoiseshell glasses, he furrowed his brow in concentration and stared fixedly ahead as if deep in thought.

Grace glanced across and out of the corner of her eye

watched as he reached inside his breast pocket and pulled something out.

'This is for you.' He smiled falteringly.

In her lap he'd placed a small vanilla-coloured envelope. Puzzled, she looked at it for a moment, before turning it over in her hand. She slid her fingers underneath the flap and opened it. Inside was a small white card. On it, written in pale gold lettering, were just three words: 'New Year's Eve.'

'What is it?' she asked curiously.

'A date,' he answered, his smile widening.

Bewildered, Grace stared at him.

'For our wedding,' he continued, his voice wavering slightly. 'Well you said you wanted me to set a date,' he finished, his hand reaching across and brushing her hair away from her face, '. . . and I thought seeing as we've had such a long engagement already it wouldn't matter if the wedding was in only a month. Like you said – what are we waiting for?' His nervousness began to disappear as he explained: 'although of course we'll have to knuckle down and start getting things organized immediately . . .'

All at once Grace saw how the story ended. And as Spencer's voice faded into the background, her mind thumbed through the rest of the evening: the flirting, the celebratory glasses of champagne, the expensive dinner where they would discuss wedding arrangements and guest lists and honeymoons. Fast-forwarding past the journey home, the cognacs and the candles, the slow undressing in front of the fire, *the sex*.

Of course it would be fantastic, because making-up sex always was. Just as everything would be in those first blissfully heady few days of reconciliation. And everything would be as it should be. Everything she'd wished for would come true. She'd have Spencer, her home, her stability, her life as she knew it. They'd get married, go on honeymoon, and in a couple of years she'd be one of those women in Wandsworth with two privately educated kids, a successful lawyer husband, and a wardrobe of elegantly cut, classic dresses.

Only they'd be sensible little black dresses, thought Grace, thinking back to the morning of her birthday and Spencer's suggestion that she wear her dowdy A-line number. Not floaty, flimsy dresses from New York that were beautiful and sexy and see-through.

And that Jimi bought for me.

And it was then, at that moment, on a double yellow line outside St Mary's hospital in a Jeep Cherokee with Coldplay playing on the stereo, that Grace realized you can't really know what you want until you've got it. She loved Spencer, but she wasn't *in* love with him any more, and to be honest, she didn't think he was in love with her either. She was the wrong woman for him, just as he was the wrong man for her, and it wasn't to do with all those nagging doubts, it wasn't even about Spencer's drinking, or their engagement, or her stupid dresses. It was because they'd lost their magic. For whatever reason it had trickled through their fingers, and getting married wouldn't make it reappear.

A voiceover played in her head. '*It's what's inside the heart that counts. That's the magic.*' Grace shuddered. She couldn't ignore it any longer, couldn't pretend any longer, couldn't deny it any longer. Inside her heart, it was stuffed so full of love she could barely breathe. And every single, magical drop of it belonged to Jimi.

The truth sent her reeling.

'Oh Spence . . .' She shook her head. 'I'm sorry, I can't marry you.'

A deep cleft split down Spencer's brow. He looked shocked. Confused. *Indignant*. 'But I thought that's what you always wanted?'

As the words registered, the realization hit. And looking sadly at Spencer, she said quietly, '*So did I.*'

Chapter Forty-nine

There simply wasn't a cloud in the sky.

A spotlessly clean canopy the colour of faded denim stretched over the entire city, beating bright Easter sunshine upon the blossom trees lining the streets and breathing a deliciously warm breeze through every open window and car sunroof.

For once, the weather had played a pleasant trick on the capital. Instead of waking up to the usual Bank Holiday drizzle, frost, and even a few gales, it was basking in eighty degrees and, despite the forecasters' killjoy warnings of sunburn, UVA and air pollution, its residents were celebrating with picnics in the parks, jugs of Pimm's outside pubs, and barbecues on every balcony, patio and roof terrace in London.

High up on one particular small, decked roof terrace, Grace sipped her champagne and gazed out across a leafy corner of Ealing Common. Savouring the bubbles bursting on her tongue, she breathed in the mouth-watering aroma of charcoal-blackened burgers, roasted corn-on-the-cob, and fluffy Maris Piper potatoes baked in tinfoil and dripping with gloops of melted butter and listened vaguely to the Peruvian Panpipes playing on the stereo, the chinking glasses, buzzing chatter and whooping laughter of the party. Her leaving party.

Closing her eyes she lifted her face to bask in the warmth of the sunshine. She was going to have to get used to this kind of weather, she told herself, allowing herself a small smile of excitement as she thought about her suitcases all packed and ready to go, her British Airways ticket tucked safely into her passport, her new life waiting for her on the other side of the world.

It had all happened so quickly. Less than four weeks ago she'd been sitting at her desk at work, redesigning a brochure for a worldwide chain of hotels, the next she'd received a phone call from the MD asking if she'd like to 'pop in for a chat'. At first she'd assumed it was to talk about deadlines, or new projects or, more worryingly, her ongoing battle with Janine, which since Maggie had left was fast turning into a war. So imagine her surprise when he'd sat her down, congratulated her on her talented work, and offered her a chance to work on a new project.

In Sydney, Australia.

He'd continued talking but she'd only caught the odd phrase '. . . heading up the new design team . . . generous relocation package . . . six-month contract initially . . . great opportunity . . .' as her mind had flicked back to that evening in December when she'd said goodbye to Spencer outside St Mary's, climbed out of his jeep, and walked away into the icy darkness. She hadn't been sure where she was going, or where she was heading, and those first few steps had been slow, tentative, fearful. Until – *whoosh* – she'd been hit by the wave of euphoria that comes from knowing you've made the right decision, and carried away in its swell she'd stuck her hands deep into her pockets and taken great big strides. Because she knew where she was going, and she couldn't wait to get there. It was a place called the rest of her life.

Not to say the journey wasn't without its tough times. In the weeks and months that followed she'd been forced to endure Christmas with her blatantly disappointed mother, who worried about what the neighbours would think and complained that her bridal linen was unrefundable. On New Year's Eve she'd found herself at a party having a good time until they'd started the countdown and she'd looked out upon a vista of coloured balloons and kissing couples. As for Valentine's Day, there had been more than one wistful twinge as she'd sat at her desk at work, surrounded by Interflora bouquets, but they'd soon disappeared when she'd caught the tube home and bumped into desperate gaggles of men clutching helium balloons and overpriced bunches of roses. She might have sacrificed her right to a padded card but, to be honest, she wasn't upset, merely relieved.

In fact, she'd never looked back and regretted her decision. Not when she'd stayed in by herself on Saturday night, not when she watched the other married couples at Starbucks with their rosy-cheeked babies and seemingly perfect lives, not even when she heard a rumour that Spencer had been cited in Tamsin's divorce. Only now, with hindsight, she could see they should have broken up years ago but they'd stayed together for all the wrong reasons. She'd wanted more than he could give her, and she'd stayed with the wrong man for fear of being alone.

But ironically, being single hadn't turned out to be too bad. In fact, Grace had discovered with a shock that not having a man in her life was pretty damn good. She actually enjoyed her new-found freedom, welcomed the return of her old independent spirit, revelled in the liberating feeling of being able to do, quite frankly, anything she sodding well liked. Having moved out of her tiny rented studio in Earls Court, she'd taken that first scary step onto the property ladder and was now the proud owner of a lovely little flat in Shepherd's Bush which she'd painted in rainbow colours, and not a hint of magnolia. OK, so she was the poorest she'd ever been, she had a freakishly large mortgage, and she spent her weekends following the blue line at IKEA with a yellow nylon bag slung over her shoulder, but she was the happiest she'd ever been.

With one exception. And it was one very big exception: *Jimi*. Since that morning after the night before they hadn't spoken or seen each other. She'd thought about calling him, she must have thought a million times, but every time she went to dial his number, she stopped herself. What was the point? What was she going to say? That she'd made a big mistake? That she missed him like crazy? That she missed his cynical jokes, his hypochondria, his pessimism? That she missed receiving his daft text messages, listening to whatever latest CD he'd bought, or arguing about whether man really did land on the moon? Was she going to tell him that he drove her completely nuts? That he could make her laugh till her belly begged for mercy? That despite being so wrong for her, he was so right for her? *Or was she going to tell him that she was in love with him?*

Because she was. Totally, utterly, and completely. Looking back she realized she'd probably been secretly, begrudgingly, unknowingly in love with Jimi since she was a teenager in Manchester. But now it was too late. They say it's all about timing, and her timing sucked.

She'd heard through the grapevine that he'd rented out his loft in London and gone back up to Manchester. This much had filtered back through Clive, but not much else. No details, no emotions, no feelings, no thoughts. But what did she expect? He'd told Clive that sleeping with her was a mistake – that much she did know. He'd probably done what he did to Kylie and put her in a box with the lid on.

And by the looks of it, thought Grace, scanning the party wistfully, even though in her heart she knew there was going to be no sign of Jimi, he'd locked it tightly and thrown away the key.

'Anyone for sausage?'

Adjusting his chef's hat, Clive prodded his barbecue proudly. 'I think they're pretty well done.'

448

'I think you mean burnt to a cinder,' a familiar voice chastised him.

Grace swung round. Across the other side of the roof terrace she saw a stunning brunette wearing a figure-hugging gold Chinese Mandarin dress, a pair of impossibly high emerald green stilettos and with a large white orchid tucked behind her ear, slipping her arms affectionately around Clive's aproned waist. It was Rhian. And she's looking absolutely amazing, thought Grace, watching her giggle as Clive twirled round, grabbing hold of her remarkably tiny bottom with one oven-gloved hand as with the other he plucked the orchid from behind her ear and clenched it between his teeth.

Nearly five months on and Rhian and Clive were still clearly besotted with each other. Having moved out of her housing association flat above Baltic Travel, she and Jack, along with her profusion of crystals, joss sticks, ornaments and World Music collection, had moved in with Clive in Ealing, breathing new life into his grey, shabby bachelor's flat, with splashes of colour, sprinkles of fairylights, and a never-ending splurge of laughter.

A lot of it came from Jack who immediately ditched Barbie and adopted Clive as his new best friend. In the beginning, Rhian had been cautious: she and Jack had a special bond and she guarded it like the most precious thing on earth. But one night, a few weeks later, she'd watched Jack and Clive lying on all fours on the living-room carpet playing monsters of the deep, and whatever doubts or worries she'd had disappeared. Clive wasn't going to break any bond. On the contrary, he would only strengthen it.

For the first time in her life, Rhian felt she'd found true happiness. And the funny thing about happiness is that it has a domino effect. After that first freelance job, her career was beginning to take off again, and only yesterday she'd received an unexpected, and highly exciting, phone call from the fashion editor of *Vogue* saying they'd seen her work and been very impressed, 'and would you consider doing some work for us?' Rhian didn't need to consider, but struggling to keep her voice steady she'd proceeded to make a great pretence of checking her diary and talking about 'free windows', until five minutes later she'd got off the phone with an entry in her filofax that read: '*9 a.m. Sanderson Hotel*' (and then in big capital letters, underscored repeatedly) '*GWYNETH PALTROW.*'

But the greatest surprise had been at a recent shoot. After shaking hands with a large entourage of hairdressers, stylists, PAs and magazine staff, she'd spotted the photographer. He'd been standing with his back to her, giving directions to his army of assistants who were setting up lights, reflectors, tripods and backdrops and, feeling more than a little apprehensive to be on her first job in nearly three years, she'd walked over to introduce herself. Only to realize they'd already met.

'*Phil.*' Confronted with the sight of her ex, she'd frozen with surprise, her hand extended in a redundant handshake, the smile sliding from her face. 'What are you doing here?' she'd blurted, struggling to regain her composure and failing dramatically.

'Um . . . taking photographs,' he'd half joked, his long brown fingers lifting up his Hasselblad camera in explanation.

A space had opened up. Followed by silence. And then they'd both spoken together.

'I thought you were in the States . . .' she'd begun.

'You're looking great . . .' he'd started.

They'd both stalled.

'I am, I just flew in for this shoot. I was going to call you . . .' his voice had tailed off. 'How's Jack?' he asked.

'Great, considering . . .' She'd paused, her initial temptation to make some cutting remark about how he had a father he barely saw, who only kept in touch via the odd long-distance phone call and lavish present at birthdays and Christmases. And then stopped as she realized she no longer felt bitterness towards Phil – only pity. 'He'd love to see you,' she'd said generously.

'I'd love to see him too. I've missed him.' Phil's confident veneer seemed to crack as he'd lowered his eyes and looked at her through his dark eyelashes. Eyelashes just like Jack's. 'I've missed you too,' he'd added quietly, giving Rhian a look that in the past would have sent her stomach into a succession of backflips; but now it remained unexpectedly still. 'Olivia and I are over, it should never have happened.' As he'd been speaking he'd shaken his head, his dark curly hair springing up and down, just like Jack's did. 'I was wondering . . .' Reaching out, he'd gently rubbed his thumb against the underside of her wrist, just like he used to. 'Would you have dinner with me sometime?'

The breath had caught in the back of Rhian's throat. And for a brief moment she'd paused, tempted by her age-old fantasy of them getting back together.

'I'm sorry, I can't.' Shaking her head, she'd pulled her hand away. 'I'm busy.'

And I'm in love, she'd added silently, feeling a warm enveloping hug as she thought about Clive. What they had wasn't a fantasy, it was real. Stuffing both hands firmly in her pockets she'd walked away without looking back.

'Can I tempt you?'

Grace turned around to see Rhian wafting a tray of blackened, charred lumps under her nose. She shook her head, smiling. 'No thanks, I think I'll pass.'

'I don't blame you,' whispered Rhian, stifling a giggle as she caught Clive's eye. Smiling brightly she pretended to lick her lips appetizingly, then turned back to Grace with a look of dismay. 'Oh dear, he's trying so hard but he's such a terrible cook, nobody wants to eat anything,' she wailed. 'If I even *look* at another Linda McCartney I'll explode.' Looking around for a solution she found one in the shape of a potted palm. 'I know, I'll hide them,' she hissed, tipping the whole lot in the terracotta pot and hastily burying them in the soil. 'There, problem solved.' Standing upright she reached for a glass of champagne and clinked it against Grace's.

'Cheers.'

'Here's to the chef,' grinned Grace.

'No, here's to you,' corrected Rhian quickly. 'And your new life. Even though I'm going to miss you terribly.' A tear prickled and she sniffed it quickly away. 'Who else am I going to call every morning and read their horoscope?'

'You've got Clive,' pointed out Grace, smiling.

'Oh I know, I know, but it's not the same. I know he doesn't really believe in them.'

'Actually I've got a confession to make,' admitted Grace sheepishly. 'Neither do I.'

Rhian looked as if someone had just informed her the pope was gay. And then seeing the funny side, her face split into a wide grin. 'Seeing as you're a fellow Taurean I'll forgive you,' she giggled, letting her off. 'And anyway, you look far too great,' she said approvingly. 'Is that new?' She gestured to the dress Grace was wearing, a bias-cut, scarlet swathe of satin. 'I haven't seen it before.'

'Yes you have.'

Rhian threw her a look of confusion.

'Hanging on the back of my bedroom door,' prompted Grace, giving her a clue.

'But wasn't that . . . ?' Rhian's voice faltered as she digested this piece of information. 'You mean . . . oh my goodness, that's not . . .'

Grace began smiling.

'*Your wedding dress?*'

She nodded happily. 'I ended up giving Spencer his ring back, even though he said he didn't want it. It seemed only fair. But it seemed such a shame to waste this dress so I had it shortened and dyed.' She did a little twirl, the luscious fabric fanning out just below her knees. 'White was never my colour anyway.'

'No kidding,' said Rhian, as they erupted into laughter.

They were interrupted by the sound of a jangling doorbell.

Unexpectedly Grace's stomach flipped.

'I wonder who that could be.' Rhian's forehead furrowed, as she mentally skimmed through her guest list. As organizer of this surprise party it appeared Rhian had spent the last few weeks playing detective, sneaking looks in Grace's address book and secretly ringing around her friends.

'I don't know,' said Grace, fighting to appear calm when inside she was on full alert. *Was it Jimi?* For a nanosecond she held onto the fantasy, before tossing it quickly aside. No of course it wasn't, she told herself sternly. He was in Manchester. He didn't know she was leaving for Australia. And if by some small chance he did, he certainly didn't care.

But a tiny voice within plucked up courage and began to fire a million possibilities at her. Perhaps Clive had told him, perhaps he'd travelled down from Manchester, perhaps he was going to surprise her . . . Hope raced ahead before she could stop it and all at once she realized just how desperately she wished it was him, just how much she wanted to see him again. Feeling on tenterhooks, she took a much-needed gulp of champagne.

The doorbell sounded again.

Every muscle in Grace's body tensed.

'Hell's bells,' whooped Jack excitedly, abandoning his sausage roll and charging through the legs of party-goers towards the french windows. '*Mummy hell's bells*,' he screeched even louder.

'Where on earth does he pick these things up?' tutted Rhian, turning scarlet and throwing Jack a horrified look. 'I'll be back in a sec, I'll just see who that is.' Flustered, she dashed across the roof terrace –

not an easy task when her stiletto heels kept getting wedged down between the grooves of the decking – to open the front door.

Grace strained to hear. There was the soft click of the handle, the creak of the door, and then Rhian's voice: 'Grace, come over here and see who it is.'

Could it be? Her heart bursting with hopeful expectation, Grace began excusing her way through the partygoers, her eyes darting towards the door.

'Sorry I'm late.'

The familiar voice disarmed her, and catching sight of the person standing in the hallway with a closely shaved head and a Marbella suntan, Grace's eyes widened in surprise. Her hope that it was Jimi instantly evaporated, but instead of a hollow disappointment, her face split into a broad smile. Flinging out her arms, she whooped loudly with delight:

'*Maggie!*'

Chapter Fifty

The afternoon slipped into evening with the delicious ease of an ice-cold G&T. Grace spent the rest of the party catching up with Maggie, who'd flown back especially, listening with delight to hilarious stories about her new life in Spain, marvelling at how well she looked, and congratulating her on finishing her last round of chemo.

'The doc says it's all zapped.' Maggie smiled, unwrapping a coffee-and-cream chupa chup and popping it into her mouth. Having quit smoking, lollies were now her new habit. Well, if it was good enough for Kojak, she'd joke, stroking her bald head and cackling like a drain. 'So now we just have to keep our fingers crossed the bugger doesn't come back.'

'That's great news, Mags.' Grace beamed, giving her a hug.

'Grassy-arse,' she replied, in what had to be the worst Spanish accent Grace had ever heard.

'I see your Spanish is coming along,' said Grace kindly.

'I've had a mastectomy, not a lobotomy,' chided Maggie, seeing right through the compliment. 'You're not fooling anyone, I know I'm bloody terrible. Sonny despairs, my neighbours despair, I despair . . .' She rolled her eyes melodramatically. 'I blame those tapes. You know, I'm still only on the first one. I've been stuck in that bloody restaurant saying I'm allergic to shellfish for bloody months.'

For a moment they remained straight-faced, both remembering their morning drive to work. Then slowly Maggie's shoulders began to shake, her dangly diamanté earrings rattling against her neck as she exploded into loud guffaws, setting off Grace, who snorted loudly as together they cracked up with hoots of laughter.

Far too quickly the evening turned into night and people began saying their goodbyes and drifting off home. Until finally it was just Clive, Rhian and Grace left outside on the roof terrace, toasting marshmallows and finishing off what was left of the chocolate-peanut butter Häagen-Dazs. 'Well, I guess this is it,' sighed Grace, licking the hot melted pink goo from her fingers and quickly following it with an ice-cold mouthful of ice-cream. 'Time to go.' Licking her spoon, she placed it on the coffee table and stood up.

Concentrating on digging for peanut butter chunks, Rhian looked up and let out a whimper. 'Do you have to?'

' 'Fraid so,' said Grace, smiling ruefully. 'My flight's not till lunchtime tomorrow but the company have arranged for me to stay at a hotel at the airport tonight and I need to go back to the flat first to collect my things . . .' She broke off to let out a wide yawn. 'And it is pretty late.'

'Oh, I know, I know.' Rhian nodded, untwining herself from Clive who lay half asleep on the sofa, and hurrying inside. 'I'll call you a minicab, we know a good firm, they're terribly cheap . . .' she began fussing, walking inside and pacing up and down the kitchen, flicking through the yellow pages, dialling the number and gabbling the address down the phone. Replacing the receiver, she suddenly stopped and turned to Grace. A large tear plopped off the end of her nose. 'Oh Grace, I'm going to miss you,' she sniffled loudly, and flapped her hands in front of her face to try and fan away the tears. 'Sorry, ignore me, I'm being pathetic and emotional. Too much champagne.'

'Or not enough,' said Grace, squeezing her in a tight bear hug while desperately trying to put a brave face on things herself. She'd never been much good at goodbyes, and she could feel the tears prickling. She was going to miss Rhian, and London, and her life here. Most of all she was going to miss Jimi. But then I already do, thought Grace, resignedly.

'I'm sorry he didn't come,' said Rhian, reading her mind.

Grace met her gaze, and realized that sometimes you don't have to tell friends anything, sometimes they just know. 'Me too,' she agreed.

Rhian squeezed her hand reassuringly.

'If you ever see Jimi . . .' began Grace.

'Yes?' asked Rhian hopefully. For months she'd been trying to persuade Grace to just pick up the phone and call him. But she was too stubborn. For whatever reason, she'd always steadfastly refused. 'Do you want me to give him a message?'

Grace hesitated. Over the last few months she'd thought of a million things she wanted to say to Jimi, but right there, at the moment, she couldn't think of a single one of them. 'No. No message.' She smiled sadly, shaking her head.

A loud hooting from outside signalled the arrival of the minicab. Gathering up her things, which lay strewn around the roof terrace, she walked downstairs followed by Clive and Rhian. 'Bye you two.' Giving them one last hug, she climbed into the waiting Datsun.

'Bye . . . safe journey,' called out Clive, one arm stretched across Rhian's bare shoulder.

'And don't forget to send us a postcard,' Rhian reminded her. Standing together on the doorstep, they waved her off until their arms ached.

*　*　*

Ten minutes later the doorbell rang.

'Who on earth can that be?' gasped Rhian, trotting to the door in her pyjamas and marabou slippers. She picked up the intercom, 'Hello?'

There was a hissing crackle, and then a faint voice. 'Have I missed the party? It's me . . .' followed by lots more crackling.

Rhian squashed the handset to her ear. 'I can't hear you properly, you'll have to speak louder!' she yelled, making a mental note to get the intercom fixed. Clive had been saying he would do it for months, but then Clive, she'd discovered, was a member of the gnu species. He was always '*g'nu*' do something or other.

Losing patience, she pushed the buzzer. Tugging open the door to the flat, she listened to someone hurrying up the stairs. She waited expectantly to see who their very late partygoer was. Or were, she thought, as she realized there was more than one set of footsteps, heard the sound of loud panting, and saw two shapes loom up in the dimly lit hallway.

It was a man and his dog.

'You're late,' said Clive, before anyone else had a chance to speak.

'I know, I blew a tyre on the M1 . . . I tried to get here as quickly as I could.'

'*Excuse me,*' interrupted Rhian, annoyed at being ignored. She turned to eye the stranger in her living-room. Something about him seemed strangely familiar. Holding out her hand, she said pointedly, 'And you are?'

'Oh I'm sorry,' apologizing, he held out his hand and smiled. 'Please to meet you. I'm Jimi.'

'*Jimi?*' Rhian was flabbergasted. Of course – the man from the restaurant – the blast from the past – the man who broke Grace's teenage heart – *the man she was in love with*. Spinning around to face Clive, she said incredulously, 'You knew he was coming? *You were expecting him?*'

'Of course.' Clive shrugged, puzzled that she should ask such a thing. 'I invited him.'

Watching Clive and Jimi slapping each other on the back as they walked into the flat and out onto the roof terrace, Rhian could only marvel. Why was it that men never told you the important details? 'Is there anything else you feel the need to tell me?' she asked tartly.

'Only that I think you're the most damn wonderful woman alive,' winked Clive, rolling up a cigarette.

Rhian's disgruntlement vanished in an instant and, disappearing into the kitchen, she began busying herself making coffee and nibbles.

'So, how are you, old son?' asked Clive, passing him a beer and offering him what was left of the marshmallows.

'Is Grace here?' asked Jimi, cutting to the chase.

Clive fidgeted uneasily on his buffet. 'Well, that's just it.' He frowned and began to scratch his head vigorously, wondering how to break the news. 'She's already left for the airport,' he blurted out. Tact was never his strong point.

Jimi's face visibly paled. 'The airport?' he repeated quietly. For a moment he remained slouched in his deckchair staring catatonically into space. After Clive had telephoned him in Manchester to tell him Grace was moving to Sydney and they were having a surprise leaving party for her, he knew he had to see her before she left. Now the realization that he'd missed her was unbearable.

Clive ventured carefully. 'Are you OK, old chap?'

'No, I feel terrible,' groaned Jimi, clutching his head. 'Look into my eyes – can you see anything?' he demanded, staring at Clive. 'I'm sure I've got a tumour.'

Humour him, just humour him, thought Clive. 'You're fine, honestly,' he said.

'Then why do I feel like this? I don't want to feel like this. I want my old life back. *I want the old me back*.'

'Believe me, you don't,' said Clive quietly, shaking his head.

'What do you mean?' asked Jimi, frowning.

Pulling off his chef's hat, Clive eased himself down onto the rattan garden chair. He grimaced as he sat on something, and foraging around underneath a cushion, tugged out Jack's one-legged Action Man. He cleared his throat awkwardly. 'You're an old friend, and I love you dearly . . .'

Jimi looked alarmed at this outburst of emotion. OK, so they hadn't seen each other for five months and admittedly he had missed him. Even so . . .

'But you used to be a total shit,' Clive blurted. 'Not just to women, but to your friends.' He swallowed, his Adam's apple bobbing up and down nervously as he broke off to stare into the middle distance, his forehead screwed up as he struggled to find the right words. 'And then Grace came along and well . . . well, I don't know her terribly well, but she's got to be something special because she's changed you. For the better, I might add. You're now a much nicer person.'

There was silence. The muscle in Jimi's jaw clenched and twitched agitatedly.

Watching it, Clive questioned the wiseness of his honesty. What on earth did he have to go and say all that for? Who the hell said honesty was the best policy? Afraid he'd overstepped the mark, he nervously swigged back his beer and waited for the inevitable onslaught.

But there wasn't one.

'Is that a roundabout way of giving me a compliment?' asked Jimi, turning to look at him and smiling ruefully.

Clive's face relaxed into a lopsided grin. 'Absolutely,' he said and nodded decisively.

'Good, so now it's my turn to give one.' He paused to look across at Rhian, who was busily drawing whiskers on Jack's face with an eyebrow pencil. Refusing to go to bed, he was intent on being a tiger. 'Rhian seems lovely . . .' He looked pointedly at Clive, who'd blushed the colour of his hair, '. . . Jack looks

460

like a pretty amazing kid, and from where I'm sitting you three have got it sussed.' He took a swig of his beer. 'And so, although I never thought I'd see the day when I'd ask your advice about women, now I am.' He turned to look at Clive. 'Tell me. What do I do?'

'First you've got to tell me what you want.'

'Simple. Grace.' He shrugged, stubbing out his cigarette. 'But . . .'

'But nothing,' said Clive cutting him off. 'If you really want this woman you've got to fight for her. You've got to pull out every stop you can because you can't lose her, Jimi. Not again. Last time it was for thirteen years, this time you might not be so lucky. This time it might be for ever.'

For ever. Jimi balked at the word. It was so final. Irrevocable. *Unthinkable.* For ever meant never having the chance to tell her how he really felt, never being able to say just how much he loved her, never being able to explain why he had never made that phone call thirteen years ago . . .

It was too much.

Springing up from the deckchair like a superhero, Jimi thrust his beer into the hand of a startled Clive and planted a large kiss on Rhian's cheek. 'I have to leave,' he announced urgently.

'Leave?' stammered Rhian. Having armed herself with a tray of nibbles and the barbecue leftovers, she stared at him open-mouthed. 'But you've only just arrived.'

'I know, but when you decide you want to be with someone for ever, you want for ever to start right now.'

Rhian looked even more bewildered. What on earth was he talking about? He wasn't making any sense.

But to Jimi it made perfect sense. It was as if every-thing suddenly snapped into focus and he was seeing things with such amazing clarity, such sharp-ness, in such vivid Technicolor, that he couldn't believe he'd been blind to it before.

'So you won't be wanting anything to eat?' Rhian

held out the redundant tray hopefully. After hearing so much about the famous Jimi, meeting him for the first time was almost like meeting a celebrity and she was rather disgruntled that she wasn't going to be able to impress him with her role of party hostess.

'Thanks, but no. I don't want anything to eat. I don't want anything to drink, and I don't want to waste any more time. I've wasted enough,' he declared, gripped by a rush of euphoria that caused him to lift his face to the heavens and broadcast to the audience of glittering stars. He wanted to shout it from the rooftops and that's exactly what he did, his loud, broad Pennine voice booming across Ealing Common.

'There's only one thing in the world I want and it's Grace. Grace, do you hear? I love Grace. *I'm in love with Grace.*' Feeling as if his lungs would burst he turned and charged out of the flat. With Flossie scampering after him, he vaulted down the stairs three at a time and ran into the street where his Citroën was parked.

Left behind on the roof terrace, Clive and Rhian turned to each other.

'My goodness, that's so incredibly romantic,' whispered Rhian, her eyes brimming with tears. 'Jimi's in love with Grace, and she's in love with him. They're a perfect match. Two soulmates. The yin and the yang. It's just so amazing, so wonderful, so thrilling, so . . .' Then reality began to dawn. '*Tragic,*' she gasped. 'Oh my goodness, it's terrible, he's too late, Grace has already left.'

'I think he's gathered that, darling,' consoled Clive, squeezing Rhian's shoulder. 'Don't worry, he'll drive over to her flat.'

'But she's not staying there tonight,' cried Rhian. 'She only went there to pick up her suitcases and then she's going to stay at some airport hotel, she didn't say which one.' She looked as if she was about to burst into tears.

'Don't worry, we can call her on her mobile,'

suggested Clive brightly. As he was speaking he saw Rhian turn ashen and pounce on something glittery lying next to her geraniums.

It was Grace's mobile phone.

'She's forgotten it . . .' Her voice broke off as they heard the roar of an engine. Peering down into the street-lamp darkness, they caught sight of a white Citroën screeching around the mini-roundabout at the bottom of their road, and then disappearing.

'Oh dear,' whispered Rhian, snuggling into Clive's T-shirted shoulder. 'I hope he finds her. I hope they can finally get it together.'

'Me too,' said Clive, and then smiling to himself he quipped drily, 'For all our sakes.' He pulled her closer, and standing high up above the rooftops they stared out into the night and held each other just that little bit tighter.

Come on. Change, you bastard. *Change.*

Stuck behind a queue of traffic at the lights, rapping his fingers impatiently against the steering wheel, Jimi eyeballed the red light like an enemy in battle and willed it to turn green. It remained stubbornly scarlet.

'Typical. Bloody typical. Nearly midnight and I'm stuck in bloody traffic,' Jimi swore loudly under his breath and thumped the horn impatiently.

Flossie whined and stuck her snout underneath her paws.

The lights changed. 'Finally,' he said grimly, scrunching the gearstick into first and screeching away from the lights.

The baseball-capped driver of a BMW in the next lane mistook his haste as the desire to race and, grinning wildly, attempted to overtake. It wasn't much of a competition. The shiny white Citroën DS might be a style icon, an exceptionally cool classic that, when he merely sat behind the wheel, made Jimi appear achingly cool as well, but in reality driving it was like steering a cruise liner through the Suez Canal.

Whereas the electric blue BMW, with a spoiler the size of an iceberg that sank the *Titanic* welded to its arse, and a suspension so low it literally dragged on the tarmac, might raise more than a few derisory sniggers – and by having the sheer nerve to drive around London in it, so did its baseball-capped owner – but in reality it went like a bloody rocket.

Normally Jimi's competitive spirit would have cried battle, but he barely noticed as the BMW whizzed past, the driver grinning jubilantly and honking his horn as he burned off down the dual carriageway. Instead he was too busy concentrating on working out shortcuts. 'Not far now, just a few more streets, nearly there,' he muttered under his breath while mentally tracing the *A-Z* route in his mind. He'd already been driving for twenty minutes and now, as he neared Earls Court, he felt relief begin to seep up through his body. Finally he was nearing Grace's flat. Finally he was going to get to see her.

He rounded the corner, and as he did, he caught a glimpse of Grace in the distance. His breath caught in his windpipe. She looked gorgeous: red dress, sparkly flip-flops, hair all loose . . . His heart soared, and then crash-dived . . . suitcases, holdall, trolley. Lurching over a speed bump he braked sharply. Forced to slow down just as he needed to be speeding up he stared, horrified, as her luggage began to disappear into the boot of a Datsun minicab, witnessed her disappear onto the back seat, watched the minicab disappear down the street.

Panic erupted with volcanic force. All at once, his confession, his speech, his declaration, his hope, disintegrated before his very eyes. Alarmed, he whacked his foot on the accelerator and sent the car crashing over the speed bumps, the chassis crunching painfully on the tarmac as he attempted to follow the cab, whose driver suddenly speeded up and began to weave in and out of traffic. Almost as if he knows he's being tailed, thought Jimi, who'd watched far too many cop-car chases over the years and had now found himself in one. Only I've got no chance because I'm driving a bloody P&O ferry, he fumed, rapidly changing his mind about choosing a classic car. Looks were not everything. In fact right now, I'd give anything to be driving an Astra.

As the minicab jumped the lights at amber, Jimi attempted to follow, but the small matter of nearly being squashed by an articulated lorry heading in the opposite direction forced him to screech to a halt. He slammed his hands on his steering wheel in exasperation. This called for a major rethink. He reached for his mobile. He was going to have to call Grace. There was no other choice. He was going to have to say over the phone what he wanted to say face to face. Watching the tail-lights of the cab vanishing into the distance he stuffed his earpiece tightly into his ear and rang her mobile. It connected. His heart shot into his mouth like a bowling ball.

'Hello?'

'Grace, it's me, Jimi,' he blurted, any attempt at a cool one-liner flying right out of the window.

'Oh Jimi, this isn't Grace, it's me, Rhian,' apologized a Welsh voice on the other end of the phone.

It was at that precise moment that Jimi realized what it would be like to be stranded on a sinking ship and discover that the one life-jacket on board had a hole in it.

'Grace left her phone at the party by accident . . .'

But Jimi wasn't listening any more. The lights had changed. Tugging out his earpiece and dropping the phone onto his lap, he gripped the steering wheel with both hands and put his foot down. The engine growled as he raced ahead, the warm night wind blustering in through the open windows, ruffling Flossie's fur. But there was no sign of Grace's minicab. He pressed the sole of his Puma trainer to the floor. The dial read 55 m.p.h. . . . climbing to 60 . . . up to 70 m.p.h. He raced towards Heathrow, but he couldn't see the Datsun. Oh

Christ, he wailed silently, this just can't be happening. Where has she gone? He scanned the traffic ahead frantically. What if I've lost her again? Only what if it was like Clive said? What if this time it's *for ever*.

The words seared into his brain, leaving him with no doubt. This called for desperate measures. This called for a plan. This called for action. Brow furrowed, body hunched over the steering wheel, he felt like something out of a Bond film. This would be the time that 007 pulled out his secret weapon, he thought grimly. But what was his? What could he do? He frowned even harder. Think, Jimi. Goddamnit.

Think . . . Think . . . *Think.*

And then an idea came to him.

He dismissed it immediately. Oh no he couldn't. He just couldn't. There had to be another way . . . His mind batted it backwards and forwards, searching for a way out like a rat running up and down a maze in a laboratory experiment trying to find an alternative route. Except there wasn't one. Oh Jesus. *No.* His heart fluttered wildly and he could feel the sweat prickling on the palms of his hands. He breathed in – one long, deep inhalation, holding it as if he had the hiccups – and then out again. But it didn't make a blind bloody bit of difference. His heart was still thudding like the bongos.

And there was still no other solution.

As the idea began to form, shame screamed. Embarrassment curled his toes tightly. Whatever shreds were left of Jimi's ego threatened to fly right out of the window. But there was no other way. He didn't know what else to do. He loved Grace, and if there was even the smallest, tiniest, craziest chance that this might work, that Grace might just understand and forgive him, he had to take it. He checked his watch. There was still plenty of time.

Reaching out with a quivering hand, he clutched the black dial on his radio. Quickly pressing it down to turn it on, he flicked it backwards and forwards, whining past stations, blasting segments of songs. 'C'mon, c'mon,' he cursed under his breath, until eventually . . .

'. . . *so for all those of you who need Dr Cupid to fix it for you in the love stakes, call us here at* Do You Come Here Often? *. . .*'

As the number was read out Jimi grabbed his mobile, put the barrel to his head and pulled the trigger. And there, right at that moment, he committed street-cred suicide. He started dialling . . .

Chapter Fifty-one

Feeling the balmy night breeze on her face, Grace rested her elbow on the edge of the minicab window and stared out as they raced over the flyover towards Heathrow airport. Watching the buildings whizz past, the familiar London skyline receding, she thought about everything she was leaving behind: her family, her life, *Jimi*.

Stop it. Stop thinking about him, she chastised herself. He's not thinking about you. He didn't come to your leaving party. He didn't even bother to say goodbye. He's two hundred miles away in Manchester. He'll be with his latest squeeze. He'll have forgotten all about you . . . Chewing her lip, she stared out towards Heathrow. In the distance she could see the flashing tail-lights of planes, landing and taking off. That will be me soon, she thought, feeling a rush of excitement, followed by a deep, intense pang of regret. She never got to say goodbye. Never got to explain. Never got to tell him that she loved him.

Well, it's probably for the best. You'd probably have made a complete fool of yourself, she told herself firmly, leaning back against the soft upholstery and winding up her window a little. Without the wind rushing in her ears she vaguely became aware of the radio, a familiar voice. Was that . . . ? She strained to hear and then recognized the voice. Dr Cupid. Her mind flicked back. She hadn't listened to him since that night with Jimi, and hearing him now brought the memories rushing back.

'Excuse me, could you turn that up a little, please?' she asked, leaning forwards to talk to the back of the thick-necked minicab driver who hadn't spoken a word throughout the entire journey but had remained resolutely motionless smoking filterless cigarettes.

There was a grunt of affirmation and the volume increased.

'. . . *and tonight we've had lots of callers, it seems that this sunny weather has brought out all those broken hearts that need fixing . . .*'

And you're going to fix them, are you? thought Grace wryly, a smile breaking over her face as she thought about Jimi. How he would have loved to have known that Dr Cupid had got divorced. It would have appealed to every cynical, pessimistic, disbelieving, scoffing bone in his body.

'. . . *but tonight we have a very special show. Tonight I'm not going to read you a letter, because there isn't one. Yep, that's right, listeners. Coming up next we have an SOS from a heart. A plea from a man who's quite literally running out of time . . .*'

Closing her eyes, Grace settled back in anticipation of what would no doubt be a highly entertaining story.

'. . . *a man who knows, more than most, how love waits for no-one . . .*'

Grace smirked. 'Love waits for no-one,' she murmured under her breath, shaking her head with derision. Then was abruptly flung sideways as the cab swerved left and swung into an Esso garage.

'Petrol,' grunted the driver in explanation as he cranked on the handbrake and, flinging open the door, yanked the keys out of the ignition. As the engine died, so did the radio.

Plunged into silence, Grace was disappointed. Damn, I wanted to listen to that, she cursed, watching as the driver lumbered over to the pump, his large frame nearly bursting out of his ill-fitting shiny suit as

469

he reached for the nozzle and began to fill up the Datsun. Oh well, he'll only be a couple of minutes, she thought and sighed, breathing in a lungful of warm petrol fumes. Flopping back onto the seat, she waited. Impatiently.

Deep breaths. Deep breaths. Deep breaths.

Jimi was having his very first panic attack. White-knuckling the steering wheel, he raced down the flyover towards Heathrow trying to negotiate the lanes of traffic, nearly causing a pile-up by braking hard for the speed cameras, accelerating madly to overtake the blue rinse crawling along in the Mini Metro, while at the same time desperately on the lookout for Grace's minicab, which seemed to have vanished into thin air.

Oh, and then there was the little fact of the *faux*-American voice whooping in his ear. The voice which just happened to belong to the producer of 'Do You Come Here Often?' *'Get ready to pour your heart out to the nation, Jimi! Ten seconds and you're gonna be talking to Dr Cupid.'*

His heart ran screaming into his mouth. *Oh shite.* Oh fucking shite.

'I'm counting you in now . . . 10, 9, 8, 7 . . .'

This was his every nightmare and more rolled into one. Forget the dream where you're running down the high street with no clothes on, he was about to get naked on national radio. And this was about more than just baring his manhood. This was about baring his soul. To millions of strangers. Or, even worse, thought Jimi, feeling as if he wanted to projectile vomit all over the walnut dashboard. *People that knew him.*

'. . . 6 . . . 5 . . . 4 . . .'

Every cynical, sceptical, negative, scoffing, scornful, contemptuous, derisive, mocking, sneering, cocky, vain, arrogant, conceited, self-important, egotistical, proud, self-respecting, dignified, cool, hip, trendy, unbothered, self-possessed, laid-back, hip gene inside his body raised up in revolt. *Don't do it, don't do it, don't do it!* they screamed inside his head like a Shakespearian tragic chorus. Back out. Put the phone down. Run for your life. You'll never live this down. You'll never recover from the shame. You'll never again be able to hold up your head in society.

'... *3* ... *2* ...'

On the verge of taking their advice, bottling out, hanging up, and luxuriating in the relief that he'd saved himself before it was too late, he heard a much louder voice deep inside himself.

You'll never see Grace again.

As the thought struck, the show suddenly went live in his ear and the producer's bark was replaced by Dr Cupid's, in all its full-Cheddar cheesiness, '... *so tonight you're going to hear it straight from the heart* ...'

Oh Jesus, this is much, much worse than I thought. Jimi cringed. His heart hammered a drumroll, his body tensed, his brow dripped with sweat. But despite every apprehension, every excruciating moment he knew was yet to come, he didn't put the phone down.

He couldn't.

'... *because he's on the line to tell his story ... Hi, are you there, Jimi?*'

Because although Grace was probably never going to hear what he had to say, he couldn't keep it inside any longer. He had to tell someone, and if he couldn't tell her, he was going to tell the whole of goddamn London.

And so, with a deep breath, he swallowed his pride, said farewell to his self-respect, and answered,

'... Er ... yeah ... yeah ... I'm here ...'

Jesus Christ, how long does it take to fill up a bloody Datsun?

Bored and restless, Grace chewed her fingernails and watched the digital display on the pump climbing with agonizing slowness. It seemed to be taking an eternity, and it was still only on £4.37. She sighed, looked at her watch for the umpteenth time, glanced back at the minicab driver who was slumped against the car, perspiration trickling down his face, then across at the petrol station. A gang of girls spilled out clutching handfuls of chocolate. Immediately her mouth watered.

'I'm just going to pop to the loo,' she fibbed, climbing out of the cab and running across the forecourt, her mind already debating whether or not she should go for a four-finger KitKat or if she was really more in the mood for a bag of Maltesers. And then . . . *thud* . . . there it was – the memory of Jimi demonstrating how he could fit a Malteser up each nostril, and there she was, collapsing with snorts of laughter on his suede sofa. She felt a pang of sadness. Salty tears sprang up, and she sniffed sharply, blocking the image out of her mind as she hurried through the automatic sliding doors and into the illuminated glare.

Walking past the shelves of magazines, down the aisles of crisps and biscuits, Grace came to a stop by the counter and tried to concentrate on the display of shiny-wrapped confectionery. She eyed it miserably. If ever there was a time to comfort-eat, it was now, she decided, listlessly picking up a Flake, a Twix and a bag of Revels and handing over a fiver to the attendant at the cash register. Waiting for her change, she heard a radio playing in the background and the sound of Dr Cupid.

'*. . . So tell me, who are you sending this SOS to tonight?*'

She tried not to listen. She didn't need to be reminded of Jimi, she didn't want to think about him any more.

'*There's no need to hold back, just let it all out, Jimi . . .*'

Jimi? Grace jumped. What a coincidence.

'*. . . erm . . . well actually, it's not an SOS, it's an explanation. And it's for Grace . . .*'

Oh. My. God. An incredibly nervous voice stuttered out of the radio. No, that couldn't be. It just couldn't be.

Except it was. Grace reeled with astonishment. *Jimi was on the radio.*

'. . . *because there's something I've been meaning to tell her for a long time . . .*' There was a nervous clearing of the throat, '. . . *since August 15th, 1988 . . .*'

Grace's jaw dropped with astonishment. He'd remembered the date.

'Excuse me – your change,' prompted a customer behind her who was waiting to pay for his petrol.

'Sssshhhhh,' she gasped, feeling her head spinning. 'Turn it up,' she pleaded to the till attendant, who took one look at the expression on her face and obediently increased the volume. To be honest, his curiosity had been aroused, as had that of the customer, who paused from pulling his credit card out of his wallet to listen with bemused interest.

Jimi's voice filled the petrol station.

'. . . *back then I was eighteen years old and nuts about a girl at school. Her name was Grace. She was gorgeous and funny and popular, but she never gave me the time of day. I tried everything to get her attention, and believe me, I did some pretty stupid things, but she completely ignored me. Then, one day, out of the blue she did more than just look in my direction, she saved my skin and spoke up for me. When everybody else was too scared to, she showed just how brave she was. It takes guts to do what she did and I never thanked her properly enough, to be honest, I tried to pretend I was the hard guy, when really I was so frightened. So shit scared that if you'd got close enough you'd have heard my knees knocking together.*

'*We made friends that day. It was one of those idyllic teenage days that seemed to go on for ever. We ate McDonald's, even though she was a vegetarian, we bought records, even though her taste in music was pretty dire, and we drove out to the country. And we talked, and laughed, and sat by the side of this beautiful river, by this beautiful abbey and we watched the sun set and made love. I know, it sounds real corny stuff, and maybe it was, but to me it was really special. She was special. She is special. It was just magical. It was one of those moments that you want to wrap up in cotton wool and keep in a safe place for ever.*

'Afterwards I drove her home and I promised to call. Only I never did. I never called. And I never told her why, to this day I've never given her an explanation why I didn't. Instead I've let her think I was a complete and utter bastard who broke her heart, that I didn't care, that I didn't love her. When in fact the opposite was true. The truth is I was too embarrassed. Too scared to call up a girl I was nuts about because I thought she'd laugh at me. Because you see I had a secret and I thought she'd discovered it. Because despite all my bravado Grace was the first girl I ever slept with, she was my first love. And until right now I've never told anyone that secret. I've never told anyone that until Grace I was a virgin . . .'

In the petrol station there was a collective sigh from the assistant and the growing number of customers who'd crowded around the counter to listen to the radio and to look across at Grace, who was reeling from his revelation. *Jimi Malik hadn't called her because he'd been a virgin?* The idea was as astounding as it was ludicrous. It was crazy, it was totally unexpected. And it suddenly explained everything, she thought, unable to stop her face splitting into a joyful smile.

'And so I want to say sorry, to say I wish I'd been braver, and that I wish more than anything I'd called. And Grace, if you're listening, I want you to know that it wasn't because I didn't care, it was because I cared too much . . .' He broke off and laughed nervously. *'I know I'm a bit late, give or take thirteen years or so, but . . . well . . . I'm hoping it's never too late if you love someone. And I do love you, Grace. I love you so*

bloody much I'm calling a radio station, and I'm telling hundreds of listeners . . .'

'Half a million,' corrected Dr Cupid, interrupting.

'. . . *when really there's only one person I hope is out there listening. And that's you Grace Fairley. Because you're the only woman I know who sucks ice-cream from the bottom of her cornet, who can wear stripy tights and glittery flip-flops together and still look amazing, and who could even make me want to request this next record . . .'*

Grace's smile was already wide but it grew even wider as she heard the opening bars and recognized the song: 'Perfect', by Fairground Attraction. And as the familiar tune began to fill the petrol station, she heard a car screech onto the forecourt, saw two slanted headlights like cat's eyes shining right at her, and watched as the door flew open and the driver jumped out.

Catching his breath, Jimi scanned the tarmac. Yep, it was definitely the same minicab, he recognized the last bit of the number plate and that funny plastic frog stuck to the rear window. He heaved a sigh of relief. Thank God he'd spotted it as he was racing past, he thought, taking a few tentative steps towards it before realizing Grace wasn't inside. Gripped with icy panic, he spun round.

And then there she was, walking towards him across the forecourt, the lights of the garage illuminating the sparkly beads on her flip-flops, her cherry red satin dress that rippled and shone, her dark hair that seemed to have grown much longer, swinging across her face.

Looking at her looking at him, something deep inside tugged sharply. Only a few moments ago he hadn't been able to stop talking, but now he couldn't think of a single word to say. He felt ridiculously nervous. More nervous than he'd ever felt in his whole life. His breath held tight inside him with anticipation, he stared at her as she stopped a few feet away from him, watched her tuck a piece of hair behind her ear. And then break into a smile. A huge, daft, delighted smile.

'That was some speech,' she whispered.

He smiled shyly. 'It's not finished yet. There was a PS.'

'And what does the PS say?' she asked, hope catching in the back of her throat.

He took a deep breath. 'Stay.'

Grace gazed at Jimi. Overwhelmed by everything that had just happened, that was happening right at that very moment, she couldn't answer. She loved him, of that she was certain. And there was a great big romantic part of her that wanted nothing more in the world than to just climb into his Citroën with him, drive back to his flat, and never leave. Only there was a tiny realistic part of her that couldn't, wouldn't give up this chance of a lifetime. Heading up her own design team was something she'd always dreamed of, something she'd worked so hard for. If she gave it up she might regret it for ever. She shook her head. 'I can't.'

Jimi felt a sickening thud in his stomach. 'Why not?'

'Because I've got to do this for me.'

'Can't you do this for us?'

Us. The word sounded so good. So right. So obvious. What the hell had taken them so bloody long? 'This is for us,' she said quietly. 'This is for you and me.' Nervously she looked at him, her heart hammering inside her ribcage. She was taking a huge risk. She was asking him to wait for her, to believe in her, *to believe in them*. Being 10,000 miles apart wouldn't be easy, they'd have to trust each other, they'd have to be faithful to each other, they'd have to love one another. Taking a deep breath, she eyed him daringly. 'We've waited more than thirteen years, what's another six months?'

Jimi drank in Grace: the small pulse beating in her neck, the freckles across her forehead, her dark eyes flecked with tiny grains of amber. And the expression in them. Nobody had ever looked at him like that before. It said more than any words, more than anything he could ever write, or say on the radio, or hope to articulate. It left him in no doubt. You don't throw away a look like that, you wrap your arms around it, hold it tightly, and you never, ever let it go.

He took up the challenge. 'Make that three months,' he bargained determinedly.

She threw him a look of confusion.

'I'll meet you at Ayers Rock, at sunset . . .' Remembering his commission for *Chic Traveller* he'd had an idea.

As he spoke, Grace got it.

'On a Harley-Davidson . . .' they chorused together, breaking into wide, giddy smiles as they remembered the plans they'd made as teenagers.

'It's a deal,' laughed Grace, her eyes shining as she felt a hot, treacly surge of joy, as if she'd just been dipped in melted happiness.

They looked at each other, locked into the moment, until finally Jimi spoke.

'Oh by the way, I nearly forgot.' Ducking back inside his car, he reached on to the dashboard, and re-emerged holding a chunky paperback. 'Something for you to read on the plane.'

Curiously, Grace turned it over in her hands, her eyes widening with astonishment as she read the title: *One Giant Step* by Jimi Malik. 'Oh my God, you did it! You wrote it!' she gasped, her voice thick with admiration and pride. 'That's just amazing.'

'It's not the real thing yet, it's just the proof.' He smiled modestly, trying to hide his obvious delight. 'It's out in the autumn. At all good bookshops,' he added, unable to stop himself. He still couldn't believe it himself. When his agent had rung with the news that he'd been offered a two-book deal, he'd been almost delirious. Him? A published author? What could beat that?

Now, looking at Grace, he realized. *She could.*

'Wow.' Grace beamed, nodding approvingly at the slick design on the cover, tracing the lettering of his name with her fingers, eagerly turning back the first few pages. And then she saw it: two lines of neat black text on a white page.

'*For Grace. For making me believe man really did land on the moon.*'

It was as if everything held its breath. Time froze, the world stopped spinning, Grace stopped breathing. She looked up at Jimi. He was watching her, his face unsure and anxious as he waited for her reaction. Their eyes met, and for one delicious, perfect moment they gazed unblinkingly at each other. No games. No arguments. No misunderstandings.

And then Grace did something she'd been wanting to do since that first time in the taxi. Only this time it's not an accident, she thought, pulling him towards her, feeling his arms entwined tightly around her waist as she tilted her face towards his. Getting ready to take a good look at those fireworks again, she tightly closed her eyes. And she kissed him.

There was a collective sigh from the audience that had gathered at the window of the petrol station and the sentimental voiceover of Dr Cupid, drifted out into the darkness.

'*So if you think Grace and Jimi should be together, give us a call here at* Do You Come Here Often? *After all, they say the best things in life are worth waiting for . . .*'

It's past midnight. Warm and muggy. Across the length and breadth of the capital, thousands of different people, in thousands of different places, living thousands of different lives turn to look at the person they love. On a roof terrace in Ealing, Rhian and Clive smile at each other, half asleep in a hotel bedroom Maggie and Sonny cuddle up in their pyjamas, and on a garage forecourt somewhere near Heathrow, two people, one dog, and a whole future ahead of them, finally make it happen.

Epilogue

As the sun began to set Ayers Rock came alive. Magnificently rising up against a papaya sky streaked with flashes of copper and tinged with gold, it seemed to the tourists watching from the nearby motel almost as if it was on fire.

Sitting outside at a small wooden table on the viewing deck, Grace looked up from writing her postcard to gaze with wonder at Uluru, the sacred Aboriginal home, as it changed from flaming scarlet to brooding magenta. As the red orb of the sun began to slowly sink, the huge monolith seemed to come alive, displaying a whole range of emotions to its captive audience, from burning anger to glowing serenity.

Captivated, Grace sipped her ice-cold gin and tonic glistening with crystal beads of condensation, relishing the cold liquid after the dry, dusty heat of the desert. It was three months now since she'd moved to Australia, and it was everything she'd hoped for. Looking back down at her postcard, she smiled at the irony of what she'd just written. *'Finally made it to the desert. And guess what? I've never been happier.'* It was addressed to Clive, Jack, Rhian and the bump. With a baby due in six and a half months, she wasn't the only one who'd swallowed a happy pill.

Her new job had turned out to be hugely enjoyable and her team had been so successful there was every possibility they would want to renew her contract. Not only that, but she was renting an amazing flat on Bronte beach, which meant she woke up every morning with a sweeping view of the ocean. She'd made some really good friends, and she'd really settled into her new life. In fact I can't ever imagine going back, mused Grace contentedly, watching as the sun began to sink lower and lower, casting a ruby sheen over the magical stillness.

And then she heard something. A faint rumbling far away in the distance, gradually growing louder and louder. Pushing her sunglasses onto her head, she scanned the vista, but there was nothing, just dust and barren scrubland. And then she spotted it. Far away on the horizon, a cloud of dust, a glint of metal shimmering in the sun. Mesmerized, she stood up to watch the blurry image growing closer, to listen as the noise grew ever louder until it was recognizable as the roar of the engine. A motorbike engine. A Harley-Davidson. Her heart somersaulted.

Everyone says you learn from experience, and if breaking up with Spencer had taught Grace one thing, it was that being single was better than being with the wrong man. If only because then you're free to meet the right man, she thought happily, picking up the helmet that was lying beside her and walking towards the swirling cloud of dust. Quickening her pace until she was running towards it, her feet catching in the short clumps of grass, her breath catching in the back of her throat.

And how do you know when you've met the right man?

The motorbike stopped, the rider lifted his visor and, meeting each other's gaze, Grace and Jimi shared a smile. A happy, newlywed, *magical* smile.

It was just like Maggie said.

You'll know.

And she did.

THE END